Homicide 69

Homicide 69

SAM REAVES

CARROLL & GRAF PUBLISHERS
NEW YORK

HOMICIDE 69

Carroll & Graf Publishers
An Imprint of Avalon Publishing Group, Inc.
245 West 17th Street, 11th Floor
New York, NY 10011

First Carroll & Graf edition 2007

Library of Congress Cataloging-in-Publication Data is available.

ISBN-10: 0-7867-1812-9
ISBN-13: 978-0-78671-812-2

9 8 7 6 5 4 3 2 1

Interior design by Bettina Wilhelm
Printed in the United States of America
Distributed by Publishers Group West

Acknowledgments

ONCE AGAIN THE author must thank many people whose generosity with their time made possible the writing of this book. Foremost among these is John DiMaggio, whose labors in educating the author about police work were cheerful, tireless, and utterly indispensable. Art Bilek reviewed the manuscript and then told the author how it really was; further thanks go to Robert M. Lombardo, Ed Dams, Hy Roth, Bruce Clorfene, Bob Kelty, and David Walker. Many thanks to all of you.

With so much expert help, it should be clear that any inaccuracies or implausibilities that remain are entirely the fault of the author.

Part One

Something Really Bad

One

"IT'S GONNA RAIN all over our dead guy," said Olson.

The sky was the color of a nasty bruise, a serious contusion gone a deep wicked purple, a day or so after a bad beating. Somebody beat the hell out of that sky, thought Dooley. "Turn your headlights on," he said.

Olson reached for the knob. "They'll never get that ball game in. They've already had a couple of delays and they're gonna run out of daylight soon."

Dooley watched lightning flicker in the void far out over the lake. "Who they playing?"

"Astros. Jenkins throwing for us. They win today, that's six in a row."

"Break out the champagne."

"Hey, it's their year. Who's gonna beat 'em? You gonna tell me the Cards are gonna catch 'em?"

Dooley shrugged. "What'd he say, Weed?"

"Weed and the river. Just south of North."

"You shoulda took Elston."

"Why? Weed's on this side of the river."

"Now you gotta double back on North. From Elston you come on east across the river and you're there."

"Ah, what's the difference? We'll get there."

"Not before the rain, we won't."

The sky had opened up again by the time they found the squads parked at the end of Weed Street where it dead-ended at the river in an industrial nowhere of train tracks, chain-link fences and long factory blocks. Nobody wanted to get out and stand in the rain, but they all did eventually, Dooley and Olson and the four officers from the squads, huddling together in the lee of a warehouse.

"Those two little colored kids found her," said one of the uniforms, nodding at the farther squad. The dome light was on and Dooley could see two small dark figures on the seat through the streaming glass.

"A woman, huh?" said Olson.

The copper gave a single shake of the head. "I didn't get too close. But it looked like a woman to me. Through the fence there."

There was a fence at the end of the street but nobody had mended it where the wire had peeled away from the post and there was a gap big enough to step through with a little bit of a stoop. Dooley took a look at the trampled grass around the gap. "You guys go through here?" he called back to the nearest uniform.

"Just far enough to see the body. There weren't any prints or anything."

Not now there aren't, thought Dooley. He ducked through, trying to step over the trampled patch, and stood where the riverbank fell away into brush and debris down to the revetment four feet above the water. Rain stippled the leaden surface of the river. Small trees clinging to the bank gave a little shelter. Dooley stood with his shoulders hunched, hands in the pockets of his raincoat, looking down at the problem. All he could see was an expanse of naked back, pale in the twilight, and a tangled mass of hair. Through the fence Olson said, "I don't know how he can be so sure. You seen the hair on some of these hippie guys these days?"

"That's a woman," said Dooley.

"If you say so."

Dooley stood and looked down the slope for a long moment, scanning for signs but finding nothing but rivulets of water taking evidence into the river. Rain spattered on leaves above his head. Dooley pulled a handkerchief out of an inside pocket and wiped water off his forehead. "She's nestled right into the weeds. There's no trampling."

"Yeah. So somebody just threw her down there after she was dead."

"Or she walked down there and laid down to die."

"Without her clothes?"

"I didn't say it was likely. Who gets to get his shoes dirty?"

Olson said, "I just bought a new pair of Florsheims. And you're already there."

Dooley moved up the bank, away from the body, looking for a place to go down where he wouldn't disturb any evidence. When he'd gone ten or twelve feet he stepped onto the slope and slipped, going to a knee to stop the slide. "To hell with your Florsheims," he said. "I just got this suit cleaned."

Where the slope leveled off at the edge of the revetment, Dooley found some footing and started working his way back along the bank toward the body, trying to ignore the rain in his face. He saw the soles of two feet, smudged black; he saw the swell of one bare buttock above the weeds. Dooley knelt, a hand to the ground for support, and felt for that place inside him where he could regard this poor massacred soul as nothing but a paycheck. When he had it he bent closer and parted the weeds."Ah, shit," he said gently.

The woman lay face to the river, legs and arms drawn up in front of her. Beneath the tangle of dark brown hair there was a face still there, but nobody was going to look at it and say "That's my girl." The eyes were closed, swollen to the size of plums and about the same color, and the nose had been smeared sideways. The lips looked like blood sausage, split open in a couple of places. Looking at the dead woman's face Dooley saw the color of the sky.

Olson called down, "What's she doing, saying her prayers?"

"She's tied up." Dooley tugged gently at the taut twine at the ankles. "They hog-tied her."

Olson said, "Call it a homicide, Professor?"

"I don't think we're gonna get an argument on that. Get a wagon, get the mobile lab over here, call the sergeant."

"Roger wilco. Don't fall in there, 'cause I ain't pulling you out."

Dooley heard Olson hustling away to get out of the rain. He knelt there with water trickling down the back of his neck and ran his fingertips over the dead woman's back. Her skin was cold and slick, the smooth white surface dotted with small round patches of discolored skin, rough to the touch. Dooley shifted his feet, rose to a crouch. He grabbed a tree limb for support and leaned over the woman, looking at the mottled patches of dark skin on shoulder and hip. He took another long look up the slope and bet himself the evidence technicians weren't going to find much today.

Back at the end of the street Dooley spoke to the nearest uniform. "Let's have a word with your witnesses."

On the back seat of the squad sat two boys maybe eight or ten years old, big white eyes in small black faces. They looked wet and cold and either scared or thrilled to death, Dooley couldn't quite make up his mind which. He slid onto the passenger seat in front and put an elbow over the back of the seat, wiping his face with the handkerchief. "How you boys feeling?" In response he got one OK and one widening stare. "What's your name, son?" he said to the one who had managed to answer.

"Jerome."

"Jerome what?"

"Jerome Hayes. We gonna get in trouble?"

"No, you're not gonna get in trouble. I just need you to tell me how you came to find that lady down there."

The silent one piped up all of a sudden. "She's dead, ain't she?"

Dooley nodded. "I'm afraid she is."

"What happened to her?"

Dooley thought of two or three different things he could say while he stared at the kid. "Something really bad," he said finally.

• • •

The rain stopped; the sky cleared; the sun went down. Dooley barely noticed. While Olson talked into the radio and started bossing patrolmen around, Dooley walked the streets: Weed, Kingsbury, Blackhawk. He stood looking up Kingsbury to North Avenue, thinking *I have her body in the trunk and I have her clothes. What do I do?* The book said canvass the area but there was nobody to canvass, just closed-up factories and warehouses. He and Olson walked down alleys, checking doors, rattling gates, looking in trash cans, looking for ways through to the river, looking for a shoe, a purse, a bundle or a scrap of cloth.

The sergeant arrived, a busy man and a hard one to please. Dooley spent a few minutes justifying his existence and watched the sergeant drive away. The setting sun found him and Olson half a mile from their murder scene on a twelfth-floor high-rise walkway that was wired in like the lion's cage at the zoo, knocking on doors and looking for a mother, a grandma, anybody to take charge of his two witnesses and verify an address for them. They spent a tense fifteen minutes convincing a posse of male relatives the boys weren't being charged with anything but there were procedures to follow; Cabrini-Green was not friendly territory for two white cops. It was a long walk down a dark stairwell and back to the car.

Dooley watched evidence technicians root through weeds in the fading light; he watched a wagon roll away, in no hurry.

"Flip you for it," said Olson.

Dooley shrugged. Partners had their preferences; Olson could type better than Dooley and he was a good detail man, but he didn't have Dooley's iron stomach. "Drop me at Polk Street and go get a start on the paper," Dooley said.

• • •

The medical examiner was a thin pale man who looked as bad as some of his customers under the fluorescent lights; the coppers joked that if he ever dozed off on the job the assistants would have him up on a table in an instant. "Got our make-up smeared a little, did we, dear?" he said to the woman on the table.

"I need a cause of death," said Dooley.

"Slow down, cowboy. I'm looking at a smorgasbord of injuries here. You're going to have to give me a minute. You'll notice she's in rigor." The medical examiner pushed on a knee and let the body rock back, still in its fetal position.

"I saw that."

"Which means she's been dead at least eighteen hours. And looking at this lividity, I'd say she lay somewhere for a while before she was dumped. Maybe in the trunk of a car. But then I don't want to prejudice your investigation."

"So sometime yesterday afternoon or evening."

"Probably. Stomach contents may tell us more."

"And what killed her?"

"You want a wild guess? Just looking at her neck here? Cause of death was strangulation."

"Yeah." Dooley was looking at her back. "Somebody used her for a God damn ashtray."

"And she looks like she went about ten rounds with Sonny Liston," said the examiner. "With no gloves. And that was the easy part." He was pulling gently at limbs, craning to look at what her legs had been hiding.

"I'm seeing a lot of blood all of a sudden," said Dooley.

"And in bad places."

Dooley nodded. "She was alive for all of this, wasn't she?"

"All but the last bit." The medical examiner straightened up, a look of faint distaste on his face. "I'd say strangulation was probably the best thing that happened to her yesterday."

• • •

"So what do we got?" said Olson, leaning back on his chair. He looked like somebody had chased him around the block a few times. His brow glistened where his hair had beaten a retreat and he had loosened his tie for comfort. He looked a lot like a homicide dick sometime after midnight with nothing to put on paper and a lot of paper to fill.

Dooley, who felt worse than Olson looked, shook his head. All the windows in the third-floor Homicide/Sex office were open but the cool night air wasn't finding its way in. "We don't have shit," he said. "We got a dead girl with no face and no name. We got no crime scene, no witnesses. If she was a nice, ordinary girl her prints aren't going to help us. We got no grieving mamas, no worried girlfriends, no jealous boyfriends. We don't even have her clothes. Until somebody tells us who she was, we got nothing at all."

Olson nodded. "When it hits the news the phone'll start ringing."

"Let's hope. We gotta find the clothes."

"Think they're down there close somewhere?"

"Maybe not. They took them off her before they killed her. What did they do with them?"

"Depends on how smart they are. I'd burn them or put them way down in deep water, a long way from where I put the body."

Dooley nodded for a few seconds, mechanically, looking far away. "Well, we got an autopsy to keep us entertained."

A few seconds went by and Olson said, "Want me to go?"

Dooley shrugged. "I'll go. You get on the missing persons reports."

Somebody laughed out in the hall; a car hissed by on the rain-washed street outside. Olson ran a hand over his face. "What do you think, Mike? It's a pretty short haul from the projects to the river."

"That's never a bad first guess. But I don't think Jerome and Claudell had anything to do with it."

"But they might have an idea who did. You really think they were back there looking for pop bottles?"

"I think if they knew who did it they wouldn't have flagged down that squad. And they had a bag full of pop bottles with them. I'll tell you what else I think."

"What's that?"

"I think they're not going to find any semen in her tomorrow."

Olson considered that like a man weighing a remark about the weather. "How come?"

"I don't think you take so much time with the rough stuff if you're gonna rape her. Somebody really worked her over."

"OK, so the guy can't do it anymore. That's why he beats her so bad. The rage. We've seen it a hundred times."

"I don't know, all those shallow puncture wounds. The cigarette burns. That didn't look like rage."

"All right, it's late and I'm getting a little punch-drunk here. What did it look like?"

"It looked to me like somebody wanted something from her."

Olson let out a long sigh as his front chair legs hit the floor. He put his hands on the edge of the desk and hauled himself to his feet. He put his hands in his pockets and stood looking down at Dooley with his washed-out blue Swede eyes.

"I'd like to meet these guys, I really would. Want to hit J.J.'s?"

"Sure." Dooley stood up and reached for his jacket. "Look on the bright side."

"What's that?"

"We probably will, before too long."

• • •

J.J.'s had nothing to recommend it to a thirsty copper but its location across the street from the old red-brick station at Damen and Grace. It had a pool table in the back, a jukebox on the wall, and a wide selection of whiskeys kept corked to avoid evaporation. The two brothers who ran the place were fastidious, abstemious and long-suffering; the only thing the cops loved as much as a drink was a prank. Dooley had seen horseplay that would make a junior-high kid blush. The brothers put up with the nonsense because a room full of armed policemen was about the best clientele a barkeeper could ask for.

Tonight there was a celebration going on; Frank Finley had made lieutenant and was moving downtown. "Whiskey for the gentlemen, please," he called out as Dooley and Olson pushed toward the bar. Finley and Dooley had shared a patrol beat for a year or so in the early fifties and Dooley respected him.

"I'll take one, too," Dooley said. "When you're through serving the gentleman." He shook Finley's hand. "Congratulations, pal."

"Thanks, Mike. I'll miss you."

"No, you won't."

"Nah, you're right. OK, how's this? I'll try to remember your name for a while." Finley was half in the bag and having a good time.

"That's more like it. Seriously, you earned it. I hope you go a long way." Finley was a good cop, just possibly good enough in Dooley's estimation for his integrity to survive his ambition.

"I appreciate that." Finley's grin faded and he leaned in close to Dooley as the whiskey was delivered. "Listen, Mike. You could be doing the same thing, moving up. You don't have to be a homicide dick on third watch for the rest of your life."

"I don't want to be anything else."

"Ah, don't bullshit me, Dooley."

"Third watch is where the action is. And I get to eat dinner anywhere I want."

Finley looked at him with drunken benevolence. "You're one stubborn mick, aren't you?"

Dooley drank and said, "I don't like the games, that's all."

"Jesus. So you have to throw a sawbuck in the desk drawer now and then to get the vacation time you want. It's life, Mike."

"I know. I don't have to like it."

"No, you don't. Ah, hell, here's to you. A career dick and one of the best. God bless you." Finley practically cracked Dooley's glass with his own, then turned his back on him.

Dooley nursed his whiskey along for a while, enjoying the banter, mostly listening. When he finished it off he slapped Olson on the shoulder. "Bedtime. See you tomorrow."

"Sweet dreams."

"You know it." Dooley got in his car and drove. The city had that washed-clean feel after the rain and Dooley rolled the window down and let the damp air blow on him. The traffic was thin and he made good time out of Elston.

Merrimac Avenue was asleep, happy and ignorant. Out here in the M streets there were no weeds for bodies to lie in. Sometimes Dooley felt guilty sneaking home in the middle of the night, bringing corruption and death out to the Northwest Side.

Dooley sat in the car in the dark for a while after pulling into the garage. He made sure to switch off the ignition, tired as he was; one of these nights he was going to forget, fall asleep in the car and die of carbon monoxide poisoning. *Cop's suicide stuns family, friends.* He could see the headlines.

After a while he climbed out of the car, pulled down the garage door and felt his way to the door that led into the kitchen, key in hand. Dooley always tried to leave everything in the dark garage; he hated to bring bad things into Rose's kitchen with the single light on over the sink, dishes shining in the drainer, the table top cleared and the chairs squared away. He draped his jacket over the back of a chair.

He made his way through the hall, up the stairs, sticking close to the wall so the steps wouldn't creak, listening for soft voices in the dark. Once in a while Kathleen or Frank would be awake and call out "Hi Daddy" or "Hey Pop" to him; when he was little Kevin used to do that a lot and Dooley would wonder if he ever slept. Dooley hated to wake his kids up but liked putting his head in the door and telling them to go back to sleep.

Rose never called out; she would just wait until he came to her. Tonight she stirred and murmured "Hi darling," half asleep, as he stepped softly across the rug toward her. He sat on the side of the bed and leaned down to kiss her, lingering for a moment with his nose in her hair, lips on her soft damp temple. She found his hand and squeezed. Dooley straightened up and then just sat there for a while holding her hand, waiting for her to go back to sleep. This was just about the best part of his marriage these days.

After a time he kissed Rose again and let go of her hand. He took off his holster and locked the .38 and his star in the drawer. He sneaked out of the room and back downstairs and into the kitchen again. He took the bottle of Jameson's out of the cupboard and got a glass from the drainer. He poured an inch of whiskey into the glass and put the bottle back. The clock over the door said two twenty-two. Sometimes Dooley sat in the kitchen for his nightcap, just looking at the pattern in the Formica table top, but tonight he walked up the hallway into the living room and found his armchair in the dark.

He knew drinking alone in the dark wasn't a good way to drink and he knew that sometime after dawn he would have to get out of bed and piss, long before he had gotten enough rest, but he didn't care because he liked to drink his Jameson's and he figured he had earned it.

It would be two twenty-two in the afternoon in Quang Tri province, Viet Nam. Dooley had worked it out looking at a globe: Viet Nam was just about exactly halfway around the world from Chicago. It would be hot, like it had been on Bougainville or Luzon. Two in the afternoon and hot as hell. Dooley could still feel it.

Dear Father don't let anything really bad happen to him, Dooley prayed, the only thing he ever prayed anymore. He took a sip of whiskey.

One way or another Dooley had been dealing with bad things for a little over twenty-five years, but out in the Pacific he had learned all about degrees of bad. Getting shot was what you hoped for sometimes. The first time Dooley had seen a man burned black and crisp, screaming on the ground, he had started to learn about really bad things.

The woman on the riverbank had run into it. She hadn't been lucky enough to get a knife in the chest, a bullet through the head or a few quick whacks with a baseball bat. She had run into the thing that Dooley felt had been stalking him since 1943, when the Japanese 17th Army had taken his education in hand on Bougainville, the thing that he feared would not be content until it had his son. She had run into Something Really Bad.

I'll find them, Dooley promised her in the dark, raising his glass.

Two

THE GOVERNOR WANTED a 4 percent state income tax but his own party wasn't buying it; the feds were trying to figure out if the Chicago mob was manipulating the stock market. Where the hell have you guys been, thought Dooley. Accardo, Cerone, Alderisio. Dooley had been hearing the names for twenty years and he wouldn't have been surprised to read that the Outfit owned the stock market. He turned the page. The FBI had been busy; they'd raided Panther headquarters on the West Side with a fugitive warrant and scooped up a couple of wagon loads; eight of them were right back out on bond. Dooley kept on scanning. The VC had hit Saigon and towns in the Delta with terror bombs but there was nothing about the Third Marines up in Quang Tri province.

The Cubs had gotten the game in after all; six in a row. Dooley folded the paper and shoved it away. He drained his coffee cup and went to put it in the sink. Rose came in with a handful of flowers from the garden and put them in a vase. She was wearing a sleeveless blouse and a pair of baggy shorts that did nothing to hide the size of her rear end. Dooley had to look away.

"You're up early. You have to go to court today?" Rose set the vase on the table and looked up at him.

"Nah. Just a nice little autopsy."

She came over to him, arms folded, wearing the tight-lipped look with which she met all his flippancy. "Any chance you can swing home for lunch?"

"After an autopsy? Depends on what you're serving."

"Tripe." Rose gave a fleeting smile, and for a second Dooley caught it, a vision of her the way she had been, his Irish Rose circa 1948. He wished he could see it more often, in there beyond the hair streaked gray and the extra weight, the complexion that had been peaches and cream and was now just patchy red. He had a middle-aged Irish lady on his hands and he didn't know where the hell she'd come from. "Nah, it's a long way to drive to come home for lunch. I'll just go straight to work. Where's Frank?"

"Still in bed, I guess."

"Jesus, it's nearly ten."

"He was up late last night, listening to music."

Dooley shook his head. "The kid needs a job. Something to get him out of bed in the morning."

"He's working on it. The summer just started, he deserves a little vacation."

"When I was his age I worked year round. After school, all summer."

"And you found plenty of time to play ball."

Dooley shrugged. "Sure. I kept busy. I didn't lay around listening to records all the time. Hell, I'd love it if Frank got interested in playing ball."

"He'll be OK. Francis will be OK."

Dooley let it drop and turned to rinse out his cup. "I saw the ticket Kathleen got. I'm not gonna try and fix it. She can pay the damn thing. She needs to learn."

"She ran a stop sign. I've run stop signs. So have you."

"I need to take her out some time and teach her how to drive. She's got a lot to learn."

"So take her out the next time you're off. You're never around."

"Yeah, well, people keep dying."

Rose had that look again when he turned around. "You could get off third watch, couldn't you? Haven't you earned the right to work days yet?"

Dooley didn't want to go down this road again. Shaking his head, he said, "It's not that simple."

"I know, you like working evenings. It's where the action is."

Dooley had never yet lost a stare-down to his wife, and she gave it up after a couple of seconds. Then he felt bad and put out his hands; Rose stepped in close to him, her arms going around him. They stood there listening to somebody's lawn mower, somewhere down the block. "We haven't had a letter in a long time," she said into his throat.

Dooley held onto his wife and tried to think of the right formula. "Two weeks, that's not so long. You get busy. You get tired. You get a break and all you want to do is sleep." And sometimes, he thought, there's nothing to say except things you couldn't ever put in a letter. "He'll be all right."

Rose pulled away far enough to look at him. "How do you know that? How can you possibly say that? What if he's not?"

Dooley hated the rise in her voice, the panicked look in her eye; he wished she could keep a lid on things."It's all odds, Rose. It's a roll of the dice. You gotta believe in the odds. Look at the casualty figures and you see the odds are really in his favor."

She pulled away from him, and Dooley could see she didn't buy it. He didn't really buy it himself, knowing that the longer you were in the field the shorter the odds got, but he wasn't going to tell anybody that.

• • •

The medical examiner got a cigarette going one-handed with his Zippo, flipping over pages on the clipboard lying on the desk with the other hand. "You want the Classic Comics version or the full-length novel?"

"You better stick with the comic book," said Dooley. "I'm a slow reader."

The medical examiner shook his head. "Nobody appreciates my work."

"Hey Doc, tell me who she is and the drinks are on me."

"That's all you need, is it? Well, I can't tell you who she is, but I can tell you what she is. She's a white female, which you probably figured out already, roughly thirty years of age give or take a half-decade either way, and she's dead."

"Well, thanks. I guess I'll be going then."

"Hang on, cowboy. She's been that way somewhere between thirty-six and forty-eight hours. She was stuffed someplace, like maybe a car trunk, shortly after death and then stayed there for half a day or so before being tossed out on the riverbank. Rigor mortis had set in fully by the time you found her, so she'd been dead at the very least eighteen hours. That means she died at the latest around midnight Tuesday, probably earlier that evening or afternoon. She hadn't had anything to eat for at least a day before she died. And she hadn't had sex in a while, either. At least, nobody ejaculated in her."

"Did they tie her up before or after she died?"

"Both."

"Both?"

"Some of the ligature marks were pre-decease and some were after. It looks like they tied her up, let her loose, tied her again, several times. When she died they trussed her up for the last time, maybe to make it easier to carry her."

Dooley met the medical examiner's utterly blank look for a second or two. "All right. I guess I have to ask you what all they did to her."

"I wrote it all up for you, Latin words and all. Comic-book version, they beat her face to a pulp with brass knuckles or something similar, they burned her with cigarettes, they jabbed her with a sharp object, like an ice pick, in some very tender places. Find the place where she died, you'll find a lot of blood. Unless they're really good at cleaning up."

Dooley stood there nodding slowly and looking down at the clipboard. "Did she manage to put up a fight at all?"

"Not enough to get anything helpful under her fingernails. The only thing I can tell you is there was grime on the soles of her feet and her hands and knees that looks like motor oil and dirt. Like she walked and crawled over a garage floor at some point."

"OK, how about ID? You took her prints, how about dental records?"

"Her jaw was broken in three places and a lot of her teeth were knocked out of kilter. You'll need a hell of a dentist."

"Scars, birthmarks, tattoos?"

"Nothing too helpful. She'd had a few stitches on her right elbow at some point a long time ago but that's about it. I'd pray you've got her prints on file if I were you. Or somebody who knew her well enough to recognize a mole or a freckle here or there. The face isn't going to be much help."

"Terrific. You got a package for me to take back?"

The examiner pointed at a cluster of tagged plastic bags on a counter. "Right there. Hair, blood, twine, the works. Give me fifteen minutes to finish up the paperwork."

"Take your time," said Dooley. "I'll be right outside."

• • •

"There's a lot of women missing in Chicago, you know that?" said Olson. "You'd think they'd be easier to keep track of."

Dooley shrugged out of his jacket and hung it on the chair. "What are we looking at?"

Olson blew out a puff of air. "Crossing off anybody too young, too old, too black, too blonde or with too many missing fingers, I come up with six possibilities. All of them have been missing for at least a week."

Dooley frowned across the desk. " A week."

"Yeah. Does that rule them out?"

"I wish it did. Nothing's for certain. But this is somebody that probably got killed on Tuesday. And I don't think she was out of circulation for a long time before they killed her. I don't think you grab somebody and then let her sit around for a week before you start in on her. I think we're looking for someone that was still saying hi to the neighbors on Monday. So she hasn't been missed yet. She lives alone, maybe. One of these big apartment buildings where nobody knows anyone else."

"Well, she was in the papers this morning. If she's got any friends at all, if she's got a job she hasn't shown up at for a couple of days, that ought to get somebody worried." Olson thought about it for a second and said, "Unless the person that would normally call her in missing is the one that did it."

"Yeah, I know. Always the best guess."

"He catches her playing around or something. He's had enough and goes ape-shit. He doesn't rape her because all he wants is to teach her a lesson."

"Could be."

"You still think it's more cold-blooded than that, don't you?"

Dooley leaned back and clasped his hands behind his head. "She'd been kept in a garage. Jealous rages don't happen in garages. They happen in kitchens and bedrooms. If it's a little more premeditated, maybe he lures her down to the basement. What the hell do I know? I'm just thinking out loud. All I'm saying is, I think somebody wanted something from this girl. Jealous husbands use what's laying around. Bricks, pipe wrenches, the carving knife. With this girl, somebody had a plan."

"A man with a plan."

"And a garage."

"Yeah. There's a hell of a lot of garages in this city."

"Not too far from Weed Street. I don't think they'd want to drive a long way with a body in the trunk."

"Unless they're real sharp. In which case they might drive all across the city just to throw us off."

"Could be." Dooley scowled at his partner. "She had to make some noise. It had to be someplace where they knew they wouldn't be interrupted. We're not looking for a garage out behind somebody's house."

"OK, we've eliminated all but a few thousand places."

"The clothes may be long gone," said Dooley. "They took them off her early and got rid of them. But you never know. Get it in the bulletin, discarded women's clothing in a garbage can, a pair of high heels in the incinerator, whatever. Somebody turns in a woman's purse, we want to see it."

Dooley and his partner looked at each other for a few ticks of the clock, two men with shovels looking at each other over a pile of manure.

"We could just sit here all day, wait for somebody to call and tell us who she is," said Olson.

Dooley smiled. "There's a reason they dumped her in Weed Street. We go back and look, we may figure it out."

• • •

"You come off of North Avenue, you take the first right that leads to the river."

Olson shrugged, looking out the windshield at the corner of Weed and Kingsbury. "Or you come up from Division."

"If you come up from Division, you dump her down there closer to Division. There's a million places to get through to the river."

"Could be."

"Look, if it happened down there in the projects, how'd she get there? What was a white woman doing in there? You telling me they snatched her off the street or something? I think we'd have heard about it."

"I don't know, I'm just covering all the bases. So they came off North, fine."

"I think that's more likely. And I think they were coming east."

"How come?"

"What's east of here, in the way of industrial areas? Not much. You get into Old Town there pretty quick."

"All right, so they were coming east. Where from?"

Dooley drummed with his fingers on the metal of the car door. "Someplace east of Crawford. Pulaski, I mean. Or say Cicero."

"OK, I give up. Why?"

"If you're west of Cicero, you take her out to the forest preserve to dump her."

"As long as we're guessing, I guess that's a good one. So you're saying Humboldt Park. We looking for a bunch of Puerto Ricans?"

"Maybe. But there's another way to look at it."

"What, after you got me believing in this? Don't let me down."

"Say you're right. Say they didn't want to dump her in their own back yard. We're talking about people with some savvy, not just a bunch of derelicts on a bender. Still, they don't want to drive all night. So they think of the river, 'cause that's their closest option, but they go up it or down it a ways to find a place. They still started out east of Cicero, and I bet they were south of North, because there's more industry down that way, more areas where you could beat up a woman in a garage and nobody'd hear her. They came up Halsted maybe, or Ashland, from the near West Side. Ashland, because if they came up Halsted, they'd have run into the river and other places to turn off before they got to North Avenue."

"Jesus, you're a hell of a guesser. Let's go write up the guess report and go home."

"There's a million garages in this city, but there can't be too many of them on the near West Side where the owner either doesn't know or doesn't care what goes on in there in the middle of the day. I think we're looking for a place with a reputation. We're looking for a place the auto theft people know about, or the local patrol guys wonder about, driving by it. Be worth a talk with somebody over at Monroe Street."

Olson reached for the ignition. "It's gonna turn out she was killed in New Orleans and brought up the Mississippi and thrown off a boat. And then you won't look so damn smart."

"If they ever had her on a boat," said Dooley, "she'd be at the bottom of the lake."

"You got all the answers, don't you?" said Olson, shoving the car in gear.

• • •

"Sheesh, take your pick," said the sergeant with the six strands of hair plastered across his shiny dome. "There's so many places to hide around here you could lose a fuckin' army. Since the riots, anybody with any sense has found someplace else to do business. Go a few blocks west and you got your pick of empty buildings."

Dooley had a feeling he was not getting through. "I don't know if we're looking for a place that's derelict. I don't mean some burned-out shell where the junkies go to shoot up. I'm thinking about places you've had your eye on. Chop shops, fencing operations, a place where you see cars parked outside but you don't know exactly what goes on in there. The type of place you wonder about."

The sergeant shrugged. "It's a big district. Chop shops, I don't think so. Not around here. Fencing, I could show you half a dozen places where I know they're taking in stolen goods. But I don't think they're renting out the back room to sex maniacs."

"No, I know. But there's got to be places where things get

stored, places where things get hidden. Places that are, number one, secure; number two, a bit isolated; and number three, not part of a going concern with employees going in and out all day. Your patrol guys would know."

"You want to know the truth, around here my patrol guys worry mainly about not getting shot by some spade who thinks it's time to start the revolution. Stolen TVs are the least of our worries. It ain't fun out there."

"That I can believe. But you can announce it at roll call. You can ask anyone who's got an idea about a place to give me a call. Anybody who knows a place where things go on late at night, where cars turn up at odd times, where they saw something that looked funny last Tuesday, whatever. Just put out the word and have 'em give me call." Dooley slid his card across the desk.

The sergeant took it and gave Dooley an amused look. "Sounds to me like you're all out of leads and down to the guessing."

"I never had any leads. I got a corpse with no name, I got no witnesses, no crime scene. You got any bright ideas, I'm listening. All I can think of to do is start shaking trees and see what falls out."

"You start shaking trees," said the sergeant, "you better be ready to duck."

• • •

"You think you're gonna spot it like this, huh? Just driving around?" Olson sounded bored but he was scanning the street like a good cop.

"No, we're just taking the scenic route home." Dooley was driving for a change, cruising west on Madison. "We're tourists, that's all. I don't know about you, but I can't afford to take the family to Wisconsin this summer. I'm thinking of bringing them down here, show them a foreign country."

Olson made a little puffing noise that might have been a laugh. "The heart of darkest Africa. Jesus, they tore the place up, didn't they?" Half the buildings on the block were gone, burned to the ground, and the ones that were left had no glass, just plywood and padlocked grates over the doors. The West Side looked like a flight of B-29s had unloaded on it. "You'd think someone would have said, 'Hey, remember we gotta live here.'"

"If you can call it living."

Dooley and Olson had spent some frantic hours out on the West Side in the riots the year before, the first time Dooley had been shot at since 1945.

"Look—natives." On a corner, five or six black men with giant Afros glared at them as they rolled past. "Geez, Mike. How come they don't like us?" said Olson, mock-plaintive.

"Because they know we don't like them."

The scenery got worse: Dooley remembered what Madison had looked like when he was a kid and wondered where the hell everything went.

"There," he said. "That's the kind of place we're looking for."

It was an island now, a single intact building in a block of charred rubble and a few cleared demolition sites. It was hard to say whether any of the storefronts still housed a going concern, but at least the windows were intact behind the accordion grilles and there were no scorch marks up the façade. There was a faded, peeling sign that said Auto Repair over a big overhead door, but the door was shut tight and there were no vehicles parked anywhere near the place. "Something like that," said Dooley. "That's where they took her."

"Well, that really narrows it down now, doesn't it?" said Olson. "I'd bet we've narrowed the field to a couple hundred places over two or three square miles. Let's go get lunch."

Dooley swung up Ashland and went north. "They left tracks," he said. "Had to. They always do."

Three

RAIN AGAIN, ON a Saturday; June so far was a poor excuse for summer. Dooley drove to Damen and Grace with his wipers on, tires hissing on the pavement. Upstairs, at least, the temperature was bearable, the only good thing about the weather. Somebody had left a *Daily News* on a desk and Dooley paged through it looking for the story, knowing he was only going to find the same wire service reports he'd seen at home. There was another picture of Nixon and Thieu at Midway, more D-Day reminiscences. Dooley didn't give a damn about D-Day; twenty-five years ago yesterday he'd been on the other side of the world from Normandy with his own problems. And here was the Viet Nam report: Da Nang shelled, the 25th Infantry Division hit in the Delta, and action up in Quang Tri near the DMZ, no units specified but ten marines dead in an ambush. Dooley tossed the paper onto a chair.

"You see where Namath called it quits?" Olson sat down across from him clutching a cup of coffee.

It took Dooley a second to stop thinking about dead marines. "What happened, his knees give out?"

"No, he says he won't give up the bar. He'd rather hang out with his mobster pals than play football."

"Well, he's got his money in the bank."

"Yeah. Be nice to have enough you could walk away like that. Son of a bitch sure could throw the ball."

"Who needs him?" Dooley was leafing through message slips. "You look at these?"

"I just got in myself. I can't look at a piece of paper until I have some coffee."

"Well, get ready to look at a lot of it." He slid a message across the desk. "Somebody came up with a name for the guy that was seen with the dead kid over on Hoyne last week. Let's find out what the B of I's got on him."

"Anybody call to tell us who our dead girl is?"

"Doesn't look like it. You looked at everything that came in on the teletype this week, right? No missing girls that might be ours?"

"Nobody that matched the description." Olson drank coffee and said, "She's been dead four days and nobody's reported her missing. We're talking about a lady of the evening, maybe."

"I talked to Vice already. We can try and match her prints up with somebody they know."

"Man, till we get a name I don't know what we're gonna do with her."

"Me neither. Hey."

"What?"

Dooley waved a message slip at him. "Guy from Monroe Street called. 'May have info for you. Off today, call at home.' Here's my alert patrolman, I bet you."

"Probably some rookie who got excited about a broken window."

"I think it probably takes more than a broken window to get people excited out on the West Side," said Dooley, reaching for the phone.

• • •

"Yeah, right, they said you were looking for a possible murder scene in our part of the woods." Over the phone Donald Gray didn't sound like a breathless rookie. He had taken his time getting to the phone but Dooley was used to that; he spent half his life on the phone.

"Just trolling," said Dooley. "Looking for a place where somebody could get away with murder."

"We got a lot of those. The reason I called was, they mentioned Tuesday."

"Yeah. That's when we think it happened."

"Well, all I can tell you is, Tuesday night we picked up one of our regulars, an old wino that lives on the street mostly, around Madison and Halsted, in there. Somebody complained because he was panhandling at a bus stop. Last thing in the world we wanted to do was put him in the squad, believe me, the way he smelled, but we had a couple of irate citizens standing right there. So anyway, as we're taking him around the corner, he starts hollering about how come we're bothering him when people are being murdered all over the place. We thought he was just ranting at first, but then he says a couple of things that get our attention. 'They're killing women back there,' he says, 'and you're wasting your time with me.' So we stop and ask him what the hell he's talking about and he says he can show us the place. So we start driving around, Jackson, Adams, west of Halsted a few blocks, with him saying down there, and then no, it musta been the next street over, and I'm starting to think he's full of shit and trying to get him to tell us what he saw or heard and he's talking nonsense. Drunk on his ass. And just as I'm losing patience he says there, right down that alley, and this time he's pretty definite and shows us where he was trying to sleep when he heard somebody screaming. It was an alley between Adams and Monroe west of Sangamon, there's this factory or something with a door on the alley, and he claimed he heard a woman scream inside there, sometime that day. He was sleeping off a drunk in the alley and had just woke up, he said. He said he laid there and listened to her scream for a while, real faint, inside a building somewhere, and then she quit."

"And he ran to the nearest phone to report it," said Dooley.

"I asked him about that. He said he wasn't sure at first he'd really heard it and anyway he knew we wouldn't believe somebody like him. I asked him if he was sure now if he'd really heard it and he started to back down and finally said no, maybe he hadn't really heard it. We couldn't pin him down. We tried to raise somebody, checked the doors, and everything was locked up tight and we couldn't see much through the windows and so we just noted the address and called in and asked about reports of incidents around there and there weren't any. So frankly I just told him to get lost and kind of forgot about it, because with these old half-dead winos you never know. They do hear things a lot of times. But when they announced this at roll call I remembered and thought I oughta call you."

"It's good you did. Can you give me the address?"

"Sure. The building's on Adams, it's 952 Adams, and there's a sign in front that says Mid-America Screw Company or something like that. There's an overhead door in back on the alley."

Scribbling fast, Dooley said, "OK, now can you tell me who your wino is and where to look for him?"

"I can give you his name, I've booked him enough times. Ernest McGill, age forty-four, or so he claims, but he looks about seventy. He's an Indian. They call him Chief, but then they call all the Indians Chief. He hangs out sometimes at the Jack Pot on Madison and panhandles up and down Halsted. The wagon guys can probably scoop him up if you put out a stop order on him."

"OK, thanks, Don. I appreciate it."

"I gotta tell you, it's been bothering me, thinking I should have maybe done more. I didn't know if it was just the DTs or what, and then the night got kinda busy and I didn't have time to think about it any more. But I'd hate to think I could have prevented something and didn't."

Dooley considered. "This was Tuesday night?"

"About nine in the evening."

"Then I wouldn't worry about it. If it was the place we're looking for, it was probably all over by then."

• • •

The rain had stopped but a creeping fog had taken its place. Everything in the glistening streets was muted, remote, furtive: pedestrians with their heads down, scuttling into the streets without looking, the murmur of traffic outside the closed car windows broken by a sudden squeal of brakes, a long blast on a car horn. Olson nearly rear-ended a Bonneville on Halsted when it balked at a yellow light.

The 900 block of Adams was intact; the riots had missed it, but economic decline could wreck a block just as badly, only slower. The Mid-America Screw Company was long gone, leaving one story of sturdy brick industrial plant with wired-over windows, empty. Through a window on Adams Dooley and Olson could see scarred linoleum and a gutted filing cabinet lying on its side. Sometimes you had to try to find somebody awake at the County Clerk's office to find out who owned a building, but sometimes it was easy: there was a sign on the door in front that said *Managed by Athens Realty 812 W. Jackson*. Olson wrote it down and they walked around the corner.

In the alley in back they found the overhead door and a regular one next to it. There were windows here, too, but they were too grimy and it was too dark inside to see anything. Dooley stood looking at the cracked pavement in front of the overhead door and saw it wiped clean by the rain. "Let's go find our wino," he said.

"You don't want to go talk to Athens Realty first? That's a couple of blocks away."

Dooley shook his head. "I don't mind finding out what we can about Athens Realty, but I don't want anybody over there to have any idea we're interested until I've got probable cause for a search warrant. I want to have a stick to hit somebody with."

Olson looked at the sky and jammed his hands deep in the pockets of his raincoat. "We could just wait till the local guys haul him in."

"What else were you planning to do today? You got a date or something?"

"I'm just thinking, there's a lot of winos on these streets."

"They won't be on the streets today," said Dooley. "They'll be looking for a roof."

Dooley had worked on Skid Row as a young patrolman twenty years earlier. Not a lot had changed, though the high and mighty were always making noises about bulldozing it. West Madison Street was like a weed with tough roots: it looked bad but it was easier to leave it in place and pretend it belonged there. From Clinton west across the expressway all the way to Ogden, Madison was crowded with the type of establishments designed to make a buck off men who had no money. On Madison Street you could sell your shoes for the price of a bottle of port and have only a few feet to walk in your beat-up relievers to get the wine. Madison Street was where you wound up when you'd run out of drive or run out of options.

"Try the bars first, then the missions, then the flophouses. We're lucky the weather's lousy. Not a great night to sleep out." Dooley pulled the Plymouth to the curb and put it in park. "Here's the Jack Pot. Maybe we'll hit it, first time lucky."

The Jack Pot Inn, like all the Skid Row bars, let you know right up front what you were going to have to pay; the clientele usually didn't have much of a margin to work with. Big painted signs in the window announced *Schooner Beer 15¢—Shot Whiskey 15¢—Shot & Beer 35¢* and the ever popular *Sweet Wine 15¢.* Inside was a long gloomy room with a moderately populated bar stretching down the left side and bare light bulbs hanging from the ceiling. There was a strong smell of spilled beer that had never gotten wiped up. There was black linoleum on the floor and cardboard boxes stacked against the wall. Nobody who cared about decor ever drank here; it was as close to purely functional as a place could get.

The bartender knew what they were, if not who; Dooley didn't even bother with ID. The bartender was a broad heavy bald man who looked as if he had won a lot of fights in his life but was starting to tire in the late rounds. "You got a customer named Ernest McGill?" said Dooley. Olson strolled slowly on down the room, hands in his pockets.

The bartender shifted a couple of glasses behind the bar. "Could be. I don't know 'em all by name."

"They call him Chief. He's an Indian."

The bartender looked down the bar to a knot of drinkers who were long past worrying about a couple of coppers. "Hey, anybody know an Indian named Chief?"

That brought a rumble of laughter, but Dooley wasn't in the mood to join in. "How many Indians you got that drink in here regularly?"

The barkeep shrugged. "I don't keep a list."

Dooley gave him the look, the one that said I can make things just as hard as you want. "Two? Three? Five?"

"A couple."

"OK, I want you to think hard for a second and tell me what you can about those two individuals. Names, where they sleep, where they eat, who they run with. What time of day they normally drop in to your fine establishment here. Whether you ever cash checks for them and what the name on the check is."

The bartender put on an injured look, not one that he did particularly well. "I'm not a social worker, for Christ's sake. I'm a saloon keeper."

"Yeah, I know. You just pour the drinks. They got names?"

A barkeeper who didn't at least try to protect his customers from the law could start to lose them, but the man knew he had to stay on the good side of the cops, too. Olson had returned from his little tour and stood backing up Dooley's patient stare. The bartender swiped at a couple of wet spots with a towel and said, "I think you must want Mac. Haven't seen him in a few days. I don't know where the hell he bunks, but I know he eats next door sometimes, when he bothers to eat."

• • •

"Mac? You mean the Indian guy, wears the plaid jacket? Yeah, he comes in here. Haven't seen him in a couple days. He knows better than to come in here when he's drunk. He only comes in to eat when he's made a couple of bucks. I don't know what he does, collects bottles maybe. I think he sleeps up at the loading docks, on Kinzie. That's mostly where the Injuns flop. Mac's OK, when he's sober. I've seen him outside the missions sometimes. Try the Bible Rescue Mission."

• • •

"They'll start lining up for the missions in a while and we can work the lines. Then there are maybe fifteen hotels between here and Ogden. Rule out the ones that are all black and it won't take that long."

"What do you say, want to try the Holiday Inn there, just in case?"

"That one I think we can rule out."

• • •

"I think Mac went up north."

"Where's that, the reservation?"

"No, shit, you kidding me? Mac ain't seen the reservation in thirty years. I mean up on Wilson Avenue. He goes to the Indian bars up there. He knows people, I think he's got a place he knows up there to flop at. He'll be gone a few days, then he'll show up around here again. What the hell'd he do, anyway?"

• • •

"I can't believe what I'm seeing here, Mike. It's pouring rain and they're making these poor bastards stand out here."

"The mission doesn't open till six."

"But I mean, Christ, they're standing there inside looking out at all these fuckers getting soaked. You'd think they could open the damn doors five minutes early."

"I don't think that's what they mean when they say it's a rescue mission."

• • •

"Mac. Never heard him called that. You mean Chief. Indian guy in a plaid jacket, yeah. Hey Danny, you seen Chief around?"

"Big Chief or Little Chief?"

"What the hell, Chief. That Injun that hangs around here. In the plaid jacket."

"That's Little Chief. Big Chief's the one with the eye patch. Yeah, I seen him the other day in Rothchild's. Who wants to know?"

"The officer here needs to talk to him."

"I don't talk to no fuckin' bulls."

"Excuse him, officer, he's got a little drunk on, you know? Say, listen, as long as I been helpful and all, I don't suppose you could help me out with a starter on a jug, could you?"

• • •

"I run a clean place here. You got no call to bother me."

"Nobody's going to bother you. I need to see your register, that's all."

"Who you looking for?"

"Ernest McGill. You know him?"

"No, I mean what's he done? We don't never have no trouble-makers here. I run a clean God damn shop."

"Let me see the register."

"I don't allow no women upstairs, I don't let no jackrollers in here. I run a tight God damn ship."

"You're going to run the ship right up on the rocks, drinking on duty like this. Don't bullshit me, I can smell it on your breath."

"You don't need to tell me my business, mister. I been running this place more years than you've been alive."

"Lemme see the book, Grampa."

• • •

"I need a shower. I might need two showers." Olson turned the ignition key and revved the engine. "Mike, promise me something, will you?"

"What?" Dooley finished jotting down notes and slid the legal pad into his briefcase.

"If I ever take to drink, promise me you'll shoot me before you let me wind up down here."

"OK, I promise. I'll shoot you like a dog."

"We ready to call it a night? We've pretty much covered the street."

Dooley smiled at his partner. "We haven't done the alleys yet."

Four

"CUBS GOT WASHED out today," said Olson. "That's gotta hurt, losing a big Sunday crowd like that."

"It hurt me, that's for sure," said Dooley, sifting through papers. "My kid was gonna go to the game, and when it got rained out he couldn't find anything better to do than lay around the house and be a pain in the ass. Coming to work was the good part of my day, and that was pretty much a washout, too."

"Oh, I don't know. I think we gave the taxpayers pretty good value for money today."

"What the hell did we accomplish?"

"We knocked on doors. We put miles on the odometer. We showed the flag and cowed the populace. What else do you want?"

"I want the R.D. number on that rape out on Belmont. Where the hell'd it go?"

Olson tapped a finger on a form. "Right there. You're getting punch-drunk, pal."

"I wish to God I *was* drunk."

"We can probably arrange that."

"It could only help. What are we missing on this rape?"

"Nothing. I did the submission forms to the bulletin. It's all there. We did a good day's work."

"Shit. We chased our damn tails all day."

"Man, you need a vacation. Or a shot and a beer, at least. What's eating you?"

Dooley jammed his ballpoint into his shirt pocket. "The girl on the riverbank."

"Hey. We got our feelers out, got our sentries posted. We just have to wait for something to come in."

"She knew somebody," Dooley said, pushing his chair away from the desk. "Everybody knows somebody. Somebody misses her. How come they haven't called us?"

Olson brought a fist down on the stapler. "Because they don't know she's dead. She'd have to be out of touch for more than a week before they get worried. And they don't read the Chicago papers, don't get Chicago TV, so no bells have gone off yet. So she's from out of town, or at least her folks are out of town. Or maybe her folks are dead. We really don't know shit about this girl."

"No, we don't. Except she had something somebody wanted."

"Or they thought she did."

"Good point. If you stuck an ice pick up my ass, I'd give you whatever you wanted in a hurry. I wouldn't sit there and take that kind of abuse if I could help it."

They sat and looked at each other for a few seconds before Olson said, "Well, how many hotels and motels are there in Chicago? We could call every one of them and see if they've had any female guests go missing."

"It may come to that. A shortcut would be to look at complaints of people skipping out on their hotel bills. But I don't know, I don't think she was at a hotel. I think she was hiding."

"That would make sense. Where?"

"I don't know, but I can do some more guessing. Let's say you've got problems with somebody in Chicago, so you leave town. But you don't go too far, for whatever reason. You're close enough that when they catch up with you, they throw you in a car and bring you back here to work you over instead of doing it on the spot. Just far enough that we don't get the missing person report."

"I see. Like maybe over a state line."

"Yeah. I think we need to do more than just look at the teletype. I don't think a disappearance necessarily goes out on the teletype unless somebody has a reason to think the victim's going for a ride. I think we need to talk to the state police in Wisconsin, Michigan, and Indiana for starters, see who they're looking for, who didn't come home last week."

"OK. I can do that tomorrow."

The phone rang across the room. Harper answered it and after a few murmured words put his hand over the mouthpiece and yelled, "Dooley! Twelfth District for you."

Dooley took the phone. "You looking for an Ernest McGill?" said a voice at the other end.

"Yeah. You got him?"

"Scooped him up in the last wagon load for public intoxication. Somebody saw your stop order, we thought we ought to give you a call."

Dooley looked at his watch: close to midnight. "Thanks, I appreciate it. I tell you what, I'm not going to do anything with him tonight. Hang on to him after court in the morning and I'll come and take him off your hands."

• • •

The Monroe Street lockup was a second home for a good many men on Skid Row; if you spent a lot of your time drunk, the ritual of the wagon, the lockup, the bullpen and the Call Court was going to be a big part of your life. This time though, as he came through the barred door from the cells, Ernest McGill looked like a first-timer, dazed and bewildered in his filthy plaid jacket. He looked at Dooley standing there waiting for him and flinched as if someone had walloped him. He limped over to the desk. Dooley could see he was stone cold sober and suffering for it. He signed the paperwork while McGill reclaimed his personal effects and then said, "Come on, Mac. Let's go have a talk."

"What the hell did I do?" said Ernest McGill in a ragged bass. He was a little bandy-legged man with a dark seamed face and a wild thatch of black hair. He looked a little like a picture Dooley had seen of Sitting Bull, if Sitting Bull had had his hair cut with garden shears and spent a few nights in the gutter. "They let everyone else go but me."

"You didn't do anything that I know about. You got something on your conscience today?"

"I don't know nothing."

"Me neither, Mac. That's why I need to talk to you." He turned to the officer at the desk. "Can we borrow one of your interview rooms?"

"Be my guest."

In the room with the door closed Dooley said, "They treat you OK back there?"

McGill sat sideways on his chair, an elbow over the back, slumped like a man in pain. He looked like hell and smelled worse. "What's it to you?"

"You're my witness. I don't let people mess around with my witnesses."

McGill blinked at him. "They took ten dollars off me. Worst God damn jackrollers out here, the men in blue."

Dooley had seen cops rob drunks blind in his time on the street: not many, but it didn't take many to make a reputation. He said, "You get a name?"

"Huh?"

"Do you know the name of the arresting officer?"

McGill's hand trembled as he passed it over his mouth. "Sure I know his name."

"Well, you want to go out there and make a complaint, I'll back you up. But then, I get to drive out of the neighborhood afterwards, so that's easy for me to say. It's your call."

A cop as an ally was a brand new concept for McGill, Dooley could see. He watched the Indian making all the necessary calculations. Dooley hoped like hell he would decide against it, because he was going to have a busy enough day as it was, but he needed Ernest McGill on his side and figured this might be part of the price. "Forget it," said McGill. "It ain't worth the trouble."

"If you say so." Dooley pulled out his wallet and took out a ten. "Here."

McGill thought about it long and hard; where he came from nobody ever gave you anything for free. But ten bucks was a lot of money for a man like him and in the end he put out his trembling hand and took the bill just like Dooley knew he would. "This is about what I told that cop the other day, ain't it?" said McGill.

"About what you heard in the alley, yeah."

"I don't want to get in no trouble."

"Who with? You worried about someone?"

"No, I mean, I can't go to no court or nothing."

"Well, Mac, I don't know that it's going to come to that. I need two things from you. I need you to tell me exactly what you heard, and I need you to show me exactly where you heard it. Can you do that?"

"Like I said the other day, I was sleeping off a drunk. I might have dreamed it."

"I don't think so. If you'd dreamed it you wouldn't have brought it up the other night. You told Officer Gray about it because you were sure, weren't you?"

Dooley watched his witness fighting it, watched his head sag and watched him clasp his hands to stop them trembling. "I don't feel so good," said McGill.

"What do you need, Mac? You want to eat something? I'll buy you breakfast."

"I could use a drink."

"I could probably spring for that, too. But you got to help me out." Dooley gave it three or four seconds and said, "Look at me, Mac." To the Indian's sidelong squint he said, "Somebody got hurt the other day. Real bad. And you know it. And you wouldn't have said anything about it if you didn't want to help us catch the people that did it. You got a chance to do a good thing here, Mac."

Ernest McGill held out for nearly half a minute while Dooley stared at him. Finally McGill said, "I could show you where I heard it."

• • •

"He took me right to the spot," said Dooley into the phone. "Same place he took the first officer to. No hesitation this time, no confusion. He showed me where he was sleeping and pointed out the building in question, just across the alley. He was positive about it."

"Well, sounds like you might have what you need then," said the State's Attorney at the other end of the line. "Just one thing. What was he doing in the alley?"

Here we go, thought Dooley. "He was sleeping."

After a brief pause the State's Attorney said, "Sleeping? This was what time?"

Dooley clenched the phone and said, "He was sleeping off a drunk. Look, if he woke up he had to be almost sober."

The lawyer puffed into the phone. "You're going to have a hell of a time selling that to a judge."

"Listen, you got to talk to the man. You'll see. He was positive."

"I'll tell you what, the *judge* is going to want to talk to the man. You want him to sign off on a search warrant, he's going to want to look your man in the eye and hear him tell it in clear bell-like tones."

"Shit," said Dooley, with passion. Back in the interview room he handed McGill a cup of coffee and said, "Mac, here's the deal. You're gonna get a shower and a meal and a pint of vodka. Only thing is, you get the vodka a little at a time, just enough to keep you going, because we have to go talk to a judge."

"A judge? What do I gotta talk to a judge for?" Ernest McGill had put up with a lot, and Dooley could see he was getting close to his limit.

Dooley clasped his hands on the table and waited for McGill to focus on him. "Let me explain what I'm trying to do, OK? I need to get a search warrant to get inside that building. To do that, I have to convince a judge that I have what's called probable cause. That means I have a good reason to look inside there, good enough that some sharp defense lawyer can't poke holes in it. Used to be, the judge would just take our word for everything, but they've made things a little harder. I have to get a State's Attorney to rule on everything I do so they don't throw it out of court later, and the one I just talked to says I need to take you in to let the judge have a look at you. If the judge thinks you're just a hopeless drunk who hallucinated the whole thing, he won't give us our search warrant and we'll never find out what happened in there that day. But if you can hold things together long enough to go and look that judge in the eye and tell him what you heard, leave no doubt in his mind that you're in possession of all your faculties and you're an upstanding citizen and everything, then we get our warrant and we can maybe see what happened in there and maybe catch somebody. And then, by God, Mac, I swear I'll do what I can to make things easier for you around here. I'll put the word out that you helped me out and nobody should mess with you. And I'll buy you dinner at the Pump Room if you want."

McGill looked at Dooley and did the last thing in the world Dooley expected. He shook a few times like an old jalopy trying to turn over and he gave out a string of sucking, gasping sounds that

Dooley finally recognized as laughter."You're a hell of a psychologist, officer, you really are," he said finally. "There's just one problem."

"What?"

"I don't drink vodka."

"You do this morning," Dooley said, rising. "He won't smell vodka on your breath."

• • •

The judge had gray hairs coming out of his ears and tufts of steel wool where most people had eyebrows. Dooley stood watching him skim the affidavit. "You say you were asleep?" the judge said without looking up. He spoke brusquely, with the voice of authority: penetrating, imperious, unused to modulation. Dooley had a feeling the man would use the same voice asking his wife for more coffee in the morning.

"Yes sir." Ernest McGill sat on the edge of his chair, looking like a waif in the oversized seersucker jacket Dooley had bought him at a second-hand shop on Madison, his hands resting on his thighs, knuckles just barely showing. "I had done a lot of work that morning and I was tired."

The judge looked at McGill from beneath the eyebrows. "What kind of work do you do, sir?"

"That morning I was collecting bottles." After the judge's blare McGill's voice was a hollow rumble, a barrel rolling slowly over gravel. "There's a feller on Sangamon that pays for empties. I'd spent the morning picking up bottles and I'd just turned in a load. Then I was tired and needed to lay down."

"Had you had anything to drink?"

Dooley frowned at a ragged fingernail, trying hard not to look as his search warrant went through the rail and over the cliff. "Yes, Your Honor, I had," said McGill. "But just enough to calm the shakes and put me to sleep. They only pay you half a cent per bottle, so all I'd managed to raise was the price of a pint of wine."

"I see." In the silence the judge flipped over a page of the affidavit. "And a pint of wine is not sufficient to inebriate you?"

"No, sir. You see, sir, I'm an alcoholic. I know it's a bad problem, it's pretty well wrecked my life and all, but that don't mean I'm drunk all the time, sir. A pint of wine is just about enough to settle me down a bit. Most times it don't even put me to sleep, but I'd walked a hell of a lot all day picking up bottles, and the night before I didn't sleep a whole lot 'cause I got chased out of the docks by a feller I had a beef with and had to carry the banner most of the night. I mean just walk around. So when I got a little wine in me I went to sleep for a couple of hours in this stairwell I know about in that alley." McGill passed a hand over his mouth, a fairly steady hand, and let it fall to his thigh again. His eyes were watering a little but he was looking straight at the judge.

The judge let the affidavit fall to the desktop. "And what woke you up?"

"I don't exactly know. I just kind of came to, and just set there for a little while, feeling OK but not ready to move, and then I heard her scream. Faint like, a long way off. Or on the other side of a wall. But I heard it."

"And did you investigate?"

McGill's gaze fell away from the judge, and his hand went back to his mouth, and Dooley shifted his weight and started thinking about new approaches. "No, judge, I didn't," said McGill. "I just set there. I wasn't sure at first, and then when she screamed again I was scared, and then finally I came up out of the stairwell and went to listen at the door, and I heard her one more time. And then I got scared and left."

"And did you give any thought to finding help, or reporting it?"

McGill was looking at the judge again, and it was the look of a haunted man. "No sir. Well, yeah, I thought about it a little. I even walked a little ways looking for a policeman, but I didn't see any, and then—I don't know. I kind of tried to forget about it. It wasn't the first time I ever heard somebody scream. And you want to know the truth, the police aren't always real helpful when you need their help." He shot a quick look at Dooley. "But . . ." McGill's hand rose, fluttered, and fell back to his thigh.

"But what?"

"But I felt bad about it."

The judge gave McGill a long look that said a lot about the judge's opinion of McGill's feelings, and then he looked up at Dooley. "If I understand this affidavit correctly, you have no real evidence that this man's account is connected with the crime you're investigating."

"Just the fact of the time, Your Honor. We believe our victim was killed that afternoon."

"But the speculation as to where your victim was killed is just that, speculation."

"It's a guess, sir." Dooley had learned that trying to bullshit a judge was always bad policy. "But it's a damn good one."

The judge made a noise in his throat that might have meant just about anything and turned over the pages of the affidavit again. Seconds ticked by while McGill wiped his mouth and Dooley jingled change in his pocket. Finally the judge pulled back the sleeve of his robe and looked at his watch. Dooley thought it was all over. "I've seen stronger affidavits," the judge said. "But I've seen a lot of worse ones, too." He reached for a pen.

• • •

The sun had started sliding down the sky by the time they came out of the Cook County Criminal Court and walked down the steps onto California Avenue. Dooley folded the search warrant and slipped it into the inside pocket of his suit jacket. He slapped Ernest McGill on the shoulder. "Mac, you're a hell of a man."

"Can I have the rest of the bottle now?"

"You can have whatever you want. You hungry?"

"A little bit."

"Where do you want to eat?"

"I don't know. You can drop me on Madison, I guess."

"Hey, I can do better than that."

"That's all right. Just drop me there. I'm OK."

"Whatever you say, Mac."

The ride up Ogden was silent. For a while Dooley could hear a faint sloshing as McGill put the bottle to his lips, and then as they neared Madison Street there were gentle snoring sounds in the back seat. When Dooley pulled over on Madison, McGill took a few seconds to come around. He focused on Dooley watching him over the back of the seat and struggled to sit up. "Hey, sorry. Kinda tired, I guess. Thank you for the ride."

"My pleasure, Mac," said Dooley. "And listen, I will put in a good word for you over at the district. You been a big help. Anything I can do for you, let me know, OK? You got my card."

Ernest McGill steadied himself with a hand on the seat back and looked at Dooley with a lost and forlorn expression. "Just one thing, mainly," he said.

"What's that?"

"Catch 'em." In the dim light inside the car, McGill's eyes shone wide and white in the wrecked face. "See, there are times, Christ, I can still hear her screaming."

Five

"NOTHING I HATE more in the world," said Stan Kowalczyk, holding a lighter to a Pall Mall. "Taking next of kin to the morgue." He flipped the lighter shut and put it away in a pocket of his shirt. "I've had people faint on me, I've had 'em go nuts and beat their heads on the wall, I've even had people come after me, like it was my God damn fault somebody killed their kid."

Kowalczyk was in the region of forty but his vocal cords were going on sixty, eroded by too many cigarettes, possibly a few too many drinks, and too many years of laying down the law to people who didn't know how to listen. He blew smoke and said, "This guy I felt sorry for. Drove up from Kankakee thinking we might have his daughter. Looked like a walking dead man. The guy was a wreck."

"Why'd he think it was her?" Dooley was scanning the Supplementary Report Kowalczyk had tossed on the desk.

"He read about your stiff in the paper. His daughter's been gone a month. He talked to somebody at Eleventh and State who said sure, come on up and have a look at her. Never saw a man so happy to waste a day. I wouldn't say he exactly had a spring in his step walking out of there, but at least there were signs of life."

"OK, how's he sure it's not her?"

"His daughter's got a mole on the back of her neck and a vaccination scar on her arm. Your girl doesn't."

"OK, thanks for handling it."

"Always glad to clean up after the night shift. I'm just glad this one had a happy ending."

"If you can call it that," said Dooley. "His daughter's still missing."

"Well, hell with it. Who needs happy endings? We're coppers, for Christ's sake."

When Olson came in Dooley was staring out the window into the haze over the distant Loop. The rain had moved on after spoiling the weekend and left the first hint of steamy weather to come behind it.

"You don't have to wait for me," said Olson. "You want to open that file without me, I give you permission."

"Don't worry. Kowalcyzk's doing the work for us."

"Jesus. Are you sure that's wise?"

"He had a guy come in for a possible ID on our mystery girl this morning, but it was a false alarm."

"Well, shit. That's what you get for letting a Polack take care of it."

Kowalczyk flipped him a casual finger and went on packing up his briefcase. "How'd it go with your wino?" said Olson, settling onto a chair.

"Perfect," said Dooley. "We got a warrant."

"You're kidding me."

"I told you it would fly."

"Damn. You sure know how to sweet-talk a judge. So, we ready to go wave it at somebody?"

"I didn't get it to wipe up your damn coffee spills. Who's driving?"

• • •

The realty company was on Jackson just around the corner from Halsted. *Athens Import-Export* was painted on the glass, with Greek characters below it. The display window was filled with candles, souvenir tablecloths bearing images of the Acropolis, books in Greek. Inside there was a counter and shelves crowded with knickknacks: statuettes and glassware. There was nobody behind the counter but when Dooley called out, a man came through a door from the rear.

"Is this Athens Realty?" Dooley said.

The man was middle-aged and bald, scrawny and a little stooped, with a gray moustache. He looked from Dooley to Olson, not liking what he saw. He had slightly watery eyes. "Who wants to know?"

Dooley pulled his star out of a pocket. "Officers Dooley and Olson, CPD Area Six Homicide. You got a realty company back there somewhere?"

The man looked at the badge and then at Olson and Dooley in turn and seemed to sag just a bit, like a little air had gone out of him. "That would be my brother you need to talk to," he said. "He's not here."

"What's your brother's name?"

"Theodore Athanasopoulous. I'm Michael."

"Where could we find your brother, Mr. Athanasopoulous?"

The man's eyes flicked back and forth between the two cops. "He went back to Greece."

"When was that?"

A shrug. "Maybe two months ago."

"When's he coming back?"

"I don't know. He had some problems there to deal with."

"I see. And he's the owner of Athens Realty?"

"That's right. Athanasopoulous is too long to fit on a sign, he said."

"So who's running it while he's gone?"

That was a tougher question than Dooley had anticipated, apparently; at least, Michael Athanasopoulous seemed to be having trouble with it. After frowning down at the countertop for a couple of seconds while he rubbed at something on it with his thumb, he looked up and said, "Well, I guess I am."

"OK. You have a building at 952 West Adams?"

"Maybe. I don't know all the addresses. Normally, see, I don't have anything to do with the real estate. I mainly just run the store."

"There was a factory there. It's empty now. Who do we talk to about getting in there?"

There was a pause while the watery eyes blinked a few times. "What happened?" he finally said.

"Maybe nothing at all. We've been given information that may indicate that a crime took place there. We'd like to take a look at the premises if we could. Who would I talk to about that?"

Dooley could see the man trying to guess what his legal rights and obligations were and having trouble with it. After a few seconds, Michael Athanasopoulous said, "Don't you need a warrant?"

"You mean one of these?" Dooley pulled it out of the inside pocket of his jacket, unfolded it and laid it on the counter.

Athanasopoulous stood looking down at it as if he were afraid to touch it. Finally he looked up and said, "Well, I told you, Ted's in Greece. He's the owner."

Dooley stared at him for a few ticks of the clock, watching the watery eyes blink. "I'm just guessing, but I'd say if I took a look at the papers I'd find out Ted's a partner in the import-export company. Am I right?"

A suspicious look was followed by a shrug. "Yeah."

"And I'd also guess if I looked at the papers I'd find out you were a partner in the real estate company. Am I right?"

"Yeah, OK, officially. But it's mainly Teddy's project. He does real estate, I run the import business. We run 'em both out of this office. But we pretty much stick to our own thing."

"OK. But you could let us in."

Michael Athanasopoulous closed his eyes. He let out a long breath and his head drooped. For a moment Dooley thought he was praying, leaning on the counter. Then he raised his head and looked Dooley in the eye. "I tried to tell the stupid son of a bitch," he said.

Dooley had had a lot of practice waiting for people to tell him things that would make their lawyers blanch. He had a special look he put on: impassive, not too intent, patient.

Michael Athanasopoulous sighed. "You gotta help me out," he said. "I got a hell of a problem on my hands."

• • •

The office behind the store had a couple of desks littered with paper, some filing cabinets, stacks of cardboard boxes. Athanasopoulous cleared chairs for them and collapsed on another one behind a desk.

"The first thing you have to understand is that my brother is an idiot."

"Everyone's got a brother or two like that," said Dooley. "What'd he do?"

"I told you Teddy had some problems over in Greece? I lied. The problems were here."

Dooley thought he could predict how this was going to go. "Go on."

"I don't know what to do now. Maybe you can tell me."

"Only if you tell us what's eating you first."

"My brother got himself in big trouble. Money trouble."

"It happens."

"See, he's got a problem."

"Yeah, and so do you. You told us."

"OK, look. My brother likes to gamble. Thinks he's a genius, can't lose. God damn expert, always studying the papers, thinks he can beat the odds. Says it's a science. I says to him, it's a science for those bookies, that's for sure. Thing is, for a while he was winning. Then he starts to lose, and so he starts to bet more, to catch up.

And then before he knows it, he's in so deep he won't ever catch up. The dumb son of a bitch dropped thousands of dollars on bets over the last couple of years."

Athanasopoulous paused, eyes watering, looking forlorn, maybe waiting for sympathy.

"You were saying," said Dooley.

"So they started coming around."

"Who did?"

"The goons."

Dooley nodded, thinking, yeah, them. "You get any names?"

"Names, are you kidding? They don't give names."

"From your brother. Did he tell you who he owed money to?"

"No. He didn't want to talk about it. He knew I didn't like it and he tried to keep it a secret. These goons who came looking for him kinda blew his cover, though. Finally I caught him monkeying around with the books, trying to hide the fact he was taking money out of the company to cover his losses. Then he had to tell me about it. The dumbshit."

"Did he give you the name of the bookie?"

"No. All I know is he had a guy he called things in to. He'd go pick up his money at a bar somewhere when he won. But I don't know the name of the place. I didn't ask. What the hell was I going to do? I just wanted him to pay off the debts and stop gambling."

"So what happened? He ran away?"

"He cut some kind of deal with them. He came to me one day and said he'd worked out a deal and it was all square and they weren't gonna bother us no more. And then a week after that Ted tells me he needs a vacation in Greece and I'm in charge of things till he gets back. Don't worry about the real estate, the rents will come in the mail and Steve's the guy to call for maintenance problems and just refer anything else to him, he says. OK, I'm referring you to him. I can give you a number in Athens."

"What do you think the deal was?"

Athanasopoulous was having trouble looking at Dooley. "I'm pretty sure I know what the deal was. One thing he told me before he left was that 952 Adams was not for rent anymore. Just forget about it for a while, he said. Anyone asks, say it's been rented."

Dooley nodded slowly. "You have a key?"

Athanasopoulous sighed and pulled open a drawer in the desk.

"Here's where we keep the keys. I looked. There's none for 952 Adams."

"How about your maintenance guy? Would he have one?"

"He might. But before we go any farther, can I ask you a question?"

"Sure."

"Do I need a lawyer?"

Dooley knew the correct answer to that one from the other man's point of view: hell, yes. But he wasn't going to say that. "I don't see that you've done anything that I would want to charge you with."

Nodding, Athanasopoulous said, "You gonna protect me if somebody objects to my letting you in there?"

Dooley knew he had to give that one some serious consideration; he looked at it for a while and said, "Anybody gives you any grief, you show them the search warrant. You were forced to let us in, you didn't have any choice. And you didn't tell us a thing."

Athanasopoulous stared at him and Dooley could see a faint light of hope in the watery eyes, and something else, maybe, besides: relief. "I think I can live with that," said Michael Athanasopoulous.

• • •

Dooley stood patiently on the sidewalk while an elderly man fumbled with keys, Athanasopoulous muttering in Greek at his elbow. The door gave, and Dooley motioned Athanasopoulous in ahead of him, with Olson bringing up the rear. Inside it was dark. Athanasopoulous found a light switch. They were in a small office with a counter. A window in the back wall gave onto a larger space, darkened, and there was a door beside it. The maintenance man tried several keys in the door. One of them worked.

They followed him into a large workshop which lit up gradually as fluorescent lights flickered on. The concrete floor showed traces of the machines that had been bolted there. Dooley and Olson took diverging paths through the room, walking slowly. Their steps echoed in the emptiness. The two Greeks lingered by the door. Dooley scanned the floor, working his way toward the back of the shop.

In the far corner there was a broad doorway into another big room, and enough light shone through to outline the overhead door in the back wall. Dooley paused in the doorway and looked for a switch. He found it and more lights came on, showing a space big enough for a sizable truck to back in. The concrete floor was smudged with years of grease and dirt. Dooley walked along a wall toward the front of the building, Olson trailing him. There was a small office tucked into the corner of the garage opposite the overhead door, two partitions at right angles with a window in each forming a roofed cubicle ten feet square. Dooley shoved the door open with the toe of his shoe. He leaned in and flicked a switch.

He and Olson stood looking at cheap gray linoleum, cheap fake wood paneling with scraps of masking tape still holding torn corners of paper, some graffiti scrawled in black, and a desk. The desk sat obliquely across the middle of the office and there was a straight-backed wooden chair next to it. In the bleak fluorescent light the room looked like the end of the world. "What do you see?" asked Dooley.

"Nice and clean," said Olson after a minute. "Where's the dust?"

"And what do you smell?"

Olson sniffed a couple of times, just perceptibly. "Pine-Sol," he said.

• • •

A mobile crime lab van was parked in the alley, one squad drawn up behind it and another one beside it, blocking the alley. The overhead door was raised and inside the garage the lights were on. Through the windows of the cubicle in the far corner Dooley could see men moving with great deliberation around the little office. "I'm amazed you got a judge to go along with this," said the man with wavy gray hair who stood next to Dooley.

Francis McCone had retained a touch of brogue despite forty years on the streets of Chicago, possibly because he considered Chicago merely an extension of his native Ireland. From County Cork to County Cook, he was fond of saying by way of autobiography. McCone was the third watch detective supervisor and no fool despite the jovial manner. "You don't even know if a crime was committed here," McCone said. "When you have some evidence something happened here besides somebody spilled coffee and wiped it up, come talk to me."

"They'll find something. Nobody can clean up that well."

"Did you get in touch with the owner?"

"We sat and watched his brother talk Greek into the phone for a while. He said his brother's traveling, somewhere outside Athens. He's going to keep trying to track him down. We got anybody with good enough Greek to call over there and make sure he wasn't trying to pull the wool over our eyes?"

"Steve Dimas always claims to speak it."

Dooley nodded. "And he gave us a couple of names, people that might know who the brother bet with. We need to work both ends. Run down the brother over in Greece, run down his associates here. Am I forgetting anything?"

McCone jerked his head toward the interior of the garage. "Just this little matter here. If they don't find anything, all you've done is stir up a hornets' nest. It all depends on that. Either this was brilliant police work, or it's an irresponsible waste of time and money."

Out of the door in the corner office came Pete Olson. He walked across the garage, hands in pockets, skirting patches of the floor that had been marked off with chalk. "Bingo," he called as he came.

"What?" said Dooley.

"They found blood. At least that's what they think it is. In a crack on the chair."

Dooley nodded, tight-lipped, being careful not to look at McCone.

Olson reached them and said, "Of course, in a place like this people are always skinning their knuckles and bleeding on things while they get a Band-aid from the first aid kit."

McCone said, "That's right. Doesn't mean a thing until they match it up with the victim's. If they can. Still too early to say whether you're a hero or a bum, Mike."

Dooley thought McCone was smiling as he turned away, but he couldn't be sure.

• • •

"I don't know how you do it," said Olson. "A man of your modest talents."

"I only look brilliant next to you," said Dooley, jabbing at the typewriter.

Olson chuckled and said, "I mean it, though. You were right, you son of a bitch."

"Maybe," Dooley battered the last sentence of his Supplementary into submission and jerked the form out of the machine. "Until they match that blood with our girl's it looks a lot like nothing at all. A drunk had a bad dream outside a building with a lousy gambler for an owner. Coincidence."

"Ah, come on. You don't believe that."

"I don't believe anything. I just write the damn reports."

"I know. You're just trying not to be cocky."

Dooley shot his partner a look. "If we have found the place where she was killed, we were pretty God damn lucky. You know that as well as I do. And I think that's just about it for our good luck on this one. From here on out, it's going to be pure hell, because if it's an Outfit thing, you know nobody's going to talk. Ever. About any of it. Unless we can find a big enough stick to wallop somebody with. When was the last time anyone got convicted for a mob hit?"

"Hey, there's always a first time."

"Yeah," said Dooley, rising wearily from his chair. "So they say."

• • •

The letter was lying on the kitchen table, facing Dooley as he came in from the garage. His heart leapt when he saw it, but he made himself go through his routine calmly before looking at it: hanging the jacket over the chair, getting the bottle out of the cabinet and a glass out of the drainer. He poured his inch of Jameson's into the glass with great concentration and put the bottle back. Then he sat down and pulled the single sheet of paper toward him, covered with Kevin's careful, slightly meandering handwriting in blue ballpoint.

May 26, 1969

Dear Mom, Dad, Kathleen, Frank—

First of all, don't worry, I'm OK, things have been pretty quiet recently and we're hoping they'll stay quiet. I know I haven't written for a while and I'm sorry. We've been in the field for a couple of weeks and even when there's not much action it's hard to find time to write.

You walk the trails all day and then you have to set up a perimeter and before you know it it's dark and you can't see to write. But I'll try to do better. We're back at base now and I got your last 3 letters. Hey Kathleen, that's neat you got your license. Be careful and don't hit anyone. Frank, I hear the Cubs are doing good, fill me in.

We have seen some action this month, but we haven't run into anything too heavy, and we haven't taken too many casualties. Everyone's hoping for a nice quiet summer. Maybe we'll get in some time at the beach! That would beat the jungle by a long shot. I never thought I would say it, but camping out is getting pretty old.

Well, 9 months down, 4 to go. It will be good to get home. Mom, thanks for the care package. Dad, I guess you know how it is out here, don't worry about me, I can take it OK. Pray for me please, I miss you all and love you and will SEE YOU IN OCTOBER.

Love,
Kevin

Dooley cried a little like he always did over his son's letters, silently, being careful not to let any tears fall, wiping his eyes with his sleeve, taking a couple of deep breaths and puffing out his cheeks to get over it, hearing his son's voice in his head. *I guess you know how it is out here.* Yeah, Kevin, I have a pretty good idea. *I can take it OK.* Dooley knew what that meant; that meant *It's hell, Dad, the worst thing I've ever been through, and I wish I had listened when you tried to tell me, but I have to take it; I don't have any choice.* And then that *please,* which tore Dooley's heart out.

Nothing really bad, Dooley prayed. Don't let anything really bad happen to my boy, please.

Dooley drained his glass and went up to his wife.

Six

DOOLEY WONDERED WHAT the hell was happening in his living room. From the head of the stairs it sounded like a bad industrial accident was in progress. He came down the stairs and walked into the living room with his hands in his pockets, frowning. Frank was lying on the couch, tapping his fingers on the edge of the album cover in time to the music. He caught sight of Dooley and froze with a wary look on his face. Dooley grimaced at him and mimed turning a knob counterclockwise. Frank took on a sullen look and swung his feet to the floor. Moving with calculated slowness, he shambled to the stereo and turned down the volume.

"How many times do I have to tell you not to put your feet up on the couch?" Dooley said.

"I don't have my shoes on," said Frank, flopping back on the couch.

"I don't care. I don't want to see your feet up there." Dooley stood peering at the record spinning on the stereo. "This guy's in pain," he said. "The music's so bad it's making him scream."

"That's so funny I forgot to laugh," said Frank.

"Who's this then?" said Dooley, holding out his hand. Frank glared but gave him the album cover and Dooley peered at it, a smile spreading slowly. "Holy Mother of God, it's my Aunt Mary," he said.

"Cut it out."

"I'm serious. She looked just like that, when she let her hair down. Homeliest woman on earth." Dooley squinted at the name on the cover. "This is a *man*? I don't believe it."

"Gimme that, will you?" Frank grabbed for the album cover.

Dooley shook his head. "Listen, you're not gonna lay here all day."

"I know it. I'm going out later."

"Not before you've painted the trim, you're not."

"I'll get to it."

"You'll get to it today."

"But I'm supposed to go to the lake with Terry."

"You can go to the lake when you get the painting done."

"Aw, come on. You said I didn't have to do it right away."

"I'm tired of seeing you sitting around on your butt. It better be done when I get home tonight. And it better be a good neat job."

"Aw, come on, Pop."

Dooley left the room before he got mad; his younger son just had that effect on him these days. In the kitchen Kathleen was perched on a chair underneath the wall phone, listening to somebody at the other end, winding the cord around her finger, long tan legs crossed. She freed her fingers from the phone cord and waggled them at Dooley. He poured himself a cup of coffee from the percolator on the stove and doctored it at the table, looking down at the newspaper lying there.

John L. Lewis was dead, eyebrows and all. Nixon wanted to keep the tax surcharge; the Russians and the Chinese were shooting at each other. The more the merrier, thought Dooley. He went and got himself a bowl of Wheaties and sat down. On the South Side a gang of Negroes had stuck up a tavern, kidnapped a white girl, and raped her in an abandoned building. Dooley shook his head but turned the page; not his problem. Here was the real news: A convoy from the 4th Infantry Division had been hit north of Pleiku, and up in Quang Tri, where things had been pretty quiet recently, James

Stewart's stepson, a lieutenant in the Marines, had been killed in action. Dooley gave up on the paper and poured himself more coffee.

Kathleen finally hung up the phone. "Hi, Daddy."

"Hi, sweetheart."

"Can I go to a movie tonight with Carol?"

"Depends on what it is."

The hesitation told Dooley what kind of movie it was; he looked up in time to catch Kathleen's calculating look, her lips just parted. "It's called *Midnight Cowboy.*"

"A western, huh? I thought you didn't like westerns."

"Um, this is kind of a modern western."

"What's the rating on it?"

Kathleen was wandering toward the sink, not looking at Dooley. "I'm not sure. Probably *M.*"

"*M*, what's that, *mature*? Now why would that be, I wonder?" Dooley reached for the paper again. "Let's see what it looks like."

"Daddy, *M* just means it's a serious drama. It has an adult theme or something. It doesn't mean it has lots of naked people running around or anything."

"These days you never know. Where the hell?" Dooley thrashed at the pages; he never went to the movies, so he could never find the movie section. "Your aunt Barbara said that thing last year—*The Graduate*—was the dirtiest movie she'd ever seen."

"Oh, God, Aunt Barbara. She'd think *National Geographic* was dirty."

"It is."

"*Daddy.*"

"Relax, I'm just kidding. Here we go. What's the name of this thing?"

Kathleen hesitated again. "*Midnight Cowboy.*"

Dooley found it. "*X*? What the hell's that? *Under eighteen not admitted?*"

He looked up at his daughter.

Kathleen's eyes were wide. "You're kidding! *X?* "

"You knew that, didn't you?"

"No! I had no idea."

"Don't lie to me. I'm a detective, remember?" He stabbed at the ad with his finger. "Look, isn't this the guy that was in *The Graduate*? Yeah, I'm sure that's the same guy. There is no way you're going to this movie."

"Daddy, I'm almost eighteen."

"Well, kiddo, 'almost' ain't gonna do it for you. You got to be eighteen to get into this one. It's out of my hands. God, I can't believe what they're getting away with nowadays." He threw the paper on the table. "You were figuring on passing for eighteen, were you?"

"I didn't know it was *X*. And don't call me a liar!"

"Don't try and pull the wool over my eyes."

"I wasn't. And I'm tired of being treated like a child."

Dooley'd had enough. "I'll treat you like you deserve to be treated. As long as you're under my roof, you go by my rules. *And don't you walk out on me when I'm talking to you!*"

His bellow froze her in the doorway, and she turned slowly to stand staring at him, pale and stiff with defiance. "Are you done?" she said quietly.

"Not quite." Dooley heaved a great sigh. "Kathleen, there's a lot of unpleasant things in life. I see them every day. I'm just trying to protect you from that. Don't be in such a hurry to grow up."

She folded her arms and said, "I'm not your little girl anymore."

Dooley could see that; it was one more thing that made him sad. "I know."

"Can I go now?"

Dooley waved her away. "Yeah. And go tell your brother to turn that crap off."

• • •

There was no such thing as a simple job, Dooley had learned. Something always went wrong. There wasn't enough lumber or the screws were stripped or there were severe structural problems under the wallpaper. In this case the stringer had rotted out at the bottom, meaning the whole flight of steps up to the porch had to be rebuilt. From a quick morning's work it had turned into a two-day job.

Dooley measured again, marked his cut, and stuck the pencil behind his ear. He wanted to finish the job and get the hell out of there and put some lotion on his sunburned neck, but he resisted the urge to hurry. "Hurry up and make a mistake," his father had always told him when he was breaking him in, standing there watching him with his eagle eye. At sixteen, Dooley had chafed at the bit but learned the old man was right about that like he was right about everything else: hurrying only got you in trouble.

He straightened up from the sawhorses when Rob's truck pulled into the driveway. Rob got out of the cab and walked over, giving the new steps a critical eye. "Thought you'd be done by now," he said. "Got a beer in the cooler for you."

Dooley wiped sweat off his brow with the back of his hand. "I had to cut a new stringer from scratch. And I had a hell of a time taking out the old steps without tearing up the siding. I'm gonna have to re-caulk it when it's done, too."

"Shit. Well, how much longer you think it'll take?"

"I got maybe an hour of work left."

Rob ran his eye over things and shrugged. "OK. Do what you have to. Want to stop by the house later for your dough?"

"Sure."

"When are you off next? I got a lot of jobs coming up. I can keep you busy all summer if you want."

Dooley picked up the saw and bent to his work, not answering. The truth was, he was tired as hell of working for Rob Devlin; every year it got harder. Dooley and Devlin went way back to the West Side. Their fathers had worked together, and after the war Rob had taken over his old man's business while Dooley went on the department. But maybe just for old times' sake Dooley had moonlighted doing carpentry for Rob all these years instead of doing what most cops did, finding some way to parlay their status into a cushy second job that was easy on the feet. It had always been a good deal for both of them, cash in hand for Dooley and reliable occasional labor for Rob, but Dooley was starting to wonder if it wasn't time to look for something indoors. He made his cut and shut off the saw. "I don't know. I'll have to check."

Rob stood there looking at him, squinting a little into the late afternoon sun. "You're getting tired, aren't you?"

Dooley brushed sawdust off the plank. "I'm OK."

Rob laughed softly. "Look, Mike. You don't have to keep doing this just for me. I been wondering when you'd get sick of it."

Dooley looked up at him finally. "I could maybe use a little break, ease off a little. I don't want to leave you high and dry."

Rob nodded. "I appreciate that. But I got other guys. I just hired a young guy that looks pretty good. Strong as a fuckin' ox."

"Like we used to be, huh?"

"You said it. Look, the truth is, I could use you this summer but I won't have any trouble replacing you. It's up to you."

Dooley shrugged. "Let me think about it and give you a call."

Rob slapped him on the shoulder. "Do that." He turned and made for his truck. "We're not twenty years old anymore, Dooley."

"Thank God," said Dooley.

• • •

Dooley stood in a corner of his back yard, hands on his hips. He had been standing that way for some time, staring into the angle of the high board fence where Rose had planted her hydrangeas. Every once in a while a car purred along a street somewhere near at hand; very faintly he could hear pop music on a distant radio. Dooley wished he could go on standing there forever.

The screen door slammed and Rose's steps sounded on the patio. Dooley turned toward her as she came across the grass with two glasses of iced tea. "What you doing?" she said.

"Looking at the fence. It needs to be repaired."

"What's wrong with it?"

"There's a couple of cracked boards down there. I'd try and get Frank to do it, but I don't trust him to do the job right."

"Well, we've lived with it that way for this long, we'll probably survive a few more years."

Dooley took a glass of tea and sipped it. There was not enough sugar in it, as usual; as usual he drank it without complaint. "Sure. Like we live with the peeling paint and the water damage in the basement. There's a million things to do around this God damn place. I fix one thing and another one breaks."

"Thanks for taking care of the toilet."

"I got to start teaching Frank to do that kind of thing. There's nothing hard about it."

"Frank would love it if you taught him something. Anything."

"Think so? Every time I try and tell him something he rolls his eyes like I'm not worth listening to."

"Well, you go at him like a cop all the time. Try approaching him like a dad."

Dooley made for the patio. "Aw hell, I'm tired of worrying about Frank." He sank onto a chair. "I'm tired of worrying about Kathleen, too. I got enough to worry about with Kevin over there."

Rose sat down across from him and he was sorry he'd mentioned Kevin; he was going to set her off again. But she only frowned into her tea and said, "What about this troop withdrawal they're talking about? You think Kevin might get to come home early?"

"Who the hell knows? Laird was saying in the paper this morning both army and marine units would be included. We could get lucky, I guess."

Rose stared into swirling ice cubes for a while and said, "Frank and I started a letter. It's on the kitchen table."

"I'll get to it."

She looked up at him. "I don't mean to make another chore for you."

"Nah, I know. I'll get to it."

She let a few seconds pass. "You want to get off by yourself, go see a movie or something?"

"A movie? When was the last time I went to a movie? I think the last movie I saw was in black and white. It was a talkie, I remember that."

"Just an idea. Sorry."

"I'm sorry, Rose." Dooley looked at his wife and shrugged. "I don't know what I want. I just got a lot on my mind these days."

"Yeah," she said, looking at him with what he thought of as her Martyr of the Faith look, "me too."

• • •

Dooley sat at the kitchen table with a ballpoint pen in his hand, staring at the paper in front of him. He could hear the faint hum of the clock on the wall. *Dear Kevin,* he had written, some time ago. There was a lot of blank paper below that. His eye ran over Frank's hurried scrawl on the top half of the page for the tenth time: *Williams and Santo are hitting a ton and Jenkins and Hands are having a good year. Everyone says this is their year and I think it is. I've been to a few ball games and it's really cool, lots of people in the bleachers acting crazy and having a good time. Maybe you'll be home before the Series and we can get some tickets. Be real careful and I'll see you then.*

Dooley had learned to squeeze a serviceable report out of a typewriter, but writing was not something that came easily to him. What could he put on a piece of paper that would get across what he wanted to say to his son and that he could let anybody look at? He sure as hell wasn't going to let Rose see the things he really wanted to tell Kevin. *Now you know what I know, son. Nothing's ever going to be the same for you.* There was no way Dooley was going to put that in a letter. Maybe when Kevin got home they could go off some place together, go fishing or something, and maybe over a campfire or leaning on a bar they could talk about it. Dooley would have loved to have somebody to talk about it all with when he got back from the Pacific, but he never had.

Nothing much to report here, Dooley wrote. *Just lots of work. People keep getting killed.*

• • •

When Dooley walked in, Olson was already at the desk, leafing through papers. He looked up and said, "You look like a new man. Enjoy your days off?

"You bet. Nothing I like better than screaming at my kids and fighting with the old lady. What the hell are you doing here?"

"You're the only one who's allowed to come in early, are you? I been on the phone with our neighbors across the state line, like you said to do. I never got to it the other day, with all the excitement. Got 'em to send me some things on the wire."

"Come up with anything?"

"Could be. Here's a girl with brown hair who's been missing for a week in Marion, Indiana, but she's only eighteen."

"Probably too young, but you never know."

"This one could be a little more promising. A thirty-year-old woman was reported missing near Elkhart Lake, Wisconsin, last Thursday. The report says she was last seen the previous Monday.

Brown hair, right age and size, it looks like. Then there's a couple more. I just started looking through these. I'll get on the phone if something looks good."

"OK. Where's the case file? Let's see what second watch came up with on Athanasopoulous and his friends."

"I looked already. Doesn't look like anybody did a damn thing."

Dooley scanned. "Lazy bastards. What do they do all day?"

"They're busy, too, I guess. ."

"All right. Look, let's go track down some of these jerks. Christ, I take a couple of days off and things go all to hell."

• • •

"Teddy Athanasopoulous? What about him?" The butcher had thick black eyebrows and thinning white hair. There was sweat on his brow and blood on his apron. He had paused in the act of slicing steaks off a hunk of beef, and the size of the knife in his hand made Dooley glad there was a counter between them.

"I need to talk to him."

"Haven't seen him in a couple of months. I heard he went back to Greece." That was a dismissal; the butcher put knife to flesh again.

"You're still here." Dooley had on his patient look.

A couple more steaks came off onto the block. "I'm not Teddy Athanasopoulous."

"You'll do. You've gone through enough drinks with him."

"Who says?" The knife stopped moving. Dooley gave the butcher a look that said you should know better than to ask me that. "Look, you want to talk about this in front of the customers, or you want to discuss it in private?" Dooley had gotten the undivided attention of the three women with their shopping baskets as soon as he'd pulled out his star.

The butcher's scowl began to look a shade more thoughtful. He turned to call through a door into the back of the shop. "Panos!

Get out here for a second." A younger man came through the door. "Take care of these people, will you? Six steaks for the lady here." The butcher yielded the knife and came around the end of the counter. "Let's go outside."

There was an awning over the door that protected them from the sun. The butcher pulled a pack of Chesterfields out of a pocket and lit one. "What do you need to know?"

"I need to know who Athanasopoulous placed his bets with."

The butcher blew smoke at Jackson Boulevard and said, "What bets?"

"The bets that lost him so much money he had to leave the country. Those bets."

"How the hell should I know?"

Dooley moved, just close enough to the butcher that he had to take notice, had to turn and look him in the eye. "If you weren't in a position to know, you'd be shocked and asking questions right now. If you know he had to leave town because of his betting, you know who he bet with. Now, don't bullshit me anymore."

The butcher looked away, smoked, and said, "That prick little brother of his told you, huh?"

Dooley was almost starting to feel sorry for Michael Athanasopoulous, almost. "I need a name," he said.

The butcher watched cars go by. He dragged on the cigarette, squinting at something over Dooley's shoulder. "We never bet that much, for Christ's sake. Teddy just had a run of bad luck."

Dooley could see he had a slow learner on his hands. "Look, Nick. You weren't paying attention when I introduced myself, were you? I'm not a vice cop. I don't give a damn about your gambling."

The butcher looked at Dooley. "What are you then?"

I'm a *homicide* cop. You know what that means?"

Starting to sound shocked, the butcher said, "Who got killed?"

"I'm the one with the questions. Now who'd you bet with?"

Dooley watched as it spread across the butcher's face, the

dawning awareness of the depth of the waters around him. "What's gonna happen if I tell you?"

"To you? Not a damn thing. You think I'm likely to tell your man who gave me his name? Give it up and I'm done with you."

The butcher gave a shake of the head. "I don't know."

Dooley sighed. "Like I said, Nick, I'm a homicide cop. But I do know some vice cops. And they might be interested in what you do with your folding money. They don't need to know, of course."

Dooley watched the butcher's face harden, and he watched the butcher come to the inevitable conclusion. The butcher sucked hard on the cigarette and said, "I only know the guy's nickname. Charley Sawbucks." He threw his Chesterfield away into the gutter. "Italian guy."

• • •

"Italian guy. The plot thickens." McCone looked amused, leaning back on his chair behind his desk. "Anybody surprised?"

"Italian guy with a dumb nickname. No, I'm not surprised."

"So, you know where to find this Charley Sawbucks?"

"I've got a trail to follow. But I'm going to talk to somebody in Intelligence first. I want to know who the hell I'm dealing with."

"Call Ed Haggerty at Maxwell Street. He's been in all those guys' hair for years."

"First thing tomorrow. Now we have to sit down with the phones. We've got some out-of-state missing reports to follow up."

"Go run up the city's phone bill, then." McCone was already reaching for a pen, dismissing him. Just as Dooley reached the door, though, he stopped him. "Mike."

"Yeah?"

"Good job."

Dooley swung the door open. "It's a little early to say, isn't it?"

• • •

"Mrs. Victoria Radke, please."

"Um, speaking, that's me." The voice was small and far away, the tone uncertain; Dooley was used to hearing that note of apprehension in response to his no-nonsense phone voice.

"Mrs. Radke, this is Officer Michael Dooley of the Chicago Police Department. I understand you filed a missing person report on a Sally Kotowski last week?"

It took her a couple of seconds to find her voice. "Have you found her?"

"We're not sure, Mrs. Radke." Dooley had learned long ago that it wasn't his problem to deal with the emotions. That was the other person's problem; all he could do was lay it out there in a neutral tone of voice and be ready for the fallout. "We have an unidentified homicide victim that may fit the description you gave in your report."

"Oh, God." For a moment Dooley thought he'd lost Victoria Radke, and then she was back, her voice barely making it out of a tightened throat. "I can't believe it. Not that. What happened to her?"

"Well, like I said, we're not sure at this point who the victim is. What we need from you is any information you can give us that may help with an identification, even if it's negative. If you're lucky you might help us rule your friend out." Give 'em something to hang on to, an old dick had once advised Dooley.

She was trying, Dooley could tell; he could practically hear her fighting for control. "What can I tell you?" she said finally, in a steady voice.

"First you could go over your description with me if you would, just clear up a few points. Your report states that Sally had brown hair?"

"Yes, that's right. Kind of a light brown."

"I see. And could you tell me approximately how long her hair was, how she wore it? At the time she disappeared?"

"Well, it wasn't too long, not like a lot of girls wear it. Maybe like just touching her shoulders, you know? And she styled it so it had some body, so it didn't just hang there, it curled in toward her neck, you know what I mean? Kind of like, I don't know, like Barbara Feldon wears it on TV, if that helps. She had on one of those hair bands that last night she went out, to hold it back behind her ears, you know?"

"Yes." The hair on Dooley's dead girl had been matted with mud and grease and any style it had possessed was long gone, but the length sounded about right. Dooley had a feeling this was going to be one of those conversations where two people were rooting for opposite things. He thought it might be time to be careful with his verb tenses. "Could you tell me if Sally has any distinguishing marks that might help us? Any scars, birthmarks, tattoos, that kind of thing?"

"Tattoos? God, no. I can't think of . . . birthmarks, no, none that I ever saw."

"What about scars? Any old stitches, surgical scars, anything like that?"

"I don't think so. Not anything big. Uh . . . I remember once when we were kids she had to get some stitches in her elbow after she cut it on a broken window, but I don't know if that would still show up."

Dooley had to take the phone away from his face while he took a deep breath through his nose. Here was the hard part: what made him want to celebrate was devastation for the woman at the other end of the phone line. Carefully he said, "Mrs. Radke, do you have any possessions of Sally's still with you?"

"Oh yeah, all of them. We just packed them up and put them in a storeroom." A second or two went by. "Why?"

Not your problem, Dooley reminded himself, hating this

moment as he always did: “Mrs. Radke, I think we’re going to need you to come down for a possible identification.”

“No.”

“And if you can bring any objects that might have Sally’s fingerprints on them, that would be a big help.”

Somewhere up in Wisconsin a woman was in pain, her voice fading farther and farther from the phone receiver. “Oh, no. Oh, God. Sally, Sally, Sally . . .”

Seven

"CHARLEY SAWBUCKS. THEY still call him that, do they?" At the other end of the phone line Ed Haggerty had the fraying voice of a man well into middle age. Dooley had never met him but had heard the tales: in an Intelligence Division that some people said was there to stifle intelligence as much as gather it, Haggerty stood out. He had busted everyone from Alderisio to Yaras at least once and had probably torpedoed his own career by the stubborn habit of doing his job. "Well, you're talking about Mr. Charles Scaletta, if I'm not mistaken, An old hand at the business."

"Bookmaking, you mean," said Dooley. "I'm assuming he's not a killer."

"Oh, hell, no. Charley's a numbers guy. All Charley does is take bets. And he's good at it. I don't think he's ever actually done any time. Charley's never there when the sheriff's guys kick in the door. It's always his employees crowding into the back of that wagon. Charley pays the bail, pays the fines, sets up another room. Just a cost of doing business. He's been at this since Nitti and Guzik were dealing out concessions in the thirties. Nah, Charley doesn't hurt people. Charley's got people who take care of that for him if necessary."

"OK, here's the situation. One of his customers got in over his head and people started coming around to muscle him. The customer's left the country but we think he made a deal before he went and part of the deal was to hand over the keys to a vacant building he owned. Now it appears there's been a homicide inside the place and I'm trying to follow the chain from Charley to whoever has the keys."

"A homicide? Who got killed?"

"We think maybe the girl on the riverbank was killed there."

There was a brief silence. "That would surprise me. That would surprise me a lot. They don't go in for that type of thing usually."

"We're thinking they wanted something from her. But we don't even know for sure that's where she got done. I'm just following a trail."

"Well, first of all, if there was any muscling done, Charley won't know a thing about it, even if he does, if you know what I mean. Any muscle he ever needs is just a word-in-the-ear type of thing, pick up the phone and say hey, I've got a guy who's getting behind here, could one of your guys have a talk with him, that kind of thing. Charley'll give you that innocent look and probably deny he even knows the poor sap. You got solid information on the deal?"

"Inference. Before he left, the customer told his brother basically the place was off limits, and the keys are missing. I'm pretty sure the brother's clean and more or less in the dark about the whole thing. He's been cooperative."

"I see. I'd say you better find the other brother, because you're not going to get anything out of Charley."

"I didn't think so. I just wanted to know where he stands in the scheme of things. Who does he answer to, whose ear did he put that word into?"

"Well, Charley answers to Taylor Street, which means Joey Aiuppa, at the top. But that crew has a lot of soldiers, a lot of guys Charley could call on. And I don't think Charley Sawbucks has any use for a vacant building. My guess would be that the muscle, or whoever lent Charley the muscle, took the keys as part of his own side deal, just saw an opportunity. An Outfit guy can always find a use for a nice anonymous building with a good lock on it. Was there anything in there? Like stolen merchandise, I mean?"

"Not that I've heard of. The evidence people went through it pretty good."

"OK. I don't know right off the top of my head who takes care of Charley's problem collections. I'd have to make a couple of calls and get back to you."

"All right, you got my number."

"I got it. I think you got your work cut out for you. On something like this, if the Outfit did have anything to do with it, mouths are gonna be shut real tight."

"We're used to that," said Dooley. He hung up the phone and looked up at Olson, who was standing by. "What's up?"

"Got a call from the Radkes. They just pulled into town. I told them to meet us at the morgue."

• • •

Victoria Radke was a blonde who might have qualified as a looker a few years or even a few days earlier, but grief tends to do bad things to a woman's posture and complexion. Dooley could see the first faint sketch of the old woman, broken by cares, in the thirty-year-old female slumped across from him with her head on her husband's shoulder, a fistful of Kleenex pressed to her nose.

"I'm sorry," said Victoria Radke. "I don't know what happened. I've never fainted before."

"Don't worry about it," said Dooley. "You sure you're OK now?"

"I'll never be OK."

"She shouldn't have to see that," said the husband, who sat with one arm around his wife and his free hand planted on his thigh. He was close to forty, tall and horse-faced and going gray, and he was one of those people who react to shock by getting angry at the world. "I could have gone in there by myself. You shouldn't have to put her through that."

"You're right about that," said Dooley. "Are you certain about the identification?"

Radke shook his head fiercely. "I don't know if I could say certain. It looked like her, but I couldn't swear to it."

"Well, the fingerprints will tell us for sure."

His wife stifled a sob and said, "It's so awful. I can't even be sure it was her. Her hair was that color, that's all I can tell you. And she had a scar there. But . . . God, what did they do to her?"

Dooley shifted his notepad a few inches. "They beat her pretty badly."

"How did she die?"

"She was strangled."

"Oh, God, that's awful."

And you don't know the half of it, thought Dooley. He said, "It's over for her now. She's at peace. Now it's up to us to catch the people that did it."

"It was the Mafia. I'm sure that's who it was."

"Is that what she told you?"

"She had a mobster boyfriend. He got shot last winter."

Dooley had interviewed thousands of witnesses over the years, but he could count on one hand the ones that had jerked his head up from the notepad like this. "She told you that?"

"Yes. She called me from Chicago in, I don't know, February maybe, the first time we'd talked in a while. She said she was thinking about leaving Chicago and asked if she could come and stay with me for a while if she did. That's when she told me about the boyfriend. Sally didn't have very good luck with men. Or maybe she had bad judgment. I don't know."

"Can you tell me who the boyfriend was?"

"Herb something. That's all I know. She talked about Herb this, Herb that. He was a gambler or something and he spent a lot of time in Las Vegas. He took her out there with him a few times."

Dooley thought hard about the previous winter. The syndicate wasn't his area of expertise but he had heard all the names. "Was it Herb Feldman by any chance?"

"I don't know. I don't think she ever told me his last name. She just said he was a gambler and he had lots of friends in the Mafia and then he did something wrong and they killed him."

Dooley remembered the hit but not the details; he thought it had happened somewhere in the western suburbs.

"And that was why she had to leave town?" he said.

"That's not what she said. She just said she wanted to be out of that life. She'd had enough of gangsters finally, she said. Anyway, that was in February and she didn't come to stay until early May."

"Had she been associating with gangsters for a long time?"

"I couldn't really tell you." Victoria Radke dabbed at her nose and rallied, sitting up straight and exhaling heavily. "See, Sally and I grew up together, in Aurora, but we hadn't seen each other in a long time. She always wanted to go to Chicago and she took off right after high school and got a job there and never came back. We kept in touch but not all that close, you know? I went to see her a few times in Chicago the first few years, and then I met Bob and got married and moved to Wisconsin and we kind of lost touch for a while. Until February. She'd called my mom to get my number. And then in May she called me up again and asked if she could come stay with me. I'd written her about the resort and she asked if she could stay with us for a while and work there or something. So I said yes."

"Sorry, what resort?"

"Bob's family owns a resort on the lake. We live there and run the place. We gave Sally a room and let her do odd jobs. Help out in the kitchen, clean rooms, stuff like that. Just till she decided what to do next."

"I see. Do you know how she got involved with gangsters in the first place?"

"Not really. Except that was kind of the lifestyle she got into. Nightclubs and bars and all that. It probably started when she was a bunny."

Dooley's brow wrinkled. "A bunny?"

"At the Playboy Club.

"I see."

"Sally always wanted to get into show business. She was really glamorous, really good-looking, and after she'd been in Chicago for a while she got the job at the Playboy Club. She sent me a picture of herself in the costume. She was perfect for it."

"How long did she work there?"

"At the Playboy Club, I don't know, a couple of years maybe. Then she got a job dancing in some bar somewhere."

"Rush Street," put in the husband. "It was some place on Rush Street."

Dooley waited for more but Radke just sat scowling at him. "You remember the name?"

"No. All's I know is she said she worked on Rush Street. I couldn't tell you where. I don't think she ever said where."

"Did she mention any associates, any friends?"

"She had a friend," said Victoria Radke. "Another girl that worked at the Playboy Club, another bunny. I think they roomed together. Laura, her name was. I remember that."

"No last name?"

"I don't think she ever said it. She just said Laura was her best friend in Chicago."

"OK, we can probably track her down through the club. Now, can you tell me what happened the day she disappeared? That was what, last—Monday of last week you said? That would have been Monday, the second?"

After a look at her husband the woman said, "Nothing really happened. We just didn't see her after that Monday night. She went out to the bar after she finished up in the kitchen and she never came back. She came and went pretty much like she wanted. She didn't even have a regular job really, she just pitched in where we needed her. We didn't even start to wonder until the next afternoon. Bob wanted her to tend bar down on the beach that day. We have a little sort of cabana thing where people can buy drinks, and he couldn't find her."

Radke frowned. "I was irritated, because I was counting on her and she didn't show up. I didn't have any idea anything had happened to her."

His wife sniffed. "And then that night we started to get a little worried. We asked around town but nobody'd seen her."

"Where was the bar?"

"Just down the street. It's a small town. There's, like, two bars. She used to go to the one just a few blocks away. She'd made some friends there, just people from town."

"And she told you that was where she was going?"

"Well, she came by the office and said she was going out for a drink and did I want to come. I had stuff to do and I said no."

"She was at the bar," said Radke. "I went by there the next day and asked. She had a couple of drinks, talked to some people, and then left around ten."

"You're sure she didn't come back to your place? Could she have come back without your seeing her, then left again? Slipped out sometime in the night? Met somebody and gone off with them?"

The Radkes exchanged a look and the husband said, "I don't think so. Well, sure, I guess. I mean, she had her own room up on the second floor. She could have gone up the back steps, I guess."

"I think somebody would have seen her," said Victoria. "There's always people around, even late. People sit up on the porch till all hours. Even around back, especially out back. There's always people around."

Radke said, "But I guess she could have come back. All I can tell you is we didn't see her and nobody mentioned seeing her after she left for the bar."

"I see." Dooley pondered for a moment and said, "Did she ever get any phone calls?"

They exchanged a look and Victoria said, "Yeah, a few. She'd made a couple of friends."

"Guys," put in her husband. "She was a hit with the local guys." There was a brief freeze and he added, "I just mean she was a good looking woman. Guys noticed. But the cops checked that out. The names I was able to give them, they went and asked them. And I think they all checked out, had alibis and stuff, I mean."

"You don't remember any particular calls that day?"

Victoria said, "She worked in the office for a while that afternoon. I heard her take one call, and she might have gotten others when I wasn't around."

Dooley nodded. "Uh-huh. Was she on foot that night?"

"Yeah. She didn't have a car."

"How'd she get up there from Chicago?"

"She took a bus to Sheboygan and we went over and picked her up."

"OK. So she walked. Anybody see her going to or from the bar that night?"

"Not that anybody's said. But you wouldn't expect them to. We're right at the edge of town and between us and the bar it's not real well lit at night. It's really almost a country road until you get to the block where the bar is. There's some houses, but they're set back from the road. Nobody saw any strange cars or anything. That's what they told us anyway. The sheriff's officers went over it all when we finally called her in missing on Thursday."

"That was three days after she left. You weren't worried?"

Victoria was starting to crumple again, fist to her mouth. "We just figured she was a big girl and she'd gone off somewhere on her own and we'd missed a message somehow. We looked in her room, we asked around. Nobody had seen anything that sounded like anything bad had happened."

"To tell the truth, we figured she'd found herself a boyfriend," said Radke. "I thought she was holed up somewhere with a man and just hadn't gotten around to calling. It wasn't really my business, I thought."

A single sob made it past his wife's fist and she said, "I knew something was wrong. If we'd called the police sooner . . ."

"You don't know that it would have made any difference," said Dooley mechanically, getting a glimpse of rough nights ahead for the Radkes. He pulled the teletype from the Wisconsin cops out of the folder. He'd read it already but it was something to do while Victoria Radke cried. He looked up as Olson came into the office. From the look on his partner's face Dooley knew pretty much what he was about to hear.

Olson pulled up at the desk and stood looking down at the Radkes with professional gravity. "I'm afraid it's her," he said. "The fingerprints check out."

• • •

"Well, we got our victim." Olson tossed a wad of paper at a distant wastebasket and missed by a mile. "They can put her in the ground now."

"Thanks for handling the call." Dooley had won the coin toss and chosen the paperwork.

"Hey, my pleasure. My favorite part of the job. 'Hi there. Did you know your daughter was tortured to death last week?' It's all tone of voice, you just handle it like a lost wallet. People love talking to me."

Dooley had made his share of those calls and recognized the bitter tone. "She say anything useful?"

"She didn't even know Sally was missing. You know what she said? She said, 'I gave up on that girl when she was about fourteen.' I don't think this was the closest mother-daughter relationship, somehow."

Dooley signed the supplementary and shoved it away. "OK, we got our victim, we got our crime scene. Now I want witnesses."

"Well, that ought to be a piece of cake. I'm sure we'll have a regular parade of Outfit guys through here anxious to talk about it."

"Feldman. We get in touch with Intelligence and find out what they know. This and that, you know it's the same case."

"You're sounding kind of cocky all of a sudden."

Dooley leveled an index finger at him. "Why do syndicate guys get killed?"

"They talk. Or somebody thinks they're about to talk."

Dooley nodded. "Or they hold out. That's a big no-no. Maybe the biggest one."

The light of understanding shone in Olson's eyes. "Oh my God, the poor stupid bitch."

"Maybe she was stupid. Maybe she was loyal. Or maybe she was just unlucky."

Olson frowned at it for a couple of seconds. "Why did she wait until May to run?"

"Maybe she didn't wait. We don't know where she was between February and May."

"And why didn't she just give it up when they caught her? Put me in that situation, I'd hand it over so fast they wouldn't know I ever had it."

"I bet she tried. I bet she tried like hell to give it up."

Olson shook his head, thinking about it. "Jesus Christ."

"Yeah. We're not dealing with a bunch of God damn altar boys here. Anyway, the question is, where is it? I think if she had it with her, she would have given it up when they grabbed her. I don't think she would have let them bring her back here if the money was sitting in her room up there or something. What happened to her suggests to me she didn't have it and couldn't get to it when they grabbed her. So what did she do with it?"

"Stashed it somewhere."

"Yeah. The Radkes cleaned out her room, after the cops up there had a look at it, and they swear everything she had was in that suitcase and that box they brought with them. I went through it all and there's no locker keys, no bank slips, no address book, nothing. If she had something like that, it was probably in her purse, and Mrs. Radke says she's pretty sure Sally took it with her that night. The Wisconsin cops might have found something. We need to call up there and check. But who the hell knows? It's all guessing. Maybe she coughed it up right away, came back to her room and pulled it out of her sock drawer and handed it over."

Olson watched him shove papers around for a moment and said, "In which case, what they did to her was just—"

"Punishment," said Dooley. "Or worse than that."

"Worse?"

"Maybe it was just fun."

Eight

THE GIRL LAY dead in an armchair, in a blue and yellow bikini, a basket with an orange beach towel peeking out of it at her feet. Her head lolled to one side and blood had trickled out of the hole in her temple and run down her neck and chest to seep under the bikini top between her breasts. Her eyes were open, but the lids were drooping; she looked bored, as if death had been a real disappointment so far.

"I don't know what the hell happened," said the man on the couch. He had on bathing trunks and sneakers and a loud sport shirt. He had sandy hair and with his vacant eyes he looked like somebody had rung his bell with a two-by-four. "I could have sworn it was unloaded," he said.

"I want to make sure I have this right," Dooley said. "You wanted to scare her?"

"I didn't even want to scare her. I was just fooling around."

"So you pointed the gun at her and pulled the trigger."

"I didn't even mean to pull the trigger. I was just gonna say boo, have her look over and see the gun, you know . . ."

"Scare her," said Dooley.

The vacant blue eyes met Dooley's but didn't linger. "I guess so. I don't know how it went off. I didn't try and pull the trigger. It just went off."

Dooley looked at Olson, who stood frowning faintly at the man on the couch, pen poised over his notebook. Olson's eyes flicked to Dooley's and his lips tightened. The patrolman who had been waiting for them in the basement apartment gave a silent shake of the head in the doorway.

Dooley jutted his chin at the automatic lying on the carpet. "Where'd you get the gun?"

"My cousin gave it to me when I moved to Chicago. He said I'd need it living up here."

"You ever fired it before?"

"Uh-uh. Just kept it in a drawer."

"And why'd you pull it out now?"

"I don't know. I guess I just wanted to show her I had it. We were gonna go to the beach but we got to talking and she asked if I was worried about burglars here, and I said no and I was just gonna show her why not. So I went to get it. Jesus, I took the clip out."

"Uh-huh. You took the clip out." Dooley looked at his partner again, and Olson read his face and took over, allowing Dooley to turn his back on the man and pace slowly away, stifling his disgust.

"Did you clear the chamber?" Olson said, a third-grade teacher leading a dim child through an arithmetic problem.

"What do you mean?" said the man on the couch.

In the silence that followed Dooley turned around and saw the whole sick mess: the girl dead in the chair, the moron on the couch still looking more bewildered than guilty, Olson looking down at him with contempt. Hours of work ahead even if it was just what it looked like, a death too stupid for the word tragedy. Dooley wanted to knock the moron around the room a bit; he wanted to feel facial bones break under his fist. "She a good friend of yours?" he said, calmly.

There was nothing at all in the blue eyes that met his, no remorse, no shame, no awareness. "I just met her," the moron said.

"Well," said Dooley. "I'd say you made quite an impression on her."

• • •

"So what can we charge this dumb son of a bitch with?" said Olson. He had loosened his tie in the heat; sweat had beaded on his broad and shining brow. Up here on the third floor there was no place left for the heat to go except down a man's throat.

"Homicidal stupidity," said Dooley, easing onto the chair across from his partner. "Being an asshole in the first degree."

"No chance he did it on purpose, huh?"

"No chance we could ever prove it." Dooley ran his handkerchief over his face, sapped by four hours of interviews. "Her parents never heard of the guy, no indication of any history between them. The neighbors barely knew he existed, he never made any trouble. He's got no record, not in Illinois anyway. Only thing I can think of, if the autopsy shows she's pregnant or something and he's the father, maybe there's something there. But that's just wild optimism. I sure as hell couldn't shake him. The son of a bitch just sat there and looked at me and kept saying the same thing. 'I thought it was unloaded.' I think maybe he really is just as stupid as he looks, which ought to be a crime all by itself."

"You could fill a fuckin' jail with people like him."

Dooley snapped a pencil in two. "If he did do it on purpose, then he was willing to do time for it, because with manslaughter, reckless endangerment and any weapons charges we can pile on with, he's sure as hell going to Stateville for a while."

"McCone OK with that?"

"He can listen to a State's Attorney as well as I can. There's no case for murder here. If he did want to kill her, he pretty much got away with it. He behaves himself, he'll be out in a few years. Fuck him. Maybe somebody'll slip a shank in between his ribs."

Olson gave him a musing look. "Jeez, Mike. The guy got under your skin a little, huh?"

Dooley gave one of his weary shrugs, his signature. "Nineteen years old, pretty girl, all she did was agree to go to the beach with this idiot. Bang. You tell me what the moral of the story is."

A phone rang as Olson was thinking about it, and if there was a moral Dooley never got to hear it, because the dick who answered the phone called out his name. He took his time going across the floor to take it; Dooley was starting to run out of gas. "Yeah," he said into the phone.

"Ed Haggerty here, how you doing?"

"Oh, hey, thanks for getting back to me. Still in there pitching."

"Good. You wanted to know all about Herbie Feldman."

"Yeah, we got an ID on our girl on the riverbank and we were told she used to be Feldman's girl."

"No kidding. Hold on, Sally what's-her-name?"

"Kotowski."

"That's her. Wow. That's tough luck. She didn't do it, you know."

"Do what?"

"Blow the whistle on Herbie."

Dooley sank onto a chair. "You're gonna have to fill me in a little. I don't handle much mob stuff."

"OK, here's the background. Herb Feldman was one of the Outfit's guys in Vegas. You know they control some of the casinos out there. The Stardust, the Riviera, the Desert Inn."

"Yeah."

"And they skim. They skim like hell. It's a perfect setup for them. They rake off unbelievable amounts of cash that nobody can keep track of. They got a guy out there, Caifano, that oversees everything, and a few other guys that haul the money back here. Feldman was one of those guys. That's why he got shot. He was awaiting trial on federal charges and they were afraid he was going to cut a deal and blow the Vegas operation out of the water."

"I see. How'd the feds get to him?"

"He was stupid and greedy, that's how. He tried to work some kind of extortion deal on a bank out there and somebody went to the feds. Herbie skipped town last December ahead of an indictment and came back here and went to earth with Sally, holed up in her apartment. But in January the FBI found him and arrested him for unlawful flight to avoid prosecution. And they didn't arrest her, which looked bad as hell for her. You know, people would figure she fingered him. Only I talked to the feds and I asked them how they found Herbie and they said it was the stupidest thing in the world—he called somebody in Vegas on a line they had a tap on and said where he was. And Sally didn't get charged because in their estimation she was under duress. So I made a few phone calls and put out the word—it wasn't her that fingered him. I guess somebody didn't believe me."

Dooley thought for a moment and said, "Any chance he gave her money to hide? I mean, it looked like they wanted something from her."

"I guess it's possible. He might have tried to get away with that month's skim or something. It would have been stupid, but those guys are so greedy they'll try anything. And yeah, if they thought she had helped him stash it somewhere, that could explain it."

"All right, so who are we talking about? I'm ready to go knock on some doors."

"Well, I don't know how much we really have. He got killed out in Oak Brook and the police out there weren't much help. They don't get too many homicides. They came to us right away when they saw what kind of thing it was, but they didn't have too much to give us. The shooters wore masks, nobody got a plate number, the usual. There's a limited number of people they use for this kind of thing. I can give you five or six names and it was probably two of them, but I'll never prove it. As for the girl, if it was because Herb used her to hide money, then you're probably looking at the same five or six names."

Dooley let a couple of seconds pass. "What they did to her was a little different from a nice clean shooting. I'm wondering if there's somebody with a reputation for that type of work. Say an ice pick specialist. I'm thinking of something like what happened to that bookie they found in a car trunk a few years ago on lower Wacker."

"Old Action Jackson? Well, we did have our suspicions on that. But I don't know that anybody's copyrighted it."

"That would be something to go on."

"Well, at the head of the list you'd have to put Mad Dog D'Andrea, I guess."

"Mad Dog?"

"Mad Dog Joe D'Andrea. Juice loan collector with the Grand Avenue crew. They say he's got a way with tools. We think he got his licks in on the Action Jackson business, but we couldn't ever prove it. And he probably killed Andy Sparks last year."

"The guy they found in the sewer out near Harlem?"

"That's the one. He pulled off that big score down in Alsip and tried to get by without paying his street tax. He'd been perforated pretty good before they finally cut his throat. That's the type of work D'Andrea does. But we've never been able to nail him."

"Who does D'Andrea answer to?"

"I don't know that Mad Dog answers to anybody. He's a little bit of a loose cannon. But like I said, he mainly works for the Grand Avenue crew, and that would be Joey Lombardo. But on something like this, I don't know if Lombardo would call the shots. The Vegas skim goes right to the top, and that's where the order to go after the money would come from."

"The top. Meaning who these days? Ricca? Accardo?"

"Well, that's an interesting question. Ricca's retired for sure, out of the game. Prison took it out of him. Accardo, well, it looks like he's doing his best to stay out of things. He's made his pile and just wants to enjoy the good life now. I'm sure money still goes up to him, but he's being real careful, and he's keeping his kids out of it.

Accardo's like the king. He just wants a competent prime minister to keep things running. If Tony wanted to get back into it he'd have done it when Giancana went off the rails. Instead he basically told Giancana to take a long vacation and put Battaglia in his place."

"But Battaglia went to jail, didn't he?"

"Yeah, a couple of years ago. Then the word was it was Joey Aiuppa for a while, but he wasn't quite up to it. Now, as far as we can tell, it's Milwaukee Phil."

Dooley had to think for a second. "Alderisio."

"That's right. And if that's the best they can do, they're in trouble. Philly's an old hit man. He's no genius. The guy they really miss is Murray Humphreys. He was the real brains."

"So where do I start? Who gave the word to go after Sally Kotowski?"

"Probably somebody we just mentioned. But you'll never prove it. The best you'll ever do is nail somebody that actually helped kill her, and that will take a hell of a lot of luck. If I were you I'd concentrate on physical evidence, because nobody's going to talk to you. If you can get prints or something, you might get lucky. Otherwise you're swimming upstream."

Dooley sat with the phone to his ear until Haggerty asked if he was still there. "Still here," Dooley said. "Where do I find Joe D'Andrea?"

There was a mild chuckle at the other end of the line. "I get a feeling you're one of these guys that likes to bang his head against the wall."

"That's me. I got a hard head."

"Well, sometimes that's what gets the job done. I'd say you'd be most likely to find him at the office, like any businessman. Remember the old Armory Lounge?"

"Heard of it. That's where, on Roosevelt Road?"

"Just past Harlem, yeah. In Forest Park. They've renamed it since the days when Giancana ran things out of a booth in the back, but a lot of guys still hang out there. It's called Giacomo's now. That's where I'd look for Joe D'Andrea first."

"OK. What's the local situation? Am I better off contacting the Forest Park department, or doing an end run around them?"

"That's a real good question. They definitely have some people on the pad. Don't just call up and announce you're coming to town, because then I don't think you'll find D'Andrea there. If I were you I'd just go in cold. You ever dealt with D'Andrea?"

"No."

"You're in for a treat. Handle with care, because there's a reason they call him Mad Dog. He can blow up like a firecracker if you rub him the wrong way. Of course, sometimes that's half the fun. Joe gets so mad sometimes he can't talk right. He'll start spluttering and mixing up words and it can be pretty funny. But you want to watch it, too. He's no joke."

"I'll try to keep that in mind," said Dooley.

Nine

THERE WERE ADVANTAGES and disadvantages to working at night; one of the advantages was that if you wanted to talk to hoods, you were more likely to find them up and about after sundown. Hoods liked the night shift; their office hours tended to correspond to business hours at taverns, strip joints and supper clubs.

Giacomo's, *née* the Armory Lounge, sat on the north side of Roosevelt Road, a long low building slouching back from the street with a parking lot on the west side and a big Z-shaped neon sign over the door that said *Giacomo's* on the top bar, *Lounge* on the bottom, and *Restaurant* on the diagonal stroke. Olson turned into the parking lot and rolled slowly past the handful of cars parked there: a couple of Lincolns, a Caddy or two, the odd Riviera or Toronado. Dooley was looking at license plates; he rapped on the window as they passed a dark blue Torino. "There it is. He's here."

Olson parked at the edge of the lot closest to the street, nose out for a fast getaway. Dooley wasn't expecting any problems, but there were things you did just in case. They got out and strolled toward the door beneath the big neon sign.

"Let's hope he's been here a while," said Dooley. "Booze never made these guys any smarter."

"It has been known to make people ornery," said Olson.

Dooley paused with his hand on the door. "I'd like that," he said. "I'd love to arrest somebody tonight."

"You're just in that kind of mood, aren't you?"

"Yeah, I'm in a mood tonight." Dooley pulled open the door.

They walked into a long dimly lit room with a bar stretching down the right side and booths along the left-hand wall. At the rear the space opened out into a restaurant area with a scattering of tables. Music from a jukebox was playing: Johnny Mathis oozing around a tinkle of piano. Heads turned at the bar as they walked in, and the looks were not especially welcoming. Dooley had mastered the art of walking into tough bars as a young man in khaki, and he had never forgotten the fundamentals: you walk in like you own the place. He sauntered down the bar with his hands in his pockets, looking at each face in turn and seeing variations on a theme: surly, hostile, belligerent. He'd been looking into faces like these for a couple of decades now. There were a couple of women, young and decorative, with their hair puffed up like LBJ's daughters wore it, hanging on men's arms, earning their keep.

In a booth near the back he found the face he'd studied in a photo back at Damen and Grace. The man sat facing the front with his elbows on the table, two others across from him craning over their shoulders to see what had caused the sudden freeze. Joe D'Andrea was a stocky little man in a rumpled gray suit with the tie loosened and the top shirt button undone. He had greasy gray hair combed straight back from his forehead and a broad jowly face featuring a mouth with a permanent downturn at the corners. He looked like the type of man who would take a swing at you for nudging his elbow in the checkout line.

Dooley pulled up at the booth. "Joe? Joe D'Andrea?"

The blunt chin came up a few degrees and he said, "Who the hell wants to know?"

Dooley pulled out his star. "My name's Dooley. This is Olson. We're from CPD Homicide."

D'Andrea sat back slowly, his face going sly. Flicking a look at his audience across the table he said, "Oh, good for you. Your mommas must be real proud of you."

The other two laughed. They were old men with ravaged faces, hard cases whose years of bad living had caught up with them. Dooley waited out the snickers. It reminded him of grammar school, twelve-year-old bullies laughing when the ringleader wanted them to laugh. His eyes never left D'Andrea's. "We need to talk to you."

"So talk. Who's stopping you?"

"Not here. In private."

"These are my friends. I got no secrets from my friends." D'Andrea took in the whole bar with a gesture. Dooley knew everybody in earshot was listening hard.

"I do. Now cut the shit and come with us."

D'Andrea just stared at him; he wasn't used to taking orders from coppers, especially not on his turf. "You tryin' to tell me I'm under arrest?"

"You could be. Easy. That's a trick they teach us on the first day at the academy. Now let's go."

"Fuck you. This ain't Chicago. You can't do a fuckin' thing to me here."

D'Andrea had it right; on this side of Harlem, Dooley was just a private citizen. But Dooley was tired of seeing mobsters hide behind the rules; it bothered him that D'Andrea and his pals felt so safe here. "Wanna bet?" he said. "We'll make it a hot pursuit if we have to. You refused to pull over to talk about your broken tail light."

"Kiss my ass. I don't have no fuckin' broken taillight."

Dooley smiled at him. "You checked it lately?"

Dooley watched D'Andrea's face go red. D'Andrea said, "Fuck you, you fucking cocksupper cocks."

"Say what?" Dooley squinted at him. "What the hell's a cocksupper?" The other wise guys might have known better, but they couldn't contain themselves; there was an explosion of laughter.

D'Andrea started up out of the booth at him, jarring the table and slopping a little beer onto it, then thought better of it and sank back onto the seat. He jabbed a finger at Dooley. "I'm gonna show you what a fucking cock*sucker* is, you prick."

"Cut it out, Joe. Let's get moving. Cooperate and we'll have you back here for last call."

"What the fuck, Joe?" said one of the men in the booth. "They're just coppers."

D'Andrea snorted, wiped his mouth with his sleeve. "Yeah. Hey, how much money you make last year, copper?"

"Enough to afford a new suit. Let's go, move." Dooley stood aside to let him out of the booth.

D'Andrea slid out, glaring at Dooley. "Have a cold one waiting for me," he said to his pals, and started stumping toward the door. Olson led the way and Dooley trailed, watching faces again. Now the faces were mostly amused; Dooley could see that nobody thought there would be any problem about Joe D'Andrea coming back before closing time.

Outside Dooley led him to the car and said, "Put your hands up on the car, Joe."

"Fuck you, I ain't carrying nothing."

"You'd be even dumber than you look if you were, but I don't take any chances. Put your hands on the car."

D'Andrea leaned on the Plymouth as Olson patted him down. "This what you poor fucks driving this year? My fuckin' kid drives a better car than this."

"Your kid probably sticks up liquor stores. We don't have that option."

Spittle came flying back over D'Andrea's shoulder. "My kid don't stick up no liquor stores, you piece of shit. He's goin' to college. And he could kick your lousy cop ass, I guarantee it."

"Pipe down, will you?"

Olson held up a thick roll of bills in a rubber band. "You planning to buy a house tonight?"

"Cheap fuckin' bastards. I bet you don't see that much money in a year. Go ahead, steal it. Greedy prick cop fuckers."

Olson stuffed the roll back in D'Andrea's pocket.

Dooley said, "Joe, you're starting to get on my nerves. You cuss at us one more time and I'm gonna put the cuffs on and book you for drunk and disorderly."

"Ahhh . . ." There was a brief battle, and the pro in D'Andrea won by a hair. "Go take a hike, will ya?"

They put him in the back and Olson drove east on Roosevelt. "Where the hell we goin'?" said D'Andrea.

"Austin district. 5327 West Chicago."

"Aw, hell with that. You got questions, ask 'em. We don't need to go to no station."

"Joe, I don't want to start any rumors. 'Two cops gave Joe D'Andrea a ride around the block the other night.' How do you think that sounds? This way it's on paper, we took you in, we questioned you. There's a record."

"What the fuck you wanna know about? I ain't done nothing."

"Save it till we get there."

"You're ruining my God damn evening, you know that?"

Olson made good time up Austin, and by eleven-thirty they had Joe D'Andrea in an interview room. Dooley found coffee and put a cup in front of D'Andrea. He sat down next to Olson, who had his legal pad and his pen on the table.

"I don't want no coffee," D'Andrea said, glowering, disheveled. "I gotta take a piss already."

"You can take a piss just as soon as you answer one question for me."

"That's about what I got time for. One question."

"Where were you on May thirty-first? That was a Saturday."

D'Andrea's eyes widened. "How the fuck do I know? It's June now. That was a month ago."

"It's June fourteenth. That was two weeks ago. It rained, remember? Come on, two Saturdays ago. Make an effort."

"I don't know. What the hell you want? Daytime? Nighttime? Saturday's a whole fuckin' day."

"Daytime. The afternoon."

"Fuck, I don't know. Probably at home. I work around the yard on Saturdays. Yeah, I was at home."

"Mowing the lawn? In the rain? Come on, Joe, you don't even mow your own lawn. You're a top syndicate guy. You've got eager young punks to cut your grass for you."

"Fuck you. I was at home. I remember now, yeah, it was raining. I watched some TV, fooled around in the basement some. Ask my wife."

"Don't worry, we will. How about that night? Saturday night."

"You said one question."

"It's the same question. Where were you?"

"You prick, you said I could take a piss."

"You can, in a second. Just answer the question. Where were you that Saturday night?"

"I was probably at the lounge, like always."

"Probably?"

"I was at the fuckin' lounge. Ask anybody."

"Who? Who can put you there?"

"Ahhh . . ." D'Andrea waved both hands at him, disgusted. "Anybody. Ask Freddy, the bartender. Same guy that was there tonight. He'll tell you. I'm always there."

"Who besides him?"

"I don't fuckin' know besides him. Anybody. Johnny Muscia, Tony Messino, Sammy Carlucci, I don't know. A lot of guys were there."

Dooley let him stew for a few seconds, gauging how long he had before D'Andrea blew up. "OK, how about Tuesday, June third? The Tuesday following that."

"Jesus, I'm gonna piss down my leg here in a second."

"Drink the coffee, piss in the cup. Tuesday. The third of June. Daytime. Where were you?"

"Shit, I don't know. I don't keep no fuckin' diary."

"Tuesday last week. Wednesday was the day we had the thunderstorms. I'm talking about the day before that. The Cubs had the Astros in town. Remember?"

"Fuck, no. I don't pay no attention to baseball."

"OK, you don't like baseball. You noticed the thunderstorms though, right? Where were you the day before? Tuesday."

"All right, all right, I remember. I was in bed."

"In bed? Who with?"

"Your mother."

"You talk about my mother again, you'll spend the night here. Now give me a straight answer."

"You said daytime. I sleep late, for Christ's sake. That day I slept till two or three in the afternoon. I was up late the night before. There was a card game."

"Where?"

"At Pete McGuire's place, in Cicero. I was there till sunup, then I went home to sleep. I didn't get up till the afternoon. Ask my wife, she'll tell you."

"OK. Now how about the evening?"

"I went to the lounge."

"Again?"

"I go there all the time."

"That's convenient."

"I ain't making it up. You can ask anybody."

"You went straight there from home?"

"Yeah. I got up, had something to eat, drove to the lounge."

"What time did you leave home?"

"I don't know. Late afternoon. Five o'clock maybe."

"And what time did you get to the lounge?"

"Fuck, I don't know. Traffic was bad, it was rush hour. Five-thirty maybe."

"All right. Who can put you there on Tuesday?"

"Ah, lemme think. I had a talk with Sammy, Sammy Carlucci. He'll tell you. And then Vince Palermo was there, I remember that 'cause he don't usually come by no more, I hadn't seen him in a while. And Freddy. The bartender. That's three people can prove I was there."

"How late did you stay?"

"Till closing. Four o'clock."

"You were there for what, eleven hours, you're telling me? Ten and a half?"

"So what?"

"You never once left the place?"

"I like it there. I have a little dinner, talk with my friends. What's it to you? Freddy will tell you. He'll vouchsafe for me, the whole fuckin' time."

Dooley shook his head. "OK. Now. Last Sunday. Afternoon and evening. Where were you?"

D'Andrea closed his eyes and exhaled, raggedly, a persecuted man. "At the lounge. I was at the lounge."

• • •

"Perfect," said Dooley. "He was at the lounge. He's always at the lounge."

"Yeah." Olson steered with one hand, cruising down Austin, past midnight, through light traffic. "Interesting, though. He was vague about every day but Tuesday. For Tuesday he had his witnesses right at his fingertips."

"Yeah. Carlucci, Messino, Palermo and the bartender. I'll tell you one thing, that's four guys we can figure are cooked."

"How about the wife? You want to hit her tonight, before he has a chance to talk to her?"

"I don't think so. If he's got the guys at the bar fixed up, you know the wife's already on board. I think we just go back and throw them a few curveballs, see if somebody swings and misses."

When they walked into the Armory Lounge the music was different but only a few faces had changed. One of the ones that had been there earlier called out, "Hey, where's Joe?"

"He's taking a piss." Dooley pulled up at a vacant stretch of the bar and flagged down the bartender. "Freddy?"

"Yeah." Freddy was a walking cadaver, a thin hairless man who had spent too much time indoors serving drinks to hoodlums in inadequate light. "What can I do for you?"

"I need you to remember something."

Freddy looked for something to do, a glass to polish, anything. He came up empty and said, "I'll do my best."

"Did you work here on Tuesday, June third? That's Tuesday of last week, not this past Tuesday."

"I work every night but Monday."

"OK. Last Tuesday. I need you to tell me who was in here, as many as you can remember."

Freddy stared at him for a moment. "I don't know. The regulars, I guess. One night's pretty much like another around here."

"You know a guy named Vince Palermo?"

"Know who he is."

"Has he been in here recently?"

"Yeah. Matter of fact, it was last week some time. Might have been Tuesday."

"OK, so you remember the night."

"Yeah."

"OK, now who else was in here that night? Think about it."

Freddy thought about it. "A bunch of regulars. Sam Carlucci was here, I remember. Oh yeah, Tony Messino, too."

"Who else?"

Freddy had been pushed to his limit, apparently; he made an elaborate shrug and said, "I don't know. A bunch of guys. I can't remember 'em all."

"Who did Palermo talk to?"

"He talked to Joe D'Andrea."

"Anyone else?"

"Not that I noticed. Maybe Messino. Yeah, I think he talked to Messino. Look, it was a couple of weeks ago, right? How am I supposed to remember?"

Dooley stared him down until somebody down the way called for a drink. "You mind?" said Freddy.

Dooley pushed away from the bar. "Go ahead, go take care of business."

A sallow dog-faced hood two stools over grinned at Dooley and said, "Fishin' again, huh? I think you just lost another lure."

• • •

"Of course they cooked it all up. He picked three guys and briefed 'em. D'Andrea was there all evening, and funny thing, each of them only remembers the other three being there. If we track down Palermo he'll say the same thing. If we had a way to throw all those mopes in separate cells and go at 'em one by one we might cross somebody up. But we don't have the time or the resources to do that. We're stuck with what we got. But all it does is make me even more sure he wasn't there that night. Shit." Dooley was getting tired of this stretch of Austin, going by in the night. "You know what pisses me off?"

"What?" Olson was down to two fingers on the wheel, elbow out the open window.

"They were laughing at us the whole time. They know."

"That's hoods for you."

"They own the fucking city and they know it."

"Mike, you need a beer. Let's cut this asshole loose and go hit J.J.'s."

"I don't need a beer. I need a win."

Back at the district the sergeant gave them a look as they walked in. "Your guest in the penthouse suite ain't too happy with the accomodations," he said. "You gonna charge him?"

"Nah," said Dooley. "We're gonna give him a medal."

"Well, just get him the hell out of here. He's disturbing the lieutenant's beauty sleep."

When Dooley opened the door of the interview room, D'Andrea stopped pacing and started yelling. "Where the fuck you been? I been sitting in here for an hour. I wanna see my fucking lawyer and I wanna see him now."

"Relax. You don't need a lawyer. You need a ride, and if you don't shut your mouth, you're going to see what it's like to walk around the West Side at night."

D'Andrea stopped in the doorway and stuck a finger in Dooley's face. "I'm gonna remember you, Dooley." He looked like a stroke waiting to happen, flushed and with a sheen of sweat on his brow.

"I hope so, Joe. I hope you remember to take a shower soon, too."

Go ahead, thought Dooley, watching veins throb in D'Andrea's forehead. Take a poke, see what it gets you.

D'Andrea looked like he was considering it, but he said, "You think you got what it takes to mess with us, huh? You maybe got another thing coming."

Dooley looked down into the blotched face, six inches away, and said quietly, "I think it's just a matter of time before I nail you to the fucking wall, that's what I think."

The ride back to the lounge was silent. Olson pulled over in front and said, "Here you go, Joe. We'll waive the fare because you're such a good customer."

"Kiss my ass." D'Andrea got out and slammed the door. He

tore open the door of the bar and went inside. Olson pulled a U-turn in the street and headed back east. He said, "He's got a winning way, doesn't he?"

"Pull into that lot there."

"Huh?"

"Pull in there and wait. I'm just thinking."

Olson turned into a parking lot next to a darkened building. "What are you thinking?"

"Put it in the shadows there, where we can see back to the bar. I'm thinking he's maybe going to pass the word to somebody about what happened."

Olson spun the wheel, maneuvering to where they could see the door of the lounge, half a block back.

"So?"

"It might be somebody back there, it might not. He might do it by phone, but I don't think so. I think they're careful about phones now. So I think there's just a chance he might come out of there in a couple of minutes and drive some place. Be interesting to see where."

Olson wasn't happy, Dooley could tell; he'd been looking forward to his beer. He threw it into park. "If you say so."

"We'll give him fifteen minutes, OK? If he's still in there we'll call it a night."

There was still a little traffic on Roosevelt, to and fro; it was a Saturday night and people were out and about. The first five minutes seemed like an hour; then Dooley settled down and managed to watch without thinking about the clock. At twelve minutes he was ready to admit it was a pointless hunch, but he decided to give it another minute. At thirteen minutes Joe D'Andrea came out of the door of the Armory Lounge and turned toward the parking lot. Olson turned the ignition key. "Right again, you bastard."

"Maybe. Maybe he's just had enough to drink finally."

The blue Torino came peeling out of the lot and headed east, picking up speed fast. Olson gave him a block and eased out after him. The Torino's tail lights were pulling away. "How much of a chase do we give him?"

"Reasonable. If he goes too fast let him go."

Olson managed to keep the Torino in sight, hanging a couple of blocks back. D'Andrea crossed Austin going hard, then slowed. At Cicero he turned north and headed up into bad streets.

"Where the hell's he going?" said Olson.

"Well, he's not going home. He lives near Harlem and Diversey."

D'Andrea had slowed considerably and Olson had to hang back, pulling over and dousing the lights at one point. It was not a nice place to park at one in the morning; even before the riots these hadn't been happy precincts. There were a lot of broken windows and padlocked grates, a few liquor bottles moving in the shadows.

He's just cruising," said Olson, pulling out again.

They saw what he was cruising for a turn or two and a few blocks later. The ladies had started to appear here and there in doorways and under street lamps: high boots and short skirts, fishnet stockings and cigarettes hanging from blood-red lips. Some were black and some were white; some were young and some were old; all of them had the patient wary look of the survivor

"Son of a bitch," said Olson, as D'Andrea pulled over a block ahead.

She had on a white minidress and she came out of the shadows to lean down at the passenger-side window for no more than five seconds before she got into the car. The Torino pulled away from the curb and Olson said, "There you go. He's passing the word. There's the secret head of organized crime in the city of Chicago. A twenty-buck whore."

"Keep after him, just for a bit."

"What, you want to surprise him? Shine the brights in on him, cause a little coitus interruptus?"

"Right now I'm thinking about what happened to Sally Kotowski."

Olson put it in gear. "You don't think he does it just for fun, do you?"

"I don't want to think about what he does for fun. But I don't think we can just drive off and leave him, not now."

In these streets the traffic was sparse and mainly there for one thing, and Olson had no trouble keeping the Torino in sight. It didn't go far; the first dark alley was the customary venue for this type of transaction, and the Torino had gone only a block or so when it turned off the street. Olson rolled slowly toward the mouth of the alley.

"What do you want to do? Go after him?"

"Just pull up so we can see him. Hit the lights."

As they pulled across the mouth of the alley they looked to the right and saw the Torino halfway down, parked. As they watched, the lights went off. A few seconds went by.

"What do you think?" said Olson.

Dooley watched the dark car sitting a couple of hundred feet away, trying to figure odds. "I don't know. I guess I think if he was going to hurt her he'd probably take her someplace. I think he's probably just getting his Saturday night blow job. But I'd hate to be wrong. Let's just sit for a second."

The passenger-side door of the Torino flew open and the whore came tumbling out onto her hands and knees. Her dress was up around her waist but she didn't let that slow her up; she made it to her feet and started running as best she could on her high-heeled boots.

"Go," said Dooley.

Olson reversed and then wheeled into the alley in a squeal of rubber. He grabbed for the knob and the headlights caught the girl running toward them, eyes wide and hair flying. With the lights in her face she dodged to the side and flattened herself against the wall. The Torino took off with a screech, its lights coming on as it reached the street at the far end of the alley.

Olson braked as they reached the girl. Dooley pushed open the door and got out. She was just outside the halo from the headlights, but he could see her panting, pushing her tight skirt back down her thighs. "Police," he said. "You OK?"

She panted some more and then made a sound: she sobbed. She stifled it and gasped, "You cops?"

"Yeah. Did he hurt you?"

The whore was getting her breath and her courage back; she straightened up and said in a slightly quavering voice, "No, I'm OK."

Dooley had taken a couple of steps toward her, not crowding her. "Sure you are," he said. "I can tell you're having the time of your life."

She blew out a breath and said, "To hell with you."

"Look, we're not going to arrest you. Tell us what happened in that car just now."

She hadn't survived this long by being slow; she caught Dooley by surprise, taking off on her high heels and getting past him, shaking off his grab. He took two steps and quit; he wasn't going to chase her.

"Hell with it," he said, watching her go back the way they'd come. They got back in the car.

"His Saturday night blow job, huh?" said Olson, rolling down the alley.

Dooley shook his head. "He didn't just scare her," he said. "The son of a bitch did something that's pretty hard to do."

"What's that?"

"He made a whore cry."

Ten

"WIPE YOUR FEET." Dooley barely looked up from the paper as his family trooped in from the garage, bringing the rain with them. Frank shot him a peeved look and stepped back onto the mat, blocking Kathleen and Rose in the doorway. For a moment the three of them clustered there, milling and shuffling, before spilling into the kitchen. Rose sighed as she went past with her usual reproachful glance. Dooley had long ago established the principle that a man who worked into the wee hours most Saturday nights should not be expected to make it to Sunday morning mass, but Rose had never quite conceded the point.

"You see this?" Dooley said, tapping the newspaper.

"What?" Rose halted in her tracks; she seldom looked at the paper but was fully aware that it carried signs and portents, clues to the life or death of her first-born son.

"They're going to pull out the Third Marine Division."

It was the first good news Dooley had seen in the paper in a long, long time, and he had been sitting here at the table trying to keep a lid on a surge of optimism ever since he read it.

"*What?*" He had everybody's attention instantly and they crowded around him, craning over the table. "When? You mean Kevin's coming home?"

The joy in the female voices irritated Dooley; he should have known better than to spring it on them like this but he hadn't been able to resist."Now just hold on a minute. All it says is, some elements of the Third Marine Division are to be included in the withdrawal, starting with the Ninth Marines. Kevin's in the Third Marines. That means the Third Marine Regiment, which is also part of the Third Division, so they may come out, too. But it doesn't say when. Look, it's the military. Nothing happens fast." Except death, he thought, as they pawed at the newsprint to get a look at it.

"But it's good news, right? It means maybe before October, right?" Rose was pleading with her eyes, wanting him to tell her things he couldn't tell her.

"Potentially," said Dooley. "But it doesn't mean he's coming home tomorrow. They'll put them out unit by unit. They're not going to just abandon ship. And things could always change. They're in a war, for God's sake."

"Jeez, Pop. Don't be such a wet blanket."

"I'm being realistic." Dooley scowled at Frank and tugged the paper out of his grasp.

"*Kevin's coming home! Kevin's coming home!*" Kathleen and Frank started jumping up and down like idiots. Dooley winced at the noise.

"All right, cut it out! You're shaking the damn house."

They ran off down the hallway and Dooley pushed away from the table and went to rinse out his coffee mug. When he turned around he saw his wife standing there with a wondering look on her face. "What's the matter?" he said.

She came toward him, arms tightly folded. "I know you're just trying to avoid being hurt. But we need hope sometimes. It's not wrong to hope."

"I know that." He opened his arms and she stepped into the embrace. After a moment he said, "I just know how it goes. Out in the Pacific we'd hear we were going home about once a month. And we never did. Not till it was all over."

She drew back. "You pray for him, don't you?"

"Of course I do."

"He needs it. He needs all the prayers he can get. And I believe they work, Michael. I really do."

"Sure," said Dooley, just audibly.

Dooley had an ambivalent attitude toward prayer. He had prayed like hell for his brother Patrick in the first year of the war, only to have Patrick wind up at the bottom of the Coral Sea in the dark flooded hulk of the *Lexington.* Dooley knew that sometimes God treated prayers the way a man treats a fly buzzing around his head. After Patrick died Dooley had never bothered to pray for his own life; from Bougainville to Manila he had prayed nothing more than *let me die like a man*. He figured the best strategy was not to ask for too much.

Nothing really bad, he prayed, holding his wife in his arms.

• • •

"It was a good thought, but I'm afraid I can't help you," said Haggerty at the other end of the telephone line. "We can't watch them all twenty-four hours a day."

"I know that," said Dooley. "I figured it was worth a try."

"Yeah. The last time we had any surveillance on D'Andrea was a couple of years ago. I could tell you where he had lunch and when he went to the can for that week, but I can't tell you where he was on June second or third."

"That's OK. I knew it was a long shot."

"Now, the feds are always tailing people around. Maybe they could help you."

"That'll be the day. But I'll keep it in mind. Thanks, Ed."

"Don't mention it. Keep after 'em."

After he hung up, Dooley sat looking at the file. "I want to try and find this friend," he said, tapping a finger on a name. "This Laura. We need to zero in on Sally's last few weeks, and this may be one person who can tell us about it."

"OK." Olson was holding a pencil poised over his coffee cup, a thoughtful frown on his face. He started to put the point into the cup, hesitated, reversed the pencil, and stirred the coffee with the eraser end. "That the one that worked at the Playboy Club?"

"Yeah. The bunny."

Olson took a sip and looked at Dooley with innocent eyes over the rim of the cup. "Want me to call 'em up? Save us the drive?"

Dooley looked up at him and said deadpan, "I think we need to go over there. Maybe we can catch her before she starts work or something."

"Or something," said Olson, setting down the cup. "All right, suits me."

The Playboy Club was on Walton, just east of Rush, in the heart of the nightlife district. Dooley had never much cared for the area, but he was in a minority; Rush Street drew crowds in any weather, on any day. Most of the joints were the high-roller kind, with lots of neon flashing and a clientele in suits and ties, but there was a scattering of lesser places, narrow bars that went back a long way from the street, a few sandwich shops, and here and there on the side streets the strip clubs and peep-show joints. Late on a damp gray Sunday afternoon, the sidewalks were full of people, mostly men walking in packs with eager looks on their faces.

The Playboy Club had a canopy over the sidewalk that stretched the length of the façade, flags flying on poles angled out from the wall above. As Dooley and Olson bore down on him a doorman jerked awake and pulled open the door for them. Inside they went up a dozen or so steps and stood in a hall on a carpet with the bunny-head symbol repeated endlessly as far as the eye could see. In front of them was a board on the wall labeled *In the Playboy Club Tonight* above slots holding name plates. To the left was a pool table where a blonde in a purple bunny suit was lining up a shot. Her opponent, a man in a suit with his tie loosened, stood with both hands on his cue, a sheepish smile on his face. His rooting section, three other men with drinks in their hands, watched as the bunny bent over the table. They did not seem overly interested in the shot.

To the right was the entrance to what looked like a bar. Dooley and Olson went through the door and stood just inside, letting their eyes adjust to the gloom. The main source of light was an array of illuminated transparencies on the walls, naked girls everywhere, glowing in the dark. "It makes you feel kind of reverent, doesn't it?" said Olson. "Like stained glass."

"Good evening. Are you gentlemen key holders?" The bunny teetered toward them on her heels. Her hair was piled up on top of her head, the satin ears perched at the crest; her smile was dazzling and almost sincere; and her breasts were threatening to spill out of the inadequate bodice.

"We're police officers," Dooley said. "We need to talk to your manager."

She wasn't trained for that; she gaped at them, and for a second or two she looked almost real. She felt for her smile and said, "Um, why don't you have a seat right here and I'll go speak with him. Would you like something to drink?"

"We're working," Dooley said. "Thanks."

He'd stumped her again, he could see; with an anxious look she pointed them to a booth and tottered away. Dooley watched her cotton tail wiggle as she went. His look met Olson's and they laughed at each other, shaking their heads. "I think I've seen some of these," Olson said, looking around. "I remember *her*. Miss June, I think."

"Yeah," said Dooley. He had seen the magazine at the barbershop, where it was kept up on the top shelf of the coatrack, but he didn't look at it unless someone had left a copy where he could reach for it casually. "You think they have a lot of spilled drinks in here?"

"I bet a lot of drinks go over on purpose in here. Just for the fun of having the help come deal with it. A lot of drinks go onto laps, I bet."

"You got a dirty mind, you know that?"

"Sex isn't dirty anymore, Dooley. Haven't you been reading the papers?"

A man in a suit with well-tended gray hair came across the carpet toward them. They got up to shake his hand. "I'm Jack Barton," the man said. "Can I offer you gentlemen a drink?" His voice was professionally smooth and his handshake practiced and firm.

"No thanks, we're on duty. We were hoping to speak to one of your, uh, people. If she still works here."

Barton frowned. "I hope nobody's done anything wrong."

"No, we just want to interview her. In connection with a homicide." Dooley saw Barton's eyes widen and dart toward a nearby table where two men were pretending not to listen. "Look, would you rather talk about this somewhere else?"

Barton flashed a smile to cover his relief. "Maybe that would be better. I'll ask Martha to join us. She's our hutch mother."

Two minutes later they were seated in an office that was well lit, free of decoration, and cluttered with papers. Barton was behind his desk and a well-preserved middle-aged woman in a sleek blue dress and with reading glasses on a chain around her neck sat to one side. She looked just a touch bewildered. "This is Martha Willis, who's in charge of our bunnies," said Barton. "Now, who are you looking for?"

Dooley said, "First I should tell you that we're working on the murder of another former employee of yours. She was just identified a couple of days ago. Her name was Sally Kotowski."

Willis gasped. "Oh, my God, that's terrible. That's awful."

Barton said, "She was one of ours?"

Willis nodded. She closed her eyes, opened them again, and said, "I remember her. What on earth happened to her?"

"She was strangled. We found her on the riverbank last week."

"That was Sally? Oh, dear God. I read about it." She slumped on her chair and for a second Dooley thought she was going to faint. The three men tensed, ready to jump and catch her, but she rallied. "Sorry. I'm all right," she said. "Oh, my Lord, how terrible."

Barton was scowling at Dooley as if it was all his fault. Dooley had things figured out; Barton's only interest was professional. Scandal-smothering would be part of his job. "So who was it you were looking for?" Barton said quietly.

"We're looking for a friend of Sally's who might be able to tell us things we need to know about Sally. We don't know if she still works here, and all we have is a first name."

"All right, what's the name?"

"Laura. We're told she worked here at the same time as Sally but we don't know if she still does."

Barton looked at Martha Willis, who blinked back at him and then turned to Dooley. "That would be Laura Lindbloom, I think," she said.

"Ah," said Barton. "I remember."

Olson was writing down the name. "Bloom like a flower? Two *o*'s?"

"That's right. She left us, I think, in 1966, if I'm not mistaken."

"Any idea where she went?" Dooley said.

"None. I know she and Sally shared an apartment after they moved out of the club, but I remember Sally telling me at one point she'd moved on from there. I couldn't tell you where."

"OK. Well, we've got a name."

"Laura Lindbloom. Yes. Handle that one with care," said Barton.

"Jack," said Willis in a tone of reproach.

Barton shrugged. "Well, she was a bit of a tiger. I mean, she stood right there where you're sitting and called me a pig. Screamed at me."

There was a brief silence and Martha Willis said, "We had to ask Laura to leave."

Barton said, "She tried to pull the old 'you can't fire me because I quit' thing, but she was fired, believe me."

"Why was that?" said Dooley.

"She was rude to the customers." Barton threw up his hands, an open and shut case. "Not to mention me. She was insubordinate."

Wearily, Martha Willis said, "Laura wasn't a good fit for the organization. Not everyone's cut out to be a bunny."

"I can imagine," said Dooley. "Well, thanks for your help."

"Certainly." She rose a little unsteadily, looking dazed. "I'm devasted. Poor Sally. Please catch them," she said.

"We're working on it," said Dooley.

When she had left, Dooley pointed to a shelf on the wall. "Can I have a look at your phone book?"

Barton flapped a hand. "Help yourself."

Dooley took down the directory and leafed through it. There were a handful of Lindblums and Lindblooms in Chicago and one of the latter was a Laura with an address on Cleveland. He dumped the book in Olson's lap and tapped the page with his index. "There you go." He turned to Barton. "Tricks of the trade."

"I'm impressed." Barton smiled. "Listen, I'm hoping . . ."

"Yeah?"

"I know you have to keep the press abreast of these things. But if it comes up at all, it should be made clear that Sally was not currently working at the Playboy Club. I'd hate for that previous connection to become . . . an angle. The papers can play havoc with a reputation."

Dooley just stood there, thinking about how Sally had looked lying in the weeds. He wished there was a way he could show that to this mutt, make him look at her. "We'll try and be discreet, Mr. Barton."

• • •

The address on Cleveland was just far enough north to be Lincoln Park instead of Old Town. The street had lots of trees, old narrow houses, and no place to park. They left the Plymouth at a corner and walked back. The house was a Victorian pile that could have used a lick of paint and some remedial carpentry. It had a round turret at one corner. There were four doorbells by the front door. The second from the top was labeled *Lindbloom*. Dooley pushed it. A few seconds went by and they heard a scraping sound somewhere above them. They stepped back from the door and looked up to see a girl put her head out of a window on the second floor. "Hi," she said. She had long blonde hair that fell past her face as she leaned and she looked like she could have been one of Kathleen's friends, no older than eighteen.

"Miss Lindbloom?"

The girl said nothing; she just stared down at them, her friendly look fading. Dooley was starting to wonder if she'd heard him when she said, "She's working."

"We're police officers," Dooley said. He pulled out his star and held it up for her to see. "We need to talk to her." The girl stared at them some more, starting to look a little alarmed. Dooley was used to the reaction, but he wasn't going to stand there all day. "Look, is Laura here or not?"

"Um, she's—she's in the studio."

Dooley waited. He said, "OK, where's that?"

It appeared to take her a while to remember; after chewing her lip for a few seconds the girl said, "Go around to the back and up the stairs." She pointed to the side of the house.

"Thanks." Dooley and Olson made their way down the gangway and went through a wooden gate into a walled garden where nobody had done much in the way of gardening besides setting a couple of chairs on a brick patio. There was an external staircase built on to the rear wall of the house. Dooley and Olson labored up the stairs, their footsteps creaking. At the top there was a landing and an open door. Through the door Dooley could see a white-painted attic space that ran most of the way up toward the front of the building, with a skylight in the roof that gave it ample light. As he stepped closer he saw a man standing at an easel, scowling. The man wore glasses with thick black frames and had hair that fell into his eyes. Dooley paused on the threshold.

"What the hell do you want?" said the man.

Dooley was used to discourtesy; a civil answer was a rarity in his line of work. Nevertheless, something about the man's tone of voice, the look he shot him, irritated Dooley. This man was maybe forty years old but he was trying to look younger with the hair, and he hadn't bothered to shave that morning.

"Police," Dooley said. "I'm looking for Laura Lindbloom."

"That doesn't answer my question." The man had been holding a brush, leaning toward the canvas on the easel, but now he set it down on a palette that lay on a stand next to the easel and turned to face the detectives, hands on his hips.

Dooley was used to denial, evasion, and stalling. He was used to criminals, professional tough guys taking a hard line with him. He wasn't used to taking shit from citizens, not quite yet. "I'm a *police* officer," he said with careful articulation. "I was told she was here."

The stare-down lasted about three seconds. The man with the glasses had just conceded by opening his mouth to say something when a voice came from Dooley's left, just out of sight around the door frame. "What is it?" This one was female.

Dooley took a step into the studio and stood with his hands in his pockets, frozen. The woman was standing on a raised platform a foot off the floor, and she was buck naked. For a moment all Dooley could do was stare. He saw a fair number of naked women in the course of a year, but just about all of them were dead. This one was distinctly alive. She was a honey blonde with hair that touched her shoulders, and she stood with one hand on her cocked hip and the other resting casually on a tall stool. She had breasts that went just over the fine line between jutting and hanging, crowned with light brown nipples, and a smooth hard belly and a perfectly triangular patch of dark brown hair that started six inches below her navel and disappeared into Wonderland at the convergence of her legs. When Dooley got around to looking at her face he saw that she had frank brown eyes. As he watched, the woman exchanged a glance with the man at the easel and then shifted, stepping to the edge of the platform and then gracefully down onto the floor. Dooley watched her breasts sway with the movement.

She plucked a terrycloth robe from a sofa and in a second the vision was gone and she was knotting the belt at her waist. "Well?" she said, stepping toward Dooley.

Dooley hadn't blushed since sometime before Pearl Harbor, but to his chagrin he felt himself going red as a fire engine. "Excuse me," he said.

"It's all right, officer. We're all adults here, I think. What can I do for you?"

Dooley was reeling from a rare insight; it wasn't often that the momentous truth that women are naked twenty-four hours a day under their clothes was so vividly brought home. "Are you Laura Lindbloom?" he managed.

"Yes. What have I done?" She glanced at the artist again and seemed to get some kind of encouragement from him; her look went a little sly. "Danny's not a minor, so you can hardly accuse me of corrupting him." Behind Dooley the artist snickered. Dooley took a time-out to get his composure back, studying her face. She was closer to thirty than twenty and hadn't left home just yesterday. Her skin was free of makeup and a couple of years beyond glowing girlhood; it showed the first faint traces of experience: laughter and hard knocks. Dooley knew better than to put too much stock in first impressions but his first guess would have been that there were brains behind the pretty face. "You know a woman named Sally Kotowski?" he said.

Whatever she'd been thinking before, that got her attention; the sly look went away like a light going out. "Yes," she said. "What happened?"

"I'm afraid I have bad news." That was the formula, and it usually did the trick. After you hit them with that one, they were ready for the payoff. "You may have read or heard about a woman found dead near the river last week."

"Oh, my God." Her hands went to her mouth, a classic response; Dooley had seen them all.

"The body has been identified as Sally Kotowski."

First she looked past Dooley at the geek by the easel. Then she turned around and marched to the sofa, wheeled, and sat down. Sitting on the edge, her back straight and her hands clasped in her lap, she stared out the window and said, "I can't believe it."

Dooley took a couple of steps toward her, just wandering. "I'm afraid the identification's definite. What we're trying to do now is to gather as much information as we can about Sally from people who knew her."

She looked up at Dooley and he could see her recovering from the shock. "How did you connect me with her? I haven't seen her in months."

"The person who identified her told us about you. We traced you through the Playboy Club."

"I see." She took a deep breath. "May I get dressed?" At Dooley's nod she rose and padded quickly on bare feet toward the end of the room. She went through a door and closed it behind her. Dooley turned. The artist had taken the palette to a workbench along the wall and was scowling at his brushes. Olson was standing at the easel, surveying the canvas. Dooley hadn't fixed on it when he'd come in, but now he took a look. It was a disappointment. He and Olson exchanged a glance.

"Do you guys mind?" The artist shouldered his way between them. "This is where I work. This is my office. OK?"

"Don't let us stand in your way," said Olson.

"Sorry to interrupt," said Dooley. "I hope this won't take too long."

"I'm paying her for her time, you know." The artist leaned close to the canvas, smoothed a patch of paint with his thumb.

"Oh, is this supposed to be her?" said Olson.

The artist straightened up slowly and turned to face him. "I'm not a portraitist," he said coolly.

"You can say that again." Olson gave him a smile and moved away.

A frosty silence reigned until the door at the end of the studio opened and the woman emerged. She had put on a leather vest over a blouse with billowy sleeves and a skirt that left a fair stretch of thigh uncovered. She had hooked her hair behind her ears. "Danny, I'm sorry. Can we do this another time?" she called to the artist.

"Sure. Whenever." He had gone back to the workbench and was fiddling with rags and brushes.

She came to a halt in front of Dooley and Olson, looking pale but composed. "Now, what can I tell you?"

"Is there someplace where we could talk in private?" said Dooley.

A second went by and there was a brief abrupt clatter from the workbench. "For Christ's sake," said the artist. "I'll just go step out for a while, shall I? Make yourselves at home." He stalked to the door, where he paused long enough to say, "Don't bother to lock up when you leave. I like to run a kind of open house up here, you know?"

After the door slammed she gave Dooley a harried look. "He hates to be interrupted when he's working."

Dooley nodded. "Me too. Why don't we sit down?"

Laura Lindbloom sat on the sofa, legs crossed. Olson perched at the other end, notebook in hand. Dooley found a chair and pulled it up opposite Laura and tried not to look at her legs. He had her give Olson her full name and address and then he hesitated. "Uh, what's your occupation?" he said finally.

She waved a hand at the platform where she had stood naked. "Not just this, if that's what's bothering you. I tend bar over on Wells Street. This is just moonlighting. It's still selling my body, I guess, but it's in the service of art. Or at least that's what Danny would tell you."

Dooley met her gaze for a moment. "OK. Can you tell us how you knew Sally Kotowski?"

She drew a deep breath. "First, can you tell me what happened to her? I don't really read the papers."

Dooley just said, "She was strangled."

Laura put her hands over her face. "Oh, God. Poor Sally." After a few seconds she lowered her hands, and Dooley could see the fight for composure going on. When she had won it she said, "Well, I got to know her at the Playboy Club. We both started there about the same time, back in sixty-four. We lived in the club for a few months and then when that got old we decided to get an apartment together. We shared a place on Pearson for a while."

"And you left the Playboy Club in 1966?"

"That's right. I'd started to see through the whole thing by then."

Dooley blinked a couple of times but didn't ask her what she meant. "What about Sally? When did she leave?"

"She stuck it out until some time in sixty-seven. Then she'd had enough, too. But I guess she got what she wanted."

"What do you mean?"

"She had her man. That's what a lot of girls are looking for, somebody rich to take care of them."

"And who was the man?"

"Well, she went through a few of them. When she quit she was with this guy Herb Feldman."

"What can you tell us about him?"

"I think he was a hoodlum."

"Why do you say that?"

"Because he looked like a hoodlum and acted like a hoodlum. And he bragged about all the hoodlums he knew. He wore expensive clothes but he had the manners of a ditchdigger. He treated Sally all right except when he was drunk. Then he treated her like a dog. I don't know why she put up with it."

"When was the last time you saw her?"

"Last fall sometime. We'd kind of drifted apart. Herb had set her up in her own apartment and we just moved in different circles."

"Was she still with Feldman at the time?"

"Sort of, but she told me she was about to give up on him. I think she'd finally started to get smart."

"Did she say anything specific about why she was giving up on him?"

"He was never around, for one thing. He was spending a lot of time in Las Vegas but expecting her to be on call when he came back here. He wasn't faithful to her but he expected her to be faithful to him. She was tired of being pushed around. And she'd realized he was never going to marry her. She was just an ornament for him. Just a toy."

"But she hadn't actually made the break?"

"I don't think so. She talked about him in the present tense, like 'Herb says this, Herb says that.' It still sounded like a going concern."

"Did she say anything about his business?"

"Not much. I never got a clear idea of what he did. She told me once he was a gambler. I didn't think that was actually a career, but I guess I was wrong. Herb seemed to do OK out of it."

Did she talk about what he did out there?"

Laura's brow wrinkled. "Not that I recall. I assumed he was just gambling."

"She never mentioned anything else, never hinted about anything?"

She gave Dooley a long, grave look. "That's why she was killed, isn't it? Something she got mixed up in."

"We don't know. We're looking for answers. There's always the chance it was just a random thing. But Herb Feldman was a hoodlum, all right. And that's always something to look at. Did Sally ever talk about his friends?"

"Sometimes. In a really juvenile way. Like a high school girl getting a thrill out of hanging out with the tough kids. Do you know who Herb and I had lunch with today, that kind of thing."

"Remember any names?"

She shook her head, making an effort. "Italian names, that's all I could tell you. She would get all mysterious and vague. Herb knows some really heavy people, she told me once."

"OK. Did you know she'd gone up to Wisconsin?"

"Wisconsin? No, I didn't know that. When did that happen?"

"In the spring. That's where she was when she was abducted. It would be really useful to know how they found her up there."

"Like I say, I hadn't seen her since last fall. And she didn't say anything about moving. She was talking about acting jobs, here in the city. She was going to get an agent. I don't think she could act worth a damn."

"Do you know if she actually had an agent?"

"No. I never saw her again after that."

"Can you point us to someone who might have been in closer touch with her in the last few months?"

"Boy, I don't know. Her mother's in Aurora, I think."

"We've already talked with her. They seem to have been estranged."

Laura shook her head, eyes going away, out the door onto the landing. "Poor Sally. I don't know. I don't think Sally had a lot of friends, you know, close friends she would confide in. There was me, for a while, but then we lost touch. I mean, she knew people, but she was very man-oriented. She wanted to snare a man. She thought that would solve everything."

Dooley waited for more but nothing came. He nodded, glanced at Olson, and stood up.

"All right. Thanks for your help." He fished a card out of his jacket pocket and handed it to her. "If you wouldn't mind, I'd like you to keep thinking about this. Any information you can come up with about Sally's associates, someone else who could tell us about her last few months, any disputes, enemies, anything that might have led to her death, please give me a call."

She took the card but didn't get up. "OK." She stared at Dooley's card, looking dazed, as the two dicks made for the door. Just as they reached it she spoke. "Did you see her body?"

Dooley halted. "Yeah, we did."

"Was it really bad for her?"

Dooley took two seconds to decide that this was one of the people you didn't lie to. "Yeah," he said. "It was pretty bad for her."

"Then do me a favor and find them," said Laura Lindbloom, looking up at him. The dazed look was gone and in its place was something else, the beginnings of anger maybe.

"OK," said Dooley. "For you."

Eleven

"WHAT YOU READING?" Dooley stood in the doorway to the living room, looking down at his son. Frank swung his feet off the couch with a guilty look and blinked up at Dooley for a second or two. He looked at the book in his hand as if he were noticing it for the first time.

"A book," he said with a straight face.

Dooley didn't have the energy for this today. "No kidding? I've heard of those. Look, wise guy, I'm trying to make conversation. What's the book?"

Frank stared at him in wonder. "It's just a science fiction book."

Dooley could see the title from where he stood: *Stranger in a Strange Land*. It seemed to him he had heard of the book in a vaguely disreputable way but he couldn't remember enough to make an issue of it. "Is it any good?"

Frank shrugged. "It's OK."

Dooley nodded, waiting for more but knowing it wasn't coming. "Terrific," he said, and left the room. In the kitchen Rose was at the table, cookbooks stacked in front of her, making out her grocery list. "We need sugar," Dooley said.

"There was more in the cabinet. I refilled the bowl."

Dooley poured himself a cup of coffee from the percolator. "When does Frank start at the hot dog stand?"

"Monday. And it's a Dairy Queen."

"Whatever. Get him off his duff, finally."

"He's looking forward to it. Don't be so hard on him."

Dooley sat across from her and pulled the paper toward him. "I just hate to see him sitting around doing nothing. It's bad for kids."

"He's not doing nothing. He's reading."

Dooley scanned the front page. Nixon wanted the troops home by the end of the year; Ogilvie had sent the state cops to Cairo. What the hell was Rockefeller doing in Paraguay? "He's just reading trash."

"What would you like him to read?" Rose asked the question in an abstracted tone of voice without looking up from her list, and Dooley knew she was baiting him. Dooley made sure his kids did their homework, but he liked to joke that the last book he had read had been *Tom Swift and His Flying Boat.* "I just think he needs to get some exercise," he said. "Reading's fine. But he never gets any exercise."

Rose finally looked up at him. "Why don't you take him out and play ball with him, then? Like you used to do with Kevin?"

"I've tried. He always says no."

"When was the last time you asked him?"

It was a direct challenge; Dooley knew this look of his wife's, artfully blank and expectant. "He'll say no," he said into his coffee cup.

"If he does, you can say I told you so," said Rose, returning to her list.

After he ate breakfast Dooley wandered up the hall toward the living room. He knew he had to do it or Rose would be giving him dirty looks all day; he also knew he didn't really want to go stand in the hot sun and throw a baseball to a kid who was just going through the motions. He stuck his head in the living room again. "Hey, Frank. You want to go out and play catch or something?"

Frank looked up at him and frowned: why is this man bothering me again? Then his look softened and for a moment Dooley wasn't quite sure how he felt, whether he was hoping for a yes or a no. Finally Frank said, "Nah, not really."

Dooley went back to the kitchen, where Rose was on her feet, putting things into her purse. "I told you so," Dooley said.

"You happy now?" said Rose.

"Yeah," said Dooley, reaching for the newspaper. "I'm thrilled."

• • •

The store was on Ridge Avenue near where it slashed across Clark Street, a couple of blocks from the sprawling hulk of Senn High School. The storefront was plastered with big painted signs, white on red: *Farmers' Market, Wholesale & Retail, Garden Fresh Fruits and Veg., Direct from Farm to You.* Inside was the usual jumble, apples and tomatoes and ears of corn in heaps, a moist vegetable smell, stacks of cardboard boxes, snacks and soft drinks near the register for the after-school crowd. The walk-in cooler was in back, down a short passage.

The grocer lay on the floor of the cooler, with three bullet holes in his head and one in his chest. His eyes were open and he lay on his back with his legs bent and splayed like a frog's, one arm across his belly and the other flung out across the floor. He was a plump man in his fifties who had gone a little bald and cultivated a natty little moustache. He looked absolutely fresh and alive, as if he would spring up at any moment and apologize for the prank, wiping the trickles of red paint from his high shining forehead.

"Register's empty," said Olson from the doorway.

"Surprise, surprise." Dooley stood with his hands in his trouser pockets, trying to see it. The gun had been a small one to leave such neat holes; maybe the grocer had not taken it seriously and made a swipe for it. A cold-blooded execution would probably have meant a shot in the back of the head, but there were no rules; some killers liked to see panic in the victim's eyes at the last second. "She coherent yet?"

"Well, she hasn't moaned in a couple of minutes. Wagon's on the way."

Through the street door Dooley could see people outside the shop, milling. The squads had drawn a crowd as always. The little fat woman in the gingham dress sat on a chair behind the counter, purse in her lap, wringing a handkerchief and trembling. Her eyes were red and her breathing seemed to require a lot of effort, but she was no longer making noise. Dooley looked for another chair but didn't see one, so he squatted in front of her with a hand on the counter to steady him. "Do you think you can talk to us now, ma'am?"

She nodded, took a deep breath and said, quavering, "I saw him. I saw him run out of the store."

"Who? Someone you know?"

"A boy. Just a boy. He had long hair."

Dooley nodded. "We'll get a description from you in a little while. Can you tell us just what you saw, starting from the time you approached the store?"

Her face began to go, screwing up into a grimace, and Dooley thought he'd lost her, but the little fat lady had her share of courage, and she got control and looked Dooley in the eye and said, "I was coming in to do my shopping, and when I was just a little ways from the door I saw him run out. He was stuffing something in his pocket, and I thought he was maybe stealing something, and it made me mad because Mister—Mister Pappas—he had trouble with that all the time. I came in to tell him about it, and then I didn't see him, and I thought he must have left the store for some reason, and then something made me walk down there . . ." She was fighting hard but losing; she made another stab at finishing and then started wailing again.

One of the patrol cops wandered back up the hallway from the cooler, shaking his head. "Fuckin' asshole kids," he said. "They'd come through here in packs after school and rob him blind. I always figured it was a matter of time before something like this happened."

"You know the kids around here?" said Dooley.

"Lot of 'em, yeah."

"I see a few kids on the sidewalk out there. Get out there and start collaring them. All the kids you can find. Throw them in the squads. When she's able, I'm going to get a description from her."

The lady on the chair sniffed and wailed, "Who's going to tell Chrissie? Who's going to tell her?"

"Where's my father?" The shriek came from the doorway, where a uniform had put out an arm to stop a girl from coming into the store. She was maybe sixteen, skinny in blue jeans, with long black hair and braces on her teeth and big frantic eyes. "Where's my father?" she demanded, looking at Olson.

"I got a feeling she knows," said Dooley, quietly.

• • •

"These sketches are fucking worthless," said Olson. "This could be half the kids in the city. Hell, it could be my wife."

Dooley was sifting through interview reports, looking for gold. "Don't worry, we'll get the little prick because somebody will tell us who it is. Right now, as we sit here, the word's going around that neighborhood, from house to house. We hit the street tomorrow, somebody'll give him up." Dooley slapped the folder shut. "Will you type up this God damn thing? You're a hell of a lot faster."

"What's it worth to you?"

"You can drive tomorrow."

"I always drive."

"See how good I am to you?"

Olson shook his head. "What a mind. I don't stand a chance against that Jesuit logic."

"Look, you do the report, I'll see what the hell these people want." Dooley picked up the three message slips that had been waiting when they returned.

"OK. But the first one to J.J.'s buys."

"That's a deal."

Dooley moved to a desk with a phone. The first message was from a dick in Area Three who wanted information about a wife-beater Dooley had arrested back in April. The dick was long gone; Dooley left a message at the Area. The second message was from an old Polish shoemaker on Augusta Boulevard Dooley had once left his card with who called every month or so with half-intelligible warnings about impending crime sprees that never happened. Dooley skipped it. The third message was from Laura Lindbloom. *Has more info.* There was a phone number. It was after eleven at night. Dooley checked his watch and dialed the number. A man answered with a shout at the other end; Dooley could hear music and tumult. "Laura Lindbloom, please."

"Who?"

"Laura Lindbloom. She gave me this number."

"She's busy right now."

Brusqueness was just about always the wrong approach to take with Dooley. "Not half as busy as I am," he said.

"Well, that's your problem."

Dooley knew better than to get into shouting matches on the phone. He knew it was a waste of time to throw your weight around unless you could hit something with it. "Who am I talking to?" he said calmly. "What's the name of your establishment?"

"The Mad Hatter."

"On Wells Street?"

"That's right."

Dooley hung up without another word. He walked back to the desk where Olson was working and took his jacket off the back of the chair. "Thanks for doing that," he said.

"Don't mention it. You shoving off?"

Dooley hesitated, taking his time putting on the jacket. "Gotta go talk to a witness." If he asks, I'll tell him, Dooley thought.

"What, no J.J.'s?" said Olson.

"Maybe later."

Olson looked up from the report. "Who's the witness?"

Dooley put a lot of effort into keeping a straight face. "The naked lady. The artist's model."

Olson gaped at him and then his eyes narrowed, with just a hint of a smile. "You sly bastard. No wonder you wanted me to do the report."

"Pete, I swear to God, I never looked at the message till after I asked you to do it."

"Yeah, sure."

Irked now, Dooley said, "Look, you want to change places? I'll do the report. You go talk to her. Hell with it. I'm not trying to put one over on you."

"No, no. I agreed." Olson threw up his hands, a look of long-suffering saintliness on his face. "Go ahead. I'll sit here and toil in solitude while you get another look at her."

"I mean it, Pete. Say the word."

Grinning now, Olson said, "Nah, go ahead. Just promise me one thing."

"What?"

"Try to keep *your* clothes on, OK? For the honor of the department."

Dooley swore at him and walked out. Going down the stairs, he put his finger on why Olson had irritated him: he knew. He knew that from the instant he'd seen her name on the message Dooley had been thinking about what Laura Lindbloom had looked like up on that platform with her clothes off.

Old Town had been around forever, though it hadn't always been the zoo it was now; Dooley could remember when this end of

North Avenue was the main drag of an old down-at-the-heels German neighborhood, complete with taverns where the bartenders pretended not to know English. The Germans had given way to the artists; Dooley had arrested a remorseful beatnik saxophonist who had stabbed his male lover in a Wells Street dive some time in sixty-one or two. And then just a few years ago the place had exploded. The intersection of North and Wells had become the hub of a nightlife, tourist-trap, clip-joint jungle that sucked thousands of drifters, grifters and slumming accountants into a four-block neon-flashing strip every night. The developers had gussied up the old row houses on the side streets and sold them to stockbrokers; they had turned derelict factories into shopping arcades. They had thrown up old-style gas lamps along Wells Street, and every bright son-of-a-bitch with a half-baked idea and a handful of cash had opened a bar. In Old Town you could watch go-go dancers on pedestals or listen to hippies with guitars who couldn't sing but insisted on trying. You could take LSD and stare at shifting lights while the music damaged your ears or you could drink beer and throw peanut shells on the floor while watching miniskirts go by on the sidewalk outside. You could get drunk, get laid, get rolled, get flat broke in a hurry. Dooley didn't much like Old Town.

He found the Mad Hatter in the first block south of North and parked at the next corner. Walking back to the bar he parted packs of teenyboppers who looked about sixteen and navy recruits on their first pass from Great Lakes who looked younger than that in their starched whites. A drifter with hair in his eyes started to ask him for money and thought better of it.

The bar had a sign over the door with a picture of the Mad Hatter on it and a big front window through which Dooley could see walls of unfinished brick and a long bar stretching to the back. Inside there was music coming from a jukebox and, shouting to each other over it, a Friday-night crowd that looked at a glance to average just over legal drinking age. There were two people working behind the bar, a man with shaggy black hair and Laura Lindbloom.

Dooley found a space at the end of the bar just big enough to squeeze into. His neighbor on the left gave him a dirty look but scooted over, fast. Dooley caught the male barkeep's eye and crooked a finger at him. The look on the barkeep's face as he walked over was a touch on the sullen side, but Dooley was used to that.

"Yeah?"

"I need to talk to her." Dooley pointed at Laura, making a drink down at the far end of the bar. "And don't give me any grief this time."

The barkeep knew a cop when he saw one. He glared at Dooley for just a second and went to get Laura. She looked up at his touch, listened, fixed on Dooley, and nodded. When she had delivered the drink she came up the bar toward Dooley. She was wearing a dress that was short but not too short and hung loose on her, hiding the shape of her body. She wore sandals that showed her painted toenails. As she drew near, Dooley was careful to keep his eyes on her face.

"I got a message you called," Dooley said as she leaned over the bar, close enough to hear over the noise. She still had the frank brown eyes, and up close Dooley couldn't help but notice that her lips had a pouting look that wasn't entirely a bad thing.

"Yes. I didn't expect you to show up like this. I thought you'd call."

"I did. Your pal didn't want to let me talk to you."

She threw a look over her shoulder, bit her lower lip, and said, "Look, why don't we go to the office?"

Dooley waited for her at the rear of the place while she put a few words in her partner's ear and then stepped out from behind the bar. She led Dooley down a hall past the bathrooms to a third door. Behind it was a cramped windowless office with a cluttered desk and one chair. Laura shoved the chair toward Dooley with her foot and cleared a space on the desk. She turned, hiked her buttocks up onto the desk and sat with legs dangling, presenting Dooley with an interesting prospect. He settled on the chair with an uncomfortable feeling that he had lost the advantage. "I must have made a bad impression on your friend out there," he said.

She smiled. "We're not exactly fond of cops around here."

"And why is that?" Dooley said, knowing the answer.

Laura cocked her head slightly, lids drooping a little, a who-are-you-trying-to-kid look. "Well, let's see. It might be the payoffs. Yeah, I'd say that's it. It's the bag full of money we have to give your colleagues every month."

"You're not talking about my colleagues."

"I'm talking about the car that pulls up out front with the plainclothes guy in it that my boss addresses as 'sergeant.' The one that set us up on a phony after-hours charge before we started paying off. Would that be one of your colleagues?"

"I'm not a vice cop."

"The patrolman who comes in here every month for his envelope isn't a vice cop, either. But he wants his piece of the pie, too. We pay him just to make sure somebody shows up if we ever have trouble. That's a hundred a month to two different factions, if that's what you call them. That's on top of our taxes, of course. I guess I was naive, thinking the taxes covered police protection."

Dooley conceded with the barest of nods. "I'm a homicide cop. I don't give a damn who you serve drinks to or what time it is when you do. My job is to catch killers, and I don't expect anything for it but a paycheck. Are we on the same page?"

Her look softened. "Sure. I was just blowing off steam, and I guess I had to wait until a cop came along that I could tell wasn't going to make me pay for it."

Dooley worked on that one for a couple of seconds, hoping it was a compliment. "Your message said you had something more to tell me."

"Maybe. I don't know if it's useful."

"Nobody knows till we take a look at it. Any information's good."

"OK, well, there were a couple of things. First, we buried Sally the other day. Out in Aurora. Me, her mother and sister, a couple of friends. That was it. And I didn't get the impression her mother wanted to be there. It was kind of sad."

"It usually is."

"Yeah. Anyway, I was talking with her sister, and she mentioned Sally had left a lot of stuff with her before she went up to Wisconsin. A couple of boxes. She sublet her apartment, left all the furniture, but took her stuff to her sister's out in Elmhurst."

She had Dooley's attention now, all of it. "That's good. That could be very important." He pulled his notebook out of his jacket pocket and said, "Can you tell me how to get in touch with the sister?"

"You could try her mother again. All I know is she's in Elmhurst. I'm afraid I didn't think to get her phone number."

"That's OK. When was this? Did she say?"

"Just before she took off for Wisconsin. She didn't say when that was. She just said Sally came by and dropped off her stuff and said she was going to stay with some friends in Wisconsin for a while."

"All right, I'll have a talk with her. Was that it? You said there were a couple of things."

Laura shrugged. "Maybe nothing important. I just did what you said. I kept thinking about Sally, and that meant thinking about her boyfriends. And there was one guy that I thought maybe I should mention to you."

"Besides Feldman, you mean?"

"Yeah. This was before Herb. This was back in sixty-five. She started going out with a guy she met at the Playboy Club. We weren't supposed to date customers, of course, but it happened all the time. This guy was a cop of some kind, not a city cop, I don't think, but some kind of cop. Or he had been. An ex-cop, I guess. But there was something crooked about him, too. Sally told me once he had been indicted but never convicted for some shady thing he'd been involved in. She went out with this guy for months, and I thought it was kind of serious, but then he left. Left the country, I mean. To go to Mexico. And Sally swore he was going to come back for her, or send for her, or something, but he never did, and she finally gave up on him. It hurt her, and I held it against the guy, because he had seemed OK."

"Who was the guy?"

"His name was Tommy Spain."

Dooley frowned. "Tommy Spain? No kidding."

"Why? Do you know him?"

"I know about him." Dooley had heard all about it, but it was a few years back and he had to think for a second. "He was a crooked cop, like you say. Actually he was with the sheriff's department, I think. I don't remember what it was he got in trouble for, but I remember he had a bad reputation."

"The funny thing was he was really a charming guy. He was polite, he seemed like he had some education, he acted like a gentleman. I remember wondering if Spain was his real name. I think he was really Italian, because he spoke it. I saw him order in Italian once, in a restaurant down on Taylor Street."

"The rumor was he was connected, yeah. That wouldn't surprise me a bit."

"So I thought you might like to know."

Dooley nodded, frowning. "Was there any contact between them after he left for Mexico?"

"He would write letters and occasionally call her, but that petered out over the course of the next year or so. And then she took up with somebody else."

"When did he go to Mexico?"

"Oh, I don't know. Sixty-six, maybe?"

"So as far as you know she had nothing to do with him after, say, the end of that year?

"As far as I know. Maybe he has nothing to do with anything. But you said to call if I thought of something, and this was a shady guy she once went out with. I thought you might like to know."

He held her gaze for a moment; she was a hell of a looker. "I appreciate it. You never know. You did the right thing to call me."

"Is there any . . . progress? Are you any closer to finding out who did it?"

"Hard to say. You build a case a little at a time. We know a few things. But we're not close to making an arrest, no."

"Did the mob kill her?"

Dooley put his head on one side, flapped a hand. "Too early to say."

"And if it did, is anyone ever going to be prosecuted for it?"

Dooley returned her stare for a moment before he said, "You really don't think much of us, do you?"

"I'm a skeptic, that's all. People with more experience than me have told me it's kind of hard to tell the difference between the cops and the mob sometimes."

She was starting to get to Dooley a little; he had to take a deep breath. "Look. I've been a cop for twenty-two years. I've seen it all. There's good cops and bad cops, like there's good plumbers and bad plumbers. There's some dirty games that get played. But don't think we all play them. There's a reason I'm still just a homicide dick after twenty-two years. There's a reason I'm still working two jobs and worrying about how I'm going to pay to send my kids to college. You get the picture?"

She looked at him for a while, thoughtful, and then she nodded, very slightly. "Yes, I do, officer. I think that's sad."

"That's life. I don't waste time crying about it. I just do my job."

"It would be nice if more cops did."

"Listen, lady. People like you don't always know what the job is."

The door swung open and the male bartender stuck his head in. He ignored Dooley and said, "Laura, I could really use you out here."

"I'm sorry, Scott. I'll be right out." The door slammed and Laura slid off the desk. Dooley figured his interview was over and he jotted a couple of things down in his notebook. When he looked up she was standing there with her arms folded, that candid gaze on her face. "I'm not much of a lady," she said. "You can use my name."

Dooley shrugged and finished jotting. He put away the notebook and said, "OK."

"I'm sorry if I offended you, officer. Or can I use your name too?"

"My name's Dooley. No offense taken."

"Dooley." She gave him a wry smile. "OK, Dooley, can I ask you a question about the job?"

"Sure."

"Would it include arresting somebody who was recruiting teenage girls into prostitution? Would that be part of your job?"

"Not *my* job."

Her look hardened. "I've lost you, haven't I?"

Dooley put his hands on his thighs and stood up. "No, you haven't lost me," he said after a moment. He slid his hands into his trouser pockets and stood there rocking on his heels. He felt better now, looking down on her.

"Then I'm going to tell you something and ask for your advice."

"All right."

"You remember that girl you saw at my apartment the other day?"

"Yeah."

"She was staying with me so she didn't have to sleep on the street. She'd run away from her pimp because she'd gotten tired of turning tricks every night for three months. She's sixteen years old."

Dooley waited a second and shrugged, just a little hitch of the shoulders. "Did you report it?"

"She wouldn't let me. She's afraid to talk to the cops because she says they're in it with the pimps. She says she's fucked cops. For free, of course."

Dooley stared at her. He didn't like hearing that kind of language from women. "There's a Youth Division. They're separate from Vice but they handle this kind of thing. I could give you a phone number."

"I don't know if she's able to make distinctions between different types of cops at this point. Look, I'll take care of the girl. I was hoping you might take care of the pimp."

Dooley was getting irritated. "What do you want me to do? I'm a homicide detective."

"I know. You're not part of the system around here. That's why I thought you might be able to go around the system, at least pass the word to somebody who could do something effective. I mean, I would think that your professional pride would get involved at some point."

Dooley had been through this before, with other people. There were always outraged citizens who wanted to know why the world wasn't perfect. Dooley had given up trying to explain to them. He knew he couldn't be responsible for anybody's conscience besides his own, and he knew it was time to thank her for her information and walk out. Instead he looked at the floor and said, "I'd need to know a little more."

Twelve

"THEY HAVE LIKE, three or four different places they take us to," said the girl on the couch with the dirty toes peeking out of her sandals. She had long straight blonde hair just like every other girl these days and a sweet round face, and close up Dooley decided he'd been wrong. She looked too young to be one of Kathleen's friends. "I don't know all the addresses. They just like, drive you there and drop you off, and you go upstairs and somebody lets you in. They have beds in all the rooms except like the living room, and you just sit around and listen to music and stuff and wait for the customers. They're supposed to ring in this like secret pattern, like ring-ring, ring-ring-ring. When a guy comes in, he talks with whoever's in charge that night and picks somebody out and if it's you, you go down the hall and fuck him." She looked up at Dooley for the first time and he changed his mind again; what he saw in her eyes was sullen and tired and thoroughly grown up.

Dooley looked across the room at Laura, who stood by the window with her arms folded, looking out into the street. He turned back to the girl. "So what made you want to quit?"

She stared at her nails for a while without saying anything, slumped on the couch. "I just got fed up, that's all. At first Ray was really nice. He like gave me money and let me stay at the hotel for free and all, but once I started working it was like, well, first you gotta pay off what I lent you, even though he never said it was a loan, and then it was, oh yeah, you're doing great, I owe you a couple of hundred, but I've got expenses to cover and shit like that. Here's ten bucks, have a ball. I like finally realized I wasn't ever going to see my money."

Dooley had heard this all somewhere before. "You don't know Ray's last name?"

"No. I never heard any last names."

"How many other girls are involved? Do you know?"

"I know there are four of us at the hotel. I've seen a couple of others, you know, on the job, but I don't know where they live."

"Mm-hm." Dooley sat there nodding for a bit, wondering about his judgment. He had purposely come here on his own time, before his shift, so this was all off the record. He looked up to see Laura watching him with those frank brown eyes. Dooley gazed back and realized suddenly that he didn't trade looks like this with complainants; Laura was already in some other class, he didn't know what. Something about it excited him and something bothered him at the same time.

He said to the girl, "Are you willing to testify? You willing to go into court and look these people in the eye and say what happened?"

She shook her head. "No way. I don't want to get hurt."

"You'll be protected."

"Yeah. For how long?"

"If you want to put an end to this you've got to be willing to go on the record, stand up and testify."

The girl glared at Laura and said, "I told you this would happen."

Laura came away from the window. "Jenny didn't want to talk to you. She was afraid you were just going to tell these people where she is."

"I wouldn't do that."

"I know. I told her you're outside the system."

"I'm not outside the system. I'm just in a different part of it. I'm still a cop. If people won't testify we can't do anything."

The girl said, "I don't want anything to do with cops anymore. The cops are in it with them."

Dooley frowned at her dirty toes. "Now, how do you know that? I need to know why you say that."

She shot a look at him. "Because I had to give a cop a blow job. For free. Ray said it was part of the service."

Dooley sat there with his lips squeezed tight together, like he'd just eaten something bad. "Ray told you the guy was a cop?"

"No, he didn't like, introduce him or anything. He just said look, a guy's gonna come up the back way and wait in the last bedroom and you're gonna do him for free, whatever he wants. And then later he said I hope you took good care of him because he's the one that decides if we go to jail or not. Oh, and the guy had a gun and handcuffs, too. It's hard to hide that stuff with your pants down."

"Could you identify him?"

She thought about that one for a few seconds before answering. "No way."

"OK, let me put it a different way. Could you describe him for me?"

She blinked a couple of times and said, "Bald. A real chrome dome. That's all I can tell you. But he's not the only one. One girl said Ray told her all the cops are on the take."

There was a silence.

"Well." said Laura finally. "There are cops and there are cops."

"Sure," said the girl listlessly.

"I'm not sure what you want me to do," said Dooley.

Laura perched on the arm of the couch. "You can put the word in where it'll be heard. You can find somebody in the police department who's willing to go after the pimps. There must be somebody."

"OK." Dooley put his hands on his knees and stood up. "Jenny, you have to do one of two things. You have to file a complaint and be ready to go to court, or if you don't want to do that, you have to get the hell out of the neighborhood, maybe out of town. If pressure comes down on these people they're going to wonder who blew the whistle, and it won't be that tough a guess. You see what I mean?"

"Yeah, I see." She was absorbed in her painted fingernails again.

Dooley stood looking down at her. He was feeling for his paternal instincts and not finding them. Girls like this were past help; they should have listened to their parents. "I'll see what I can do," he said.

Laura walked down the stairs with him. "Thanks for coming," she said at the street door.

"Sure." He cocked a thumb up the stairs. "How long has she been with you here?"

"A couple of weeks."

"You planning on adopting her?"

Laura gave him that look, her head on one side. "What if I am?"

"You want my advice? Drive her downtown, put her on a bus. A kid like that will freeload off you as long as you let her."

"She's being tough, but I've sat with her through the tears at night. She's a screwed-up little girl inside."

"She got a home? Parents?"

"She's got a stepfather in Missouri that started feeling her up when her mom wasn't around. That's why she hit the road."

Dooley gave up with a shrug. "I'm not responsible for her home life."

"Of course you're not. And you're not responsible for all the prostitution around here, either. I know that."

She left it dangling, but the challenge was there; Dooley didn't need to have it spelled out. He looked into those brown eyes and felt that thrill again, that same little warning stir. What am I doing here? he thought.

"I told you, I'll see what I can do," he said.

• • •

"Michael Dooley, how you been? Long time no see." A policewoman's uniform was about the worst thing there was for setting off a woman's looks, but Katie Conway had a glowing Irish complexion and hair that it would take more than an ugly hat with a badge on it to spoil.

"Hey, Katie." Dooley had never worked with her but had thrown back many a drink with her and her three brothers at Emerald Society gatherings. "You coming on or going off?" Dooley had taken a chance on catching her at her desk at the Chicago Avenue station; he was going to have to hustle to make roll call at Damen and Grace.

"Coming on. Youth Division gets busy at night, Dooley." Katie pulled a stack of files toward her. "You still working homicide?"

"What else? People keep on dying."

"Then I have to say I have mixed feelings about you walking in here. Please don't tell me you've got a dead kid for me."

"Nah, just another one having second thoughts about life in the big city."

"What's up? You taking in runaways now?"

"God forbid. I got enough problems with my own kids. No, I just came in to pass on a tip, really." Dooley dragged a chair over from a neighboring desk, scanning the office as he did, just noting who was in earshot and how interested they looked. He lowered his voice a shade and said, "What have you heard about the Princeton Hotel, on California Avenue? Anything?"

Katie Conway frowned a little, fishing in a drawer for a paper clip. "Nothing, I don't think. It rings a bell, maybe. That's where, near Humboldt Park somewhere, right?"

"California and North, yeah. The thing is, I ran into a kid who says she's been living at the hotel and turning tricks for the guy that owns it. The guy has a whole string of girls. He and a couple of associates use a bunch of different apartments around Old Town. All the girls are underage."

He had her full attention now. "Jesus. What do you mean, you ran into this kid?"

"A friend told me about her. She's kind of taken the kid in. Asked if I could do anything. The kid ran away from the hotel but she's scared to talk to us." Dooley waited a beat and said, "She says there's coppers in on it."

Katie Conway's mouth set in a firm line. "How does she know?"

"She serviced one, she says."

"Jesus Christ." Dooley sat there and watched Katie Conway's Irish blood rise. She exhaled, shook her head. "I don't know, those vice guys. Shit, that would surprise me though. Call girls and dancers and so on, everyone knows there's dirty stuff going on. But underage girls? God, I'd hate to think there's sworn officers out there that would put up with something like that."

"Me too. Look, I did my best to get this girl to come in and talk. But she won't. She gave me all the particulars she could, and I'm passing them on to you. I don't know what you want to do with it."

"Well, we sort of have to look into it, don't we?"

Dooley smiled at her. "That's what I was hoping you'd say."

Katie walked him to the street door and said, "How's your boy—Kevin, is it? He still overseas?"

"Yeah. Supposed to come home in October. We're keeping our fingers crossed."

"They're talking about bringing them home early. Maybe he'll get lucky."

"We're hoping."

"God bless him." She squeezed Dooley's arm. "Thanks, Mike. A lot of coppers wouldn't have bothered with this."

Dooley couldn't talk for a second. He found Katie Conway's hand, squeezed back. "Hey. I got a daughter, too."

• • •

"Son, I'm going to do my best to help you," said Dooley, with all the fatherly concern he could muster. Across the table from him the kid with the hair on his collar and the pimples on his chin sat looking at him like a dog that has just been kicked and is waiting out the storm under the kitchen table. "There's a State's Attorney out there that wants to put you in jail for the rest of your life."

"I didn't do it,"said the kid.

Dooley clasped his hands on the table and gave him the Father Confessor look. "We have witnesses. They saw you running out of the store."

The kid's face clouded and he sank lower on his chair. "I was in the store, but I didn't kill the guy. I just took the money 'cause I didn't see nobody there."

It was the best line for the kid to take, and it might even have been true, but Dooley didn't think so. He knew he had come to the crossroads, the point where he made his case or threw it out the window, depending on what he said next. "Son, the gun has your prints all over it."

Dooley watched the kid's face for three seconds and knew he'd nailed the little bastard. Even the stupidest kid, if he was innocent, wouldn't take longer than that to come up with *What fucking gun, I never touched no gun, what are you trying to do to me?* It took this kid nearly ten seconds to work through the logic and say, "You're bullshitting me."

Dooley shook his head. "OK. I'm lying. We'll let the State's Attorney have a look at the lab report and see what he thinks." He pushed away from the table.

"I want a lawyer," said the kid.

You lose, thought Dooley. You just lost. He sank back on the chair and said, "Fine. I can bring in a public defender. That's your right. But I want you to consider this. If I bring in a lawyer, it's over. The lawyer's gonna tell you to shut your mouth, and it'll all go to court and the evidence is gonna put you in Joliet. The minute that lawyer walks in here I won't be able to help you."

There was just a hint of panic in the dull eyes. "What do you mean, help me?"

"I can tell the State's Attorney about any mitigating circumstances. I know you didn't go in there intending to shoot that man. What did he do, grab for the gun?"

Dooley waited the kid out, watching a slow mind run clumsily through the options, with fear creeping around the edges.

"He called me a dumb hillbilly."

And was he ever right, thought Dooley. "Man, that's rotten," he said.

• • •

"He threw the gun down a storm drain on Granville. A block west of the train tracks." Dooley tossed the signed confession on McCone's desk. "Olson's meeting a Streets and San crew out there to retrieve it."

McCone leafed through the pages. "Once they start talking, they don't shut up, do they?"

"That was the only tricky part, walking him through the statement. 'Don't forget the part about the gun,' I told him. I had to make like I was just reminding him."

"You're a devious bastard, Michael Dooley. And thank God for it."

"We all have our talents." Dooley went back to his desk and saw a message waiting for him: *Call McKinley at Monroe St.*, with a phone number. Jack McKinley was a dick Dooley had known since they were green-as-grass patrolmen. He ran into McKinley now and again and listened to his tales of mayhem and chaos out on the West Side. This time McKinley made him wait nearly five minutes before coming to the phone.

"Dooley, you worthless mick bastard, how the hell are you?"

"Tired of sitting here with this phone to my ear. Where the hell were you, on the john?"

"Hey, don't knock it. I never get a chance to go at home, with five kids clogging the place up."

"Tell me about it."

"No, the reason I called was, I got a guy sitting in an interview room over here who says he knows who killed your girl on the riverbank."

There was a thump as Dooley's feet slid off the desk and hit the floor. "You're shitting me."

"That's what he says."

"Who is this guy?"

"Fellow by the name of Billy Gaines. He claims to be a friend of the guy that turned up in the car trunk out by Cicero today."

"What guy? Sorry, I've been busy all day."

"They found a guy dead in the trunk of a Buick Electra just off Roosevelt Road this morning. Dead and messed up quite a bit. He's been identified as Chuck Steuben, and the word is he was connected. This guy Gaines walked in here about an hour ago and said he had information about this murder and the girl by the river. I sat him down and he started talking. Soon as I heard what he had to say I called you guys, and they told me it was your case. You might want to get over here. He's got quite a yarn."

Dooley thought for maybe two seconds: wait for Olson to get back or not? "I'll be right there," he said.

• • •

"Why are you here?" said Dooley.

"Because I don't want to die." Billy Gaines was maybe forty, a rough forty with a lot of late nights and booze and a few lost fights showing in a round pug's face with tired heavy-lidded eyes. He wore a plaid flannel shirt open over a dirty white T-shirt, and with sprigs of greasy brown hair going every which way on his head he looked like he had spent a couple of nights in the gutter.

Dooley just stared at him for a while. He'd never heard of Billy Gaines but McKinley had done some homework and filled him in: Gaines was a thief, a veteran hijacker of trucks and burglar of warehouses. He'd spent a couple of years in Stateville and too many more plying his trade around the south and west fringes of Chicago where rail yards and truck depots lay open to the enterprising. "You don't want to end up like Chuck Steuben, in other words," said Dooley.

"That's right. They don't like it when people don't follow orders. And they don't like heat."

"Mm-hm. So what happened?"

Gaines had told it all before, but he was used to the tedium of the interview room and showed only a hint of weariness as he started telling it again. "There was a rail car full of liquor, down by Canal Street. Chuck had scoped it out and he just needed a place to stash it. He'd paid a guy at the railroad to look the other way. And he talked to somebody on Taylor Street and worked out a deal. They gave him the key to the warehouse and he was supposed to give them half the booze."

"Who'd he get the key from?"

"How the hell should I know? From one of Aiuppa's guys, I guess. I didn't set the thing up, Chuckie did. He just came to me and said let's go, I need a hand and there's a lot of money in it for you. So I went."

"What day was this?"

"It was—fuck, I don't know. A few weeks ago, near the start of the month."

"What day of the week was it?"

"Ah, hell. It was a Monday night, I think. Yeah, it was Monday night, because the place where I like to eat in the evening was closed. I had to go somewhere else, and then I went to meet Chuckie."

"And what happened?"

"The fuckin' guy at the railroad had sold us out, or maybe they busted him, I don't know. Anyway, there was railroad cops all over the place where we were supposed to be able to get into the yards. We had to make tracks in a hurry. We went looking for the guy but we couldn't find him. Chuckie was really steamed, I mean ready to do some damage. But we couldn't find the guy. Finally we gave up and went to get a drink."

"Where?"

"Place Chuckie liked in Melrose Park. On Lake Street. Angelo's, it's called. There's a lot of connected guys go there."

"OK."

"So we go in there and have a few beers, and Chuck's still like steaming, and then in walks Herbie Feldman's girlfriend."

"You knew her?"

"Not me. Chuck looks at her and says, 'Shit, that's Herbie Feldman's girl.' He knew Feldman some, I guess. He knew a lot of the syndicate guys. I says, 'Who?' and he tells me about Feldman. I'd heard about Feldman getting killed and all, but I didn't know him."

"Hold on a second. What'd she look like?"

Gaines blinked a couple of times and said, "What do you mean? She was a broad. A nice-looking broad. She looked like a nice-looking broad."

"What color hair?"

"Brown."

"What was she wearing?"

Gaines frowned, getting impatient. "Christ, I don't know. She had on a dress, I think. Yeah, 'cause I remember looking at her legs. A light-colored dress, I think."

"What time was this? When did she walk in?"

"I don't know, Christ."

"Early? Late?"

"Oh, it was late, 'cause we'd been out on the job and then driving around looking for the railroad guy. This was probably past two in the morning, by that time."

"All right. Go on."

"Anyway, we sit there and watch her for a while and then Chuck says, 'That bitch, she's got a lot of fuckin' nerve coming around here,' and I says why, and he says because she has to know where Feldman's money is."

Dooley looked across the table at him for a few seconds. "You sat there and watched her. What was she doing?"

"Just waiting. She was like waiting for someone. She had a drink and she sat there and smoked cigarettes and looked up every time the door opened."

"And nobody talked to her, nobody bothered her?"

"Oh, a couple of guys talked to her, but she would just look at 'em, maybe answer, and go back to smoking. She wasn't there to be picked up."

"So who was she waiting for?"

"I don't know. Nobody ever showed up. When they said last call she asked the bartender to call a taxi for her. And then Chuck says to me, he says look, we're gonna take this bitch and we're gonna find out what she did with all that money. I come up empty tonight and I gotta have something to give the Italians. And I says, forget it, I ain't getting involved in none of that. But Chuckie, I don't know, you just couldn't resist him when he had an idea in his head. He'd been sitting there getting drunker and drunker and madder and madder about missing that score at the railroad yard, and he just was in a mood, know what I mean? So

I says OK." Gaines paused, rubbed at the bridge of his nose, eyes squeezed shut. He opened them, grimaced, shook his head, gave a broad shrug. "I was kinda drunk myself. So I says OK. And we went outside."

"And what happened?"

"Chuck went and got the car and told me to stick my head back in and say her taxi was there, and when she came out I was supposed to throw her in the car. I told him fuck that, I ain't gonna beat up on no woman, and he says OK, you drive then. And I got behind the wheel and watched him go back in the bar, and then he comes out and waits by the door and when she comes out he's got his knife in his hand and he puts it to her throat and makes her get in the back seat of the car with him."

"And nobody saw this?"

"It's four o'clock in the fuckin' morning. Who's around? The only thing was, if somebody came out of the bar with her, but nobody did. So off we go."

"Where?"

"To the garage. The one he had the key for. He gave me directions."

"Where was the garage?"

"On one of them streets near Skid Row there. We came up Halsted from Roosevelt and turned on, shit, Adams I think it was, and went up some side street and into an alley. And he gives me the key and tells me to unlock the door and he takes her in."

"What, he drove the car in?"

Gaines looked up at him and his mouth hung open for an instant. "Nah. He brought her out of the car, with the knife to her throat."

"So the car stayed in the alley?"

"Yeah."

There was a long silence while Dooley waited for more, but it never came. "What happened on the drive? She say anything?"

Gaines gave a half-hearted heave of the shoulders. "She started begging, you know? 'What do you want with me,' that kind of thing. And Chuck's telling her she has to cough up Feldman's money and she gives him what she has and he says where's the rest of it and she's saying she don't know nothing about no money and she starts crying. And that's about it."

"OK, what happened at the garage?"

"Chuck took her in the office in back and put her on a chair. And he told me to tie her up. There was some twine lying on the floor. So I tied her up and then he starts in on her. And I'd had enough, so I got the hell out of there."

"You'd had enough, huh?"

"Yeah. I wasn't gonna get in on that. I don't beat up on women."

"You just help kidnap them, huh?"

Gaines had mostly avoided Dooley's eyes till now; now he met him with tired eyes, no light behind them. "I just went along. I didn't know until right at the last what he was gonna do to her. And then I left."

"Yeah, I can see how it must have been tough to figure out what he had in mind."

"Fuck you. You weren't there."

"No, I wasn't. But you were. And you let him kill her."

Gaines was staring at the table again, and Dooley could barely hear his next words. "I tried to talk him out of it."

"I bet you did." Dooley sat shaking his head for a few seconds. "What do you want, Gaines?"

"I want to plead. I'll take the rap on the kidnapping, I'll do the time. Just don't let 'em kill me like they did Chuck."

"How do you know they did Chuck?"

"He called me yesterday, he says watch your ass, the Italians are pissed about what we did to the girl. And I says what do you mean we, white man. And then today I heard about Chuckie and I came right in here."

"To do your civic duty."

Gaines's eyes were closed again; he looked a few heartbeats away from expiring on the chair. "Call it what you wanna fuckin' call it."

Dooley sighed and stood up. He felt like throwing up. "Congratulations, Gaines. You're a hell of a citizen."

Thirteen

"IT COULD BE. If she left Elkhart Lake by ten in the evening, she could be in Melrose Park by one-thirty or two in the morning. It's not that far. But why did she come back?" Dooley drummed on the desk with a pencil, looking from McCone to Olson and back. "Why would she go hang out at a place she knew was full of hoods if she was afraid of them? She left town to get away from them."

McCone shrugged "Maybe she'd got the word it was safe. You said Haggerty put out the word she didn't rat on Feldman."

"How'd she get the word? She was hiding."

"Somebody called her. Or she called someone. Somebody told her it was safe."

"Who was she there to meet? And who brought her back?"

"Almost anybody," said Olson. "Somebody she called on the phone to come get her. If she was planning to leave, she'd call someone."

"We can check that. We can look at their phone records up there."

"If somebody called her, that's a different story. Someone could have called her, arranged to pick her up."

"So why would he just dump her at that tavern, so she had to call a taxi when it closed?"

"OK, she hitched a ride with somebody she talked to up there. I think we gotta get the Wisconsin cops to go back and look at her evening again."

"Same thing. Why would he just dump her? And who? Why?"

After a pause McCone said, "Get out there and talk to people, see if anyone else saw her there."

"Oh, I will. What happens if I can't find anybody who did? Or who remembers? That was what, three weeks ago?"

"Then we look at other things. But if you find someone who remembers seeing her, that would go a long way. Then his story looks pretty good."

McCone was no fool, but Dooley could see he wanted to believe it, and he could hardly blame him; somebody clears a nasty homicide for you, you don't look the gift horse in the mouth.

McCone clasped his hands behind his head and said, "Steuben was worked over pretty good before they killed him. They burned him with a torch, they cut his throat and then they shot him. That looks like a lesson. That looks like he screwed up, just like Gaines says. And if Gaines thinks he's about to go the same way, prison might look like a pretty good option."

Dooley gave up on the pencil and tossed it on the desk. "Yeah, could be."

Olson said, "What don't you like about it?"

"The dead suspect, that's what I don't like. I don't like it when I don't have a warm body to stand up in front of a judge. It's easy to blame it all on a dead guy."

Olson scratched at his neck, grimacing. "Yeah, but we got a guy practically begging to go to jail here, saying he helped. That doesn't happen much. To me that means he's scared shitless, and that makes him credible. I can see it happening just the way he says it did. I can see the bosses getting real pissed off at these two characters doing the girl that way."

Dooley waggled his head, not conceding. "Sure. It has that feel to it. I just don't like the dead guy taking the rap. That's too convenient for me."

"You think Gaines had more of a hand in it than he's saying?"

"Maybe. I think something like that's a two-man job. Something like they did to her, I think you need one to control her, one to do the dirty work. But I could be wrong. And I don't know how the hell we'd ever prove it. Look, I just think there's too many God damn loose ends here. I haven't had a chance to get out to Elmhurst and go through the stuff Sally left with her sister, for one thing. Maybe there's something there. And I'd really like to know why she came back. *If* she came back on her own. I still think the whole thing could be cooked up."

McCone said, "Tie up the loose ends. Go get the stuff from her sister, talk to people at the bar. If anything you find makes a difference, I've got an open mind. But taking into account all your reservations, we've got a plausible account of the killing by a man claiming to be a witness. And I don't see an angle for him, what he'd have to gain by lying, unless he did help kill her. Say he's willing to plead to the kidnapping to avoid accessory to murder. Even in that case we get him off the street for a while. That's hard to turn down."

"I know," said Dooley. "I'm not saying we should turn it down."

"You're just hard to please, Mike." Olson was smiling.

"Yeah," said Dooley. "I'm hard to please."

"That's good," said McCone. "I like that in a copper. But I think this one may be just good enough."

• • •

Elmhurst was a real town that had gotten swallowed up since the war in the steady creep of shopping centers and housing developments west from the city, and now it was just another suburb, a moon in the orbit of a huge planet. Mrs. George Eggers, sister to the late Sally Kotowski, lived in a shingle-sided house on a tree-lined street that could have been in any one of a hundred little Illinois towns, most likely not the nicer end of town. The lawns were a little ragged and the porches sagged just a bit in this corner of Elmhurst.

June Eggers was well into her thirties and starting to wear out from riding herd on the children she had shooed out of the house when Dooley and Olson had appeared. Even allowing for the years and the fatigue, plain was about the best that could be said for Mrs. Eggers, with her lank brown hair and sallow complexion. She was evidently the type of person who was intimidated by policemen, and Dooley kept wanting to tell her to relax. After some tense preliminaries and a few soothing words she produced a large cardboard box which had once held a Zenith portable TV. Now it was full of pieces of Sally Kotowski's life.

Dooley and Olson laid out the contents on the coffee table in the living room, sitting side by side on the couch. Most of it was letters, snapshots, her high school diploma, odds and ends. A Girl Scout badge, a small silver crucifix. Some of the photos were in an album but most of them were loose in a manila envelope. Dooley and Olson went through them together. School pictures, vacation snaps, the family. This was the first time Dooley had seen what Sally Kotowski's face had looked like before somebody had beaten it to a pulp. He was mildly surprised to see that she had been fresh-faced and wholesome, an apple-pie type of girl.

"Oh, my God. That's me." The black-and-white photo showed two girls in bathing suits, with a lake and a beached canoe in the background. The taller one was recognizable as June Eggers, a not especially good-looking adolescent girl with a protective arm around her cute little sister. Dooley handed her the photo and she stood gazing at it. Dooley looked back at his work.

"Hey, look at this." Olson handed him a color print. Here was

Sally again, grown up now, the wholesome look tarted up in a skimpy satin outfit crowned by a pair of bunny ears. There were two bunnies in the picture, shoulder to shoulder, smiling into the camera, and the other one was Laura Lindbloom. Dooley studied the picture for a few seconds. Where Sally was cute, the girl next door, Laura Lindbloom smoldered a little, dark eyed and golden haired, distant. Dooley held up the picture. "You know who this is with Sally?"

Mrs. Eggers stared at it for a moment and said, "I think that's the girl that came to the funeral. Laura something, I think her name was."

Dooley laid the picture aside. "I'm going to want to hold on to some of these." He went back to sifting pictures. Dooley fished out another photo, a Polaroid of a man and a woman at a restaurant table, crystal shining on white linen. The woman was Sally, in a sleeveless dress. The man had dark hair and black-rimmed glasses and was wearing a dark suit. "Do you know who this is?"

Sally's sister peered at it but shook her head. "No idea. One of her man friends. She had a lot of them, and I couldn't keep track of them all."

Dooley turned the picture over, saw that the back was blank and set it down on top of the photo of the two bunnies. He went through the rest of the pictures but didn't find any more that showed grown men. Then he turned to the letters.

He riffled through them, looking at return addresses. There was nothing from Las Vegas, nothing from Mexico. He took a few of them out and glanced through them: Grandma writing from Iowa, somebody named Diane, off at college. A boy named Matt, writing from Fort Bliss in 1963 that he loved her. None of the letters was more recent than five years. "You know this Matt that wrote to her?" Dooley asked.

Mrs. Eggers peered at the envelope. "Matt Hill? I think that was the boy she went out with in high school that joined the army."

"You know if he's still around, if she had any contact with him?"

"No, he got killed over in Viet Nam a couple of years ago. I guess that's why she kept the letter."

Dooley tossed the letter back on the pile and took the lid off the shoe box that had sat in the bottom of the larger box. He poked through it. It was full of paid bills, old check registers and bank statements from the Uptown National Bank of Chicago at Lawrence and Broadway. Dooley took a quick tour, looking at bottom lines. At a glance, Sally had been careful with her money, paid her bills but never gotten rich. The balance in her checking account was never more than two hundred dollars and usually a lot less. Running his eye down a statement, Dooley saw *Safety Deposit Box Fee $10.00.* He looked up at Mrs. Eggers.

"Did she ever say anything about a bank deposit box?"

A nervous shake of the head. "No. We never talked about money. I don't even know how much money she had."

"Did you find any keys with her effects?"

"No. Everything she left is here. Well, most of it." Flustered, she waved a hand vaguely. "There were some clothes. I have them in a box upstairs."

"Did you go through the pockets?"

"No."

"I think that would be a good idea. Can you bring them down?"

She dashed off up the stairs and Dooley kept leafing through papers. Olson picked up the photo of Laura and Sally and said in a low voice, "Now, how come this one caught your eye, I wonder?"

"I've got a reason," said Dooley.

Sally's sister reappeared with another box, clothes spilling out of it. She set it on the floor. "I took a couple of things I thought I could use. A blouse and some jewelry. Do you need to see them?"

"No, I think that's OK." Dooley stood up and went to kneel by the box. He rummaged through the clothes: sweaters, a winter coat. He checked the pockets of the coat and found nothing. He replaced the clothes and stood up.

"OK. I'd like to take these bank documents here, and these pictures." He tapped the two photos he had laid aside. "We'll inventory everything and give you a receipt for it."

Olson had brought the inventory book and he wrote while Dooley dictated what he wanted to take. When he was finished, Dooley signed the form and gave a copy to Mrs. Eggers. He tossed the pictures into the shoe box and put the lid back on. "What did Sally say when she dropped this stuff off with you?" he said.

June Eggers looked startled, like a pupil who hadn't expected to be called on. "Not much, really. Just that she was sick of Chicago and needed to get away."

"She didn't seem afraid? She didn't say anything about people coming after her?"

"No, not at all. She just said she needed to get out of the city."

"Did she say where she was going?"

"She said she was going to stay with friends in Wisconsin, that's all. She didn't even say who, and I knew Vickie from back home."

"She didn't leave an address?"

"No, she said she'd call. But she never did. That was pretty typical. We weren't all that close, to tell you the truth. We'd talk on the phone once or twice a year, maybe. That was just the way our family was."

"So she didn't confide in you about her personal life, boyfriends, things like that?"

"Never. See, I was gone, out of school and married, by the time Sally was . . . well, going out with boys. What I heard about mostly came from our mom, and that was all pretty negative. They never got along. And I think Sally was kind of wild in high school."

"I see. She never mentioned any men by name?"

"Not that I can remember. I remember she told me once she'd met a guy at the Playboy Club that she thought might marry her, but she didn't tell me his name or anything about him. And it never happened."

"What about your mom? Did she pass on anything Sally had told her?"

"My mother and Sally never talked to each other."

Dooley nodded. "I see. Thanks. You've been a big help."

June Eggers had picked up the picture of herself with her dead sister again, and she finally started to cry a little as they made for the door. "You'll catch them, won't you?" she said.

"We'll do our damnedest," said Dooley.

The desolation in June Eggers's eyes did not improve her looks. "She really wasn't a bad girl. She was too young when our dad died, that's all. She just had bad judgment sometimes." A couple of decades' worth of regrets trickled down Mrs. Eggers's cheeks.

Dooley tried to put some sympathy in his look. "I can believe it."

• • •

"Can you get into a safety deposit box? I don't know what the law is." Olson was steering one-handed, pushing patiently through late-afternoon traffic.

"They can probably get a warrant. We'll have to give this to somebody on days. That's the bad part about working third watch. Everything's closed."

"Some of us would say that's the good part about working nights."

"That's one way to look at it. As for the picture, you have to make them choose. You can't just show them one person and ask for a yes or no. Show people the picture, ask them if they recognize anybody. If she really was in there, they'll pick her without hesitation."

Dicks could spend half their lives in the car, driving from one end of the city to another to chase people down, check out leads. Today they were lucky: the road back from Elmhurst led more or less directly through Melrose Park. "What's the address?" said Olson, cruising east on Lake Street.

"Seventeen hundred west. You got a few blocks to go yet."

Dooley watched the storefronts go by. This was a workingman's suburb, a big step up from the tenements but a long way from ranch houses on two-acre spreads. He saw a lot of Italian restaurants and delis go by.

"Angelo's, it's called?"

"Yeah. Haggerty says the real owner of the bar is Ronnie Gallo, one of the top guys in the Grand Avenue crew. So be prepared to get lied to. The barkeeper will say whatever the hell he's told to say, just like at the Armory."

"What else is new? You ever had anybody tell you the truth on this job?"

"Once. Back in fifty-eight, I think."

Angelo's was a cozy-looking tap with red neon in a small front window. Inside, it was pleasantly dark after the glare outside, paneled in blond wood, decked out with a jukebox and pinball machines, with a TV going down at the far end of the bar. There were a couple of customers at the bar, a man in a suit and another younger one in a sport shirt. Heads turned as they came in but turned away again. Dooley took out his star as the bartender approached them. The bartender was on the far side of fifty and walked with a limp. He looked at Dooley's star and held up the beer mats he had brought with him. "You won't be needing these, I got a feeling."

"Not today. You the regular barkeep?"

"I'm the only barkeep. I'll get a vacation when I drop dead back here."

"Then I'm going to need your name and address."

"What for? What'd I do?" Heads had turned back toward them again.

"You tell me. I just had a couple of questions I wanted to ask you."

Dooley had a feeling it was more than just his skill at pouring drinks that qualified this man for his job. He stood for a long moment with his eyes flicking back and forth between Dooley and

Olson, running through the usual calculations. Finally he said, "Louis Molinari." He added an address in Elmwood Park; Olson wrote it all down. "Now what's the problem?"

"I don't have any problems, Lou," said Dooley, reaching into a pocket. "I just want you to look at a picture."

"What for?"

Dooley laid the picture of Sally and Laura on the bar. "Do you recognize either of these women?"

Molinari pulled the snapshot toward him and whistled once. "Hot shit. Yeah, I think I had a wet dream about them once."

"Come on Lou, I didn't come in here to fool around. You ever seen either of them?"

"I never even been to the Playboy Club."

"In here, I mean. Did either of them ever come in here?"

Molinari peered at the picture for five seconds or so and then cocked his head on one side. "Could be. We get a lot of nice looking girls in here. Yeah, I think maybe I've seen 'em."

"Which one?"

Molinari looked up at Dooley, and then had to look at the photo again, and Dooley could practically hear him thinking. Finally Molinari said, "I think I seen both of 'em in here."

"Together?"

"Nah, I mean I think they both been in here at one time or another. Couldn't say for sure."

"I see. When was the last time you remember seeing either of them?"

"Christ, I don't know. I don't write down who comes and goes."

"You can give me a ballpark figure, can't you? Recently? Not for six months?"

"Ah, lemme see. I think maybe I saw one of them in here a few weeks ago."

"Which one?"

Molinari hesitated, his finger hovering over the picture, and for a second Dooley thought he had him. Then Molinari said, "The brunette. This one." He tapped on Sally's face.

Dooley nodded, deadpan. "When was that? Can you narrow it down?"

"Two, three weeks ago. Maybe three."

"You remember what night it was?"

"Not for sure. Maybe a Monday? Yeah, I think it was Monday. It was a slow night."

"Early, late?"

"It was late, I think. She came in late, sat in here for a couple of hours by herself and then called a taxi to take her home."

"Anybody talk to her while she was here?"

"Nobody I really noticed. I mean, sure, guys would go up and talk to her, but not for long. She was by herself. Or maybe waiting for someone who never showed up."

"Who else was in here that night?"

"Christ, I don't know. All kinds of people."

"You said it was slow."

"Yeah, but still. You think I got a photographic memory?"

"No, that would surprise me. Think about it. Who did you see talking to her?"

"All right, wait a second. Yeah, I think I remember. There was these two guys that came in. I knew one of them. A fella name of Steuben. Chuckie Steuben. I remember he was with another guy, and they went out about the same time the girl did."

Dooley stared at him, not blinking, for a long moment. Finally Molinari threw up his hands. "What else you want? It was three weeks ago."

"Who else? Any regulars?"

Molinari was starting to look as if he had a bad case of heartburn. "Jesus. OK, lemme think. Vince Bonifazio. He was in here that night, too. I remember."

Dooley reached for the picture and slowly put it back in his pocket. "Thanks, Lou. You've been a big help."

"My pleasure." As Molinari turned away, Dooley thought he could see just a touch of sweat glistening on his brow.

Fourteen

"THEY'D BE SURE to rehearse him pretty good. I'm not impressed that he could repeat the story, and I'm not impressed that he picked her out. He took long enough to make up his mind, and he's got a fifty-fifty chance just guessing. They probably gave him some kind of description, too. They told him she was a brunette, for example. We tracked down this Bonifazio on Grand Avenue, another connected guy, and he said the same thing. He saw her, he saw them. Funny, he couldn't remember anybody else that was there that night, though. It had that same canned feel to me, but I can't prove anything. The long and the short of it is I can't prove she wasn't there, any more than I can prove Joe D'Andrea wasn't at the Armory Lounge that same night." Dooley sat there looking at McCone across the desk, knowing he was fighting a losing battle.

McCone said, "But you still don't like it."

"Not much, no. But I'm out of bullets. It smells bad to me, but I know a consensus when I see one."

McCone nodded once, slowly. "We heard from the fellow over in Greece. Dimas managed to reach him. He said he gave the key to a man he didn't know by name but had seen with Charles Scaletta. So we're talking about the Taylor Street crew, and that's who Steuben said he got the key from."

"According to Gaines."

"Yes, according to Gaines. It's all according to Gaines. He's confessing, for God's sake."

"I know. Look, I'm not arguing against an indictment. If he wants to go to jail, put him in jail. I'm just saying I've seen better cases."

"So what's your idea? Why's Gaines lying?"

Dooley blinked at McCone a few times before answering. "Because they told him to. Otherwise they'll kill him. That part of it's true—he'd rather go to jail than get killed. But the story's just a cover for the real one. She was killed for a reason, and that's what they're covering up."

McCone stared back at him for a while before saying, "The long and the short of it for me is we got a confession and we got confirmation from witnesses."

"Outfit witnesses. We have no witnesses who aren't in the rackets up to their fucking eyes."

"What do you expect? It's syndicate business. It's the type of thing the mob does. They discipline people who get out of line. That's what this looks like to me. I have to say, it hangs together for me. We'll look at the loose ends, like that safety deposit box. But I think it hangs together."

Dooley nodded. "Because they want it to. This is one they want solved for a change. Their way."

McCone breathed a faint sigh. "Sometimes things are just what they look like."

"I know. I'm not going to rock the boat." Dooley stood and looked at Olson. "Let's go write it up."

• • •

"There's a beer at J.J.'s with your name on it," said Olson. "Maybe three or four of them."

Dooley looked up from his desk. "Go ahead. I'll be done in ten minutes."

"No excuses this time."

"Save me a bar stool."

The office emptied out, Olson and two other dicks going off duty and a couple of first-watch nighthawks heading for the street. Dooley looked at the photo in his hand, the photo of Sally Kotowski and the man in glasses. The man looked familiar but he couldn't place him. He tossed the photo back in the shoe box and put the lid back on.

The phone rang, twenty feet away. He swore out loud and got up to answer it. "Homicide."

"Dooley?" said a woman in his ear.

"Yeah." There was noise in the background, indistinct music and murmur.

"It's Laura Lindbloom."

Dooley took a second to stamp hard on the little flutter he felt at the sound of her voice. "What can I do for you?"

"I need your help."

"What's going on?"

"They got Jenny back."

"Who did?"

"The guys she was turning tricks for. The pimps."

"What do you mean they got her back?"

"I mean she left my place and went off with them. Look, I was out this evening. I came back and found all her stuff gone. My landlord said he saw her drive up this afternoon with two guys in a Chevy Caprice, go upstairs with them and then leave again with her bag packed. She must have run into them on the street somewhere. I called that hotel where she was before and the man who answered said he'd never heard of her. I knew he had to be lying. If he said she wasn't there anymore, that's one thing. But he can't say he never heard of her. So I came over here in a taxi and just slipped in and started knocking on doors."

"Hold on a second. You're at the hotel?"

"Right now I'm in a bar just down the street. I got thrown out of the hotel. A guy came upstairs and kicked me out. But as I was standing out on the sidewalk trying to figure out what to do, a girl leaned out a window up on the second floor and told me they probably took her to somebody named Marge's house. She said that's where they take girls when they need convincing."

Dooley massaged his aching temple with a thumb. "All right, what do you want me to do?"

"What do you think I want you to do? We have to get her out of there."

"OK, calm down. First of all, she went with them voluntarily, right?"

"If you can call it that. They probably gave her a little money and a lot of sweet talk, but I don't like the sound of that 'girls who need convincing.'"

"I don't like the sound of it either. But I don't know if we're in any position to go throwing our weight around."

"Are you a cop or aren't you?"

"I keep having to tell you, I'm a homicide cop. Now look, I talked to a good youth officer, gave her all of Jenny's information. They're going to be on top of this real soon."

"Soon enough to help that little girl? You know what 'convincing' means, don't you? That means probably a lot of drugs, and a lot of what amounts to rape. They're going to try to break her, like you break in a pony."

"That's pretty dramatic."

"Oh, why am I wasting my time talking to you? I'll go over there myself."

"You know where you're going?"

"This other girl was better with addresses."

"Jesus. Look, hold on, will you? I'll try and track down the officer I mentioned."

"Fine, you do that. While you're tracking her down, I'll be at Marge's."

"What the hell are you going to do?"

"I'll know when I get there. What I'm *not* going to do is make excuses for doing nothing."

Dooley took a deep breath. He looked at his watch. "I'm going to need a couple of minutes to finish up here," he said. "Where are you?"

• • •

It was just a house, a two-story frame house jammed between houses a lot like it on either side, a house slapped together sometime early in the century for people who had just enough money for a house but not enough to afford any distance from their neighbors. There were a lot of other houses like it on the block, and a lot of blocks like this one north of Chicago Avenue and west of the river, solid blue-collar territory where people carried a lunch pail to work and delivered a reliable Democratic vote. "There it is," said Laura in a hushed voice. "Nine-twenty-four."

"And there's the Caprice," said Dooley as he eased past it. "A Caprice, anyway." He rolled on down the block and turned right at the corner. He parked just shy of the alley that ran up the spine of the block and threw the lever into park.

"OK," he said. "Here we are." He could just make out Laura's face in the glow from the street lamps. "We don't have any proof she's there, and we don't have any official standing. I don't have a warrant and I'm not even on duty right now. I don't even have any evidence that a crime's being committed. What we are right now is two private citizens on what may be a wild goose chase. Is that clear?"

"Then what are you doing here?" she said, her look grave in the dim light.

"That's a very good question," said Dooley, opening the door. He got out and walked slowly toward the mouth of the alley, hands in his trouser pockets, Laura trailing him. Dooley strolled up the alley, a man on a nighttime ramble, past closed garage doors. The neighborhood was asleep, the alley reasonably clean, illuminated by lights on wooden poles at hundred-foot intervals. When he reached the sixth garage on the right he tapped a garbage can with the toe of his shoe. "Here we are." The can had the address painted on it: 924. Dooley stepped into shadow between the garage and its neighbor and Laura crowded in behind him. They walked up the side of the garage until they could see the rear of the house.

"Somebody's up late," Dooley said softly. The houses on either side were dark, but here there were lights on. They could see into a brightly lit kitchen, white-painted cabinets above a sink, and upstairs there were lights in two windows behind drawn shades. Dooley stood in silence for a full minute, watching and listening. He could hear music somewhere, maybe in the house. He could hear the bass beat thumping away, very faint. At his shoulder Laura whispered, "What are you going to do?"

Dooley turned to look at her in the dark. Her face was close to his, her eyes reflecting light from somewhere, big dark eyes. "Just what I'm doing now," Dooley said.

He watched some more, and she said, "For how long?"

Dooley shrugged. In the kitchen, a man moved into view. He had dark stringy hair and sideburns and a moustache, and he wasn't wearing a shirt. Dooley could see a tattoo on his upper left arm. The man put an empty beer bottle into the sink and moved out of view again.

"That's the guy that threw me out of the hotel," said Laura, her whisper harsh with tension. "I think that's Ray."

"OK," breathed Dooley. He turned to her again. "Here's what we do. You stay right here. If they try and take her out the back, yell like hell. Don't try and stop anybody, just yell. I'm going to go around to the front and lean on the doorbell."

She nodded, golden hair shimmering in the half-light. "What if they don't let you in?"

"I don't think there's any danger of their letting me in. I'm expecting to stay right there on the porch till somebody shows up."

"Who?"

"I don't know. That's going to be the interesting part."

They traded a look, complicit in the dark. "All right," Laura said.

There was a chain-link fence barring the way to the yard behind the house, waist-high. Dooley was still spry enough, just barely, to make it over without embarrassing himself. He dropped into the yard and stepped carefully up a concrete walk and slipped into the narrow gangway along the side of the house. He went up toward the front slowly, listening, not hearing anything new.

He looked up and down the street; it looked like any other residential street at two in the morning. He went up on the porch and put his thumb on the button beside the door. He heard a bell go off inside the house, muffled and far away. He wasn't in a patient mood; after ten seconds he pressed on it again, longer this time. The third time he kept his thumb down. Dooley smiled in the dark, hearing the distant clatter; he knew how loud those old-fashioned electric bells were inside a house. When he heard locks being undone, Dooley took his thumb off the button. The door jerked open as far as the chain would let it. The face that filled the gap was a bad dream. "What the hell do you want?" snarled the woman. The voice was the best clue to her sex; her fat-neutered features, missing teeth and limp colorless hair weren't much to go on.

"I want the girl," said Dooley. "I want Jenny."

"I don't know what the *fuck* you're talking about, mister," said the woman. She tried to shut the door but Dooley's foot was in the way.

"You Marge?"

"What's it to you?"

"I want the girl, Marge."

She made another try at forcing the door shut. "I'll call the police."

"You do that. I'll be right here."

"Dave!" She vanished and he heard her trundle away. Dooley put his thumb on the bell again. With the door cracked it was a lot louder.

The man who showed up inside ten seconds was not the man they'd seen in the kitchen; this one was jug-eared and gray, with the flat hard face of a pug. He dispensed with the chain and flung the door open. He wore a sport shirt with the tail out over a solid body gone to fat around the middle, and he filled the doorway without too much effort. "You ring that doorbell again, I'll feed you your God damn finger," he said. He sounded like he'd been born somewhere south of the Ohio.

Dooley was six-two himself and not exactly frail; his whole life was pushing back when people tried to push him around. "Go ahead, give it a try. You'll be on the ground in handcuffs so fast you won't have time to blink."

That made Dave think, just for a second or two. "You ain't no cop."

"Maybe I'm not. I'll tell you one way to find out. Take a swing at me and see how fast the street fills up with squad cars."

Dave's eyes narrowed. "What the hell do you want?"

"I want the girl. Jenny. Down here. Now."

"There ain't no girl here. Somebody's steered you up a crick."

"Listen, you dumb-ass hillbilly, I'll come in there and haul her out myself if I have to. And that could get ugly. Is that what you want?"

Dave looked for a second like he was about to take Dooley up on the invitation to take a poke at him, but the second passed. "Just hold your horses for a minute. And don't ring the damn bell again."

The door slammed in Dooley's face. Dooley checked his watch and turned to look out at the street. After a minute went by he gave the doorbell a ten-second burst. He stepped to the edge of the porch and leaned around the corner of the house. He couldn't see anything in the shadows by the garage. He stood at the head of the porch steps with his hands on his hips, watching the street. At one-minute intervals he pressed the bell.

It took four minutes. A Plymouth Valiant came tearing up the block from the direction of Chicago Avenue and skidded a little as it halted in front of the house. The driver got out and slammed the door and walked toward the porch, giving Dooley a wary eye. He wore a suit and his bald cranium shone in the light from the street lamps. Dooley stood there shaking his head slowly as he mounted the steps. "I might have known," he said.

The bald man reached the top of the steps and leaned close to Dooley, peering at him in the gloom. "What the fuck are you doing here?" he said.

"Waiting to see what kind of no-good dirty copper runs a child prostitution ring. What are you doing here?"

The man vented a little contemptuous laugh. "Dooley, you always were a self-righteous prick, weren't you?"

"And you were always a poor excuse for a cop. They should have shit-canned you with the rest of that Summerdale gang."

The bald man's nostrils flared, just for an instant. "I'm gonna ask you again what you're doing here. You got a warrant?"

"I'm here to take the girl home. You don't want to see what happens if I don't, believe me."

A smile stretched thin lips. "You don't have a warrant, you don't have shit. You're freelancing, aren't you?"

Dooley had old grudges to fuel him in this one; he put his face a foot from the other man's and said, "Schroeder, you've had it. Your time's up. Even in this town they won't put up with pimping teenagers. I'm taking that girl home and if you try and stop me I'll be at the head of the pack that hounds your worthless ass out of the department."

Schroeder didn't give an inch; he wasn't used to backing down any more than Dooley was. "You'd be making a very serious mistake if you did that," he said.

Dooley had opened his mouth to tell Schroeder what he thought about his assessment when Laura's thin cry came faintly through the night air from behind the house. "Dooley!"

Dooley didn't bother with the steps; he went straight to the end of the porch and vaulted over the rail, landing on the walk with a jolt but keeping his balance. He ran down the gangway, seeing Laura now at the corner of the garage, leaning over the fence and yelling his name. As he came into the yard he saw three people standing in confusion at the foot of the back steps: Dave the hillbilly, Ray, who'd put on a shirt, and between them the girl Jenny. The younger man had a grip on Jenny's arm.

"Let go of her," Dooley said, striding toward them. Dave took a step toward him, blocking his way, raising his hands in a warning gesture. Dooley was on him in a second and unloaded a punch to his gut that doubled him over. Ray hauled on Jenny's arm, swinging her around behind him, and reached under his shirttail into his waistband. By the time he had the knife out, Dooley was aiming his .38 at his head, three feet away. "Drop it."

Ray dropped it, fast, and let go of Jenny to raise his hands. Dooley grabbed the girl by the arm as he went by and made for the fence, tugging her as she stumbled across the grass. Schroeder came out of the gangway and stopped; Dooley saw him thinking about it, a hand sneaking toward his hip, just for a second. Dooley had his gun in his hand but pointing at the ground, and he said, "It's over, Schroeder. Forget it." From his knees, Dave made a deep rasping sound of distress. Ray had put down his hands but wasn't moving. Dooley shoved his gun back in its holster and used both hands to scoop Jenny up and practically throw her over the fence.

"Take her to the car," said Dooley. He turned and faced the three men. "Schroeder," he said.

"What?"

"I've done what I came to do. Stay the hell out of my way and I'll stay out of yours. But remember what I told you. It's over."

"Fuck you, Dooley," said Schroeder.

• • •

"I don't feel good," said Jenny. She didn't look good, either, lying on the couch with a green and red Mexican blanket over her, only her dirty feet sticking out. Her face was gray and her hair was matted and dull and her lips still glistened from throwing up into the bucket Laura had put by her head.

Laura ran a hand over the girl's head, caressing. "Try to sleep."

Dooley stepped across the rug to the couch. "Before you do," he said. The girl's eyes opened and found his. Dooley leaned over her, hands on his knees. "Honey, it's time for you to find a home. If you can't go back to your family, you have to find somebody else who can take you in. You got a grandma, an aunt and uncle somewhere? You've got to know by now the street's no good for you. Right?"

He wasn't sure she'd understood him but after a moment she said, "Ray promised to pay me on time from now on."

Jesus, thought Dooley. All the looks in the world and no brains at all. He straightened up. "You go to sleep. I'm going to let Laura talk some sense into you in the morning."

Laura walked him down to the front door. "She needs to wise up," Dooley said. "Maybe the hangover will help."

Laura moved a curtain aside to look out at the street. "Are we safe here?"

"I don't think they'll come over here, but I can't guarantee it. Keep your doors locked. First thing tomorrow I'm going to leave a message with that youth officer I mentioned. Her name's Conway. I'll have her come over here and talk to Jenny. If she puts up a fuss, put your foot down. Either she talks to Officer Conway or you put her on a bus back to Missouri. Don't take no for an answer."

"I'll try." Laura was just about wrung out herself, Dooley could see. She heaved a sigh and said, "Thanks. I guess you went out on a limb for us tonight, didn't you?"

Dooley shrugged. "I can't say I didn't enjoy it. But don't push your luck. I'm a cop and I have to do things by the book."

She nodded, looking thoughtful, and said, "Anything new on Sally?"

Dooley froze; all of that had gone right out of his head for a couple of hours. "Yeah, actually. We're close to charging someone. I don't know why I didn't tell you."

"You got the people who killed her?"

Dooley hesitated; why couldn't he give her a straight yes? "We got an accomplice, we think. He says the guy who killed her is dead." He watched Laura slump with relief, or maybe disappointment, and added, "We're checking it all out."

She looked tired; she looked dazed. She looked good, Dooley couldn't help but think.

"Thanks for everything," she said. "Good night, Dooley." She squeezed his arm as he left, and Dooley felt it all the way home.

Fifteen

EARL WARREN WAS gone; somebody named Burger was replacing him. Dooley figured there wouldn't be much improvement; they would go on making things harder for the good guys. The Jews and the Arabs were fighting over the canal again; Dooley thought they'd sorted that all out a couple of years back but he didn't really follow things overseas that closely except for Viet Nam. Here it was: the Marines had been in a fight near Quang Tri City and had one marine killed in action.

Odds, Dooley thought. Trust in the odds and try not to think about it. He turned a couple of pages and counted seven obituaries for Chicago servicemen in Viet Nam. Seven.

"Hey, Pop." Dooley looked up from his paper to see Frank in the doorway. "Want to go play some ball?"

Dooley just stared at him for a moment, this gangly fifteen-year-old with hair hanging down in his eyes. The first thing he thought of was excuses, and the second thing he thought of was the sight of his son going back down the hall to lie on the couch. "Sure," he said.

"Fast pitch?"

Dooley shrugged. "Where we gonna play?"

"At the school yard. We can get some balls at the drugstore."

Dooley folded the paper. "OK."

Dooley put on his old tennis shoes, the ones he wore about once a year. Frank dug a bat and two gloves out of a closet. One of them had an old beat-up league ball in it. "Isn't that Kevin's glove?" Dooley said.

"Yeah. He said I could use it while he was gone."

Dooley drove down to the drugstore on Milwaukee and they went in and bought three rubber balls. Then he drove over to the public school four blocks away. Like all Chicago schools it had a big asphalt playground with a sign that said No Ball Playing that everyone ignored. Dooley parked and they went through a gate.

"Let's warm up a bit." They tossed the league ball back and forth. Dooley had been doubting until this moment, thinking of all the things he ought to be doing or would rather be doing this morning, but the feel of the ball in his hand, fingers gripping the raised seams, the smooth easy motion of throwing, the snap of the wrist, the little whiff as the ball left his hand, the pop of the ball in the glove, erased all that. There was nothing in the world like throwing a baseball.

His shoulder was a little stiff and his knee still hurt from jumping off that porch, but he took it easy, just lobbing it for a while, then moving back a step or so with each throw till they were seventy or eighty feet apart. Frank had gotten better. He was throwing the ball like a kid who knew what to do with it. He still wasn't all that accurate, making Dooley dance around a little, but he could wing it OK, a normal kid playing ball.

Dooley had started to work up a sweat. "Want to hit? I'll pitch to you."

Frank took his stance, right-handed, by a blank stretch of wall where somebody had chalked a rectangle on the bricks to serve as a strike zone. Frank had never wanted to learn to hit left-handed, resisting all Dooley's advice. It irritated Dooley a little; Kevin had seen the advantage right away and worked to hone a sweet left-handed swing; by the time he was in high school he was switch-hitting. Dooley put the rubber balls in his glove and said, "Batter up."

It took him a couple of tries to find the strike zone, but then it was easy to get in a groove. He threw them right down the middle and Frank chopped at them, popping them up, beating them into the asphalt, whiffing occasionally and every once in a while lining a decent one past Dooley. Chasing the balls was the hard part of school-yard fast pitch, but it wasn't that bad; the ones that weren't hit bounced right back to Dooley and there was a fence at Dooley's back to stop the ones that were. When all the balls were out Dooley ambled after the nearer ones and Frank went sprinting out to get the far ones.

Dooley started throwing a little harder and his control started to come and go. "Don't swing at that crap. I'll give you a good one." Frank swung like a kid having fun, not like a serious hitter, and Dooley started talking to him like he'd always talked to Kevin. "Keep your head on the ball. You're pulling out. Back elbow up. Stride right toward me."

Frank swung and missed and Dooley said, "Keep your head down on the ball," a little louder.

"All right!" Frank stepped out, glaring, and swung the bat one-handed at something on the ground. He took a few steps away from Dooley, not looking at him.

Dooley made sure his voice was calm. "Come on, step in there. You'll get it."

"You hit." Frank was coming toward him, offering the bat.

"Nah, come on. Step in there. Just swing. I won't say anything."

"I want to pitch to you." Frank was going sullen on him again.

Dooley shrugged and exchanged glove for bat. It was a Louisville Slugger with Willie Mays's autograph burned into it. It felt good in Dooley's hands. He couldn't remember the last time he had swung a bat other than to fungo grounders and flies to Kevin. "Take it easy on me, OK? I haven't swung at a pitch in about twenty years."

"Step in there." Frank had gathered up the balls and was toeing up the imaginary rubber, about forty-five feet away. Dooley took his left-handed stance, swinging nice and loose, bringing the bat head out over where the plate would be, remembering the feel. At that distance Frank looked like Bob Gibson. Dooley swung and missed on the first three. "You're out," said Frank, giving him the thumb.

"Get ready to duck," said Dooley. He just tried to meet the next one and slapped it right back to Frank on one bounce. Frank smiled. The next one was at eye level and Dooley let it go by. The next one came in chest high and a little outside but Dooley swung at it and it went straight up. Frank circled under it, managed to make an off-balance catch, and said "Three outs. Sorry about that, Chief."

"You got me." Hell with it, Dooley was thinking.

"I'll give you another chance. Step in there."

Dooley shrugged and took his stance. Frank had lost his control and Dooley let three bad ones go by. "Take a little off it, put it over the plate."

Scowling, Frank put one down the pipe, a little in, waist high. Dooley swung and felt nothing; for an instant he thought he'd missed it. Frank whirled to watch the ball as it left the school yard and said "Jesus" with great reverence. Dooley picked up the flight of the ball and stood with the bat in his hands, watching until it disappeared over the rooftops across the street.

"Oh my God, Pop," said Frank.

"Damn," said Dooley.

"You hit that thing a *mile.*"

Dooley gave a shake of the head. "We'll chase it later. Pitch to me."

He cut down his swing and lined a couple over Frank's head. When they went out to pick up the balls a woman was walking across the street, a ball in her hand. "Is this yours?"

She had fat knees showing beneath her lime-green shorts and her hair was in curlers. She was glaring at Dooley, caught with the bat in his hand.

"I'm sorry," he said. "I didn't mean to hit it that far."

She underhanded it over the fence. "You almost hit my daughter."

"I'm sorry. It's only a rubber ball. It wouldn't have hurt her."

"Can't you read that sign? You ought to be ashamed of yourself, a grown man."

"Sorry." Dooley scooped up the ball and turned his back on her, irritated and embarrassed. He was going to tell Frank it was time to call it a day, but the look on his son's face stopped him. Frank was grinning at him, mischievous glee and pride and sheer joy all mixed up. Dooley's heart turned over and he couldn't stifle his own grin. He held out the bat.

"Step in there, pal. I'd better stick to pitching."

• • •

A crime scene told you everything there was to know, if you could only figure out how to read it. Dooley had been told that on his first day as a detective, and he had told it to Olson and every other dick he'd broken in. What he never said was that sometimes it was like trying to read Greek.

This crime scene was in Uptown, in a second-floor apartment in the right-hand wing of one of the big courtyard buildings that stretched back from a tree-shaded street running south from Lawrence. Back before the war, when Uptown was a high-rent district, this had been a desirable address; now the money had fled west to the split-level ranch houses or east to the high-rises along the lake, and these apartments were filled with people who still had to worry about making the rent. Respectable though, thought Dooley: if parts of Uptown were a slum now, there were still blocks like this where people went to work and kept the old solid buildings clean.

This apartment was clean as a whistle, except in the bedroom where blood had spattered the sheets and a patch of hardwood floor. The victims were middle-aged, naked and very still; the woman had made it halfway out of bed before a bullet had punched out one of her eyes, and she had sprawled onto the floor with one leg caught in the covers. The man lay on his back, eyes closed and head on the pillow, one hand on his stomach and the other at his side resting on the blanket that covered him to his waist. Except for the three holes in his chest, he could have been asleep. Dooley stood in the doorway to the bedroom with his hands in his pockets and tried to read it all.

After a while he turned and looked at the two men in the hall behind him, the uniform from the squad parked out front and the little man in the white T-shirt with a ring of keys on his belt who stood against the wall wide-eyed and shaking. "The front door was locked?" Dooley said.

"Yeah," said the patrolman. "That's why I had to go dig him up." He cocked a thumb at the frightened man. Dooley frowned a little and ambled down the hall toward the kitchen at the rear. "There's no sign of forced entry," the patrolman said, trailing him. "I checked."

Dooley found the back door and saw that it was locked, bolted and chained. He looked at windows on his way back to the bedroom and didn't see any broken glass or cut screens. "OK," he said to the uniform. "So what does that mean?"

The patrolman was young and eager. "They knew him. They let him in."

"Without getting out of bed?"

The kid was a quick study. "OK, he had a key."

Dooley nodded. "And he locked up on the way out?"

"I guess so. Sure, he wanted to delay discovery as long as possible."

"That's one possibility," said Dooley.

The cop's brow furrowed just a little and he said, "What else?"

Dooley smiled and said, "He's still in here."

The patrolman's eyes got a little wider at that. Dooley said, "I'll let you open the doors. Don't touch anything else."

The patrolman moved down the hall with a spring in his step and a hand on his holster. Dooley walked over to the little man in the T-shirt. "You're the janitor?"

The little man nodded. "I was playing cards in my place, in the back. Since eight o'clock. I got four witnesses."

"Relax. Nobody's accusing you. You saw the victims?"

"Yeah, I saw 'em. Shook me up something fierce."

"You know them?"

"Sure. They live here. I see 'em all the time."

"Know their names?"

"Sure. That's the Dawkinses. Mary, I think she was. I don't know his name."

"They the only ones in here? No kids?"

"Just them. I only ever saw them, anyway."

"OK. Ever have any trouble with them?"

"Uh-uh. Pretty quiet folks. There's no trouble in this building. Mostly older folks."

"All right. Hang around for a while yet, will you? We'll need your name. Maybe wait in the hall, but don't go away."

Dooley went back to the door of the bedroom and looked at things for a while longer, hearing the patrolman jerking open doors in other rooms. Footsteps came in through the front door and Dooley recognized Olson's heavy tread. "What you got?" he said.

Olson came and stood looking over his shoulder into the bedroom. "Nobody home downstairs. The lady upstairs is the one that called it in. She heard four shots around nine-thirty. I asked her if she'd heard anything before that, and she said no. No loud voices, no banging on doors."

"How about the street door? A lot of times you can hear the buzzer go off, hear people coming up the stairs."

"I asked. She says no. But she was in the kitchen for a while, and she might not have heard."

Dooley nodded. "Well, this one's pretty easy," he said.

There was a silence and Olson moved a little closer, crowding him. "Come on," he said.

"I mean it. I can give you a name right now for the number one suspect. Give me five minutes and I'll have a plate number for him."

Olson made a scoffing sound. "You're shitting me."

"Nope. I couldn't take it to a judge yet, but I know who to look for."

"What the hell are you seeing here?"

"Everything. The situation."

There was a silence. "OK," said Olson. "I give up."

Dooley turned, smiling. "How many people of this age do you know who sleep naked?"

"I don't know. My old man used to sleep naked all the time. Some Scandinavian thing."

"People like this wear pajamas and nightgowns to bed. I'm looking at pajamas right now, hanging on that doorknob."

"OK." Olson was wearing his good-sport smile. "So?"

"They were going at it, Pete. Or had been. They were probably asleep when the shooter got in, or there'd be more sign of a struggle."

"Maybe it was their anniversary."

"Yeah, maybe. What was in that drawer?" He pointed to a dresser drawer that was standing open.

"Damned if I know. Socks? Cash?"

"Come on, Sherlock. This ain't that hard. Hold on a second." Dooley walked into the room for the first time. He walked over to a chair that had a pair of man's trousers draped over it. He picked up the trousers and felt in the pockets. "No wallet," he said. "Where's his wallet?"

"I don't know. Where should it be?"

"In his pants or out on the dresser somewhere, in sight. Where do you put your wallet when you go to bed?" Dooley kept fishing. He came up with a ring of keys. "Here." He tossed them to Olson. "Go and see if any of these fits the door."

Olson caught them and went. The patrolman leaned in and said, "All clear. Nobody else here."

"OK," said Dooley. "Why don't you go help your partner show the flag outside?" He stepped over to the dresser and picked up a framed photograph. He came out into the hall and walked to where Olson was fiddling with keys at the front door.

"None of them fits," Olson said. "What the hell?"

Dooley slapped him on the shoulder. "Now go try them on the first floor apartment. See if you can find his wallet." Olson gave him a deeply suspicious look and headed down the stairs. Dooley beckoned to the janitor, who was sitting on the steps up to the top floor. "Who's this?" he said, holding out the photo.

The janitor took the photo and peered at it. The photo showed a couple in their forties, holding hands on a beach somewhere. "That's them," said the janitor. "That's the Dawkinses."

"Is that the man on the bed?" Dooley enjoyed the effect he produced, watching knowledge dawn in the little man's face. One flight down, he heard a door open.

"Oh my God," said the janitor. "I had 'em mixed up. That's the guy from downstairs in there."

"Bingo," said Dooley.

• • •

"He wasn't supposed to come back tonight. The lady upstairs said he was a salesman, spent a lot of time on the road. He came back early and found them in bed."

"Jesus," said Olson. "Welcome home."

"Yeah. He kept a gun in the dresser drawer, and it was just too handy. I found his car insurance policy in a desk drawer. With the plate number they should track him down before too long."

McCone wore a look of affectionate wonder. "You're a marvel, you are, Mike."

"Common sense. That's all."

Olson was shaking his head. "The guy was sneaking up to bang her whenever the husband was out of town. Son of a bitch."

"You said it."

"And you figured it all out just looking at it."

"The minute I heard the door was locked, I knew the shooter had a key. Who has a key to the apartment? The guy that lives there."

"You're a genius, Dooley. What more can I say?"

"No, I'm not. It's just using your head. Nothing more."

McCone slapped the desktop and said, "Before you go."

"What?"

"They're going to indict Billy Gaines. For the abduction of Sally Kotowski."

Dooley stared, then shrugged. "OK."

"Freeman went to the bank today and asked about the safety deposit box. It turns out Sally came and cleaned it out, turned in the keys. On May the second."

Dooley thought for a second. "Just before she took off for Wisconsin."

"That's right."

"So what was in there?"

McCone said, "The bank couldn't tell us, of course. Probably money."

"So where is it?"

"Who knows? Maybe she didn't have any of Feldman's, maybe it was just hers. So it wasn't all that much, just a working girl's rainy day money. She spent some of it and had the rest on her when she was abducted. The purse never turned up, right? So Steuben cleaned it out and tossed it or destroyed it."

Olson said, "Or maybe she *was* hiding some of Feldman's. Only she had help. She left it with someone else, and that's why she came back to the city, to retrieve it. That's why she was at the bar."

Dooley gave that a couple of seconds' thought and shrugged. "Doesn't make any difference now, I guess."

McCone peered at him. "I think it's solid, Mike. It fits together."

Dooley shrugged. "You're the boss."

"If you still have any doubts, I want to hear them."

"I told you my doubts the other night."

"And I think we've dealt with them. I'm going to call it cleared."

"It's your call."

"Yes, it is. Gaines worked out a plea deal with the state's attorney that'll put him in jail for three years on the abduction charge. I'd like to charge him as accessory to the murder, but that was part of the deal, he doesn't get charged for that. I think three years is a good deal for us."

And for Billy Gaines, thought Dooley, a small price to pay to discharge an Outfit debt.

"OK," he said. "It's cleared."

And they win again, he thought, walking back to his desk. Thanks to an overworked homicide supervisor whose principles are just not quite heavy enough to outweigh pressure to clear cases, pressure not to ask too many questions about certain types of cases.

Dooley tried to concentrate on his report but couldn't. It bugged him; he didn't give a damn when people like Chuck Steuben turned up bloated and reeking in car trunks, but nothing he'd heard about Sally Kotowski made him think she'd deserved anything so bad. He remembered the promise he'd made, lifting his glass to her in the dark.

Hell with it, thought Dooley, and jabbed at the typewriter.

Part Two

One Smart Son of a Bitch

Sixteen

Dear Dad, Mom, Kathleen, Frank,

Things are OK here in bandit country. We've had a pretty easy time recently, just a lot of walking around looking for trouble. We won't be too disappointed if we don't find it! There has been a little action, not much, not many casualties so don't worry too much. I think we have the NVA on the run.

Pop, I got to know a guy in my unit from Chicago and his father is a cop too. His name is George Wilkins and his old man is a sergeant at Prairie district. George is a good guy so say hi to his old man if you run into him.

Frank, let me know how the Cubs are doing. What's Billy Williams hitting? I always liked to watch him hit, he has that perfect swing. Kathleen, do you ever see Marcia anymore? I sent her a couple of letters but I didn't hear from her. Tell her if she's going out with somebody, that's OK, I don't mind, she can still write me. It's always good to get mail.

OK, not much to say, keep the letters coming. October will be here before you know it.

Love,
Kevin

Dooley handed the letter across the table to his wife. "He sounds OK."

"He sounds just like his father. 'Not much to say.'" Rose gave him a fleeting smile and scanned the letter again, with that hungry aching look in her eyes. "This is news to me, this thing about Marcia. Would that be Marcia Borkowski?"

"How should I know? He never told me anything about girlfriends."

"I'll have to ask Kathleen. I wonder if he's still in touch with Beth."

"That the one that went off to Champaign?"

Rose sighed, folding the letter. "Yeah. That's what he should have done. Kevin should be a sophomore in college now."

It always irritated Dooley a little when Rose got started on that theme, but he didn't say anything because he was of two minds about the whole thing. One part of him was proud of his son, proud as hell, and another part of him that he would never admit to wished just as hard as his wife did that Kevin had gone off to Champaign or South Bend with all his friends instead of getting on that bus to Parris Island. Dooley drained his coffee cup. "He'd probably have been drafted anyway," he said. "Where's the front section of the paper?"

"I think Frank took it up front."

"Since when does Frank read the paper?"

"Some rock and roll star died."

"Beautiful. Who says there's only bad news in the paper nowadays?"

"Michael." She gave him her disgusted look.

Dooley went up to the living room. Frank was nowhere to be seen, but the paper was lying on the couch. Dooley scanned it walking back to the kitchen. There was a lull in the fighting all over Viet Nam; Rogers was saying it was maybe a sign the communists were serious about peace. Hanoi was releasing three POWs. Dooley wanted to believe it; he almost pointed it out to

Rose, who had put Kevin's letter back in the envelope and was sitting there holding it with a faraway look in her eyes, but he didn't want to get her started again. He sat down and skimmed through the first few pages. Rockefeller was still wandering around South America getting rocks thrown at him; what the hell was he doing down there anyway? Somebody named Brian Jones had drowned. "Here you go, here's Frank's buddy." Dooley gave a short contemptuous laugh. "Found him at the bottom of his swimming pool. Full of drugs, I bet."

Frank came into the kitchen. "Hey, Pop."

Dooley looked up. "Hey there. Off to work?

"Yeah. You see the letter from Kevin?"

"Yeah." Dooley turned over a page. "Hey, what about this Brian Jones, huh?"

Frank stared at him, amazed. "Um, yeah. You know who he was?"

"Just what I read here." Dooley gave up trying to suppress his grin. "I guess he never heard the expression 'sink like a stone.'"

Frank's look soured. "That's real funny, Pop." He made for the door.

Dooley appealed to his wife. "No sense of humor. None at all."

• • •

Dooley had a pile of phone messages waiting for him: informants with tips that would lead nowhere, a State's Attorney fretting about an upcoming trial, somebody he'd never heard of wanting to talk about insurance. One that said only *Call Mitchell* followed by a phone number Dooley recognized as the number at Austin district out on the West Side. Dooley remembered Mitchell: he had caught Chuck Steuben's homicide and he and Dooley had compared notes at the time. Dooley dialed the number and hit it on the first try.

"Mitchell," a voice said.

"Mike Dooley at Area Six. You tried to reach me earlier?"

"Oh, yeah. Hey, how you doing?"

"Keeping busy. What can I do for you?"

"Just wanted to touch base with you. I heard you went ahead and indicted Billy Gaines."

"Yeah, we did."

"Everybody over there still happy with it?"

Here it is, thought Dooley. "The supervisor decided it was solid."

"OK, I'm not going to argue with anybody. But I'm still stuck with the file on Steuben. I'll never clear this case, because you never clear a mob killing. They're too good at keeping their mouths shut. But you gotta keep working it, at least put something in the file that explains it, so you can say you did your job."

"Sure." Dooley wondered where this was going.

"So I put Gaines's story in the file and moved on to other things. And then three days ago a guy tells me Steuben got killed because he was holding out."

Dooley said nothing for a few seconds. "I see."

"The informant says Steuben and Gaines pulled off a warehouse job down on the Southwest Side last month and tried to get away without paying the tax. He had the particulars. He said it wasn't the first time Steuben had tried it, either."

"I can see where you're going with this."

"Yeah. So I go talk to Gaines again, down at the jail. He sticks to his story, but I gotta say, he didn't put as much heart into it as he did last time. He sounded like he was reading lines. But I couldn't break him. And I didn't get anything more out of Steuben's wife. She still says he didn't get home till real late on the night your girl was killed, so he could have done it. But I think she's scared out of her mind. So I thought I would talk to you, see how much you liked the way Gaines told it. You seemed kind of skeptical at the time, I remember."

Dooley sat there holding the phone and wishing he had never heard of any of these people. "Well, I did have some doubts. It seemed kind of convenient, blaming it all on a dead man. And I couldn't find anyone to back up his story except connected guys. That always bothers me a little."

"Uh-huh. I know what you mean. But your supervisor liked it, huh?"

"He liked it just enough, I guess. It's hard to turn down a confession."

"You said it. And who the hell knows? It might even be true. I just thought I'd run this by you."

"I appreciate it. I'm not sure what to do with it."

"I can't tell you that. You got a cleared case with one bad guy dead and another one in jail, I don't know who's going to care if the story's a little fishy. But I had to tell you."

"Thanks," said Dooley. "Thanks a million."

• • •

By the time Olson and Dooley got there just before midnight, the 1400 block of Orleans looked like a cop convention, with squads and unmarked cars parked every which way, and uniforms and plainclothes milling in the headlights. Dooley found McCone standing by a white Ford Fairlane, handing out orders. "Ah, Mike," said McCone. "Just in time for the fun."

"Where we at?" said Dooley. "We got a homicide yet?"

"I'm afraid so. They took the boy to Henrotin, but it didn't look good."

The door of the Fairlane was open and Dooley could see blood on the driver's seat. "A boy?"

"A youngster. And his girlfriend. They parked here and had dinner on Wells Street, then got jumped when they came back to the car. They tried to lock themselves in the car but the boy got shot."

"Jesus. OK, what's the word?"

"It's McDavid's case. He's over there, he'll give you what he has in the way of descriptions. Four youths, black, one with a gun, ran south and east when a squad came by. We need everybody who's awake canvassing. I know you two are about to go off, but that's your tough luck."

"Hey, who needs sleep when you could be earning overtime?"

"That's the spirit. I've got people working east, but nobody on Wells yet. Start at the top and work down. You know the drill."

"I know. It's going to be a zoo."

"That it will. But they might still be around. And if they're not, somebody who saw them running will be."

Cruising east along a dark block where somebody had knocked out a couple of street lights, Dooley said, "Man, that's begging for trouble, parking around here."

"Where else you gonna park for Wells Street?"

"I know. But look at it. Those fuckers come up out of the projects and just go hunting. I bet they have fifty strong-arms a week around here. They ought to put up signs—park at your own risk, mugging zone."

Dooley parked at a corner where only a cop could get away with it and they started walking. Wells Street at midnight on a Thursday was only a little less crowded than the last time Dooley had seen it. There were the same drunks, the same tourists, the same kids. Ninety-eight percent victims and the two percent he was interested in; Dooley had a professional eye for these things.

"OK, if they have any brains they're long gone, but then if they had any brains they'd be doing something else with their lives. And if anybody saw anything, it's most likely somebody that doesn't have the dough to be sitting inside these joints looking out. So start with the street kids."

"OK. Want to split up?"

"Yeah, but stay in sight. I'll take that side."

Dooley crossed to the east side of the street. He'd already picked out a group of three he wanted to talk to, lounging in a doorway next to a shop with a brightly lit window full of hippie junk, T-shirts and water pipes and jackets with fringe a foot long. He had their attention when he was twenty feet away; he saw the sudden stiffening, the turning of backs, the firefly trace of the joint as it fell to the sidewalk and was ground out under a heel. There was a lot of shuffling and then one kid was slinking away, head down and hands in the pockets of his jeans. "Hold on a second," said Dooley. "Yeah, you."

"Me? What the hell you want?" The kid had long hair hooked behind one ear to keep it out of his face, and he was doing his best to brazen it out, chin jutting.

"Relax," said Dooley. "I don't care what you're smoking tonight."

There was a nervous laugh from the doorway. Dooley could make out a girl and another boy in the shadows. "It's Mexican tobacco, man," the kid with the hair said.

Dooley pulled out his star. "Look, don't bullshit me, or I could change my mind. I'm a homicide detective, OK?"

"Fuck, man. I didn't kill nobody."

"Somebody did. Two blocks from here."

"No shit. When?"

"About half an hour ago. You hear anything? See anybody running?"

"Uh-uh, man. We been standing right here for at least an hour, right?"

"At least."

"Hell, yeah."

"Just minding our own business, officer."

And that was pretty much the way it went as Dooley worked down the block. He had to make choices, scanning and sorting and guessing: who's been out here a while, who's got the antennae out, looking for me while I'm looking for them? After ten minutes he was starting to believe not only that the killers had gone south, but that nobody who'd seen them had filtered up this way, either. And then he was standing in front of the Mad Hatter.

Dooley had not wanted to admit to himself that he'd chosen this side of the street because that was where the bar was, but now that he was here he couldn't help taking a look in through the window. And seeing Laura Lindbloom behind the bar, he had to go inside, didn't he? He looked for Olson across the street and saw him talking to a knot of kids. He wavered for a second, thinking he could just slip in and out and Olson would never notice, and then he wondered what the hell he had to be devious about. He whistled, and when Olson looked he tapped himself on the chest and then pointed at the bar. Olson waved and Dooley turned to the door; let Olson think what he wanted.

It was a slow night in the Mad Hatter, and Laura saw him as soon as he came in through the door. Her eyebrows went up just a tick, and she came toward him with an expression that Dooley couldn't quite read; at least it didn't look like dismay. She picked up a beer mat on the way, maybe out of habit, but held it suspended over the bar instead of putting it down in front of him. "Hi," she said. "You here on business or pleasure?"

"Business." Dooley had been thinking about her off and on for weeks, but the vividness of her image had faded a little; looking into her big brown eyes again was like finding lost money. Tonight her hair was tied up in a ponytail and she had a touch of something glossy on her lips and she looked good enough to eat. "A kid got shot by a mugger over on Orleans. We're canvassing the area."

"Oh, God. How's the kid?"

"I didn't see him, but they're calling it a homicide."

She sagged a little, as if air had gone out of her, and her eyes closed for a second. "Jesus, that's awful."

"Yeah. Four black males. They ran east. We're looking for anyone who might have seen them."

She was still recovering; she heaved a sigh and just looked at him for a couple of seconds and then said, “Well, they didn’t come in here.”

“Word gets around pretty fast. You didn’t hear anything? Nobody in here mentioned anything about seeing any Negro kids running away?”

She frowned faintly and said, “No, nobody said anything at all about Negro kids. When did this happen?”

“Less than an hour ago. Maybe forty-five minutes.”

Laura took a look down the bar. “I think the only person who’s walked in here in the last forty-five minutes is that old man down there, and he didn’t say anything about it.”

“OK.” Dooley knew this little side trip was a waste of time, and he should be back out on the street. “You’ll let me know if you hear anything, right? You still got my card?”

“I’ve got it. Good luck.”

“Thanks.” He turned to go, one hand trailing on the bar. “So what ever happened with Jenny?”

Laura blinked and said, “I put her on a bus, like you said to.”

“Back home?”

“No. To New York.”

“New York? Jesus. I bet she’s standing in Times Square right now.”

Laura shook her head. “She has an aunt in New Jersey. I talked to her. She’s going to take Jenny in, find her a job.”

“Good. I hope it works out.”

“Me too. She owes me the bus fare.”

Dooley returned her smile. “OK. See you.”

He was halfway to the door when she said, “Dooley.”

He turned. “Yeah?”

“I read about the arrest in the paper. The guy who helped kidnap Sally.”

Dooley just stared at her. “Yeah, well, too bad we couldn’t get the guy who actually killed her.”

"Yeah, but it sounded like you did everything you could. I wanted to thank you."

"Actually I didn't do anything. The guy turned himself in."

"I still wanted to thank you. Come around some time when you're not on duty. As far as I'm concerned you drink for free here. And it won't be resented."

Dooley stood with his hands in his pocket, trying to bring his mind back to focus on what he ought to be doing. "Thanks," he said. "I might do that."

• • •

They had started another letter to Kevin and left it on the table for him. Dooley poured his ration of Jameson's and sat down to look at it. He was dead tired but he didn't like to go to bed with tasks undone. He picked up the ballpoint they'd left there for him and scanned what the others had written. Rose had come up with her usual page of gossip and small talk; he didn't know how she did it. Kathleen's heart hadn't been in it, he could tell. She had casually broken the news about Marcia's new boyfriend and left it at that. Dooley felt a little spasm of anger toward this girl who had dumped his son; why couldn't she handle her own Dear John letter? Frank had written more: *Last Sunday was Billy Williams Day because he broke the record for consecutive games that day and he had an unbelievable day. He homered in the first game and doubled and hit two triples in the second and we beat the Cards twice. Red Schoendienst said in the paper that the Cubs will be hard to catch. I think we'll probably play the Orioles in the Series. They look like the best team in the AL. Everyone's excited about the Cubs now. Larry Lujack is calling them the "Addison Street Miracle." Even Pop is getting interested in baseball again.*

To a point, thought Dooley, clicking the pen in and out with his thumb. He drank some whiskey and put pen to paper.

Hello son from your old tired father. I hope— Dooley stopped and swore under his breath; what the hell was he thinking? *I hope you're having a good time? I hope nobody kills you before you get this letter?* The usual phrases were meaningless and you could never put in a letter what you were really thinking. *I hope they're feeding you better than they used to feed us,* he finished. He remembered the letters he'd gotten out in the Pacific, mail call coming like water to a man dying in the desert. Mainly it was just getting it that counted, no matter what was in the letter, just hearing from somebody who was having a normal life. But he could never think of anything to say. Rose had told him once, just tell him what's on your mind. Dooley almost laughed.

People are dying all over the city. The blacks hate us and the longhairs hate you and I don't know what kind of country you're going to come home to. I let them send the wrong man to jail and the most beautiful woman I ever met thanked me for it tonight.

Dooley drank some more whiskey. It was too late to be doing this; he was punch-drunk.

Dooley clicked the pen a few more times and started writing. *Like Frank says, the Cubs should win it all this year. About time, right? We sure suffered through a lot of bad years. I don't know any Wilkins at Prairie District but I'll keep an eye out for him. Tomorrow is the 4th of July and for once I'm off. We're going to cook out in the back yard and maybe Frank and I will play some ball like you and I used to. We will miss you. People ask about you all the time. I am very proud of you, we all are.*

God, I miss you my boy, please come home in one piece, if there was any way on earth for me to be out there in your place I'd take it in a second, I already went through that shit so you wouldn't have to.

There was no way you could put what you were really thinking in a letter. Dooley wiped his eyes on his sleeve and wrote, *See you before too long.*

Seventeen

"DID YOU SEE this? Did you see what happened to the Cubs yesterday?" Frank's voice was strained with outrage.

Dooley looked up from the paper. "They lost, right?"

"Yeah, they had a two-run lead and blew it. Young like, *gave* the game away. He misplayed two easy outs."

"Young, who's that?"

"Don Young, the center fielder. He did fine the whole game and then he goes blind or something in the ninth inning."

"Bad time to pick to drop a couple of balls."

"I'm starting to get kind of worried. They lost three out of four in St. Louis last weekend, and now this."

"Ah, come on. How many games up on the Cards are they?"

"It's not the Cards we have to worry about. It's the Mets. They're only four behind us now. And tonight Seaver's pitching."

"The Mets? Don't make me laugh."

"The Mets aren't that bad. This is a big series."

"Relax, it's our year." Dooley was looking at an article on page four. He'd read it once already but come back to it after finishing the paper. *Spain admits perjury plot*, the headline read, and at first Dooley had skipped over it, seeing only the name of a country, before the photo caught his eye with its caption: *Thomas Spain*. The photo showed a handsome man with dark hair and glasses, smiling a little at a point off to the photographer's right. Dooley had recognized the man right away even though there was no Sally Kotowski in this picture. Dooley skimmed the article: *Thomas J. Spain, former chief investigator for the Cook County Sheriff's office, pleaded guilty yesterday to conspiracy to commit perjury . . . a burglary and the subsequent staged recovery of $52,000 worth of . . . ordered the sentence to run concurrently with a four-year federal sentence Spain is serving in Texas . . . originally found guilty in December, 1964, but the sentence was overturned . . . fired by Sheriff Richard B. Ogilvie. . . .* Dooley had heard it all at the time but forgotten it until now.

He folded up the paper and shoved it away. He wasn't sure why the article was nagging at him. Just because Sally Kotowski had slept with this guy didn't mean he had anything to do with her death. Anyway, Dooley had written off the Sally Kotowski case; he couldn't be expected to solve all the world's problems, and if the brass wanted to believe Billy Gaines, it was none of his business; more people were dying all the time and he didn't have time to spare for girls who made lousy choices in men.

But it bothered him, still. He stood up and reached for his jacket. "You're leaving kind of early, aren't you?" said Frank.

"Gotta go to court today." Dooley pulled on his jacket. "And run an errand or two on the way. Don't worry about the Cubs. They'll be OK."

• • •

The Uptown National Bank stood at the corner of Lawrence and Broadway, a survivor of the neighborhood's glory days. Before the war you could toss back a drink at the Green Mill, maybe rubbing elbows at the bar with one of Capone's boys, then stroll a block along Lawrence, passing the bank on the way, to the Aragon Ballroom to dance the night away. Now it was hard to make the stroll without getting panhandled two or three times along the way.

Dooley pulled over to park and looked at his watch. He might just have time for this if he got fast cooperation.

Inside, the bank was a temple to a faith that had died in the Depression just a few years after it was built. The main hall was at the top of a wide flight of marble stairs, and it had a soaring vault, high windows and fancy iron grilles at the tellers' windows. Dooley liked old ornate banks like this; they looked as if they would take your money seriously. He flashed his star at a teller and was directed to a manager, who came hustling out from behind the cages.

"I'd like to take a look at the records for your safety deposit boxes," Dooley said.

The manager had gone bald but compensated by cultivating a mustache. He frowned at Dooley and said, "Would this be in connection with the Kotowski account again?"

"That's right."

"I already spoke with an Officer Freeman about this, last month."

"I know. I know she cleared out the box. I'm interested in when she had access to it in the weeks before she closed it."

The manager nodded a few times, frowning, and said, "I'll have to have somebody pull the tickets for you."

"That would be great."

Dooley waited in an office on the ground floor while an employee made rustling noises in an adjoining room. He was going to have to hustle after this to make it to Twenty-sixth and California on time. The employee, a weedy-looking kid with sideburns that looked like they were pasted on, came into the office with a sheaf of papers. "Here you are," he said, laying them on a desk.

Dooley bent over the papers. They were record slips signed by Sally Kotowski each time she had access to her safety deposit box. Dooley sifted through them quickly. There were seven of them and the dates ranged from September 15, 1966 to May 2, 1969. Dooley looked up at the employee. "You're sure this is it?"

"That's all of them."

Dooley pulled out his notebook and pen. The last date before Sally cleaned out the box in May was October 2, 1968. He made a note, thanked the young man and left.

Pushing the car fairly hard down Lake Shore Drive, Dooley gave it some thought. Herb Feldman had come back to Chicago and moved in with Sally in December, then got shot in January. It looked to him a lot like whatever was in the safety deposit box, Sally hadn't gotten it from Herb Feldman, at least not on that last visit. And even if he had given her something to hide previously, when he came into town on the run, wouldn't he have had her go and get it? Bridges burning behind him, he had to be thinking about getaways. He'd have have had her go pull the money, hand it over. But she hadn't gone to the bank between October and May.

Dooley knew it didn't prove anything, but the more he looked at it the surer he was getting that Herb Feldman didn't have anything to do with Sally getting killed, whether or not Billy Gaines was lying.

But at this point, he wondered if anybody gave a damn.

• • •

Going to court was not Dooley's favorite pastime, although the overtime was good to have. Dooley's attitude had always been that he wouldn't have arrested the son of a bitch if he hadn't been sure he'd done it; he knew the trial was a legal necessity but considered it a formality, like genuflecting in church. Nothing made him see red like a smart-ass defense lawyer trying to shake his credibility, but he had learned early on not to rise to the bait. For Dooley the defense lawyer was an irritation like a traffic jam or a stomachache; you just had to sit there and sweat it out, keeping your cool.

"Are you trying to tell the court that the defendant was able to shoot a man in a tavern at Belmont and Sheffield just before nine o'clock and then a scant five minutes later walk into a second bar nearly two miles away at Wilson and Broadway and order a drink?" said the lawyer, giving Dooley a look of theatrical astonishment, his eyebrows pushing the loose skin of his forehead into furrows as they rose. This was Cohen, one of the lawyers they talked about at roll call sometimes, a natty dresser and a nasty piece of work.

Dooley shrugged. "No."

"You would concede that it is highly unlikely that the defendant could have covered the intervening distance in five minutes."

"I'd say it's flat-out impossible."

Cohen's eyes lit up; it wasn't often a witness handed him something on a plate. "Then given the fact that we have the sworn testimony of the bartender in the tavern on Wilson Avenue that the defendant walked in at nine o'clock on the evening in question, would you concede that it is highly unlikely that the defendant could have been present when the man was shot at Belmont and Sheffield at five to nine?"

Dooley stretched it out a bit, giving the lawyer a thoughtful look before he narrowed his eyes. "I don't accept the first fact as given."

There was a brief silence and Cohen said, "Are you impugning the testimony of the witness?"

"Yes, I am."

"On what grounds?"

"On the grounds that if your son owes a man a thousand dollars and he offers to release the kid from the debt in exchange for false testimony in his trial, you're likely to agree."

Bang, thought Dooley. Right in the heart. Cohen was too much of a pro to blanch, falter or reel, but the frozen intensity of his gaze told Dooley he'd scored a bull's eye. Two days of extra digging, hours of patient stubborn interviews, had unearthed the nugget that was going to send one man to jail for murder and another one for perjury. "Your honor, I'd like to request a short recess," said Cohen, turning to the judge with a look on his face like he had just swallowed a bad oyster.

Released after his testimony, Dooley prowled the marbled halls, shouldering through hordes of the dazed and the damned. Nobody went to Twenty-sixth and California to have a good time; he went past a young black woman sobbing in the arms of an old black man. He took an elevator down to the second floor and went through an archway and nodded at a receptionist behind a high counter. He went past a door that said Edward V. Hanrahan, State's Attorney on it and turned down a hallway with doors opening off either side. He stopped at a door near the end of the hallway, rapped on it and pushed it open, revealing a small office crowded with three desks and a bank of filing cabinets. A man scooping files from a desktop looked at Dooley and said, "Can I help you?"

"I'm here to see Malone." Dooley pointed to a big blond man in shirtsleeves who sat behind a desk in the corner, absorbed in reading something on the desk before him. At the sound of his name the man looked up and smiled. "Mike, hey, how are you? How's business?"

Dooley crossed the office and shook his hand. "Business is good. They got one of mine upstairs sweating it out right now. I just need twelve good citizens to stay awake long enough to say the right words."

"That's the hard part."

"Brother, you said it. You got a minute?"

"Sure." Malone checked his watch. "Maybe two. Talk fast."

Dooley swiped a chair from a neighboring desk and sat down. "I saw your name in the paper this morning."

Malone stared for moment. "Yeah?"

"In connection with the Tommy Spain thing."

Malone's face had gone blank. He set down his pen and poked at it with his fingertips. "What about it?"

Dooley hesitated; he was used to the sight of a man getting careful suddenly but hadn't expected it from Tim Malone. "Well, congratulations, first of all. You got him the second time around."

Malone waved a hand, dismissing it. "It's just grandstanding. Spain's in prison on a federal charge anyway. This was just Hanrahan going for headlines. This was old news, a loose end."

"This was the phony bust where he let the thieves get away with most of the loot and staged a raid that recovered a few bucks?"

"Yeah. That's how he built his reputation. He was in cahoots with the black hats all along."

Dooley shook his head. "What a hell of a guy. Listen, Spain came up in a case I had recently."

Malone gave him a keen look and nodded just perceptibly. "OK."

"A woman got killed at the beginning of June," Dooley said. "It turned out she'd had a couple of mobster boyfriends."

Malone frowned. "The girl on the riverbank? Herb Feldman's girlfriend?"

"That's right."

"I thought you charged a guy for that."

"Yeah, we did. He claimed he helped abduct her and fingered another guy for the killing. A guy who happened to be dead. He said they thought she was sitting on Feldman's money."

Malone nodded. "And what don't you like about it?"

"I don't like the fact that the guy who supposedly did it is dead. I don't like the fact that there's no evidence to support the story. I don't like the fact that the girl was tortured to death and the dead guy had no record of that kind of thing. There's a lot I don't like."

"You think your guy was ordered to take the rap, huh?"

"It wouldn't be the first time."

Malone picked up his pen and studied it. "So what do you want from me?"

"An education. Before my victim was with Feldman she was Tommy Spain's girl. And I'm getting the impression that Spain's a lot more interesting than Herb Feldman. Especially since the mention of his name makes a State's Attorney I've worked with for years start acting like he doesn't trust me."

Malone looked at him then, and Dooley could see the wheels turning behind Malone's blue eyes. After a few seconds Malone said, "I trust you, Mike. I trust my wife, for that matter. But if my wife started asking questions all of a sudden about a case that a lot of people didn't want prosecuted, I'd wonder for a second what the hell she was up to."

Dooley's eyes narrowed. "Who didn't want you to prosecute Spain?"

"Good question. Whoever stole the evidence would be my guess."

"Somebody stole the evidence?"

"All the files disappeared. Right after Hanrahan decided to retry Spain. Fortunately I made photostats of everything. Just as soon as he started talking about the case. I figured somebody might try something. You want to know why I'm nervous? Because Spain and his lawyers came in here the other day expecting to win. They didn't expect to have to plead guilty. You should have seen their faces when I produced the files. I think I pissed a few people off, Mike."

Dooley gave it a few seconds and said, "Yeah, you probably did. Who the hell had access to the files?"

"Shit, who didn't? Come on, Mike. You weren't born yesterday. You know how things work around here. There's a million ways to fix a case. And a million people willing to do it."

"So what are you going to do about it?"

"Not a damn thing. I got my win. The last thing I'm going to do now is rock the boat. Anybody asks, I'll deny there were any missing files. I like my job, Mike."

"OK. Fair enough. Who can I talk to that can tell me all about Tommy Spain?"

Malone shrugged. "You could always try the feds. They put him away. Talk to the guy in charge of their C-1 squad. What's his name, Gustafson I think."

Dooley breathed a little puff of laughter. "In my experience the FBI doesn't have much time for us dumb CPD flatfoots. But I guess I could try."

Malone just looked at him for a second or two. "You want my advice? Be content with what you have. You got a guy in jail, be happy. That's all the Outfit's gonna give you, and that's more than most people get. You push on it, and all you'll get is headaches."

"That's a hell of a philosophy for a prosecutor."

Malone stiffened a little and said, "Mike, you bring me a killer, I'll do what I have to do to convict him. I'll go to the damn wall with you if I have to. You've worked with me enough to know that. But I have to live in the real world. There are limits to what I can do and keep my job. And at least in this job I can put away some of the punks that make people afraid to go out at night. That's something even the syndicate likes."

Dooley nodded and stood up. "I know. Look, that was a smart thing you did with Spain. You're the last man in the world I should be asking to justify himself. I'm sorry I said what I did."

"Forget it." Malone waved it away. "Bring me another punk sometime. You bag him, I'll stuff him and mount him."

"You got it. See you around, Tim."

Dooley had turned to go when Malone's voice stopped him. "Hey, Mike."

"Yeah?"

Malone was scribbling something on a pad. "If Hoover's boys won't help you, there's another guy you might talk to about Tommy Spain." He tore off the sheet and held it out. "I don't know his number, but I think he's in the book. He's got an office on Wabash."

Dooley took it and read: *Johnny Puig*. "Thanks. Who is he?"

"He's a private dick, but he used to work for us. He used to work for the sheriff, too. He worked with Spain way back when. If anybody can help you, he can."

"Terrific. How the hell do you pronounce this?"

Malone grinned. "I'm gonna tell you, and you're gonna laugh, and you better get it out of the way now, 'cause he's sensitive about it. You say 'pooch', like a dog."

"Pooch, huh? Here, poochie poochie."

Malone shook his head, still grinning. "Get out of here, Dooley. I got work to do."

• • •

Dooley drove nearly all the way to the Area, thinking about things, and then pulled over at a phone booth on Belmont. He didn't particularly want to discuss Sally Kotowski's death in the office at Damen and Grace, in earshot of the man who had called the case cleared. He didn't want to talk to the G yet, either, so he called Haggerty instead.

He had intended to leave a message with his home number, but it was his lucky day and he caught Haggerty at his desk. "Hey, Mike. What's up?"

"What do you know about Tommy Spain?"

"Tommy Spain? Boy, that name brings back memories. He's in jail now, you know."

"I know. But that doesn't mean he's out of the picture."

"No, it doesn't. What do you need to know?"

"Anything and everything. I found out he used to go out with my girl on the riverbank."

"No kidding. I didn't know that. Hey, didn't you grab somebody for that?"

"Yeah, but I'm not sure how much I like it. The idea is she got killed because she was hiding money for Herb Feldman, but I don't think she had anything of Feldman's. I'm wondering if Tommy Spain had anything to do with it."

"How so?"

"I don't know. That's why I'm asking you. I'm fishing."

"Well, I don't know that you're gonna catch anything here."

"Nothing jumps out at you, huh?"

"Can't say it does. When were they together?"

"Sixty-six, around then. Before he went to Mexico."

"So it's ancient history."

"Yeah, I guess so. Maybe there's nothing there. I'm just wondering, if it wasn't one mob guy that got her killed, maybe it was the other one."

"I don't think it's likely, but I can ask around a little. Boy, you must really not like the way they say it happened."

Dooley thought for a second. "Starting to," he said. "Just starting to not like it a lot."

Eighteen

"IS THAT KEVIN'S unit?" Rose leaned over the kitchen table, intent, crowding Dooley as she read the paper over his shoulder.

"No. Kevin's in the Third Marines. This is the Ninth Marines. The Third and the Ninth are two regiments of the Third Marine Division." Dooley had explained it to her before but she never retained it.

"So this means he's coming home, right? Soon?"

"All I know is what I read in the papers, Rose." Dooley looked at it again, there in black and white: . . . *200 marines of C company, First battalion, Ninth regiment, arrived in the rear staging area of Quang Tri on the first leg of their departure from Viet Nam . . . All 8,000 of the Ninth regiment are being pulled out.* "Probably the whole division is coming out," Dooley said. "But it doesn't say when."

"Soon. It must be soon. Before October."

Dooley tried to think of something to say that would deflate her; he had a superstitious reluctance to celebrate prematurely. He couldn't come up with anything and finally said, "He could be coming out ahead of schedule, yeah."

Rose put her arms around him from behind, leaning down to put her cheek next to his, and Dooley had to respond; he found her hand and squeezed it. They stayed like that for a little while and then Rose pulled away, wiping her eyes. "We have to keep praying, harder than ever now."

"Yeah." Dooley had read something else in the paper he hadn't shown Rose: the previous week had seen the lowest total of American combat deaths in six months, a trifling 153. Dooley had bad memories of men who had died in late July 1945, and he had learned that you never let down your guard until you were on that ship and the island was a smear on the horizon. He went back to the paper, trying to put it all out of his mind.

A federal appeals court had thrown out Dr. Spock's conviction for conspiracy. Dooley was confused; wasn't this the famous baby doctor? Why was the son of a bitch running around busting up draft board offices? Nobody stayed convicted anymore; Jimmy Hoffa wanted his conviction thrown out, too, because he said the FBI had gotten the goods on him illegally. An FBI guy had testified that they had bugs all over Chicago, though the bureau was denying they'd gotten anything on Hoffa with them. Who the hell knew what the G got up to? They never shared a damn thing. There was a Soviet fleet off Florida: what was going on down there?

Frank came into the kitchen. Rose said, "They've started withdrawing your brother's unit. It's in the paper."

"Outta sight! Can I see?"

"No, they haven't started withdrawing your brother's unit. They've started withdrawing the next regiment over. Don't get too excited yet." Dooley tossed him the front section and picked up Sports. Abernathy had given up four runs in the ninth to the Phillies and lost.

"Wow," said Frank. "When's he coming home?"

Dooley turned the page. "October, same as he always was. Look at this, I'm starting to think you're right about the Cubs. Didn't they get swept in New York?"

"Nah, they won the last one. Hands did it again. He's the stopper. Hey, are you off today?"

"Yeah. Why?"

"You want to go to the game? You said you could get us in."

Dooley looked at his boy across the table and for a second or two it almost sounded like a good idea. He couldn't remember the last time he'd been to a ball game. "Can't do it," he said. "I gotta go see a guy."

• • •

Johnny Puig had agreed to meet Dooley at a restaurant in Rogers Park under the El tracks across from Loyola University. "The food stinks, but you can sit in there and drink coffee as long as you want and they don't bother you," he'd said on the phone. Puig had a faint accent that Dooley couldn't quite place. Dooley had suggested meeting at his office but after finding out where Dooley lived Puig had said, "Why go all the way downtown? We're both North-siders."

Dooley was a Northwest-sider, which was not quite the same thing, but he was happy to be spared the long drive on a day off. Pushing east on Devon he saw gray clouds hanging low over the lake, but it looked like the rain might hold off for a change; they'd had rain every weekend since April.

The restaurant was called Cindy Sue's, and it shook every time a train rumbled by overhead. There was a horseshoe-shaped counter and beyond it a dining room with booths. Puig had told Dooley not to worry, they would recognize each other; they were both detectives, weren't they? Standing in the dining room checking people off, Dooley was starting to think either he was a lousy detective or Puig wasn't there yet when the man with the moustache and sideburns and hair a little too long to be a dick in any outfit Dooley would associate with looked up and waved a cigarette at him. Dooley walked back to the booth wondering if there was a mistake.

"Dooley?" said the man, extending his hand.

"Yeah. Good to meet you, um . . ." Dooley's nerve failed him.

"Johnny Pooch," said Puig. Forewarned, Dooley kept a straight face as he sat down. Puig smiled through a cloud of smoke. "That's a Catalan name, from northeastern Spain. I was born in Barcelona but Franco chased us out and we came here when I was sixteen, via France. That's the canned version, just to explain the name. You want my whole life story, you gotta pay extra."

"I'll settle for that for starters." Dooley waved off Puig's offer of a cigarette and flagged down a waitress. He ordered a cup of coffee to match Puig's and said, "I remember reading about Franco when I was a kid."

Puig's eyes twinkled. "I remember seeing Franco's bombers knock down a row of houses on our street. My old man hoped I'd get a chance to go after him once the U.S. got into the war in Europe, but I had to settle for going after the Germans. I decided that was good enough. Some of those bastards had been in Spain."

Dooley nodded. "Where'd you serve?" He was reevaluating fast; the hair was a little long but there was gray in it and the arithmetic said Puig had to be in the middle forties. He was a sad-faced man with big dark hound-dog eyes and skin that took a nice tan; Dooley had guessed Italian on first sight.

Puig said, "I rode with the Third Infantry Division from Casablanca all the way across the Rhine."

"You rode? The infantry I was in had to walk everywhere."

"Well, they put me in intelligence, because of my languages. We got to ride in jeeps mostly."

"I remember. You and the brass."

"That's right. Which infantry were you in?"

"The Thirty-seventh Division. Out in the Pacific. Bougainville to Manila."

"That's another long haul."

"Tell me about it."

Puig drew on his cigarette, exhaled, and smiled a little. "And then we came home to the brass bands and the pretty girls."

"Something like that." Dooley's coffee arrived and he took a moment to doctor it.

"So you want to know all about Tommy Spain," said Puig.

"Whatever you can tell me."

"I could tell you a whole lot. It would help to have a context. You working on a case?"

"Unofficially."

"What does that mean?"

Dooley drank some coffee and said, "That means the case has been cleared. But I don't like the way it was cleared. And I'm a stubborn bastard. So I'm spending my day off talking to you instead of going to a ball game with my kid."

"Well, I'll have to make it worth your while, then. What case are we talking about?"

"The girl on the riverbank. Last month."

"I remember. What's the connection with Spain?"

"She used to be his girlfriend."

Puig's eyebrows rose. "That's interesting."

"She liked hoods, seems like. Later she was with a guy named Herb Feldman."

"I knew Feldman. I busted every gambler in town a few times when I was with the sheriff's department."

"The official version is, she was killed because a connected guy thought she had Feldman's money. But the case stinks."

Puig shook his head. "She didn't have any of Herb's money. Herb wouldn't have trusted her with it. And if Herb had stashed anything away he wasn't supposed to, word would have gotten around, and I think I would have heard. And I didn't."

"OK, so I'm just looking for reasons why a gangster's girlfriend would get killed. And wondering if the gangster in question wasn't Tommy Spain instead of Herb Feldman."

"You got anything other than a hunch?"

"Not a God damn thing."

Puig stubbed out his cigarette. He grinned at Dooley and said, "You sound like my kind of detective. OK, here's the story on Tommy Spain. He was a mobster from the start. And I mean from the start. Tommy Spain grew up around Taylor and Racine. His real name is Tommaso Spagnola. All his friends were hoods, his father and Sam Giancana were pals. Normally Tommy would have gone to work for the Taylor Street crew like all his buddies did, but somebody had big plans. See, Tommy's a bright guy. And I don't mean just smart like a fox, like all those guys. God knows what happened, but Tommy got some actual brains. He speaks three or four languages, reads books, can tell you who's president, knows which fork to use for the salad, the whole thing. So somebody said, 'Let's get this guy on the police department.'"

"He was a cop?"

"That's how he started out."

"With his connections?"

Puig made a face. "How long you been around this city?"

"I'm not naive. I'm just still disgusted, every time I hear it."

"OK, you and me both. Anyway, that's what he was when I first ran into him, a vice cop up on Rush Street. That was about ten years ago. I was working for the State's Attorney's office, and we had an investigation going on, looking for corruption in city hall."

Dooley snorted. "Find any?"

"Christ, we didn't know where to start. But we'd drawn a bead on Daley's own corruption office. Remember? He had set up a guy named Goldblum, with lots of fanfare, to root out corruption wherever he could find it. Only in three years he hadn't come up with a single indictment. So we figured his real purpose was to cover it up instead. We wanted to see who he was meeting with and how he was spending his time, so we needed a guy to do the footwork. And we wound up with Tommy Spain."

"How?"

"That's the interesting part. He was recommended by Dick Ogilvie."

Dooley peered at him. "The governor?"

"Yeah. He was with the U.S. Attorney's office back then. We wanted their help, we got Spain. One of the crookedest characters ever to grace the CPD. What did we know? He came highly recommended. He had done some work for Ogilvie when he was going after Tony Accardo in fifty-eight or so, and Ogilvie said he was a top-notch guy. I looked into Spain's record and found a couple of things that made me wonder—he'd been involved in a shooting, where he claimed a pimp drew on him as he was arresting him. You ever heard of that? No, me neither. But this pimp wound up dead and some people wondered if that wasn't the idea, since he'd been complaining about being shook down. But the investigation supported Spain and what did I know? I took him on." Puig shook another cigarette out of the pack.

"How'd he do?"

Puig put a match to the cigarette and blew smoke out the corner of his mouth. "Well, just about the first thing that happened was that he got arrested while he was staking out Goldblum's house."

"Oh, yeah, I remember now. Goldblum's son came out and confronted him and there was a fight or something."

"Yeah. There was a hue and cry, and a bit of a scandal, and the whole thing was called off. Spain claimed it was just bad luck, but some people wondered if the son hadn't been tipped off."

"By who?"

Puig smiled through a cloud of smoke. "My guess would be Tommy Spain himself. I think he was there to make sure the investigation failed."

"Jesus. Yeah, I remember the whole thing now. He got fired, right?"

"That's right. I did, too, by the way. And there's been no serious push from the State's Attorney's office against corruption since then."

Dooley was starting to like Johnny Puig, seeing the bitterness in his eyes. "What happened to Spain?"

"He left town."

"Where'd he go?"

"That's a very good question. A man I know says Mexico."

Dooley frowned. "This was in what, sixty, sixty-one?"

"Yeah."

"I knew Spain had been in Mexico, but I thought it was later, like sixty-six."

"That was the second time. That's when he went down there with Giancana. Remember, after Giancana got out of jail?"

"I remember. I didn't know Spain went with him, never made the connection."

"Yeah, that was Tommy. They were based down there for a couple of years, but they traveled all over. They were pretty much in the spotlight, by that time."

"So hold on a second. What the hell was Spain doing down there in Mexico in sixty-one?"

"I don't know. All I know is, he was down there for maybe a year, year and a half. And when he came back, there was a new sheriff."

It took Dooley a second to remember, but he did. "Ogilvie."

"That's right."

"And he hired Spain again? After what went on before?"

"Yup. We begged him not to. I was working for the department by then, I'd landed on my feet. I told Ogilvie he'd be crazy to hire Spain, but he insisted. He said Spain was just the type of guy he needed, smart and aggressive and experienced in undercover work. That's a pretty kind way to put it, I told him, but it didn't make any difference. Tommy Spain was hired as chief investigator for the Cook County Sheriff's Department."

"Unbelievable."

"Sad but true. And he really threw himself into his work."

"I remember. Seems like he was in the paper a lot."

"Oh, yeah. And you know, some of it was legit. When he wanted to, he could do real police work. It made great cover. But the whole time, he had his own agenda. Basically Sam Giancana's agenda, when you get down to it. You know about the lie detector tests?"

"I heard about it but don't remember the details."

"He used to haul guys in and hook 'em up to the polygraph, supposedly as part of his investigations. Funny thing was, sometimes they would turn up dead after that."

"He was doing it for the Outfit."

"That's right. To find the snitches. That's how the feds finally got him. He tried it once too often, and they nailed him for conspiracy, after that bank job in Forest Park."

"I remember. That was after he'd been fired, if I recall."

"That's right. He finally went too far for Ogilvie, with the staged raid on the motel, the thing he just pleaded on the other day. Ogilvie had to fire him after that."

Dooley drank a little coffee. He was starting to want a cigarette, something that didn't happen to him very often. He'd smoked like a chimney in the army, like everyone else, and then quit cold when he got back. "Why did Ogilvie hire him in the first place?" he said.

"Yeah, that's the sixty-four thousand dollar question, isn't it?" said Johnny Puig. "There's an obvious answer, of course."

"He had something on him. But what? I mean, I could be wrong, but isn't Ogilvie supposed to be pretty clean?"

"Supposed to be, yeah. Maybe even is, by local standards. But everybody's got a skeleton or two in the closet. And if anybody would know about it, it would be Tommy Spain. That was his specialty."

"What, getting the dirt on people?"

"Yeah. Spain was a master blackmailer. He collected dirt. He was a connoisseur of dirt. He'd been a shakedown artist when he was a cop, and that was the lens he saw the world through. 'How can I get something on this guy?'"

Dooley saw a picture forming. He nodded slowly for a while and said, "So. Just assuming, which I have no reason to do except a hunch, that it was knowing Tommy Spain that got Sally Kotowski killed, what was she killed for?"

Puig blew smoke and watched it swirl up toward the ceiling. "Well, I'd say your first guess about Herb Feldman was pretty good for a first guess. That's how those things happen sometimes. Only if it was Tommy Spain that got her killed, I'd say it wasn't money she was holding."

"What was it?"

"Just what we're talking about. Dirt."

"In what form?"

"Just about any form dirt can take. Papers, photos, tapes. Spain was good with the electronic stuff. He tapped a lot of phones in his day, planted a lot of bugs."

"OK. Dirt on who?"

"Your guess is as good as mine. Spain played both sides of the fence, and you can figure he was smart enough to have a few insurance policies. At one time or another he could have been in a position to get dirt on a lot of very different people. On both sides of the law."

Dooley smiled. "That really narrows it down."

"It does, doesn't it?" Puig gave him a long thoughtful look. "I can give you a couple of names, other people you might want to talk to."

"I'd appreciate that."

Puig stuck his cigarette in his mouth and dug inside his jacket. "You're really going to pursue this, huh? On your own time?"

"Why not?"

Puig squinted at him through the smoke, putting pen to paper. "You're a glutton for punishment, aren't you?"

Dooley picked up his coffee. "I'm kind of stubborn. Everybody tells me so."

Nineteen

THE U.S. WAS sending astronauts to the moon and the British were sending troops to Ireland; Dooley wasn't especially interested in either place. He had friends who were only a generation or two removed from the Troubles, but Dooley had never had that much interest in the old country. What family mythology he'd gleaned from his dad went back to laborers on the Erie Canal and sergeants in Crook's cavalry instead of the Easter Rising. Besides that, the policeman in him had a certain reaction to rioting in the streets and he figured if the Brits wanted to send the army to Derry that was their business. He was a lot more interested in the report in column one: 1,300 marines from the Ninth Regiment of the Third Division boarding a ship at Da Nang. Dooley was starting to feel the odds were shifting in their favor.

Frank came in and said, "How about it, Pop? The Mets are in town. You promised."

Dooley looked up, annoyed. "I didn't say when."

"You're off again, right?"

"Yeah."

"Well, it's the Mets. The biggest series of the year. It'll be cool. Come on, Pop."

"Let me think about it." Dooley went on leafing through the paper. A man on Wilson had shot his neighbor's son after the boy had slugged him; Dooley wondered who had caught the case. "I don't know if we can get tickets."

"You said you knew the guy in charge of the police detail and we could get in for free."

Dooley turned a page. "I said if we were lucky and he was on, he might give us a break. I never promised a thing. We wouldn't have seats. We'd have to stand."

"That would be great. Please?"

Dooley didn't answer because he was looking at a headline that said *Old Town Teen Prostitution Ring Is Raided.* He read fast, skimming down the column looking for names and addresses: *The man, whom police identified as Raymond Moran, 25, offered her a room in his hotel at 1543 N. California Avenue and introduced her to Mrs. Marge Schenk. . . .* Dooley laid down the paper and looked up at his son.

"Please, Pop? You promised we could."

"Sure," said Dooley. "I'll have to make a phone call or two."

• • •

"We'll just roam around and maybe get lucky." Dooley bulled his way through the swarm at Sheffield and Addison, making for the gate in the corner of the old ballpark.

"I don't care if we have to stand up the whole time," Frank shouted over the din.

The kid was happy, and Dooley figured that might make it all worthwhile. Dooley spent his whole week driving around the city, and the last thing he had wanted to do was use up a precious day off fighting traffic and negotiating an illegal parking spot with a bored patrolman who was not impressed by his star.

Dooley was amazed at the crowd; how could you draw a crowd like this on a Monday? He saw a lot of bare limbs, long-haired girls in shorts and sandals, tops that didn't leave a lot to the imagination.

Where the hell have I been? he thought. He hadn't been to the ballpark in years; he'd taken Kevin once when he was small, but Kevin had started going by himself or with his buddies as soon as he was old enough to save up a buck for the bleachers and figure out how the buses ran. He'd taken Frank once when he was too young, maybe four years old, and they'd had to leave in the sixth inning because Frank had gotten bored and started whining. Dooley hadn't been back since.

At the corner of the park he stood looking through a locked gate and scanned until he found the man he was looking for beyond the turnstiles. He put his fingers to his mouth and whistled and then waved as the cop in the white sergeant's shirt with the stripes on the sleeve turned to look at him. The sergeant grinned and came ambling over.

"Hey, Mike. Good to see you. Just a second." The cop turned and beckoned to a man standing nearby and had him unlock the gate to let Dooley and Frank slip inside. "This your boy?" said the cop.

"One of them. This is Frankie."

"Frank," said Frank, shaking hands.

"Frank, Frankie, same thing," said Dooley.

"I was Frankie when I was six, Pop."

"Come on Mike, can't you see the kid's grown up?" said the sergeant, slapping Frank on the shoulder.

"Be grateful we're not still calling you Francis," said Dooley.

Frank's face clouded up and Dooley knew he'd made a mistake. "Don't," said Frank.

"Relax, I'm just giving you a hard time."

"I had a cousin named Carmen," said the cop. "A *guy* cousin. Now *that* kid had a hard time."

Dooley was desperate to change the subject and he said, "So who's throwing today?"

"I told you," said Frank. "Hands and Seaver."

"Oh, yeah."

"Should be a hell of a matchup," said the sergeant. "I don't know what kind of luck you're gonna have with seats, though. They're selling standing room today."

"Yeah, well, thanks, Phil." Frank was straining at the leash and Dooley had to cut away to follow him. Frank wanted to buy a scorecard; Dooley grumbled a little but gave in. Dooley had never kept score at a ball game in his life; he just remembered things.

The first sight of the field was always nice; Dooley always forgot how pretty a ball field could be. The ivy on the outfield walls was rippling in the breeze; a few players were running their lazy warm-up jogs across the outfield, the caps and socks a bright blue. Dooley liked the colors; even on a color TV it was never quite the same. The park was filling up and the pitchers were warming up down the lines. "That's Seaver, huh?" said Dooley. He hadn't really followed baseball for years but he still scanned the sports pages each morning and he had heard all the names.

"Yeah. He's tough. He nearly threw a perfect game at us last week in New York."

"The one that rookie broke up?"

"Yeah, Qualls. Man, that was something."

"So, what kind of year is Hands having?"

"He's ten and seven. But he's our stopper this year. I don't know how many times he's won after a losing streak."

They wandered till they found a place to stand behind the last row of seats in the far left-field corner. They could lean against the fence, look down and see the firehouse across the street, the hustlers and ball hawks with their gloves milling on the sidewalks. It was hot; even the breeze was hot.

Dooley stared, bemused. "What's with the yellow helmets out there?"

"Those are the Bleacher Bums. They're like, really organized. They do cheers and stuff. Sometimes Selma leads them from the bullpen."

"Selma?"

"One of our pitchers. Pop, you gotta pay more attention. We're gonna win the World Series this year."

"Let's win this game first, huh?"

The ball game started; for the first few innings it was all goose eggs, with Hands laboring a little but pitching out of jams and Seaver throwing smoke. Dooley was having a good time; he had forgotten what it was like to watch a good tight ball game. He didn't have time in his life for ball games any more.

In the sixth inning the Cubs scratched out a run when Kessinger bunted for a hit, Beckert moved him along on the hit-and-run, and Williams turned one of Seaver's fastballs into a long slicing single to left center. Frank went nuts, jumping up and down and screaming along with forty thousand other idiots. Dooley grinned and punched him in the shoulder.

Between innings Frank said, "Did you go to a lot of games when you were a kid?"

Dooley shook his head. "Once or twice. I was too poor."

"Too poor? Come on."

"It was the Depression. My old man was a carpenter and there wasn't much work. We had to save our pennies. And mostly I just played. A nice day like today, I'd be out all day playing with my pals. We used to play line ball, in the street, or go over to the diamonds at Columbus Park. We'd hit till our hands bled, throw till we couldn't lift our arms. That's how you learn to play."

"You were pretty good, weren't you?"

Dooley shrugged. "Depends on what you mean."

"You played in the minors, Kevin told me once."

"Yeah. I played one summer with the Eau Claire Bears."

"The Eau Claire Bears? I never heard of them."

Dooley laughed. "They're long gone. That was the old class C Northern League. My high school coach knew the manager and got 'em to sign me. It was a hell of a lot of fun for an eighteen-year-old kid." Dooley hadn't thought about it for years: little towns in Wisconsin and Minnesota, swatting at mosquitoes in the outfield, long bus rides. Making time with pretty girls, a cocky kid from the big city, innocent as hell under the swagger. Late-night walks by the river, stolen kisses under the electric hum of crickets, sneaking back into the rooming house. Dooley couldn't believe how long ago it was.

There was some excitement in the seventh when a Met bounced one high off the wall in right, but he died at second. In the eighth another Met got himself thrown out trying to stretch a single into a double, and that was about it. The Cubs went down in the bottom of the inning and Hands came out for the ninth.

Dooley was tired of standing up, tired of the noise. He was starting to think about all the things he had to do, all the reasons he shouldn't be out here wasting time. It always happened; you forgot everything for a while and then it was even more depressing to remember you had to go back to it all when you left the ballpark. Hands got two outs and then ran out of gas; Durocher came out and brought in Regan to finish up. When Beckert snagged Clendenon's liner to end the game, Dooley said, "That's it. So much for the Mets. Let's go home."

Outside the ballpark there was a party going on: music and shouting and dancing in the streets. Dooley was glad he was off duty and didn't have to worry about all the public intoxication. "We should come out here more often," said Frank as they cut across Addison Street with the crowd.

"Sure. That'd be fun."

Walking back to the car in the late afternoon sun, Frank said, "How come you didn't go on to the majors?"

Dooley made a little noise of dismissal. "I couldn't hit. Couldn't hit worth a damn."

"But Kevin told me you hit over .300 in the minors."

"I hit .329 that year, yeah."

"That's pretty good, isn't it? How come you didn't move up?"

Dooley laughed, shortly. "That was the summer of Nineteen forty-one."

"Oh." Frank was silent for a while. "But couldn't you go back to it when you got out of the army?"

"I tried." Dooley gave a single rueful shake of the head, remembering. "I had a two-day tryout with the Duluth Dukes in the spring of forty-seven, and I got cut. I couldn't hit the breaking ball anymore. I couldn't even hit a decent fastball. I'd just lost too much. The war took it out of me."

"You could have gotten it back, couldn't you? Two days isn't much of a chance."

Dooley was irritated suddenly; why couldn't the kid leave it alone? "It wasn't worth it. It was time to get on with my life." There was no way he could explain; Dooley remembered going through the motions, the sudden realization that baseball was one more thing from Before the War that was never coming back. "I grew up. That's all that happened."

Frank let it ride for a minute and then he said, "Man, I'd give anything to play in the majors."

"Maybe you will someday." Dooley didn't believe it and knew Frank didn't either.

"Not me," said Frank. "Maybe Kevin."

Dooley couldn't talk for a moment; for a second he could hardly breathe. "Maybe so," he said.

• • •

"Look *that* up in your Funk and Wagnalls," the one without the moustache said. The TV audience broke up; Kathleen snickered on the couch next to Dooley.

"Your what?" said Dooley, suspiciously.

Kathleen rolled her eyes. "Your *Funk* and *Wagnalls*. It's a dictionary, Daddy."

Dooley shook his head. "What's funny?"

"The name. It's a funny name. Oh, why *bother*? I thought you had a sense of humor."

"I do. I'm just waiting for something funny here."

"Just watch, OK?"

Dooley stuck it out till the commercial. "Now Jack Benny, he was funny," he said, getting up off the couch.

"Jack Benny, wow," said Kathleen.

Rose was at the kitchen table, writing checks. "Does Rob owe you any money?" she said. "We could sure use it this month."

"Not at the moment. He may have a job for me next week. What's the problem?"

"That new clutch cost more than a hundred dollars." She looked up at him. "And if we want to go somewhere on your vacation it would be nice to have a little saved up. Right now we might just be able to afford a day in the Dells."

"Not the Dells. I've had it with the Dells."

"OK, Mister Dooley, I'm open to ideas."

When she called him Mister Dooley it was a sign she was peeved; Dooley gave her a sharp look and got himself a glass out of the cabinet. It was too early for the Jameson's but he wanted something; he opened the refrigerator and looked at all the soft drinks and gave up. He got himself a glass of water and drank it, staring out the window over the sink.

"Want to go for a walk?" said Rose.

Dooley turned, startled. "A walk? Where?"

"Just around the neighborhood. Or we could drive over to the forest preserve." She was giving him an expectant look.

"It'll be dark soon."

"OK, forget it." She was looking at the bills again. Dooley was irritated; he'd done something wrong and he wasn't sure what.

He put the glass in the sink. "I have to go out for a while."

• • •

"Laura's off tonight. Monday's her day off."

Dooley scowled at the shaggy-haired bartender, but it was himself he was angry at; why hadn't he called first? "OK," he said. "She be in tomorrow?"

"I hope so," said the barkeep, turning away. Dooley glared after him and left. He went out on to the street and headed for his car, yielding to no one as he cleared a path through the crowd. Sitting in the car, he cursed himself out loud; indecision was not something Dooley experienced very often, and it irritated the hell out of him. Indecision and inefficiency: he had written down her home number in his notebook but left it at home. Dooley couldn't make up his mind: if he was working he should have brought his briefcase; if he wasn't working what the hell was he doing here? Finally he turned the ignition key and pulled out onto North Avenue.

He managed to park within two blocks of the house on Cleveland. It was a warm night with a hint of a breeze, and under the trees it was dark and pleasant on the sidewalk. Dooley calmed down a bit. What he was doing was legitimate, and if it gave him an excuse to talk to Laura Lindbloom again, then that was just a bonus.

He stood on her porch and put his thumb to the doorbell. A few seconds went by and from somewhere far above him a voice called out "Who is it?" He stepped down to the sidewalk and looked up at the second-floor windows, but there was no one there. "Dooley?" the voice came again, her voice, with a note of surprise. Dooley scanned the front of the house but couldn't find her. "Up here, in the tower," she called, and then he spotted her, leaning out of the fairytale turret way up at the top of the house, eerily lit by the streetlights below her. She waved at him.

"You got a minute?" Dooley felt stupid, standing there on the sidewalk yelling up at a woman in a tower.

"Sure. Come on up," she said. "Through the studio, in back."

Dooley made his way around to the back and climbed the stairs. The door to the studio was standing open but Dooley knocked anyway; when no one answered he went in. There was a new canvas on the easel, as bad as the last one. A door opened at the far end and the artist came out. "Through there," he said, pointing behind him as he shuffled toward Dooley. He was wearing a T-shirt with a wild pattern of colored splotches and had sprouted a goatee on his chin since Dooley had seen him last. He had a drink in his hand and he looked amused. "She's all yours," he said as he passed.

"Thanks." Dooley felt stupid again, though he couldn't have said why. He went through the door and mounted a flight of creaking spiral stairs he could barely see in the dark. He went up through the warm dusty air, losing track of how many turns he made as he climbed.

He came up into the turret and there she was, just visible in the dark, sitting on a chair in a very short dress, long bare legs crossed. The turret was maybe eight feet in diameter, and if it had ever had windows they had been removed; it was open to the weather except for the roof above, and a gentle breeze came through, stirring Laura's unbound hair just a little. There was no light except what came up from the street, and from all over the vast city rose a deep hollow murmur. "Hi," said Laura.

Dooley had been just standing there breathing a bit heavily from the climb, taking in the view. He could see all the way south across rooftops to the Loop, lit up in the distance. He cleared his throat and said, "Nice place you got up here."

"Thanks. Business or pleasure?"

Dooley had spotted a chair opposite hers and he sat on it. He was about level with the tops of the trees, and if he leaned out a bit he could look down through the tossing leaves to the street where parked cars gleamed in the lamplight. "Business," he said.

"I won't offer you a drink, then." Ice cubes clinked and gave off faint reflections as she moved the glass.

Dooley thought about it for a second and said, "I'm here on business, but I'm off duty."

"Does that mean you'll have a gin and tonic?"

Dooley never drank gin, but he said, "Sure."

Laura uncrossed her legs. "I'll have to go down and get you a glass."

"Don't bother, then. I don't need a drink."

She hesitated and said, "So we can share. If you don't mind my cooties."

Dooley wondered if this was normal among artistic people. "I don't mind."

Laura reached into a bucket sitting on the floor. It seemed to contain everything she needed: two bottles and some ice cubes sloshing around in the bottom. She topped up the glass and handed it to Dooley. "How's that?"

Dooley drank. It tasted strange to him but not bad. "It's fine." He handed it back to her.

"So. I read all about it in the paper," Laura said.

"Yeah. They seem to have scooped up everybody."

"Not everybody. I didn't see any mention of your colleague. What was his name—Schroeder?"

"That'll be a little harder," said Dooley.

"Is anything going to happen to him?"

"Not that I can guarantee."

There was a silence after that. Laura drank and handed him the glass. Dooley just held it for a while, not sure what the etiquette was. Finally Laura said, "I guess I should thank you again."

"I think it's the other way around. Thanks."

He made out a graceful shrug in the dark. "Did you just come over here to say thanks?"

Dooley took a drink. "No. I came over here for a couple of things. To make sure you knew about the raid for one, and then to ask you a few more questions." He held out the glass to her, but she waved it off.

"Keep it. I've had enough. I've been sitting up here all evening drinking with Danny. Maybe that's why I'm confused. Are you going to be on duty when you're asking me these questions, or off duty?"

Dooley set the glass on the sill. "I don't know. Was I on duty the night we went and got Jenny, or off duty? Seems like the line got blurred right at the start somehow."

"Well, maybe that's OK. Maybe that's what had to happen."

"Maybe. Anyway, I really came over here to ask you some more questions about Tommy Spain."

A few seconds went by, and Laura said, "You lost me there. I had to think who we're talking about."

"You remember? You told me Sally had gone out with him when she was at the Playboy Club."

"Yeah, I remember. What's going on?"

"Nothing's going on. That's the problem. The case has been declared cleared. Everybody's happy. Except me."

"You don't think they got the right guys?"

"I think they were sold a bill of goods."

Dooley sat and listened to the soft roar of the city for a while. Laura said, "I thought somebody confessed."

"He confessed to a lot less than killing Sally. And the guy he says killed her isn't around to defend himself."

"So what makes you think it's all bullshit?"

"It's just a hunch. But my hunches have twenty years of experience behind them. When I get a hunch, there's a reason."

"Who do you think did it?"

"I could give you a guess, but the name wouldn't mean anything to you. The important question is why. If I can find out why, I might have something to take to a judge. But I've got other cases to clear and a boss who says this one's history. That's why I'm here on my own time."

Laura took a deep breath and let it out again. "Wow. That's heavy."

"It's been bothering me."

"What does it have to do with Tommy Spain?"

"I don't know, maybe nothing. But if the story they're selling is that she got killed because of a mobster boyfriend, then maybe that's close to the truth. I just think it was maybe the other one. And you're the only one who's mentioned him."

"OK. What do you need to know?"

"Anything you can remember about Tommy Spain, what Sally told you. In particular, if he ever gave her anything. Money, an envelope, a package, whatever."

She gave it some thought and said, "I don't think so. Not that I recall."

"Did she ever tell you anything about what they talked about? Did she ever discuss his business at all?"

"Not really. Sally wasn't very interested in business."

"Did she get letters from him when he was in Mexico?"

"I don't think so. I remember he called her a couple of times."

"Did you overhear anything interesting? Did she say what he was doing? Did she ever run any errands for him? And was there anyone else she might have confided in?"

"God, I don't know. I'll have to think about it."

"Do that. And let me know." Dooley picked up the gin and tonic and took a drink, then another deeper one. "I'm more of a whiskey man," he said, and put it back down. "But I can see how you could get to like these." He stood up. "I should get going."

Laura said nothing for a long moment, and then she rose, a slim pale figure in the dark. "Be careful on the stairs. More than one person's fallen down those after a couple of drinks."

"I'll be careful." Dooley took a last look around. "It's nice up here. Peaceful."

"I love it up here." She took a step toward him. "Come back. On duty or off."

"OK."

She put out her hand, and he met it, just like he was shaking hands with the mayor, but she held on with both hands and just stood there looking at him. Dooley was uncomfortable for a moment, wanting to pull away, but he decided not to fight it. "Keep it up and you just might start to change my opinion of cops," Laura said.

"Cops are like plumbers. There's good ones and bad ones."

"So you said." She squeezed his hand and let go of it.

Dooley felt a little light-headed; maybe the gin was starting to get to him. "Call me," he said, and started probing for the head of the stairs.

Twenty

Jimmy Hoffa wanted a new trial but they weren't going to give him one; score one for the good guys, thought Dooley. El Salvador and Honduras, which as far as Dooley could remember were somewhere south of Mexico, were fighting a war for reasons Dooley couldn't quite make out. The lull in Viet Nam continued but somehow fifty-six communists and nine Americans had managed to get themselves killed anyway. There was no mention of any Marine units. Dooley went to the sports section and looked at the report of the game he and Frank had gone to: *40,000 see Cubs beat Mets.* Dooley skimmed the article and thought with a brief spasm of envy about the life of a sportswriter. The two teams were going to go at it again today.

The screen door opened and Rose came in from the back yard. Dooley kept his eyes on the paper but listened as she moved around the kitchen, washing her hands, straightening up. He waited for it, and sure enough she stole up behind him and put her arms around his neck, leaning to nuzzle him behind the ear. He shoved the paper away and found one of her hands with his. "Morning," he said.

"Morning. Have a good sleep?"

"Yeah, it was OK."

"I should hope so," she said, releasing him. Dooley was mildly irritated by the coyness of her tone, though he knew he shouldn't be. "It's hot today," she said. "And muggy. A good day to sit indoors in the air conditioning."

"Murder weather. We'll be busy tonight." Dooley regretted the brutality as soon as he said it; she didn't deserve it.

Rose ran a hand through his hair. He looked up to see her face gone grave. She caressed him again, and now she smiled a little. For a second Dooley caught a glimpse of a younger and happier Rose. "I wish you could stay with me," she said. "The kids are both working today. We'd have the house to ourselves."

"That would be nice," said Dooley, trying to sound enthusiastic. He managed a smile.

Dooley was having trouble with his wife's affection this morning because his conscience was bothering him a little: late the previous night he had come home, gone up to his room and dug in a drawer till he'd found a rubber and then woken his wife up, ruthlessly and without a word. She'd said nothing the whole time except to whisper that she loved him when it was all over. He'd lain there holding her, feeling relieved but ashamed; he'd been thinking of Laura Lindbloom the whole time.

• • •

Lieber and Rodkin had an office on LaSalle street with all the other lawyers, a modest suite with a receptionist and stenos working behind a window that opened off a small unpretentious anteroom with a couple of chairs. Dooley stood at the window and waited for a pretty redhead to stop typing. She finished a line and looked up. "May I help you?"

"Mr. Rodkin's expecting me."

"Who may I say is waiting?"

"Tell him Dooley's here."

"Have a seat, Mr. Dooley." She reached for a phone.

Dooley sat down and pawed through the magazines: *Time, Look, U.S. News & World Report.* He was surprised any of Rodkin and Lieber's clients could read. He gave up on the magazines and sat there thinking about lawyers and their ethics.

Inside the office a man in a tan sport jacket came into view and halted at a desk near the rear. He had gray wiry hair and a nose that went a long way toward his chin. He pulled a wad of bills out of the inside pocket of the jacket and counted off a few of them onto the desk. A middle-aged woman in glasses stacked them and wrote out a receipt. Dooley was trying to place the man; he'd seen him somewhere not too long before. By the time the man was passing through the anteroom on his way out, giving him a careful eye, Dooley had remembered. He'd seen him at the Armory Lounge, sitting at the bar. Dooley wasn't surprised; when it came to defending hoodlums, Lieber and Rodkin had the franchise in Chicago.

"Mr. Rodkin can see you now." The redhead was standing in the open doorway looking at him. Dooley got up and followed her through the front office to a door in the far corner. She knocked, leaned in and announced him, then waved him in.

Rodkin stood up as Dooley came in and reached across the desk to shake his hand. He was the type of man who had a perpetual tan, with alert dark eyes and straight black hair slicked back with Vitalis or something similar. He wore a dark blue suit with a thin burgundy tie, and the suit looked good on him. He was well into his forties but he looked like a man who might give you a good game of tennis. "Officer Dooley? Jerry Rodkin," he said. His grip was vigorous.

"Good to meet you," said Dooley. "Thanks for fitting me in. I know you're busy."

"You fellows keep us busy." He gave Dooley a big white smile, settling back onto his chair. "Now. Why do you think you need to talk to Tommy Spain?"

Dooley gave him a cool look. "I'm working a homicide. He was close to the victim."

"Who's the victim?"

"Sally Kotowski."

Rodkin froze, then frowned. "Wait a minute."

"I know. We charged Billy Gaines for the abduction. I understand he's a client of yours, too."

Rodkin nodded. "That's right."

"Well, I'm a little surprised you let him plead, because I think he was coerced into confessing."

Rodkin's expression was wary. "By the police?"

"No. By the people who really killed Sally."

Rodkin said nothing for a few seconds, and Dooley sat there looking him in the eye and enjoying the effect. Dooley didn't know how lawyers' minds worked, but he was fairly sure that Jerome Rodkin could have shot holes in the case against Billy Gaines if anybody had wanted him to.

"I'm afraid you're a little off base on this one," Rodkin said. "Gaines laid it all out for me. He helped Steuben abduct her, and then he got cold feet. Give him credit for that at least. There was nothing I could do. The man wants to go to jail because it's preferable to winding up the way Steuben did. I just got him the best deal I could."

"I'm sure you did a hell of a job. But some things have come up that make us think maybe Gaines isn't telling the whole story, and I think Tommy Spain may have something to say about it. That's why I want to talk to him. You're his lawyer, and I'm betting you can get in touch with him down there in Texarkana. You get him on the phone for me, you can listen in if you want. If one of your clients can help out another, it seems to me you'd have to go for it."

Rodkin frowned to show he was thinking about it. Dooley kept his face a total blank. He figured he had nailed Rodkin. If he refused to put him in touch with Spain, it was tantamount to refusing to help Gaines. He had to go through the motions of doing his best for his client. "I'd need to know what these things are that have come up," Rodkin said.

"You'll hear them when Spain does." Dooley wasn't about to give anything away, not even the fact that he didn't really have anything to give away. Rodkin wasn't used to having to make tough calls, apparently; he looked at Dooley for a long moment with no trace of the jaunty expression left. "Give me a day to think about it," he said.

Dooley almost laughed, thinking of the phone calls that would start as soon as he left the office; that was what a lawyer meant by thinking. He stood up.

"Sure thing." He tossed his card on the desk. "Call me at the Area. There's always someone there to take a message. We never close."

• • •

"Al Weis? Who the hell is Al Weis?" Dooley snapped his briefcase shut and took his jacket off the back of the chair. It was about a hundred degrees on the third floor and he had broken a sweat just sitting there.

"The Mets had him at shortstop today. I never heard of the guy, but he hit a three-run homer off Selma."

"Ouch."

"Yeah. You can't go giving up homers to backup shortstops."

"Strange things happen in baseball. He just had his moment, that's all. Watch, the guy will never hit another homer."

"One was enough. What's on our plate today?"

"Knocking on doors. McCone wants more witnesses for that knifing on Washtenaw last week. He says the canvass they did wasn't worth shit."

"Who caught it?"

"Second watch."

Olson lowered his voice. "Which guys?"

Dooley waited till they were on the stairs to answer. "Carlson and Pasquesi."

"What a surprise."

"Yeah." There were good dicks and bad dicks, and everybody knew who the lazy ones were. You could be a bad copper and still go a long way if you had a good Chinaman.

Outside the sun was brutal, even at four-thirty in the afternoon. It was a little better in the car, with air moving past them, but it was still the kind of day that made tempers fray and minds snap. "Hot time in the old town tonight," said Olson.

"It'll be fun."

"You hear about those guys down in Brighton Park? The ones that beat that colored guy to death?"

Dooley nodded. "Makes you proud, doesn't it?"

"Jesus. The poor bastard picked a bad place to stop and fix his tailpipe, didn't he?"

"Assholes like that, they just make things worse for everyone." Dooley hoped they all got the chair: he hated them for making him feel ashamed.

"Yeah, you know the same thing's gonna happen to the next white guy that breaks down in a black neighborhood."

"Things are bad."

"It's the heat."

"It's more than the heat. The country's going to hell. The society's all screwed up."

"Jesus, Mike. It ain't that bad."

"Yes it is. Where the hell you been? Riots, assassinations, this fucking war. Ever since Kennedy got shot, it's been nuts."

"It's a crazy time, yeah. But we'll be OK."

Dooley shook his head. "I don't know what you base that on, partner. I really don't."

Olson drove for a moment and said, "Well, hell. Here I was in a good mood, and you had to go and spoil it."

"That's me," said Dooley. "The life of the party."

• • •

It was a sacred rule in a cop's house that you didn't wake up the old man without a hell of a good reason, so when Dooley came awake with the rapping on his door his first thought was that something was burning or someone was bleeding. "What is it?" he called, swinging his feet to the floor.

"The astronauts, Pop." Frank sounded breathless through the door.

Dooley just stared at the door, not quite awake. "The astronauts?"

"Yeah."

Dooley couldn't believe his ears. "What about 'em?"

"They're about to blast off."

Dooley toppled back onto the bed. "They don't need my help."

"Pop, the countdown's starting. Come on, you're gonna miss it!"

Dooley gave up; he rubbed his face with his hands and sighed. "I'll be right down."

He put on his bathrobe and went to piss before he tackled the stairs. Rose and the kids were in the living room staring at the TV. Dooley got there in time to see the usual shaky camera view of a trail of smoke up in the sky. "They didn't blow up, huh?"

"Oh, Michael. Don't be morbid."

"They're on their way to the *moon*, Daddy."

"This is history, Pop."

"I've seen history," said Dooley. "I've seen more history than I wanted to."

"But this is bigger than *Columbus.* Nobody's ever been to the moon."

"What do we want to go to the moon for? We got enough cheese up in Wisconsin."

Rose reached for his hand. "Oh, come on, Michael. You have to admit it's exciting."

Dooley stood there and watched, holding Rose's hand, while the camera view got shakier and shakier, the vapor trail jiggling as it slanted across the TV screen. "OK, I'm excited," he said. "I think I'll go have some coffee to calm me down."

• • •

The message slip said simply *Rodkin* followed by a phone number and the words *after six.* Dooley slipped it into an inside pocket. "Ready to go?" he said.

"It ain't gonna get any cooler up here." Olson had signed for the car and stood jingling the keys.

Dooley snapped his briefcase shut and stood up. "Let's go find Mr. Easton." Dooley wanted to talk to a man who had given him a statement about the death of his business partner back in May that was starting to look like a lie in the light of some patient work done by a dick on second watch.

"Fucker did it again," Olson said, steering south on Damen through overheated traffic.

"Who did what?"

"That Al Weis. He hit another homer today."

"You're shitting me."

"No. They chased Jenkins in the second and beat us. The lead's down to three and a half games."

"Ah, Jesus. Don't sweat it."

"I tell you, they're making me nervous."

"The Mets are playing over their heads. When your backup shortstop is your power hitter, you're in trouble. I'm telling you, in September the Mets'll be in third place. The Cardinals are going to make a run at us, you watch. That'll be the real race, if there is one."

"We'll see. The Mets have a lot of pitching."

"You need some bats to win. Relax, it's our year."

The business that was running on fifty percent fewer owners since May was a machine tool concern with a plant on Fullerton just west of the river. Mr. Easton was not in his office, and his secretary could not say where he might be found. Dooley checked the file and they drove to Easton's home in Lincolnwood. He wasn't at home either, but his wife told them the names of a couple of likely bars to check. They drew a blank in both of them and decided it was time for dinner. The trail had brought them back down into the city and they stopped at a diner on Elston where the food was reliable and the service friendly to policemen. "Order me the pot roast," Dooley said, shoving the menu away and sliding out of the booth.

He found a pay phone in the back of the place and shoved in a dime. He dialed the number Rodkin had left. A secretary answered, maybe the pretty redhead, and Dooley asked for the lawyer. He only had to wait a few seconds before Rodkin came on the line. "What's the word?" said Dooley.

"I talked to Tommy Spain today."

"Will he talk?"

"Not to you."

"What, not even about Sally?"

"He says it's too damn bad about Sally but he doesn't know anything about it. He hadn't talked to her in more than two years."

Dooley leaned on the wall. "Man, I'd really like to hear that from him."

"He won't talk to you. It's hard enough for me to get him on the phone. He's in a federal prison. It takes all kinds of special arrangements to set up an interview, and he has to consent. If you're not even pursuing a current investigation you don't have a prayer."

Dooley didn't want to take Jerome Rodkin's word for anything, but he wasn't sure what he could do. "Thanks for all your help," he said, and hung up.

• • •

Dooley could feel it coming; he'd been waiting for it all day, all evening. All week, really. Everybody had, all over the city. Dooley doused the light in the kitchen, pushed open the screen door and went out into the back yard, glass in hand. After the air conditioning it was like stepping into an oven. He walked to the center of his yard and stood there in the dark, listening to the trees rustling in the rising wind, looking up into nothing, pitch black.

Somewhere up there the astronauts were on the way to the moon; Dooley hoped they made it but he couldn't get excited about it the way his kids had. He took a drink of whiskey and held the cool wet glass against his jugular. He had started to sweat again; there must be a twenty-degree temperature difference between inside and outside. A gust of wind came swirling through the yard, cooler now. The lid was going to blow off, and soon.

Dooley turned to look at his darkened house. You could take this week and shove it, as far as he was concerned. Here it came: the first ghostly flash of lightning; the first rumble of thunder. A few fat drops of rain hit Dooley in the face. He drained his glass and headed for the house. To hell with this week, thought Dooley. To hell with all of it.

Twenty-one

"MICHAEL, DO YOU want some coffee?" Rose yelled down the basement steps.

"I want to get this rug out of the swamp here, that's what I want. I could use a hand."

"I can't find Frank. I think he went out."

"Figures." Dooley swore under his breath and bent down to tug his pants legs back up above his knees. He was ankle-deep in cold water in what he liked to think of as his rec room, and even though none of the furniture down here was worth a damn, it was still an enormous pain in the ass every time water came in. This one was a doozy; Dooley hadn't seen water like this in his basement in years. He swore again and gave up; the water would drain out eventually and he would put the kids to work hauling things up to dry out in the sun. The panelling would just rot a little more around the bottom. To hell with it all.

He went upstairs and dried his feet and stood at the kitchen window drinking coffee. The headline in the paper lying on the table said *APOLLO LIFTS OFF FOR MOON*. It was another work day for Dooley; the astronauts might be on their way to the moon, but there were still cases to be cleared, cases waiting to happen. Right now all over the city people were scheming, brooding, cheating, stealing, making up their minds and losing them, setting in motion chains of events that would wind up with Dooley standing over a warm corpse. He hadn't slept well, listening to the storm and thinking about his basement filling up, and he wished he could go back to bed. He showered and dressed and strapped on his holster.

"You're leaving early," Rose said. "Court again?"

"Just trying to get a head start," Dooley said. "Looking for a guy."

"Be careful." She said it just about every day when he left. Today she came and put her arms around his neck and kissed him on the lips. Dooley knew he ought to be glad, seeing her interest in this part of their marriage revive a little, but the fact that it wasn't her that he wanted so badly made the whole thing confusing. "I'll be careful," he said.

There was flooding all over the Northwest Side; Dooley saw rugs hanging over railings, driveways full of sodden cardboard boxes. There was water standing under the viaducts on Elston and he had to nose through it slowly, hoping he didn't kill the engine. It had stopped raining but there was more to come, from the look of the sky, and the traffic hissed cautiously along wet streets.

The First Ward Streets and Sanitation garage was on Grand Avenue where it bent northwest, just west of Western. Dooley parked and walked in through an open overhead door. In a corner of the garage was a desk, and behind the desk was a fat man reading a newspaper. He looked up as Dooley came across the oily concrete floor, and the closer Dooley got the lower his thick black eyebrows went. "Afternoon," said Dooley.

"Yeah?" The fat man could have told him to get lost and the message wouldn't have been any clearer.

Dooley was used to it all. "You the receptionist?" he said.

The chair creaked as the fat man leaned back slowly, raising his chin. "Do I look like a fuckin' receptionist?"

Dooley stared him down. "I guess you'll have to do. I'm looking for Tony Bellisario."

The fat man sized Dooley up and appeared to decide there was just a chance this was somebody he had to pay attention to. He said, "He ain't here."

"Where is he?"

"He's out on a job."

"OK, where can I find him?"

"I told you, he's out on a job."

"And you don't know where? You don't have a log book, a job sheet?"

The fat man gave Dooley a look that said he was getting close to his limit. He pointed out the open door onto the street. "You seen the state things are in out there? We'll be running our asses off till midnight. There's no way I could tell you where he is right now, and even if I could he'd be gone by the time you got there."

Dooley could see how this was going, but he couldn't resist taking it a little farther. "How do you get a hold of him in an emergency?"

"He never has emergencies."

Dooley smiled, just a little, just enough to show the fat man he knew the score. "OK. Give him this, will you?" He pulled his card out of a pocket. "Tell him to call me. Tell him it's about his brother Robert."

The fat man gave Dooley a sharp look and tossed the card on the desk. "I'll tell him."

Dooley had known from the start that the odds of finding a mob-connected Streets and San worker actually on the job in the First Ward were slim, but he'd allowed for that. He turned to go, stopped, and said, "And tell him I don't give a damn how he spends his days."

"He's out on a job," the fat man said flatly, pulling the paper toward him.

"Sure," said Dooley. "Keeping his feet dry, I bet."

• • •

The apartment building was on Washtenaw, north of Division. It was a three-flat and the tipster had given nothing but the address. Dooley and Olson parked half a block away and walked back. Two young Puerto Rican guys leaning on a Dodge Charger and smoking gave them a long sullen look as they went past. It wasn't actually raining but it had been threatening all day, and Dooley was glad the weather was keeping the crowd down; normally on a hot summer evening there would be a lot of people out on a street like this, and the word would run fast: cops on the block.

In the entranceway of the building Dooley looked at the mailboxes and saw a Rodriguez, a Benitez, and a Campos. "How's your Spanish?" he said.

Behind him Olson said, "I had it in high school. If we need to know where the library is or what's for lunch, I can handle it."

"Can you say, 'We're looking for a worthless piece of shit named Wilfredo Cruz'?"

"Gimme a minute. I think *mierda* is shit."

"Well, don't worry. If we're lucky we won't have to do too much talking."

Olson nodded at the mailboxes. "So what do we do, roll the dice?"

Dooley shook his head. "We make some educated guesses. Who was the caller?"

"Didn't leave a name. Anonymous female."

"OK, what's the most common reason a female might drop a dime on somebody?"

Olson looked blank for a second or two and then said, "He ditched her."

"Right. So who we looking for here?"

Olson smiled. "The new girlfriend."

"That's enough to start with." Dooley opened the street door. "You camp out right here, just in case. If Wilfredo comes through that door, grab him."

"Where are you going?"

"To look in some windows." Dooley went outside and turned into the gangway. He walked through to the rear of the building, where the wooden back steps descended to the alley. He stood for a moment watching and listening to Spanish music coming from somewhere a couple of buildings away; then he mounted the stairs.

Dooley knew that you could see a lot more looking in people's back windows than you could in the front; he also knew how much a trash can could tell you. He figured it was not a sure bet that Wilfredo Cruz, thief, pusher, and, according to three eyewitnesses, a killer, was at home at five o'clock on a Thursday afternoon, but you never knew, especially as he was a fugitive in hiding. All Dooley really wanted was to establish who lived where in this building, preferably without tipping anybody off that a couple of middle-aged guys in suits were interested.

On the first landing he looked through a six-inch gap between lace curtains into a tidy kitchen with vegetables sitting out on the counter, green bananas, limes, little red peppers. He went up to the second floor. Here there were no curtains on the kitchen window at all, and he could see a sink with a stack of dirty dishes in it and two rum bottles, one empty and one half-full, standing on the counter. He stood looking into the empty kitchen for a moment and then stepped to the trash can standing by the door. He pried off the lid as quietly as he could and stood looking down into a welter of greasy paper, banana peels, and another couple of empty bottles. He reached into the can and shifted a couple of things, revealing a crushed Tampax box and an old copy of *Cosmopolitan*. He replaced the lid and took out his handkerchief.

Dooley was wiping his fingers and looking through the window, plotting his next move, when Wilfredo Cruz walked into the kitchen and swiped the half-full bottle of rum off the counter. Dooley had frozen, but Cruz came toward the window, taking a glass out of the sink on the way and slumping on a chair at the table, facing the window. He was a skinny street brawler with a yellowish complexion and a wild head of wiry black hair, and he didn't look as if life in hiding was agreeing with him. He splashed some rum into the glass with a sullen bored expression on his face and then raised the glass to drink and looked right at Dooley.

Dooley had had just enough time to figure out what to do; he smiled at Wilfredo and reached out to put his thumb on the doorbell. Wilfredo jerked to his feet with the sound of the buzzer and spilled rum on the table slamming the glass down; he took to his heels with a wide-eyed look, knocking the chair over as he ran.

Dooley had a choice to make and he made it fast; he guessed Wilfredo was not a deep thinker, and he would head straight out the front, not stopping to ask himself if the Chicago police were just possibly smart enough to post men at both doors. The only real question was whether he'd stop to grab something to shoot with on the way. Dooley had kept his thumb on the buzzer just to give Wilfredo a good push toward the front, but now he took it off and started sprinting down the stairs. He had no way of letting Olson know what was going on and he could only hope that his partner's fifteen years of street experience were enough schooling to make him ready for a desperate man busting out the door in his face.

He tore up the gangway listening for shouts, for shots, for breaking glass or screaming witnesses, but he heard nothing. He came out of the gangway in time to hear the street door of the apartment rattle as something slammed against it from the inside. Dooley tore his revolver out and was up the steps and at the door reaching for the handle before the sight registered: Wilfredo Cruz's face pressed against the glass, one cheek and half his mouth grotesquely flattened, his hands splayed out on either side, one of them with a gun in it, Olson's .38 jammed into his neck.

• • •

"I blew it," said Dooley. "Twenty years on the job and I pull a fucking recruit trick like that. Sorry, partner."

"Jeez, Mike. Don't worry about it. Who could have known he was gonna walk into the kitchen just then? Anyway, it worked out perfect." Olson was still high from the bust: making an arrest was the most fun a homicide dick could ever have, and collaring an armed fugitive on the fly was like running a kickoff back for a TD. Olson had talked a mile a minute on the way back to the Area, trailing the wagon that had come to pick up Wilfredo and his hostess. The adrenaline was just now starting to ebb.

"You want to go have first crack at him?" said Dooley. "He hasn't asked for a lawyer yet. All he's said is, his girlfriend can alibi him."

"What, the new one?"

Dooley grinned. "No, she's too happy to be rid of him. She's just trying to cover her own ass now. I think he's counting on the old one. Rosalia."

"Oh, that's beautiful. I think Wilfredo may be in for a surprise." Olson pushed away from the desk. "Sure, I'll be happy to tackle him first."

"Let me know when you get tired of listening to bullshit." Dooley had paperwork to do, but first he looked at his messages. One said *Tony Bellisario* followed by a phone number. Dooley checked his watch and then sat down at the phone and dialed the number.

"Yeah," said a voice that sounded like a truck rolling on gravel.

"Tony Bellisario, please."

"Who wants him?"

"Tell him Dooley."

There was a thump at the other end of the line. A few seconds later a man just a little younger and in just a little better condition said, "Yeah."

"Tony?"

"Yeah. You the copper?"

"That's right. I wanted to talk to you about what happened to your brother Robert."

"You gonna tell me you arrested the guy that killed him?"

"No."

"Then what the fuck do I have to talk to you about?"

"Maybe the guy that got him killed."

After a couple of seconds Bellisario said, "You talking about Spain?"

"Yeah, I'm interested in Tommy Spain."

"Why you calling me?"

"Johnny Puig gave me your name."

"Pooch, huh? How come?"

"He says you're the guy to talk to about Spain."

For a moment there was nothing but murmurs and faint clinks in the background. "Why would I want to do that? My beef with Spain is family business."

Dooley knew he had to play the line carefully or he was going to lose the fish. "I don't really care about your beef with Spain. I'm trying to clear a case where I think somebody got killed just for knowing Tommy Spain. So I need to know what it is about Tommy Spain that gets people killed."

At the other end of the line there was a laugh that sounded like somebody taking one in the gut. "Why the fuck would I tell you anything?"

"Because a woman got killed. In a bad way. And I don't think that's anything for the Outfit to be proud of."

"Well, I got news for you, cop. The Outfit don't give a shit about your opinion."

Dooley just waited; he'd made his case and he wasn't going to plead.

Finally Bellisario said, "When?"

"How about tomorrow? Early afternoon. You name the spot."

"OK. Two o'clock, Arco Insurance, 4724 Irving Park." Bellisario hung up with a clunk.

• • •

Dooley wondered what kind of coverage you could get at Arco Insurance; the syndicate had a million fronts, and insurance agencies were one good one. The overhead was minimal; all you needed was an office with a phone and a desk or two, maybe a back room; you could run a juice loan operation out of there and if you had somebody halfway legit up front you could even sell a little insurance on the side.

Arco occupied a small storefront in an old brick building near the Six Corners, where Milwaukee came slashing down on the diagonal to meet Irving and Cicero. Dooley had to park legally, a block away; he was doing this one on his own time and in his own car. He pushed into Arco Insurance and saw a man with slicked-back hair in a gray suit sitting behind a desk, smoking and talking on the phone, leaning back in his chair and swiveling idly back and forth as he talked. The top button of the shirt was undone and the tie was loosened; Dooley got a quick impression it was a relaxed sort of office.

He made eye contact, and the man on the phone raised his chin a half inch to show he'd seen him, but that was all the greeting he got. Dooley stood and watched him smoke, phone to his ear. It didn't take Dooley long to figure out that the man was talking to a woman; the smirk he wore and the way he murmured into the phone gave it away. Dooley gave him another five seconds and then leaned over the desk into tie-grabbing range. "I'm here to see Bellisario."

The man scowled at him and jutted with his chin toward a hallway that went toward the back. Dooley followed a faint tinny trail of jazz trumpet down the hallway and looked through an open door into another office. This was where the work got done, whatever it was: there were two desks covered with papers, telephones, a safe. The music was coming from a transistor radio that stood on the desk to his right, and smoke was coming from a cigar stuck in the mouth of the bulldog behind the desk.

"Dooley?" the bulldog said around the cigar.

"Yeah. You Bellisario?"

"Sit down." Bellisario might have made five-eight if he'd stood up, but he would tip the scales at close to two hundred. Some of it might have been muscle once; he had the hands of a laboring man at the ends of his thick hairy forearms. He had black eyes that had seen most of it, a little gray hair left on his temples and thick lips that glistened from working the cigar. He watched Dooley pull up a chair and said, "Kinda early in the day for you, ain't it? Third shift don't start till what, four?"

Dooley settled on the chair and crossed his legs. "I'm supposed to be impressed? Unfortunately it doesn't surprise me that a guy with Outfit connections can find somebody in the department to tell him all about me."

Bellisario shrugged. "I don't give a shit if you're impressed."

"Fine. Whoever you talked to, I hope they told you what kind of cop I am. I do one thing. I clear homicides. I don't do extortion or fraud or gambling or ghost payrollers or anything else. I don't care how you make your money as long as you don't kill anybody. We on the same page?"

"Sure. I'm just wondering why you're coming to talk to me outside of business hours."

"We log a lot of overtime."

"Is that right?" Bellisario puffed on the cigar, his eyes crinkling in amusement. "Must be a hell of a big case. Who got killed?"

"A woman named Sally Kotowski."

The music meandered for a while, going nowhere the way jazz always did. Bellisario said, "I get it. You don't buy what they came up with."

"No, I don't buy it."

"What the hell's it to you?"

"Call it professional pride."

"So maybe I don't mind the way it got stitched up. How's that grab you?"

"Maybe you don't. So you tell me a bunch of lies or just keep your mouth shut. But then again, maybe you've got some professional pride, too."

Bellisario looked at Dooley for a long time, smoking his stogie and listening to the thin fuzzy sound of the radio. After a minute or so he said, "You're not gonna clear every case they give you, pal. You're not supposed to. You gotta eat some of them."

"Sally Kotowski got tortured to death. Somebody beat her face to a pulp and then shoved an icepick up her. I'm not going to eat that one. And if you don't mind the way it got stitched up, the Outfit's a worse bunch of pricks than I thought."

Bellisario laughed, the same grunt he'd made over the phone. He tapped ash off the end of his cigar into a glass ashtray and said, "You're hoping I got a soft spot, huh? You might be wasting your time."

"I'll take what I can get," said Dooley.

Bellisario put the cigar in his mouth and reached for the radio. He nudged up the volume just a notch and leaned forward across the desk. "If Spain had anything to do with it, you got trouble. I'll tell you that."

Dooley put his elbows on the desk. "I got trouble any way you look at it. What do you mean?"

"I mean you're going right to the top. You know what happened to my brother, right?"

"All I know is, Puig told me he got hit after Spain questioned him about a robbery."

"Yeah. With the lie detector. Bobby had been in on a job out on the West Side, they stole a bunch of furs. And somebody snitched. It wasn't Bobby, he swore it to me, and I believe him, my brother wasn't no snitch. But Spain hooked him up to the machine and got him rattled and got him started lying about who he'd talked to and who he hadn't and then, bam. A week later he gets shot, in his garage. And you know what? Later they found out it was someone else that talked. I went to talk to a few people, I says you can't hit a guy just because this asshole Spain says he's a snitch. And all's I heard was, keep your mouth shut, whatever Spain does is because Momo tells him to do it. So I kept my mouth shut. But I haven't forgot nothing."

"Momo. That's Giancana?"

"Yeah. You talk about Spain, you're talking about Giancana. Spain's his boy."

"I thought Giancana was old news."

Bellisario shook his head, sucking on the cigar. "Giancana ain't finished, whatever they say. He still pulls a lot of weight, even from Mexico. And Spain's his boy."

"But Spain's in jail."

"Shit. For how long, a couple more years? You think Tommy Spain can't hack a little vacation in a federal can? He's just resting. And then him and Momo are gonna be back, you can count on it. And then the shit's gonna hit the fuckin' fan around here."

"What do you mean?"

"I mean there's gonna be a fight over who gets to be top dog. You think fuckin' Philly Alderisio can run the Outfit? He's a shooter, a head-breaker. Philly thinks with his fists. You need a guy with brains in the top spot."

"Like Tommy Spain?"

Bellisario shrugged. "If Giancana can't do it himself, that's who he'll back. They're just lyin' in the weeds now. And meanwhile, they still got their friends around here. So if you take on Tommy Spain, you're taking on some heavyweight clout."

Dooley watched him work on the cigar for a few seconds. "OK, so how does being Tommy Spain's girlfriend get a woman killed?"

"How the fuck would I know? Maybe she knew something, she was gonna snitch. Or he thought she was."

"The way they worked her over, it looked like they wanted something. Could she have been hiding something for Spain? Money?"

"Spain's got money all over the world. He wouldn't leave nothing worth getting excited about with a woman."

"How about information? Blackmail. People tell me Spain was good at that. Could he have given her documents or something?"

"Shit, we can sit here all fuckin' day and make guesses. All's I can tell you is that Tommy Spain is a cold-blooded son of a bitch, and if he had to push his own mother over a cliff to get an angle, he'd give her a kiss on the cheek and over she'd go. You know what I'd do if I were you?"

"What?"

"Forget all about it. Go after the spade muggers, go home to the wife and kids at night. You ain't gonna bring Sally back to life."

Dooley was starting to get tired of that line of thinking. "They ever find out who killed your brother?"

Bellisario peered at him through a wisp of smoke. "I know who killed my brother."

"He still walking around?"

"Yeah."

"And that's OK with you?"

"He was just following orders. I can live with that. Far as Spain goes, I'm patient."

"Yeah, you said you hadn't forgotten anything. Well, I'm having trouble forgetting Sally."

Bellisario made the end of the cigar glow. He blew smoke at Dooley and said, "Then you're gonna need a hell of a lot of luck."

Dooley stared at him through the smoke. He pushed away from the desk and stood up. "I'll take my chances."

Bellisario let him get to the door before he stopped him. "You heard of a guy named Arnold Swallow?"

"I don't think so."

"He was Spain's partner, back in the old days. He's a sergeant in Vice now, on Rush Street. He knows a lot about Tommy Spain."

"Will he talk to me?"

"I doubt it." Bellisario peered at Dooley for a second and then smiled. "Not unless you mention a broad named Janet that lives in an apartment on Goethe Street where Swallow goes for an hour or two a couple of times a week and where the rent gets paid by one of the top syndicate guys that don't get there as often as he used to. Just don't tell him where you heard it."

Dooley stood there for a second wondering, and then he nodded once. "Thanks."

"Don't mention it." Bellisario put the cigar back in his mouth. "And I mean that."

Twenty-two

"ISN'T THERE A ball game on?" Dooley stood in the doorway of his living room, looking at the television screen, where a man with a crew cut was explaining something to Walter Cronkite. Rose and Frank sat side by side on the couch, and Kathleen was sprawled on the floor. Nobody answered him; Kathleen looked up at him as if he had spoken in Chinese. Finally Frank said, "Pop, they're about to land on the moon."

Dooley said, "Don't give me that. The moon isn't even up yet."

Nobody thought that was funny, apparently; Dooley gave up and went back to the kitchen. He had a half-hour to kill before he had to go to work and he was restless. Normally on a Sunday he would take the family out for lunch or over to visit one of his sisters, maybe go to the forest preserve and have a picnic if the weather was nice, but today everyone in the country was in front of their TV set. Dooley had spent some time cleaning up the mess in the basement and then taken a shower; now he didn't know what the hell to do. He sifted through the paper on the kitchen table, looking for something he hadn't read yet. He paused over the front page, looking again at the small headline dwarfed by the big *MOON LANDING TODAY* at the top: *Teddy survives plunge off bridge, woman drowns.* Dooley shook his head. Part of the cop catechism was that everybody lied and the more you had to lose the more you lied, and it had been a long time since he'd read anything in the paper that screamed *lie* like this story about Teddy wandering around in a daze after the accident and then coming to his senses in the morning and calling the police. Dooley knew how Kennedy had spent the night: frantically trying to cover his ass with everything a million bucks and a seat in the Senate could muster. It was too bad, Dooley thought; he'd always kind of liked the kid brother. He figured this would just about take care of the Kennedys. He made himself a cup of freeze-dried coffee and took it out on the patio with the sports section of the paper.

The Cubs were in Philadelphia, playing two; the Phils had beaten them the day before but they were still three and a half games up on the Mets and ten on the Cards, who Dooley still figured were the real threat. The Mets were about due to crash back to earth. The Sox were at home on the South Side and going nowhere. Jackson, the kid slugger for the A's, was knocking balls out of the park at an unbelievable rate and might have a shot at fifty homers. Dooley hadn't followed the big leagues very closely in a long time but he was starting to get a little interested again; it was something to talk about with Frank.

Driving to work, Dooley put the ball game on the radio. The Cubs were handling the Phillies. Santo hit one onto the roof of Connie Mack Stadium and then Vince Lloyd said he had just been handed important news: The Eagle had just touched down on the moon.

Dooley couldn't help himself; he glanced up at the sky.

• • •

The Most Dangerous Man in the World sat slouched on a bench in the hallway outside the emergency room at Henrotin Hospital. He had an impressive Afro on his head and a wary expression on his face. Next to him a woman sat with her hands clasped between her knees, sniffling, her mahogany face glistening with tears, stiff with misery. "He's dead, ain't he?" she said to Dooley in a quavering voice.

"I'm afraid so." Dooley looked from her to the man and back, trying to maintain the sympathetic frown he had cultivated through the years for moments like this. "Can you tell me what happened?"

The woman exchanged a brief look with the man at her side, and Dooley could read it like a book: careful what you say. The woman sniffed again, took a deep breath, and said, "He fell off of the table. I was gonna change him and he fell off of the table when I wasn't looking. He musta landed on his head."

"I see." Dooley gave it a moment, eyes flicking from one to the other. "Would you come with me for a moment, please?" he said to the woman.

"What for?"

"I'd like you to talk to the doctor."

They both started to rise, but Dooley fixed the man to his spot with a look. "Just her."

"I'm comin' with her," said the man.

"You'll get your turn. Right now we need to talk to her alone."

Dooley thought for a second that The Most Dangerous Man in the World was going to make an issue of it, but under the pressure of Dooley's stare he sank back onto the bench. Dooley took the sniffling woman by the arm and led her down the hall. On the way he traded his own significant glance with Olson: watch him.

The baby lay on a gurney under bright lights, stiff and motionless. It had lasted maybe eight months before it had come to the end of the line. The doctors had taken off the filthy diaper but hadn't cleaned off the tiny genitals or the anus. The baby's eyes were half open, a little bit of white showing under the lids. Its hands were frozen in a half-clenched position, its legs splayed out. A little bit of blood showed in its nostrils. The woman stopped before she got to the gurney and sagged, starting to sob; Dooley had to grab her by the arm and pull her gently upright. "I'd like you to listen to the doctor," he said.

The doctor was a slight balding man in his forties and nobody's fool. He had seen a million cases like this one. "Come here," he said gently. "I want you to look at your baby." She trembled but complied, Dooley's hand urging her gently toward the tiny corpse. "Your baby's skull was fractured," the doctor said. "And I don't mean a little crack. I mean it shattered like an eggshell." The woman made a noise, a tearing throaty noise, eyes squeezed shut, but the doctor went on. "This child didn't fall off any table."

"Yes he did." She got the words out between clenched teeth. Her eyes were open now but she was looking at the floor.

The doctor gave Dooley a look and went on. "And then there are these marks. These are burn marks on your baby's stomach. Like from a cigarette."

"Uh-uh," said the woman.

"Oh, and one of his ribs was broken, too," the doctor said, examining a fingernail.

"I don't feel good," said the grieving mother.

Dooley led her to a chair. When he was sure she wasn't going to faint on him, he knelt by her and said quietly, "I need you to tell the truth. We'll protect you if he threatened you."

"I told you the truth." She had begun to rock back and forth, hands clasped between her legs.

Dooley let that pass. "Is that your baby's father sitting out there?"

She shook her head, still rocking. "His father's in jail."

"How long you been living with that gentleman out there?"

"About a month." Her eyes had strayed to a faraway place.

Dooley was afraid he was going to lose her soon. He said, "If we arrest him, he won't able to hurt you. There's no bail on a murder charge."

She finally stopped rocking. She looked at Dooley and he watched her focus come back. She said, "He was trying to watch the astronauts on TV. He swung my baby against the wall 'cause he wouldn't stop crying."

Dooley nodded and rose to his feet. "Thank you."

The doctor watched Dooley make for the door. "You gonna arrest him?"

"You bet," said Dooley. "That's the most dangerous man in the world out there."

"You know him?"

"Sure. You know him, too." Dooley paused by the gurney, taking a last look at the dead baby.

"Who are you talking about?" said the doctor.

"The most dangerous man in the world for kids like this." Dooley looked up at the doctor. "Mama's boyfriend."

• • •

It was all over the paper: *A Giant Leap for Mankind, Armstrong Walks on Moon, Nixon Lauds Apollo Mission, Millions Around World Cheer Moon Landing* Dooley skimmed it all and turned the page. On page three a small headline read *Kennedy to Face Charges in Accident*. Timing, Dooley thought. The guy has great timing.

When Dooley finished the paper he got up from the kitchen table and reached into the pocket of his jacket hanging on the back of the chair. He pulled out a notebook and went to the phone. He took the receiver off the hook but had to stand there for a minute staring at the number in the notebook before he made up his mind and started to dial.

Dooley was not a great fan of the FBI; he'd never been able to get the FBI to give him the time of day, and every cop he knew said the same. There was the public face, where everybody smiled at the cameras and talked about cooperation, and there was the real world, where the coppers considered the feds to be arrogant prima donnas and the feds thought the cops were all in the mob's pocket. Dooley was a grown-up and he knew both sides had a point.

He also knew he had to think long and hard about going to the prima donnas on this one: he hated to give them one more reason to feel superior, but if anyone had an incentive to take another look at Sally's killing it was them. Somebody answered the phone at the other end and Dooley asked for Norm Gustafson. He had to wait for a little while with the phone to his ear, looking out the kitchen window at his yellowing lawn, but after a minute or so he was put through.

"Dooley," said Gustafson, as if he was trying to place the name. "Are you the Dooley that was in the superintendent's office a few years back?"

There were a dozen Dooleys in the department; Dooley knew half of them. "No relation. I'm at Area Six, in Homicide."

"Homicide, huh? How can I help you?"

"I wanted to ask you a few questions about a guy you put in jail last year."

"Who are we talking about?"

"Tommy Spain."

"Spain? He was just in town the other day facing the music on some local charges, wasn't he?"

"Yeah. I missed him, though. I didn't know he was coming in." The second he said it Dooley knew he'd made a mistake; he could practically hear Gustafson's eyes rolling, listening to a dumb CPD flatfoot admitting a screw-up. "To tell you the truth, I didn't really get interested in him until he had left again."

"What is it you need to know?"

"Well, we had a girl killed a few weeks back and it turns out she was Spain's ex-girlfriend. That's the kind of thing that gets my attention."

"I can imagine."

"I was hoping I could talk to Spain about it. Only there's no way in hell the department's going to fly me down to Texarkana. I tried to go through his lawyer, but I got the runaround. The lawyer says Spain won't talk to me, which just makes me more anxious to talk to him. I was hoping I could get you interested in talking to him for me."

"And why would we want to do that? Sorry to be blunt, but homicide's not our business."

"Because I think she might have been killed because of her involvement with him. And if it got her killed, it's current business. And that mean's it's your business. At least that's what I thought."

After a couple of heartbeats Gustafson said, "Can you zero in a little bit for me?"

"I can try. She'd been treated pretty rough and at first we thought she might have been holding out something on behalf of her current boyfriend, a guy named Herb Feldman."

"Whoa, hang on a second. This was the girl by the river? Sally something? Feldman's girl, right?"

"That's right."

"I thought you had a killer there. Didn't somebody confess?"

"We had a guy claim he helped abduct her who fingered another guy for the killing, yeah. Conveniently, the other guy's dead."

"That's right, Steuben, the fellow they found in the car trunk. You're saying you don't buy it?"

"I don't like it, no."

"Why not?"

Dooley took a deep breath. "Because it smells like it was cooked up, that's why. The dead guy being the guilty one, for starters. Steuben was a thief. No record of sex crimes. I checked. And then the so-called accomplice turning himself in, supposedly because he was scared of winding up like Steuben."

"That doesn't ring true to you? They kill guys that get out of line all the time. And killing her was way out of line. That's how it read to us."

"Sure. But this is too convenient. Gaines gets three years and we stop looking for the real killer."

"You have any concrete reason to believe somebody else was the real killer?"

"Style, mainly. Evidence, not a God damn thing."

"So basically you're just going on a hunch."

"If you want to call it that. Look, you're the FBI. If you're content with the way we've handled this, it's got to be the first time."

"Now, I wouldn't say that."

"OK, whatever. But you've seen cooked-up cases before. Take a look at this one and tell me if it really looks that good to you."

There was a silence and then Gustafson said, "I'm not arguing with you, Mike. But I don't think the Bureau's going to be any more generous with the taxpayers' money than your guys are. They'd only send somebody down to talk to Spain if it was in connection with a live investigation, one of ours."

"OK. Maybe we don't need to talk to him. You already know a hell of a lot more about Spain than I do. Maybe you have something that could help me."

"I don't know. What are you thinking?"

"Well, did Spain give her something to hide, money or evidence or something. I'm looking for reasons she might have gotten killed."

"But they weren't even together anymore, right?"

"Not since sixty-six or so. But I don't know how much that means. They could have still been in touch."

"I don't think these guys are in the habit of entrusting things to their ex-girlfriends, I gotta be frank with you."

"Maybe not. Like I say, I'm just trying to cover all the bases. All I'm saying is, if you know of any connection between Tommy Spain and Sally Kotowski that might have put her in a dangerous position, I'd like to hear about it. You got a file on Spain, you probably got a file on Sally. If there's anything in there that could explain why she got killed, let me know."

There was another silence that stretched on for a few seconds. Gustafson said, "That's a little vague. But I can give it some thought."

"You want something a little less vague? You could check and see if by any chance you had Joe D'Andrea under surveillance on or about June second. If you have anything at all about his movements on the day Sally got killed, that would be a big help."

"I could take a look for you. But we don't spend every waking hour with these guys. We're not Big Brother."

Dooley had to suppress a laugh. "OK, fine. Whatever you can tell me will be appreciated. You can always leave a message at Area Six." Dooley gave him the number.

Gustafson said, "I appreciate your calling, Mike. I can take a look at it. But don't hold your breath."

"I never do," said Dooley. He hung up the phone and added, "Not with you guys."

Twenty-three

SOMETIMES IT TOOK a while, but things came through. Dooley stared at the paper in his hand and wondered what the hell to do with it. He was looking at a photostat that had come in an envelope from the Sheboygan County Sheriff's office in Wisconsin. It was a copy of a phone bill from Radke's Resort in Elkhart Lake, Wisconsin, showing sixteen long-distance phone calls for the month of May 1969. Dooley had forgotten all about sending off a request for the information, and now here it was.

Seven of the sixteen phone calls were to the 312 area code, the Chicago area. Five of them were spread out over the month of May, and then there were two at the end of the month, one on the thirtieth and one on the thirty-first, to the same number. Dooley looked at the exchange numbers and tried to figure out what part of the city the calls had gone to; he knew most of the Chicago exchanges but the two calls at the end of the month had gone to one of the unfamiliar ones. He stood up and took the paper across the office to the crisscross directory. It took him about half a minute to find the number and run his finger across to the address, and then he stood there scowling down at an address he recognized, because he'd driven out there in late June. He closed the crisscross and went back to his desk. He stood there for a little while looking at the paper and then went over to the door of McCone's office.

McCone looked up at his knock on the door frame. "Michael, what can I do you for?"

"I got this from the sheriff up in Sheboygan." Dooley laid the paper in front of McCone, who picked it up and peered at it through his bifocals.

"Translate for me," McCone said.

"She called Angelo's."

"Who called where?"

"Sally Kotowski called Angelo's Tavern in Melrose Park. Twice, just a few days before she disappeared. Angelo's was the place Gaines claimed he and Steuben picked her up before killing her, remember? Ronnie Gallo's place?"

McCone looked up at him over the rim of his glasses. "What's your point?"

"I don't know that I have a point. It should go in the file, that's all."

McCone held out the paper. "So put it in the file."

"Sure." Dooley took the paper. He flicked it with a finger and said, "Why did she call?"

McCone frowned at him. "I don't know. Does it change anything?"

"I don't know. If anything it seems to back up Gaines's story. It proves a connection between her and the place where he claimed he saw her."

"All right. Does that take care of your doubts?"

Dooley shrugged. "I just think it's interesting, and I think we still don't have the whole story, that's all. She went up to Wisconsin to get away from hoods. Then after she'd been there for a while, she called this place, which was crawling with hoods. Then apparently she came down and spent an evening there. And she got killed. I just don't understand the sequence. I'd like to know why she came back."

McCone took off his glasses and rubbed his eyes before fixing Dooley with an exasperated look. "So would I. I'd like to know why that gentleman who got himself run over by a train at the Granville El stop last night was sitting on the tracks with a bottle of bourbon, too. But in either case it's just morbid curiosity."

Dooley kept his face blank. He nodded and said, "OK. I'll put this in the file."

McCone called after him. "You're a good dick, Michael Dooley. But I think we got the right fella in jail, I really do."

"You're the boss," said Dooley.

• • •

Sometimes you got them when they were fresh; that was the ideal but it almost never happened. This time their number came over the radio when they were just a mile from the address, and they got there almost on the heels of the uniforms. The house was a frame affair with lots of gingerbread decoration, on a corner in a tranquil slice of the North Side just north of Montrose and just west of Damen. There was a squad in front and already a knot of neighbors, mostly women, milling on the sidewalk with bare arms folded and worried looks. Dooley and Olson parked and got out of the car. Dooley had taken off his jacket because of the muggy heat but he put it on over his short-sleeved shirt now. They walked slowly toward the steps up to the porch. The neighbors parted to let them pass, the murmured conversations ceasing for a moment.

A patrolman came out onto the porch and stood aside holding the screen door open for them. "Straight back to the kitchen," he said. "Can't miss it." He was old enough to have a few years on the job and it didn't look like his first homicide; he looked a little bored. Inside, the house was immaculate, with furniture that looked as if it had been in the family for a while and heavy drapes on the big west windows, drawn to shut out the afternoon sun.

In the kitchen the sunlight beat in unimpeded, making the white linoleum and the crimson pools and smears of blood shine. The other patrolman was squatting on his heels like a catcher giving the signal, elbows on knees and hands clasped, to get down to the level of the girl who sat on the floor with her back against a cabinet, cradling the dead boy in her arms. The boy's eyes were open but it didn't take an M.D. to see he was dead; a lot of blood had spilled in a hurry out of the two holes in his formerly white T-shirt. His hair was black, his eyes were blue, and his skin was the color of old Swiss cheese.

The girl's eyes were open and unblinking, too, but Dooley could tell she was alive because of the movement of her right hand, which was tenderly smoothing the hair on the dead boy's head, over and over as she stared out at nothing. She was a pretty brown-haired girl no older than eighteen, and the dead boy looked maybe a year or two older.

The squatting patrolman rose to his feet, wincing a little, when Dooley came in. "She hasn't said a word," he said in a soft voice. "I think she's in shock."

Dooley nodded once. "Then she'll be needing an ambulance, won't she?"

"It's on the way," said the uniform behind him.

"Good." Dooley stood looking at the scene, the toppled chair, the blood trail on the floor, the tracks in the mess, the soles of the girl's bare feet, the back door standing open. The smell of the gunshots still hung faintly in the air. There was no weapon in sight. "What did the people out front tell you?" Dooley asked the patrolman who had let them in.

"The neighbor lady heard shots and then screams and called it in. There's supposed to be a mother and daughter lives here. We don't know who the victim is."

"OK." Dooley looked at Olson. "Start with them out front." To the uniforms he said, "Did you search the house?"

"Not yet."

"OK. Don't touch anything, just look for people." The two cops exchanged a glance and left the kitchen on Olson's heels.

Dooley stood still a while longer, looking at the girl. When her hand finally stopped moving and settled on the dead boy's cheek Dooley said, "Where's your mother?"

A few seconds went by. Dooley had given up on getting a response when the girl said, "I don't know." She went on looking at nothing for a while. "I want to die," she said.

"I don't blame you," said Dooley. "But it'll pass."

He walked to the back door and looked out through the screen. The two patrolmen came back to report nobody else in the house. Dooley told them to stay in the kitchen. He could hear the ambulance coming up the block. He went out the back door and down a flight of concrete steps. There was a yard with a single tree in it, surrounded by a wooden fence, a garage at the back of the lot, a gate in the fence. The gate stood open. Dooley went through it into an alley. He walked slowly up the alley, hands in his pockets, scanning the ground. He walked until he came to another open gate. He went through into another yard, three houses down the block from the one on the corner. He went up a brick walk to another set of concrete steps. He climbed the steps and looked in through another screen door. "May I come in?" he said. Nobody answered, so Dooley pulled open the door and went in.

"Are you the police?" said one of the two women sitting at the kitchen table. A big blue-steel revolver sat on the table in front of her. The woman had gray hair and a calm expression on her face. Another woman about the same age sat across from her, and she was petrified.

"Yes, I am," said Dooley. "Can I talk to you outside for a moment?"

The woman just sat there, and Dooley didn't like the look in her eyes. She didn't look distraught; she looked as if she were making plans. Dooley had just started to lean, just started to think about making a smooth unhurried move for the gun, when the woman picked it up. She held it pointing toward the ceiling, but she held it with her finger on the trigger. "Are you going to arrest me?" she said.

"If I determine that you've committed a crime," Dooley said. His mind was racing. He was fairly certain he could avoid getting shot, but only fairly.

"The little bastard got my daughter pregnant," said the woman with the gun in her hand.

Dooley shook his head. "Well, then I'd say he had it coming."

"But you're still going to arrest me."

"I don't have any choice," said Dooley.

She looked at the gun, and she looked at Dooley, and for a bad moment Dooley thought she was going to use it, either on him or on herself, but finally she lowered it to the table with a thunk. "No, I guess you don't," she said.

Dooley pocketed the gun. "I'm going to ask you to come with me," he said.

The woman turned to her neighbor. "I really did it this time, didn't I, Peg?" she said.

Peg's eyes rolled up under her lids and she went slack and started to go over. Dooley caught her before she hit the floor.

• • •

"Now that's a happy family." Dooley drained his coffee cup. "Makes mine look like the *Donna Reed Show.*"

"How's the daughter?" said McCone.

"They had to sedate her. Once they pulled the kid away from her she went berserk. She's going to spend a little time in a rubber room, I think."

"The mother make a statement?"

"Olson's typing it up now. She could have been giving him a recipe, calm as she was."

McCone shook his head. "Go write it up."

Dooley sat down and stared at the typewriter, unable to begin. He was tired, tired of the whole thing. Maybe it was time to find another line of work. All he was doing with his life was cleaning up other people's messes; he was nothing but a janitor for people's failed lives. Trust Dooley to collar the housewife with the gun but give him a real case and he went nowhere.

Dooley hated to break a promise, and he'd made a promise to Sally Kotowski. But now he was starting to think McCone was right and Billy Gaines had been telling the truth and everything he'd done was a waste of time. Except, he thought, if Gaines was telling the truth, there was still a mystery: Why did Sally Kotowski call Angelo's and why did she come back to Chicago?

To hell with it all, thought Dooley. He picked up his phone messages. There were three related to other cases and one from Laura Lindbloom, saying *Call at bar, may have info.* Dooley dealt with the others first and then dialed the Mad Hatter. Laura answered, with bar noise in the background.

"It's Dooley."

"Oh, hi. Can I call you back in a few minutes on a quieter phone?"

"Sure. I'll be here." The paperwork would keep him busy for an hour. He hung up and got started. Three calls came in that were not for him, and then it was Laura again, with no background noise.

"Is this a good time to talk?"

"Sure. What's going on?"

"You told me to keep thinking about what happened to Sally."

"Yeah. You come up with something?"

"I'm not sure. I just remembered something. Was she wearing any jewelry when they found her?"

Dooley could still see Sally, lying in the weeds. "No. Nothing."

"Well, she had a locket she wore all the time. Her father gave it to her, so it had a lot of sentimental value. I don't mean literally all the time, I mean she'd take it off to go swimming or something, and of course she couldn't wear it at the club, but most of the time she had it on. I should have remembered it before, but I didn't think of it until today. That was one thing about Herb, he didn't like it and he made her stop wearing it. But I remember, the last time I saw her she was wearing it again. I asked about it and that's when she told me she was fed up with Herb. Anyway, it wasn't just a trinket. I mean it was a valuable thing. I think it was an heirloom. It was this sort of teardrop-shaped gold locket decorated with seed pearls, and inside it was a little tiny picture of Jesus, you know, a miniature. I thought maybe if whoever killed her took it, he might have pawned it or something. And that could be a clue."

Whatever else she was, Dooley thought, this gal was no fool. "You're right. I wish we'd known about this before."

"I don't know why I didn't think of it before. I'm not making this up as I go along, you know. It just comes back in bits and pieces."

"That's OK. Better late than never."

"Can you trace something like that?"

"We can try. There's a million ways it could have disappeared, starting with the kids who found the body, but you never know."

"If it wasn't with her things in Wisconsin, then I'd bet she had it on. I don't think she'd have left it with her sister."

"The sister did mention some jewelry. We can go back and check with her. I'm pretty sure it wasn't with the effects that came down from Wisconsin. You may be on to something. Of course, tracking it down would be a nightmare even if we had the manpower to put on it. I'm afraid it's a long shot at best."

"Well, it was just something I thought of."

"I do appreciate it." Dooley wanted to say something more, but he couldn't come up with the words.

Laura let the silence go on for a couple of seconds and said, "I wanted you to know how much I appreciate what you're doing, too."

"It's my job."

"From what you've said, it sounds to me like unpaid overtime."

"Well, you could look at it that way."

"I mean, the case has been declared closed, right?"

"That's right."

"But you're not giving up on it."

Dooley sat there with his mouth shut instead of telling her how close he had come to doing just that. "Not yet," he said finally.

"That means a lot to me," Laura said. "To know that somebody cares what happened to Sally. She didn't have a lot of people who cared about her. It means a lot to me that you're pursuing this when you don't have to."

"I'm stubborn," said Dooley. "Drives people crazy sometimes."

"What are you doing tomorrow night?"

Warily, Dooley said, "Working. Why?"

"It's my birthday. I'm having a party."

"Happy birthday. How old are you?"

"I'll be twenty-nine. You want to come to the party?"

Dooley sat holding the phone to his ear, the urge to laugh fighting with the urge to say yes, hell yes. "I told you, I have to work."

"I think probably we'll be going into the wee hours. You could stop by for a drink."

Instead of telling her he had a wife and children to go home to, Dooley said, "I can't even remember when I was twenty-nine. I'll stick out like a sore thumb."

"No, you won't. A lot of my friends are old enough to remember the war. You might want to leave your gun in the car, that's all."

Dooley laughed softly. "I'll have to see. But thanks. I appreciate the invitation."

"I'm counting on you, Dooley." She hung up the phone in his ear.

Twenty-four

"HEY, POP. HOW come you don't grow some sideburns?"

Dooley could see Frank in the mirror, sticking his head into the bathroom. "Because I don't want to look like a TV cowboy." He rinsed the razor and attacked another swath of cheek.

"Everybody's got sideburns now. That would look cool on you."

"I don't want to look cool."

"Man, Dad. You're no fun."

"You said it. I'm a wet blanket, all the way."

Frank withdrew, shaking his head. Dooley finished shaving and put on his tie, then went down to the kitchen and got the percolator going. Teddy Kennedy was all over the paper, trying to save his political career, sounding chastened and humble. Meanwhile, Nixon was in Manila, talking to whoever was in charge out there these days. Dooley did not have fond memories of Manila; he'd spent February 1945 taking Manila back from the Japs, street by street and house by house. Dooley had lost a couple of good friends in Manila. He turned the page. The stock market was taking a nose dive; the Dow was at a two-year low. And a woman on the North Side had shot her daughter's boyfriend; Dooley knew all about that. Things seemed to be quiet in Viet Nam. Dooley folded the paper and went to pour some coffee. No news is good news, he told himself, but he knew it wasn't always true.

• • •

"Burglary. Campbell here."

"John, how you doing? It's Mike Dooley."

"Dooley, Jesus. Long time no see. You still back at the Area?"

"Still here. I was just polishing the little brass plaque we put on your chair."

"Right. The one in the toilet, you mean?"

"Yeah. The one you sat on when you wrote all that inspiring poetry."

"I hope that's still there."

"You bet. You think anyone ever bothers to wash the walls around here?"

"It's good to know you have something to remember me by. What can I do for you, Mike?"

"I need to fence some stolen jewelry."

"Well, you've come to the right place. We offer the best prices."

"Seriously, I'm looking for a piece of jewelry that I think might have come off a dead girl's neck. I have a description of the piece and a suspect. I'm hoping you can tell me where he might have taken it, if he took it anywhere."

"Maybe. But there's a million fences out there."

"The guy I think did it is an Outfit guy, works for the Grand Avenue crew. It's guesswork, but I'm desperate."

"An Outfit guy? I didn't think they went in for that kind of thing."

"Well, that's my best guess right now. I'm hoping if he was greedy enough he might have left a trail."

"Those guys are pretty greedy, all right. But they're pretty careful, too."

"I know. Here's what I'm thinking. You take this piece from the victim, it looks like it might be worth something but you're not a jewel guy. It's not your specialty. What do you do with it?"

"If you're smart? You give it to somebody who knows the business. Get what you can from him, let him fence it. If you're really smart you make sure it goes out of town. But there's no rule book with these guys. How much is it worth?"

"I have no idea. Maybe not a lot. I got an informant who says she thinks it was worth something. But she may not know."

"You don't have a lot to work with, do you?"

"No. Mainly the Outfit angle. You're a connected guy, you have this thing that ties you to a killing but might bring you a couple hundred bucks, what do you do with it? I'm assuming there's a limited number of fences that work with Outfit guys. I just want a fingerhold somewhere."

There was a silence while Campbell worked on it. "I don't have an answer for you right away, Mike. Give me a couple of days to work on it, OK?"

"Take your time," Dooley said. "The girl's not going anywhere."

• • •

Dooley found a place to park only a couple of blocks away from the old Victorian house on Cleveland. He sat in the car for a while after he turned off the ignition, trying to decide how badly he wanted to walk into this party. He didn't especially want to meet a lot of new people who he had a feeling were not going to be exactly his peer group, but the prospect of sitting down and having a gin and tonic with Laura Lindbloom beat the hell out of going home to drink Jameson's alone in his kitchen. One thing he knew for sure: he wasn't going to leave his gun in the car. He had given one wild second's thought to stripping off the jacket and tie, leaving the gun and the star in the glove compartment, going incognito. He'd rejected that idea in a hurry. Dooley wasn't going to try to fool anyone into thinking he was anything but what he was, and if they didn't like it that was their problem.

It had rained in the afternoon, but the night was muggy and warm, a good midsummer Chicago night, with people hanging out on their porches, TV noises and rock and roll music coming out of open windows, cars cruising slowly up the block, arms trailing out open windows. Dooley could remember nights like this when his dad would take the whole family over to Garfield Park to sleep out under the trees, the park full of people escaping the heat trapped in upper-floor apartments, years ago, before air conditioning. Man, that was a different world, thought Dooley, where did it go?

Even though it was past midnight, all the windows were lit up in the old Victorian house, and here the music was louder. Dooley looked up at the tower through tree branches but couldn't see much. He thought about ringing the doorbell but decided it was probably quicker to just go down the gangway and up the back stairs.

When he reached the top of the stairs he could see he'd made the right choice; nobody in here was going to hear the bell anyway. He stood in the doorway of the studio and his nerve almost failed him. Dooley had walked into caves full of Japanese soldiers and apartments full of fresh corpses but he wasn't sure he wanted to walk into this warm, dimly lighted room full of artists twitching to loud music. A couple of heads had turned his way but most of the people were too busy dancing or shouting at one another over the music to notice him. Dooley decided that the only way to go in there was the way he went in to any rough joint.

He put his hands in his trouser pockets and went in. He had put a little bit of a smile on his face to show he was friendly, but even so most of the looks he got seemed to be somewhere between amazement and alarm. Dooley felt like a skin diver in an aquarium tank. He had almost gotten used to eruptions of hair on men's heads, but this was Longhair Central tonight; Dooley saw a white man with an

Afro the size of a beach ball. He saw a man in a shirt with frilly cuffs dancing barefoot with a woman in a leather miniskirt. The music sounded like a man caught under a pile driver and screaming. Dooley worked his way around the edge of the room, smiling at people and looking desperately for Laura. He saw people smoking and he could smell things that he knew he ought to be arresting them for.

"Are you lost?" a woman in a cowboy hat shouted at him. She gave him a great big smile and he decided she was genuinely concerned.

He leaned close to her, bumping the brim of the hat, and shouted, "I hope not. Is Laura here?"

"Upstairs." She pointed to the door that led to the tower. Dooley nodded and made for the door, stepping over the legs of a Negro passed out on a couch.

On the spiral stairs he left the music behind and started to hear voices above him. It got cooler as he climbed. As he came up into the turret he found himself looking up a woman's dress; even in the dark there was a hell of a lot to see. There were five or six people up here, and by the time Dooley was in their midst they had all fallen silent, frozen in midsentence, staring at him. Dooley stood there waiting for his eyes to adjust, wishing like hell he'd gone straight home.

"Dooley!" He hadn't seen Laura because she'd had her back to him, leaning on the sill looking out over the treetops, but she had turned to see what the hush was about, and now she was coming toward him, arms outstretched. She gave him a quick peck on the lips that caught him totally by surprise and slipped her arm through his. "This is my friend Dooley," she announced to the crowd. "The best cop in Chicago."

He could practically see the hair stand up on their heads at that; he thought a couple of them were going to jump out of the tower. "I didn't do it," said a bearded man to his left.

"Then you got nothing to worry about," said Dooley, trying to make it sound light. He could taste Laura's kiss on his lips; there was liquor in it but he couldn't say what kind.

"Dooley's very cool," Laura said. "If they were all like him life would be groovy." The tension eased as Dooley went through a round of handshaking and heard names he instantly forgot, saw faces in the gloom he would never recognize. Somebody pressed a cold, dripping wet bottle of beer into his hand, and Laura pulled him toward the window where she'd been when he came up.

The painter was standing there. His goatee had filled out a little. "Welcome to the Monkey House," he said.

"Thanks," said Dooley. "I'm afraid I forgot to bring the bananas."

Laura laughed. "I'm glad you're here."

"You win the prize for best costume," said the painter.

"I had to work tonight." Dooley couldn't tell what this look was on the painter's face; he wasn't sure if the guy was trying to start a fight or not.

"How'd it go?" said the painter. "Crack a lot of heads tonight?"

"Oh, Danny, get lost," Laura said. "Dooley's one of the good guys."

"I'm just giving you a hard time," the painter said, as if that were an excuse. He slapped Dooley on the arm, grinning, and moved away.

"He doesn't like me much, does he?" said Dooley as the painter made his way to the stairs.

"Oh, don't worry about it. That's just Danny. He's like that with everyone. It's that artist thing. Irony and all that."

Dooley worked on that for a second or two, wondering what he was missing. He said, "Look, I hope he doesn't think I'm . . ." Words failed him.

"What?" Laura's eyes shone, a foot and a half away.

"You know, trying to—to horn in on his territory or something."

Laura stared and then threw back her head and laughed. "Oh God." She eased her arms through his again and the familiarity thrilled Dooley and alarmed him a little at the same time. "First of all, I'm not his territory. Did you think we were sleeping together or something?"

Dooley was tired of feeling stupid around these people. "I wondered."

"Well, just to set your mind at ease, Danny's a homosexual."

"Oh." Dooley could feel his IQ sinking by the second. "OK."

"And even if I was sleeping with him, I invited you here, so it's cool."

Dooley took a long drink of beer. "All right. I'm not real sure what I'm doing here, that's all."

"You're doing whatever you want to do here. That's what this party is all about. Look, Dooley. I'm a very tolerant person. I like people and I don't have any prejudices. I don't see any reason why I shouldn't have a big tough cop for a friend. God knows I already have enough pot-smoking hippies in my life."

"I know. I saw them downstairs."

"Is it a problem for you?"

Dooley gave it a moment's honest thought. "Maybe it should be, but it's not. Not tonight."

"I'm glad. Come and talk to my friends." She tugged on his arm.

People had realized that Dooley wasn't there to bust them, and with Laura at his side he started to relax a little. For a while he was the center of attention, answering questions that to his surprise were not entirely hostile, and then he straightened up from the tub of ice with a fresh beer in his hand to find that everyone was trooping down the stairs, leaving him alone with Laura Lindbloom. She was leaning over the windowsill again and he walked over to stand a little stiffly beside her.

Looking out over the city, Laura said, "I should go down and party, I guess. But it's nice up here."

Dooley drank beer. He was starting to feel better. "I forgot to say Happy Birthday."

"It's not too late."

"Happy Birthday."

"Thank you. God, I'm twenty-nine. That sounds so old."

"What does that say for me?"

"I don't know. How old are you?"

"I'm forty-six."

She turned to him. "You look good for forty-six."

"I feel about eighty-six sometimes."

A feeble breeze moved her hair a little. "You married?"

"Yep. Twenty-one years."

"What's your wife's name?"

"Rose."

"Any kids?"

"Three. I have an eighteen-year-old daughter who just graduated from high school and a fifteen-year-old son. And I have a boy over in Viet Nam, in the Marines. He's almost twenty."

"In Viet Nam? That's pretty heavy."

"You could say that."

Dooley thought that was going to kill the conversation. They were silent for a while and then Laura said, "You like being a cop?"

"It's a living."

"Does it ever get you down? You ever get depressed, dealing with things like—like Sally?"

"I don't let it get to me. You get hardened after a while."

"Do you ever dream about it? I think your job would give me nightmares."

"I dream about a lot of things. I have nightmares, I have good dreams."

She was peering at him, her eyes narrowed a little. "You must be a very strong person."

Dooley shrugged. "You get used to it."

She went on peering at him for a while and then said, "So what made you decide to become a cop? Or do you come from a long line of cops? That Irish thing."

"No, I was the first one in my family. My old man was a carpenter. A couple of his cousins were in the department, though. I don't know, it just happened. After I got out of the army I fooled around with a couple of things and then applied to the department. It seemed like a natural step."

"Why?"

Dooley thought about it, looking out over the rooftops. He'd never put it into words. "I guess I figured I was already dirty, and why make somebody else get used to it when I was already used to it?"

Her brow wrinkled. "What do you mean, dirty?"

"I mean I'd been looking at death for three years, close up. Death wasn't any big deal by the time I got out of the service. So I guess being a cop wasn't much of a change."

Laura's look was grave. "That's—I don't know. That's awful, that you had to go through that."

"I sure as hell wasn't the only one. Everybody I grew up with was in the war. Some of them didn't come back. I had a brother who got killed in the war."

"I'm sorry. Were you close?"

Dooley shrugged. "He was my brother."

A few seconds went by and Laura said, "What was his name?"

"Patrick." Because she seemed to be waiting for more, Dooley said, "We were an Irish joke, Pat and Mike. Pat and Mike go to the movies. Pat and Mike play ball. Pat and Mike go on a double date." Dooley shook his head, remembering. "He was older than me and I thought he walked on water. He joined the navy that fall, just before Pearl Harbor. Everybody could see the war coming. He got killed in the Coral Sea."

"I'm sorry."

"People die. You have to deal with it." Jesus, thought Dooley, a couple of beers and I start running off at the mouth. He put the bottle to his lips to shut himself up.

Laura was staring at him intently. "Did you cry for him?"

He shot her a look, perplexed. "What's that got to do with anything?"

"Just wondering. Men have this thing about crying. But crying's good for you."

Dooley had cried like hell when Patrick died, but he'd done it in secret. He snorted. "Crying's like farting. Sometimes you have to do it, but it's nothing to brag about. And people tend to appreciate it when you control it."

Laura shook briefly with silent laughter. "You're a funny man, Dooley."

They stood in silence for a while, hearing music thumping downstairs, hearing the hollow rumor of the city spread out before them. "So what do you do for fun?" Laura said.

She had finally come up with one that stumped him. Dooley had to think about it. "I don't have time for a lot of fun. I like baseball, I guess. I play with my kid sometimes. But I don't really have much time for it."

"That's sad."

"That's life. There's a lot of work that needs doing."

"There's got to be more to life than work. God, especially in your job."

"I'm OK."

A few seconds went by and she said, "How about this? Is this fun?"

"What, talking to you?"

"Yeah. Being here, at a party. You having fun?"

"Sure."

She was staring at him, smiling faintly, and Dooley had to look away finally, losing the stare-down. "That's good," she said. "I'm glad you came."

Dooley had a brief vision of himself sitting at the kitchen table with the bottle of Jameson's. "Me too," he said.

Twenty-five

IN THE PHOTOGRAPH Milwaukee Phil was scowling, a stocky fierce-looking man in late middle age with his hair a little disheveled, flanked by FBI agents, hands in cuffs, annoyed at having his Sunday breakfast interrupted. *FBI Nabs Alderisio on Fraud Charge* the headline screamed. Dooley had read the other two newspapers' versions, and he scanned this one. The charges were nothing new; Alderisio had run one scam too many on a suburban bank and somebody had squealed. The somebody was in protective custody with his wife and daughters, the paper said.

I damn well hope so, thought Dooley, turning the page. A helicopter had gone down in Viet Nam and nine marines had died. Odds, thought Dooley. There's a lot of marines over there, a lot of helicopters.

Dooley looked up from the paper when the door to the diner opened; he'd never met Arnold Swallow but Katie Conway had given him a description over the phone. "Like a walrus with a good tailor," she had said. She hit it on the head, Dooley thought, watching the man come up the aisle, trading greetings with the counterman, winking at a waitress.

Dooley had wanted to contact Swallow without leaving tracks, so he'd called Katie. The intersection of youth and vice having brought her into contact with Arnold Swallow more than she would have liked, she had been able to tell Dooley where the second-watch vice coordinator in the East Chicago district liked to have lunch and what he looked like.

Arnold Swallow was a big man going soft in middle age, losing hair and gaining weight. He still had the walk and that particular way of scanning a room, but he didn't look like the type of cop who got his hands dirty anymore. He had started combing what hair he had left over the bald spot, the part creeping down the side of his head, but there wasn't much he could do to hide the spare tire around his middle. The best he could do was drape it in a nice dark gray suit that made him look more like a banker than a cop. He settled into a booth and took a menu from the waitress; she started to walk away but Swallow grabbed her wrist and held her while he said something Dooley couldn't hear with a sly look on his face. The waitress laughed, throwing back her head; Swallow shook with mirth, and then he let her go. Her smile faded the instant she turned away; she dealt with a couple of dozen like Swallow every day.

Dooley slid off his stool at the end of the counter and walked over to the booth. "Swallow?" he said.

Swallow looked up from the menu. "Yeah?"

"You got a minute?"

"Depends. You got a good reason to interrupt my lunch?"

"I'll let you be the judge of that." Dooley sat down across from Swallow. "Janet says hi."

That was one way to get the man's attention; Swallow froze instantly, his eyes widening just a little before settling into a guarded look. "Who the hell is Janet?" he said, laying the menu aside.

"That's what I wanted to know," said Dooley. "Who the hell is Janet that a guy would risk having his balls cut off for a little roll in the hay? She must be a hell of a lay."

A few ticks of the clock went by. Swallow rallied a little and said, "I don't know any Janet."

Dooley smiled. "Ah, OK. Sorry, I must have the wrong guy. I'll just go call my Italian friend and tell him there's nothing to the rumor and he can forget anything he heard about Arnie Swallow putting it to Janet on the sly."

Swallow took in a lot of air suddenly through his nose, his nostrils flaring and his shoulders heaving. He exhaled and said, "Who the hell are you?"

"Dooley." He reached into his pocket and pulled out his star. "Area Six Homicide."

Swallow's brow wrinkled. "Homicide?"

"That's right. Not IAD, not Intelligence. Just plain old Homicide. But if *I* know about it, you've got to be wondering who else does."

Swallow worked on it, a man watching his shipmates rig the gangplank. His eyes flicked away for a moment and Dooley could see him thinking hard about people with big mouths. His face settled into a glower and he came back to Dooley and said, "What the hell do you want with me?"

"Answers. I want some answers, Arnie. I got a dead girl on my hands and I got questions I can't answer."

"I don't know shit about dead girls."

"You know this one. Remember Sally Kotowski?"

"Who the hell you talking about? I don't know any Sally."

"Your pal Tommy Spain knew her real well."

"Jesus Christ, I haven't seen Tommy in three years."

"That would be about right. They were together back then."

Swallow blinked a few times. "You mean the bunny? That broad?"

"Yeah. You know she got killed?"

"No, I didn't know. You think I keep track of Tommy's old girlfriends? I can't even keep track of my own."

"This one was in the papers. Remember the girl on the riverbank? That was Sally."

Swallow thought for a second and his eyes got a little wider. "That case was cleared, for Christ's sake."

"The case is horseshit."

"Who gives a fuck? It's a cleared case."

"Not as far as I'm concerned it isn't."

"What the hell do you want? Problems? They clear the case, you go on to the next one, for Christ's sake. Who the hell made you the Lone Ranger?"

Dooley was familiar with the Arnold Swallow School of Police Work, and he'd never thought much of it. "The case stinks, and I'm going to clear it like it should be cleared."

Swallow leaned back, eyelids drooping a little, getting his balance back. "I get it. You're just moonlighting. You got nobody behind you on this. You don't have shit, do you?"

"I got you in an apartment on Goethe Street where you shouldn't be, Arnie. That's what I got. You can talk to my supervisor if you want, and I'll get reamed. But I won't care, because when I pick up the phone, you'll get reamed for real."

Swallow inhaled sharply again; Dooley had found the right button. "I don't know what you want," said Swallow. "I told you, me and Tommy, that's history. Tommy's in jail, for Christ's sake."

"Yeah. And that's the best alibi there is, isn't it? But I don't think Tommy killed anybody. I don't think you killed anybody. In fact, I know who killed Sally. What I need to make the case is why. And that's what I need you to tell me."

"How can I tell you that?"

Dooley leaned across the table. "Sally got killed because Tommy Spain gave her something to hide. I need to know what that was. I think you can tell me, and if you can't, you can get Tommy to tell you, and if he won't, that's tough shit, because then the word gets out about you and Janet. Is that clear?"

Swallow had lost all his color. "You're asking me to do the impossible."

"Can you get to Spain on the phone? Can you write him a letter?"

"He won't tell me. Are you kidding me?"

"Your old buddy? He'll let them put you up on a meat hook before he'll tell you what you need to know? I don't believe it."

Swallow took another deep breath, through his mouth this time, and when he exhaled, his cheeks puffed out like Dizzy Gillespie's. He leveled a glare at Dooley and said, "Look. You got the wrong idea. Let me tell you how it is. Tommy and I were partners, but Tommy's his own guy." Swallow leaned forward in turn, and now his face was a foot from Dooley's. Just above a whisper Swallow said, "I am *not in his league*. You get me? If it's a choice between me and what's important to Tommy Spain, Tommy throws me away like a used Kleenex. You get the picture?"

Dooley nodded. "I get it. You can't help me. That's a real pity. Lotsa luck with the meat hook, Arnie." Dooley slid out of the booth. He walked toward the door, but he didn't leave the diner. Instead he stopped at the pay phone just inside the door and plugged a dime into the slot. He started dialing, slowly and deliberately. Out of the corner of his eye he saw Arnold Swallow get up out of the booth, hand the menu to the waitress, and come toward him. Dooley had finished dialing the number of a carpet store that advertised a lot on TV and was listening to the rings at the other end of the line when Swallow reached him and said, "Hang up the fuckin' phone."

Dooley hung up and retrieved his dime. Outside on the sidewalk, Swallow lit a cigarette and looked at Dooley with a wonderfully concentrated look on his face. He said, "I'll tell you what I can. You can't expect me to do miracles."

Dooley made him sweat, standing there looking at him for a long moment. Finally he said, "So what's so important to Tommy Spain?"

Swallow beckoned to Dooley with the cigarette and started walking west on Division. "Leverage."

"On who?"

"Anybody. Everybody. Tommy's been at it a long time."

"What kind of leverage?"

Swallow walked with the cigarette held to his mouth, talking past it. "Tapes. Tommy used to tape a lot of conversations. He had a guy he worked with, a wire man."

"Who's the wire man?"

"Guy named Dave Novotny. He won't help you. He just planted the bugs and collected the tapes. Tommy didn't tell him shit."

"Maybe he listened on his own once in a while. Where can I find him?"

"In jail, right now. He's in Terre Haute on some federal rap."

"So what did they get that might get a girl killed?"

"I don't know. I'd be guessing."

"So guess."

Swallow flicked ash onto the sidewalk. "You want a guess? Christ, pick one. Start with the governor."

"Who? Ogilvie?"

"Yeah. He hired Tommy when he was sheriff. There was some talk about it."

"I remember. What'd he have on him?"

"I don't know."

"Don't bullshit me."

"I'm not bullshitting you. All Tommy told me about it was, he didn't have to worry, Ogilvie would go for it. He came back from a meeting and said that was it, he was in. I didn't want to know what it was about, why should I? I figured he had something from when Ogilvie worked for the feds, some rotten deal or something. You never knew with Tommy. He was resourceful, he always had stuff on people."

"So you're trying to tell me Governor Ogilvie had Sally killed, to keep this covered up?"

"Nah, for Christ's sake, not Ogilvie. Jesus, look. You have something on a pol, it's like currency. It can be swapped, and bought and sold. And stolen. Anyone who knew Tommy had it could have wanted it."

"Well, guess some more. Who knew he had it?"

"Fuck, anyone he'd tried to use it on or shopped it to would know he had it. I don't know what Tommy's been up to for the last three years. And Ogilvie's just my first guess, off the top of my head. Tommy could have Nixon and the Pope in bed together for all I know."

Dooley knew there were limits to how hard he could push; make a man desperate enough and things had a way of getting unpredictable. He said, "Find out."

"What?"

"Find out what they wanted from Sally. Find out and there's no reason why Janet's other friend has to hear about you. Do it however you have to do it, but find out."

Swallow stopped short on the sidewalk and fixed him with a murderous look. "Dooley, let me tell you something. Guys like you are the worst kind of pain in the ass. How long you been a cop?"

"Long enough to get tired of cops like you."

Swallow shook his head and took a drag on the cigarette. "You're a grown-up. You oughta know better. You're fucking with things you don't want to fuck with."

"That's the story of my life," said Dooley.

• • •

"You're famous, Dooley." Olson skimmed the paper across the desk. "'Detective Michael Dooley of the Damen Avenue Homicide Unit.' You're up there with Sergeant Preston of the Mounties now."

"I saw it this morning." Dooley hung his jacket on the back of the chair and sat down. "For once I get my name in the paper and I didn't even do anything. All I did was show up."

Olson put on a hurt look for the benefit of the dicks who were looking on. "How do you think I feel? I was there too, and you'll notice it doesn't say anything about 'Detective Peter Olson.'"

"Well, you were typing up the report when the guy was here looking for an interview. You want to get your name in the paper, you gotta learn to drop everything and start primping when the newshounds come around."

"Well, hell. You could have put in a good word for me. 'My partner Olson here, who stood there valiantly supporting me while the suspect confessed.'"

Kowalcyck leaned over the desk, coffee cup in hand. "This the guy who popped his wife and her friend, up on Argyle?"

Dooley tapped the photo. "Yeah, it was a rough one. We go up there and the guy's sitting in a chair in the living room and he says, 'Am I glad to see you. I just killed two women.' They were in the bedroom. They'd been packing to move the wife out and he came home and found them. 'I just snapped,' he says. All we had to do was stand there and listen. That's how I like 'em—the self-clearing case."

The telephone rang and Nyman picked it up and yelled across the room. "Dooley!"

It was Haggerty at the other end. "Exciting times over here," he said after the pleasantries. "You see what happened to Alderisio?"

"Yeah. They gonna make it stick?"

"If they can keep that witness alive they ought to. The feds have the big guns."

"That's what I hear. You got something for me?"

"Something. How much it means, I don't know. You asked me about Tommy Spain. Well, I went back and looked at what we had on him. He came back from Mexico a couple of years ago and got arrested on this federal rap within a few weeks."

"Yeah."

"Well, we actually had surveillance on him for a couple of days when we found out he was back in town. And guess who he had dinner with a couple of nights after he got back?"

"Sally Kotowski."

"Boy, you're sharp today. Yeah. They had dinner at the Pump Room and she spent a couple of hours in his hotel room."

"You're kidding."

"Nope. She was trailed to her apartment and identified after the evening's entertainment."

"Any indication he gave her anything?"

"Not that it says here. But we couldn't get inside the hotel room. And she probably had a purse. But that's just guessing."

"Yeah. Thanks, that's good work. Anything else interesting on Spain?"

"Nothing that points to Sally. You still unhappy with Chuck Steuben for the killing?"

"Yeah. You want to know the truth, I still like Joe D'Andrea."

"You wouldn't be getting a little obsessed, would you? Joe can do that to people."

"I don't think that's what it is. I just don't like his alibi, and I never jumped on it that hard because Gaines showed up all of a sudden."

"So you're gonna jump on it now? You're an ambitious boy."

"I'm just stubborn. What I wanted to ask you was, who does Joe D'Andrea work with? The dirty stuff, I mean. I think this was a two-man job. At least. She had to struggle like hell. I think you need two to control someone the way she was controlled. So I was wondering, does Mad Dog have somebody he likes to work with? Somebody that holds 'em while he hits 'em? I was thinking it's harder to alibi two people than one."

"Well, that's a good question. He used to work a lot with Dogbreath DiCarlo, till DiCarlo dropped dead a couple of years back."

"Dogbreath?"

"You never met him, huh? It fit him, believe me. Anyway, the word is Joe's been using a young guy recently to help him with collections. A guy named Tony Messino. Up and coming guy, did a term in Joliet for auto theft, has a reputation for going off like a firecracker, kind of like Joe. We looked at Messino pretty hard for a nasty beating out near Harlem and Grand last year but we couldn't nail him. By the time the victim's jaws were unwired he had decided he didn't really need to talk anyway. They say Messino likes to hurt people. I guess D'Andrea's grooming him to take over the family firm or something."

"Interesting. Messino's one of the guys D'Andrea claims can support his alibi. I don't suppose you have any surveillance reports on him?"

"I'll have to check on that and call you back."

"OK. In the meantime, where would I find Messino if I decided I just had to talk to him?"

"Your best bet is probably to try either the Armory Lounge again or the Italian-American Social Club at twelve forty-six Grand Avenue. That's where he spends most of his time."

Dooley jotted it down. "Thanks, Ed. I appreciate the help."

"My pleasure. Tell Tony I said hi."

"You bet."

After he hung up Dooley sat looking out the window for a moment and then went and scrounged in the wastebasket where somebody had thrown away a *Daily News.* He retrieved the paper and turned to the article about Alderisio's arrest. Here it was: the list of people named in the federal warrant as frequent guests at Alderisio's weekly sit-downs: Joseph Lombardo, Charles Nicoletti, Jackie Cerone, Frankie Schweihs. An Outfit *Who's Who.* And at the bottom of the list, Tony Messino.

Dooley stuffed the paper back in the wastebasket. Up and coming, he thought, no shit.

• • •

Dooley came into the kitchen from the garage and froze; Rose was standing there in her bathrobe with a worried look on her face. The first thing Dooley thought was *Kevin's dead*, but the look on her face wasn't quite that bad; *wounded* was the next thing he thought, and then Rose said, "Kathleen isn't home yet," and Dooley had a moment of confusion—relief and alarm tripping all over each other in a head fogged by fatigue.

"Where'd she go?" he said, dumping his briefcase on the table.

"She went out with Donna to a movie and then she called to say they'd run into some guys they knew and they were going to get something to eat. I told her to be home by eleven."

Dooley didn't have to look at his watch; he knew it was past one o'clock. "Did you call Donna's house?"

"Yeah. I woke her father up. He said he hadn't heard anything from Donna but he wasn't too concerned. He didn't seem to think midnight was very late. I got the feeling they're a little less strict over there than we are."

"Who were these guys they met?"

"She didn't say."

"You gotta ask, Rose. Jesus. You can't just let her go off like that." Dooley leaned on the counter, head down; this was the last thing he needed. "How many guys? Two, three?"

"I don't know. Don't yell at me, Michael. Please."

He looked up and saw how close to tears she was, standing stiffly with her arms folded. He straightened up and sighed.

"All right. She's probably fine. If she was with Donna, the odds are better. What theater did they go to?"

"The Gateway. When she called she said they were going to grab a bite to eat somewhere near the theater."

"The Gateway. That's what, out there on Lawrence? OK." Dooley was telling himself there was no reason to panic, but the cop in him was remembering all the nice girls who had gone off for a quick bite to eat with some guy and wound up in a case file. He knew realistically there wasn't a whole lot he could do besides wait it out, but the father in him couldn't wait. "I can call the district over there and see if they've got anything. Do we have any idea what kind of car these guys had?"

"Donna came and picked her up. They should be in Donna's car."

"I like that a little better. What kind of car does Donna have?"

"I don't know."

"Didn't you see it when she drove up?"

Wearily, Rose said, "Michael, I'm not a cop. Normal people don't look out the window to write down the make and license number every time someone drives up."

"OK, take it easy. I'm not mad at you. What's Donna's number?"

"It's there on the bulletin board by the phone. That yellow piece of paper."

Dooley scanned till he found the number. He was so tired he could hardly lift the receiver. He had started dialing when Rose said crisply, "She's here. I think this is her." Headlights came through the window as a car turned into the driveway. Dooley hung up and made for the hallway that led to the front door.

Kathleen was just pulling away from the driver's side window of a four- or five-year-old Impala when Dooley came out onto the porch. Dooley could hear her laughing, and he could hear a male voice inside the car. Kathleen came scampering across the lawn, pale legs flashing in the gloom, and stopped short when she saw him. "Sorry I'm late," she said, suddenly breathless, eyes wide, as he came striding past her.

"Get in the house," Dooley said. The Impala had started backing out of the driveway and Dooley broke into a run.

"Daddy!" Kathleen's voice strained at its upper limit.

The car swung out onto the street and rocked on its springs as the driver braked and shifted into first, but Dooley was too fast for him. He cut in front of the car and pounded on the hood just as it started to move, making the driver jam on the brakes. "Jesus!" said the kid behind the wheel.

"Hold it right there." Dooley walked slowly around to the driver's side and bent down at the window. There were two of them, and they both had hair down past their ears. Dooley couldn't believe his daughter had gotten in a car with this pair of derelicts. The driver had on a T-shirt with a pack of cigarettes in the pocket, and the one on the passenger seat had a band around his head, like Tonto on TV. "Where the hell have you two been with my daughter?" said Dooley.

"Holy shit, man. Take it easy." The driver was trying to brazen it out but his voice was a little shaky.

"No, you take it easy. You know what time it is?"

"Time for you to relax, Jack."

"Son, you smart off to me one more time and I'm going to haul you out of this car and whip you. Where's Donna?"

"Jesus." The kid was getting less cocky by the second with Dooley breathing fire in his face. "She went home in her own car. I said I'd bring Kathy home because it's on my way."

"Where have you been all this time?"

"Montrose Harbor."

"That park's closed at night. What were you doing there?"

"What are you, a cop or something?"

Dooley was about to blow the kid out of the water when his friend leaned across the seat and said, "Honest, Mr. Dooley, we didn't do anything wrong. We just sat around by the lake and the time kind of got away from us."

This one looked like a scarecrow but he at least sounded human. Dooley glared at him. He heard the front door of the house slam. "What's your name, son?"

"I'm Paul McKenna. I went to St. Tarcissus. That's how I know Donna and Kathy."

Suddenly the fight had gone out of Dooley. His daughter was

safe and he wasn't going to make these two drips into men by standing here barking at them. "You got a watch, Paul?"

"No, sir."

"Well, maybe you should think about getting one. Now get the hell out of here and go home."

Dooley ignored the squeal of tires as the Impala hightailed it out of there. When he got into the house there was no one in sight and it was ominously quiet. He found Rose sitting on the top step of the stairs, chin on her hand. "She's in her room," she said quietly. "I gave her the lecture already."

"It won't hurt her to hear it twice."

Dooley knocked on Kathleen's door but didn't bother to wait for an answer. When he pushed open the door she raised her head from the bed. "Go away," she said.

"You don't talk to me like that."

"I just did."

"I'll smack you if you don't watch it."

"That's all you understand, isn't it?"

"What's that supposed to mean?"

"That's all you understand, is violence. Pushing people around."

Dooley opened and closed his mouth a couple of times without anything coming out. He felt pressure building up inside him like steam in a boiler. He didn't have the words to explain things to this little girl. He wanted to slap her silly, shake her till her eyes crossed. She was looking at him with a sullen tear-streaked face and Dooley couldn't find his daughter in there anywhere. "You don't have the slightest idea what I understand," he said at last.

He thought she was going to put up a fight but she just let her head fall onto her arms. "And you don't have the slightest idea who I am."

Dooley stood there for a long time staring at her; she had hurt him and he wanted to hurt her back, but he couldn't come up with the words. "Well, whoever the hell you are," he said finally, "I hope you like it here, because you're gonna be spending a lot of time in this house for the next month." Dooley wheeled and left the room.

"I hate you," Kathleen said to his back.

Twenty-six

NIXON WAS IN Saigon, making small talk with Thieu in an air-conditioned palace. Meanwhile, up near the DMZ three marines had been killed in a night attack. Dooley had a feeling Nixon was getting a different view of the country than his boy Kevin was. The Cubs had beaten the Giants and were four and a half games up on the Mets; Willie Mays had been hurt in a collision at the plate.

The door to the inner office opened and a kid came slouching out like he had the weight of the world on his shoulders. He was maybe eighteen and he had hair down to his shoulders and he wore blue jeans and a loose-fitting shirt with a paisley pattern. Behind him came an older man and woman, about the right age to be his parents. The man wore a suit but didn't look like he belonged in it; the woman wore a worried frown. A fourth person stood in the doorway; he was in shirt-sleeves but wore a tie and the trousers to a nice dark blue suit. "I mean it about the haircut," he said. "Judges like the clean-cut look."

"He'll get it cut," said the older man, glowering at the kid. "I'll cut it myself."

Dooley laid the paper aside and watched the lawyer usher the happy family out into the hall. When they were gone he stood up to shake hands.

"Mr. Dooley? Bernie Shapiro. Sorry to keep you waiting," the lawyer said. "We go to court tomorrow. That boy was dumb enough to get caught speeding with a bag of marijuana on the seat beside him. I'm going to have a hell of a time keeping him out of Stateville."

Dooley didn't have much sympathy with dope users, but the thought of what a kid like that would go through in a cell block in Stateville, even with a haircut, made him shake his head. "Nothing a good spanking and a hitch in the service wouldn't fix," he said.

"That's one approach, I guess." Shapiro led him into an office with law books lining the shelves, a serviceable desk and a few wooden chairs on a worn carpet and a window with a view of the elevated tracks and beyond them the grime and sleaze of the South Loop. He waved Dooley to a seat. "Your phone call brought back memories," Shapiro said as he settled behind the desk. "Exciting times and fast company. I miss them a little every now and then. But not too much."

Dooley studied him for a second, seeing a dapper middle-aged man with dark eyes, silver hair, sideburns trimmed neatly to the earlobes. "You didn't have any trouble getting out? I didn't think you could just walk away."

"I didn't just walk away." Shapiro's face hardened for a moment. "There was a certain understanding, let's say. As long as I'm happy representing small-time drug users out of a low-rent office on South Wabash, nobody's going to bother me. But I'm afraid at this point I'm never going to make my poor widowed mother proud by becoming a judge. Not in this town."

Dooley nodded. "Puig told me you were too honest to prosper."

Shapiro smiled. "That's a compliment, I guess. Now what can I tell you about Tommy Spain?"

Dooley had tried different ways of explaining his fishing expedition but he was tired of beating around the bush. "You can tell me what Tommy Spain has to hide."

Shapiro laughed. "That's like asking what Sears has to sell. There's a whole catalogue. What department are we talking about?"

"His ex-girlfriend just got killed, after some pretty rough treatment. It looks like somebody wanted something from her. As far as we can tell, the Outfit killed her and set up a patsy for it. They went to a bit of trouble. And the only thing we can find in her background that's that important is Tommy Spain."

"I see." Shapiro held a thoughtful frown for a few seconds. "Well, Spain was always good at using people. He used his wife, so it wouldn't surprise me a bit if he used a girlfriend."

"I didn't know he had a wife."

"Yeah. He was married when I knew him. But I remember hearing he had divorced her."

"What do you mean, he used her?"

"Well, he had her hold money for him, open bank accounts, that kind of thing."

"That's interesting. That's the type of thing I think got the girlfriend in trouble."

"Could be. As for your first question, Tommy Spain has something to hide from everyone. He's played both sides against the middle for so long I'm not sure he knows which side he's really on. The one constant is that he always has insurance. He always has an ace up his sleeve."

"That's what I hear. Puig said you met him in Cuba?"

"That's right, in the good old days, before our pal Fidel turned it into a socialist paradise. Back then it was a different kind of paradise."

"And you went down there with Giancana?"

Shapiro grinned. "Is that what Puig told you? Not exactly. I went down there with the Mid-America Hotel Corporation. I had pretty good Spanish because I'd been in Panama during the war, and they needed a lawyer down there occasionally to look after their Cuban properties. Mid-America owned three hotels in Cuba before Castro came along and kicked everyone out. I spent a fair amount of time in Cuba in fifty-seven and fifty-eight. And yes, I ran into Giancana a couple of times. It didn't take me long to figure out who was behind the Mid-America Hotel Corporation."

"That was Giancana's outfit?"

"Oh, no. Not directly. But he and a bunch of other syndicate guys had pieces of it. It was a good venture for them. It was a legitimate company that ran real hotels. They used to own the Blackstone and the Drake here in town. But it was also great cover for those guys. The hotels all had casinos, and nobody's ever invented a better way to turn piles of cash into a nice secure bank account than owning a casino. Mid-America was a fabulous deal for them. And for me, to be frank. I used to love to go to Havana. A couple days' work, nothing very taxing for a competent lawyer, getting the VIP treatment, and you had a fabulous hotel suite overlooking the bay, balmy evenings, palms waving in the breeze, great food and unlimited booze, mambo music everywhere, a seat at the roulette table, women if you wanted, you name it. All you had to do was ignore the beggars and the occasional gunshot. Forgive me for getting a little nostalgic. It was all very intoxicating and very decadent. Anyway, that's where I met Tommy Spain."

"What was he doing there?"

"He came down with Giancana a couple of times. He spoke pretty good Spanish, and so he was very useful. Not that Giancana spent a lot of time mixing with the locals. I think Tommy's main job was just to keep Giancana out of trouble. You never knew when he was going to go off like a bomb and make a scene, cuss out the waiter, make a pass at the ambassador's wife, take a swing at another drunk. Tommy would roll his eyes, get Giancana calmed down, pay for the damages."

"This was in fifty-seven and eight? I thought Spain was on the police department here then."

"He was. I guess he didn't have any problem getting leave time. Anyway, we hit it off OK and sat up late drinking and talking once or twice. He'd been around, traveled a lot, had a lot of interests.

Had a broader view of the world than the rest of those guys, who were all basically Chicago street toughs when you got right down to it. Tommy was one smart son of a bitch."

Shapiro paused, looking off into a corner of the room. Dooley gave him a couple of seconds and said, "You keep in touch with him?"

Shapiro shook his head. "Not really. I'd hear about him, bump into him occasionally here in town. We had lunch a couple of times. I heard he'd been fired from the police department, and then he disappeared for a while. The last time I saw him, I ran into him in Adolph's, on Rush Street. That was in maybe sixty-two. And he said he'd been in Mexico."

"What was he doing down there?"

Shapiro gave a little laugh, shaking his head. "If you can believe him, all kinds of things. First of all, he said he'd been teaching classes in law enforcement techniques at a university in Mexico City. But he also dropped a few hints about what he called 'operations.' 'This operation I ran down in Mexico,' stuff like that."

"Operations for who?"

"He didn't say. But he hinted they had something to do with Cuba. I drew my own conclusions."

Dooley waited a beat and said, "I guess I'm a little slow. What do you mean?"

"Well, who do you think hired and trained all those poor saps that went into the Bay of Pigs?"

"You're kidding me. How did Spain get in on that?"

"Giancana."

Dooley peered at him across the desk. "You're starting to lose me."

"Sorry, I forget this isn't common knowledge." Shapiro sighed, leaned forward, shifted a paper on his desk an inch or so to the right. "This is all tied up with why I left Mid-America. By sixty-one I was starting to have doubts about the path my career was taking. I didn't like some of the things they'd started to ask me to do. I'd come to a fork in the road, really. I could go on making a lot of money and selling more of my soul to the devil each year, or I could say no and see how that went down with certain people. I chose to say no, and I think it was kind of touch-and-go there for a while as to whether I'd have a career or even a life after that. I was lucky. Somebody liked me. They let me walk away. They may even have forgotten about me. I think I can give you this, because Giancana's out of things now. But if you're going to use anything I tell you, it didn't come from me."

"OK. I'm used to protecting my witnesses."

"Fine. What happened was that the CIA used Giancana in a plot to kill Castro."

"You've got to be pulling my leg."

"I wish I was. You remember how it was when Castro nationalized everything and brought in the Russians. Panic in Washington. So somebody told the CIA to get Castro. But of course they didn't want their fingerprints on it."

"So they went to Giancana? What the hell are they putting in their drinks in Washington?"

Bernie Shapiro laughed, the laugh of a man who has seen it all and decided it might as well be funny. "Whatever it is, it doesn't help their judgment. Yeah, the CIA brought in the mob. It was a natural, really. The mob was probably already planning to go after him. He'd closed down all their operations down there. I don't know the ins and outs of it, but I know Giancana bragged about it. I heard him. He was proud of it. It let him pretend to be a good citizen, helping out the government. And Tommy Spain was his boy. I think that's what he was doing in Mexico, setting up the Bay of Pigs."

In Dooley's experience a murder investigation could take you to strange places, but this was a new one on him. "That's interesting," he said.

"Yeah. I have to say I never inquired further."

"I can understand that." Dooley blinked at him. "I don't know where that gets me to."

"I don't either. Maybe no place. Like I say, Tommy could have any number of things to hide. From any number of people on either side. All I can tell you is, step carefully, because the more you know about Tommy Spain, the more you're going to worry certain people. And the way Tommy operates, you aren't even going to know who those people are."

Dooley sat bemused for a moment. "I'd like to try to talk to his wife. Can you tell me how to find her?"

"Gosh, I don't know. I heard she moved to Florida. Maybe you can track her down there. Her name was Marlene, Marlene something. I don't know her maiden name but she might have kept his. Puig might know more. Somebody will know. I don't know if she'll talk to you, though. Mob women learn to keep their mouths shut, just like the guys. It's a survival strategy. She might be too scared to talk to you."

Dooley nodded. "Who can blame her?"

• • •

"Take off the gloves," said Kowalcyk. "They want a fight, we'll give them a fight."

Nyman nodded. "Damn right. That's an act of war. I say we bring back the National Guard, and turn 'em loose this time. No quarter."

"Hell with the National Guard. Bring in the fuckin' Marines."

"There you go. Give them a chance to send out the women and children, then go in with everything we've got. Automatic weapons, tanks. Surrender or die. You got a black beret on, you better have your hands in the air. Why should we put up with this shit?"

"Hampton, Rush, all those guys. We know where they are, we know what they're up to. What are we waiting for?"

"Fuck it. Treat the West Side like we treated Berlin. Bomb the shit out of it, then occupy it for twenty years."

They were starting to get on Dooley's nerves; he had work to do. "Why not go all the way?" he said. "Let the Russians have half of it."

Nyman and Kowalcyk stared at him. "Suits me," said Nyman. "Maybe they can do something with it."

Cops all over the city were flinching at loud noises; two nights ago five policemen had been shot at Black Panther headquarters out on West Madison. Somebody had fired on a squadrol and touched off a half-hour battle that had ended with the building in flames. Nobody had been killed, but nerves were frayed.

"I wouldn't work out on the West Side these days for any kind of money," said Kowalcyk, moving away.

"Just be glad you don't have to live out there." Dooley had grown up on the West Side and it made him sad to see what had happened to it. He looked at his phone message: *Call Campbell* followed by a number. He went to the phone and got through to Campbell after a short wait. "I got a guy who might be able to help you," Campbell said.

"Terrific."

"You gotta handle with care, because he's going out on a limb talking to you. But he owes me a favor and he said he'd help."

"I'll put on the kid gloves. Who we talking about?"

"A guy named Martin Greenberg. He has a jewelry store down on Randolph. He got robbed and pistol-whipped a few years back when I was in Robbery and I tracked down the bad guys and got his stuff back for him, so he thinks I'm God. He's also done time for fencing, and I would guess he's still in the business, but I don't look too close because he's more help where he is. You get the picture, I'm sure."

"Yeah."

"Anyway, he says if the locket got fenced by a guy on Lombardo's crew he can probably track it down. He'll need to talk to your witness."

"That can be arranged."

"He also said there are no guarantees. It's like I told you, if your killer's got any brains, he didn't fence it here."

"I'm not even sure he ever had it," said Dooley. "I'm grasping at straws."

"That's half a dick's life, isn't it? Grasping at straws and wearing out shoe leather. Anyway, he says go see him at 110 East Randolph, Greenberg's Jewelry, any time."

"I'll do that. Thanks, Johnny."

"Don't mention it. Just remember to scratch my back the next time it itches."

"You got it."

• • •

The Friday Night Fights was what Dooley called it: a busy evening for cops. Get off work, hit the bars, start drinking. Booze, women, tempers running high. People who had taken grief all week at work were in no mood to take it on Friday night. There were a lot of drunken swings that missed, a few that connected. Knives came out and kept the emergency room doctors busy stitching. The occasional gun got dragged out of a pocket. Most of the time everyone survived to sleep it off and spend a groggy Saturday making vows of cleaner living. But a small, steady percentage of the hundreds of bar fights across the city could be counted on to make more work for busy detectives. Friday nights were prime time for homicide.

Dooley had seen this one before, a couple of dozen times. The tavern was called Sammy's, one of a rank of low-rent storefronts facing the blank wall of the El embankment across a narrow street, on the far North Side. It was a long room with a jukebox, a pinball machine, a little bar-sized pool table and a dead man perched on a stool at the bar. He looked as if he had gotten tired and leaned forward to lay his head down on the bar for a brief nap. The hole just above and to the rear of his ear had dispensed a trickle of blood that had seeped through his gray hair and crept along the line of his jaw to pool by his chin on the hard shiny wood of the bar.

There were two people in the bar when Dooley and Olson got there, not counting the two uniforms and the dead man. The bartender was behind the bar and an old man in a shiny suit was huddled on a stool at the far end. "Nobody saw a fucking thing," the older patrolman told Dooley. "You got your work cut out for you."

Dooley stood looking at the scene for a moment, hands in his pockets. "You let anybody leave?" he asked.

"Hell, no. This is all there was when we got here. A couple of people tried to come in, but we shooed 'em away."

"OK, thanks. Do me a favor, though. If anyone else wants to come in, or just shows up to gawk, hold them for me." Dooley took a few paces down the bar, Olson at his shoulder. "What do you see?" Dooley said in a low voice.

"He died in a hurry, that's what I see. A nice clean shot, didn't bleed much."

"What else?"

It took Olson a couple of seconds, but he got it. "I see a lot of glasses on the bar. A lot more than I see people."

"Yeah." They stopped in front of the bartender, who sat on a stool behind the bar, arms folded. He was gaunt and morose, and this wasn't going to improve his mood. "You know the victim?" Dooley asked him.

The bartender just looked at him for a couple of seconds before answering. "Yeah. Jim, his name was."

"Last name?"

"I don't know. He never told me."

"He a regular customer?"

"Yeah. He was in here a lot."

Dooley dug in the dead man's hip pocket and pulled out a wallet. Inside it was a driver's license with the name *James Moore* and an address on Farwell. Dooley put the wallet in his jacket pocket. "OK, how about you?"

"What about me?"

"Your name."

"Philip Day."

"You the owner?"

The bartender sighed. "Till I can unload the place. I almost sold out and went to Florida last year. Should have listened to my wife."

"OK, what happened?"

"I don't know. It was pretty crowded in here. I was down at the end of the bar pouring a drink when I heard the shot. I looked up and all I saw was somebody running out the door."

"Description?"

"I couldn't say. It happened too fast."

"Short, tall? Old, young?"

The owner looked at Dooley for a long moment and said, "All I saw was the commotion, really. My view was blocked."

"Somebody saw it. What did they tell you?"

"Nobody told me anything. I just picked up the phone and called the cops. And by the time I got off the phone everyone had left. I tried to stop them but they all left."

"Before you could ask anyone what had happened?"

The owner's eyes flicked away for a second and then came back. "I asked, but nobody could say for sure. Somebody just walked in off the street and shot him."

Dooley stared at him for a moment. "OK." He took out his notebook and a pen and laid them on the bar. "I want you to write down the name of everyone you knew who was in here when it happened. Addresses if you know them."

Moving like a man under water, the owner pulled the notebook and pen toward him. He clicked the ballpoint a couple of times and put a hand to his brow. "Lemme see. Christ, I don't know."

"Work on it." Dooley moved down the bar toward the old man. When he was halfway there he could see he wasn't going to be much help; he looked like he was about to fall off the stool. "What's your name?" Dooley said.

"What the hell's it to ya?" The old man's face contracted with the effort of getting the words out, trying and failing to focus his rheumy eyes on Dooley.

"I need it for your statement."

"What statement?"

"About the shooting."

"What shooting?"

"Forget it." Dooley beckoned to Olson and led him back up the bar, past the owner frowning at Dooley's notebook, past the patrol cops at the door and out onto the sidewalk. "What do you think?" he said.

"I think the owner saw more than he's saying."

"What else?"

"I think we need to find the rest of the witnesses."

"Yeah. Why did they run away?"

Olson shrugged. "They didn't want to get involved."

"Why not? The guy was a regular customer. They probably all knew him. Somebody walks into your neighborhood tavern and shoots one of your friends, wouldn't you stick around to tell the cops who did it? At least give a description if you could?"

Olson nodded slowly. "Unless I knew the guy who did it and was afraid of him."

"That might do it. But there's strength in numbers. Usually people will stick together in a situation like that. You might be scared, but with three or four of your pals there to back you up you're more likely to have the guts to say what you saw. Even if you're by yourself you might sneak back when you saw the cops show up and hang around waiting for a chance to talk to them. But I don't see anybody." Dooley gestured at the empty sidewalk.

Olson peered at him and then smiled. "I get it. They all thought he had it coming."

Dooley nodded and started walking up toward the corner. "Yeah. He had it coming. Everybody saw who did it, but nobody wants to be the one who turns her in."

"Her?"

"The owner said he saw somebody running out the door. He didn't say 'I saw a guy.' Just 'somebody.' Maybe it doesn't mean anything, but my first guess is it's going to be a woman. The wife, probably. Anyway, somebody will tell us. We'll throw them all in the wagon and give them time to think about it on the way down."

"OK, but we gotta find them first."

"Shouldn't be too hard. I'd start there." They had reached the corner and Dooley was pointing across the street and half a block down, where a neon sign hung above the window of another bar. "It's Friday night," said Dooley. "Who the hell wants to to go home? At least half of them are in there getting their stories straight."

When they walked into the second bar the conversation stopped instantly, leaving Tom Jones on the jukebox bellowing "Love Me Tonight" all by himself. There was a knot of people at the end of the bar that had frozen solid. Dooley beckoned to the bartender. "How long have they been in here?" he said, pointing at the group.

The bartender blinked, shrugged, and said, "I don't know. Maybe half an hour."

Dooley approached the huddle. "I got a wagon coming and I got a man who's going to take fingerprints off the glasses on the bar over at Sammy's. Anybody want to tell me you weren't there?"

Nobody did; after a couple of seconds a man swallowed hard and said, "The son of a bitch had it coming. He used to beat the hell out of that poor girl."

"Slow down," said Dooley. "We got all night."

Twenty-seven

THE FIRST WEEKEND in August caught everyone by surprise: it didn't rain. It was cool at night now, sinking into the sixties after the usual eighty-degree days. Dooley came home on Sunday night, early Monday morning to be exact, and drank his Jameson out in the yard, looking up at the stars. He dozed off in the lawn chair and woke up shivering.

In the morning it was heating up again and the paper was waiting for him on the kitchen table. There was rioting in Belfast, Catholics throwing Molotov cocktails at the British army. Lots of luck, Dooley thought.

He lingered over this one: the Ninth Marines had killed thirty-nine NVA in a firefight near Duc Hoa while sustaining only two wounded. Dooley wondered if it was a good sign. He wondered when the hell they were going to pull his boy out and bring him home.

The Cubs had won in Wrigley Field; Billy Williams had swatted a three-run homer in the eighth to wipe out a two-run Padre lead. Dooley found it hard to believe there was a National League team in San Diego. He still had trouble thinking of Los Angeles and San Francisco as big-league cities. The world was starting to pass him by. The Cubs were six up on the Mets and nine on the Cards, and Dooley figured this had to be the beginning of the end.

"You're leaving early again?" said Rose as he pulled on his jacket. "I'm fixing chicken salad for lunch."

"Gotta go talk to a guy. Gotta catch him during the day."

"Why can't the guys on days talk to him?"

"It's my case. I like to keep track of things myself. Save some chicken salad for me, I'll have it when I come home."

She put her lips up to be kissed, looking a little bewildered, a little hurt. "This is all paid overtime, right?"

Dooley couldn't lie to her; he never had been able to. "Not all of it. There's some loose ends on a case we cleared that bother me. Just following up a couple of things. But I have to do it on my own time."

"You're doing all this work for free?"

"No, I'm not doing it all for free." Dooley picked up his briefcase. "Just some of it."

Rose tracked him on his way to the door. "We'll be lucky if we can afford the Dells this year," she said.

Dooley paused with his hand on the doorknob. "Think about the Skokie Lagoons. They have picnic tables there, I hear."

• • •

Greenberg's Jewelry was on the third floor of an old building with a big echoing lobby, elevators that still had old black men on high stools to run them, and long corridors floored with black and white hexagonal tiles. The shop was one of several on the floor, each with a locked door that could be buzzed open if the visitor passed muster. Greenberg himself had thinning white hair swept back from a high forehead and he looked as if gravity had pulled all the flesh off his shoulders and chest and deposited it in the round pouch that was pushing out his trousers under the constriction of his belt. He had a jutting lower lip that glistened in the fluorescent light. "Girls like you are dangerous for a man with a bad heart," he said in the throaty wheeze of an unhealthy man. He had hardly taken his eyes off Laura since ushering her and Dooley into his cramped little back room with a scattering of tools on a table and a first-class view of a blank wall across the alley.

"I'll try not to make any sudden noises," Laura said.

Greenberg laughed with a sound like a shovel scraping on concrete. "Honey, you can do anything you want to." He dragged his eyes away from her and looked at Dooley. "I'd love to take her around myself. I could tell them she's my niece or something. The problem is, I can't afford to have anybody get ideas about me. I don't want to wind up in a garbage can somewhere. I'm way out on a limb already, just talking to you, talking to your pal Campbell. I help her find this piece and then somebody gets arrested, there won't be any mystery about who pointed the finger."

"So what happens?"

"*You* take her around. You ever work robbery?"

"For a year, a long time ago. Mostly muggings, strong-arm stuff. Never got involved in jewels."

"Then they don't know you, right?"

"They shouldn't."

"OK, then you try not to look like a cop, and you do a little acting. You've got a nice young girl here you want to buy a present for. You let it slip you want to keep it a little quiet, do everything in cash so there's no checks the wife might see. That makes you the type of customer they're looking for. Can you do that?"

Dooley exchanged a glance with Laura. She gave him a cool smile. "Why not?" she said. "I always liked play-acting."

Dooley frowned at Greenberg. "I can do that," he said.

"Sure you can." Greenberg reached for a pencil. "OK, look. From the way you describe it, this is not a particularly valuable piece you're looking for. If it's genuine, it might be worth a few hundred bucks. So I don't think it landed with one of the guys up on Michigan Avenue. They only handle the real valuable stuff.

If somebody on Lombardo's crew tried to fence something like what you're talking about, then he probably took it to somebody like Steve Spanos down on Jackson. He's got a store down there and he'll sell you just about anything. He's got good Outfit connections, and Outfit guys like to go to fences they trust. Another guy to try might be Maury Fisher just down the street here. He's been known to buy a few things with no questions asked but he's not a big-time guy." Greenberg scribbled on a notepad, tore off the sheet and handed it to Dooley. "Of course, if the guy knows you're looking for it there's always a chance he might have gone outside regular channels. He might have pawned it, even though most pawnshops are pretty careful because they don't want to lose their licenses. He could even have just taken it down to Maxwell Street or something. If the thing can tie somebody to a murder the smart thing to do would be to go somewhere else. But then greed just about always trumps intelligence with those guys. Have a good time and for God's sake don't tell anyone I sent you."

• • •

"I don't know," said Laura. "It's all beautiful, but I just don't see anything that like, speaks to me, you know?"

Maury Fisher was short and fat and had more hair in his eyebrows than on the top of his head. He nodded with a sympathetic expression that looked a little forced to Dooley. Dooley figured he was running out of patience.

Dooley could lie when he had to; playing a role was a big part of being a dick sometimes, but this role didn't come easy to him. He said, "You wouldn't have anything in the back room you haven't shown us yet, would you?" Both Laura and Fisher stared at him and he thought, no, too direct.

"Nothing that's for sale," said the jeweler.

"Uh-huh." Dooley glared at him. "I mean, I'm prepared to pay cash. If there's something a little, you know, special back there."

Fisher was staring at him wide-eyed, looking as if Dooley had spit on his shoes. "I'm not sure what you mean by special," he said.

"I don't know. Something unusual."

The jeweler carefully replaced the tray on its shelf under the glass counter. "Everything I have to offer is right here," he said mildly.

• • •

"I'm no damn good at this," said Dooley. "He saw right through me." He and Laura were walking south on Wabash with an El train rumbling overhead. He had to shout at her over the noise. He felt better out here on the street, with taxis honking at one another and trying to muscle pedestrians out of the crosswalks, traffic cops yelling at the slow-witted and the stubborn, the endless stream of people.

"You were perfect."

"No, I wasn't"

"Yes you were." Laura was in a sleeveless blouse, miniskirt, and sandals today, and Dooley watched men watching her as they passed. "You came off just like a guy with a girlfriend he's trying to impress. Showing me your savoir-faire, except you weren't quite as smart as you thought you were. Believe me, I've been with men like that, a dozen times. And that's all the guy saw."

Dooley walked with his hands in his pockets, trying to figure out if she was giving him a compliment or not. "I don't know. I think we're wasting our time."

"Maybe, maybe not. Let's go see this guy on Jackson."

• • •

"It's for me," said Laura. "It's my birthday."

She flashed a killer smile and the man behind the desk cocked an eyebrow at her. "Well, well," he said. Stephen Spanos was at the tail end of his fifties, with ample dark hair shot through with gray and combed straight back off a high forehead. He had LBJ-sized ears, a long Roman nose, and a clean-shaven pointed chin, and he looked as if he might have had a fair amount of success with the ladies at one time or another. "Many happy returns. You're a lucky girl to have someone to buy you nice things." He looked at Dooley and said, "And you're a lucky man."

"Yeah." Dooley tried to fake a smile but it didn't quite come off. They were in a cramped office at the back of a long narrow shop on Jackson just west of Halsted. From where he sat Dooley could see all the way up to the front of the shop, past shelves bearing a jumble of radios, clocks, toys, tablecloths, sweaters, shoe boxes, perfume. He could see cardboard boxes stacked along the wall, some of them with names like Zenith and Norelco on them. Just outside the door of the office were clothes racks with suits on hangers. "I'm lucky all right," Dooley said. He risked a look at Laura and saw her beaming at him.

"You're so good to me," she said.

Dooley managed to stretch his lips a little and turned to Spanos. "So what have you got?"

Spanos used a key to open a drawer of the desk and pulled out a metal box. "You're looking for a necklace?"

Laura said, "Something like that. I had a locket I really liked when I was a little girl. I lost it and I've always wanted to have another one."

"A locket." Spanos opened the box. "Let me see."

"A locket, a pendant, something like that."

"There's this." Spanos laid a silver pendant on a chain out on the desktop.

"Ooh, that's pretty." Laura leaned forward and picked up the bauble. "You like that?" She showed it to Dooley.

"Very nice."

"That's a definite possibility. Can I see what else you have?"

"Of course." Spanos pulled more things out of the box: gold and silver necklaces, a pendant with a single ruby, a gold teardrop locket. Laura cooed over them but put them all down.

"I like pearls," she said. "You know, those tiny little ones. My grandmother had a brooch with little pearls on it. I always wanted to have something like that."

"Seed pearls?"

"That's right. You have anything with seed pearls on it?"

Spanos frowned, and Dooley thought immediately: she laid it on too thick. Spanos peered at her for a few seconds and said, "You're looking for something very specific, aren't you?"

Dooley was afraid she'd blown it but had to admit she was a natural actress. Laura flashed her dazzling smile and said, "Yeah, I guess I am. I want my cheap little locket that I used to love, except all nice and covered with pearls. I'm not going to find that, am I?"

Spanos's frown eased. "Not today, not here, I'm afraid."

Laura looked at the pieces on the desktop and heaved a sigh. "Well, I guess it's time to make a choice," she said.

Dooley nearly fell off his chair. "Not necessarily," he said. "If you don't see what you want, we'll go somewhere else."

"You won't get a better price anywhere else," said Spanos.

Dooley figured it was high time he took things in hand. "We can always come back." He put a hand on Laura's arm. "What do you say we look around a bit more?"

"OK, I guess." She smiled at Spanos. "Thank you so much for your time."

"It was a pleasure." They all stood up and Spanos shook hands with them across the desktop. "If I see something like what you're looking for, you want me to get in touch?" he said.

"Why, sure, I guess."

"Why don't you leave me your phone number, then? Or yours?" He looked at Dooley.

"Better make it hers," said Dooley.

Spanos smiled. "However you want to do it. Discretion is my middle name."

• • •

"I thought you were going to have a heart attack. All the blood drained out of your face." Laura was still grinning about it as Dooley pulled away from the curb.

"I thought you'd gone nuts. I thought I was going to walk out of there with a hundred bucks' worth of stolen jewelry I couldn't afford."

"I got you good."

"You sure did."

"I'll make it up to you. Let me buy you lunch."

Dooley gave her a sidelong look. "You don't have to buy me lunch."

"I want to. When was the last time a lady bought you lunch?"

"I don't know. Maybe never."

"So let me treat you. When do you have to be at work?"

"Not till four."

"Well, we've got lots of time, then. Where do you want to go?"

Dooley was of two minds about the whole thing: he had been determined to keep things strictly professional, but lunch with Laura sounded a lot better than anything else he had on the schedule till four o'clock. "There's a couple of decent places on Halsted," he said.

They had missed the lunch rush and didn't have to wait for a booth. The Greek who ran the place made a fuss over Laura and gave Dooley a knowing look behind her back. Dooley didn't want any rumors flying around but it made him feel good to be sitting there across from a beautiful woman. They got the ordering out of the way and there was a silence, and all of a sudden Dooley got nervous because he felt like he was on a date. He took a drink of water, avoiding Laura's eyes.

"Relax, Dooley. You don't have to try and make time with me." She was smiling her wry little smile.

"It never occurred to me."

"I believe you. I think that's why I like you."

Dooley couldn't think of a response to that. He had started to relax but he didn't want to talk about himself today. He said, "So tell me. How does a smart girl like you wind up in a bunny suit?"

She laughed. "I was young and stupid, what can I say? Hey, at first it was great. I thought I had it made. I was a *bunny.* It was going to be my ticket to Hollywood. They get you to buy this whole elite mentality. They keep telling you what a privilege it is to wear that costume, so you overlook what it's doing to your body. Jesus, I'd peel that thing off after work and feel my insides shift, everything falling back into place where it was supposed to be. I could breathe again. I would have these like, welts where the damn thing constricted me. You cannot *imagine* how uncomfortable it was."

Dooley could imagine other things, though: Laura peeling off the bunny costume. "I didn't get the impression you left a lot of friends at the Playboy Club."

Laura vented a little whiff of laughter. "No. I wouldn't call anybody there my friend. What did they tell you about me?"

"They said you weren't cut out for the organization. Something like that."

"They got that one right. It took me a while to see through it, though."

"What made you change your mind?"

"Besides the constant groping, you mean? The need to smile and be nice to people who made you want to puke?"

Dooley laughed. "Yeah. Besides that."

"The exploitation, maybe. The nitpicky rules. The drudgery. For an elite we were sure treated a lot like plain old waitresses. Except we were expected to be whores, too."

"I thought there was a hands-off policy. That's what I've heard, anyway."

"Not for the right customers. Hands off the bunnies doesn't apply to the really big spenders or the celebrities. With them it was, 'Look, this man's a very important customer. I'll leave it to your judgment.' And if you said no, you moved a few notches down on the Room Director's list of favorites. Things got harder."

Dooley wanted to ask if she'd ever said yes, but he didn't. "I can see how it could wear on you."

"It did. But I didn't really break through until I started to read things."

"What'd you read?"

"A book called *The Feminine Mystique*. It opened my eyes."

"I think I heard of it." This was thin ice for Dooley, a veteran reader of newspapers but no bookworm.

"It's about how women are defined only by their relationships to men. They're not allowed to establish their own identities."

Dooley worked on that for a second and said, "Who's stopping them?"

"The whole culture. Advertising, movies, TV. Woman as sexual object, woman as doting mother, that's all you see."

Dooley scratched at his neck with a thumbnail. He was being challenged, he felt, but he wasn't sure for what or how to respond. "You seem to be doing OK."

Laura laughed. "That's the point. I'm doing OK because I saw through the whole thing."

The salads arrived. Dooley worked at his, trying not to get French dressing on his tie. "So you quit at the Playboy Club because you were tired of being a sex object. So how can you stand up there in front of your artist friend with your clothes off?"

She grinned, rising to the challenge. "I know he's not going to make a pass at me, for one thing. But you missed the point, Dooley. Sex is a good thing, and it's just as bad to shove it down out of sight as it is to package it and sell it. The point is not that *Playboy* is bad because sex is dirty. *Playboy* is bad because sex is something that ought to be free and they make it a commodity like detergent or toothpaste."

"Well, I agree you shouldn't have to pay for it."

"And why do people have to pay for it? Because they can't get it freely, like the air they breathe. It's all tied up in taboos. And we need it like we need air. We have to do away with the limits that make people frustrated and crazy about sex."

"No limits at all, huh?"

"Well, some, sure. It can't be imposed, or extorted. And it's best when it grows out of friendship."

"Friendship? Whatever happened to love?"

She put her head on one side, looking thoughtful. "I'm not sure what the difference is, except just the degree. I love my friends, my friends are the people I love."

Dooley chewed on that along with his salad for a while. He wiped his mouth and said, "So I take it you're not in the market for a husband?"

She grimaced. "Frankly, I don't think a whole lot of the institution of marriage. All it ever brought my mother was misery. My father cheated on her and hit her when he got drunk. The best thing she ever did for herself and for us was to leave him."

"There are marriages like that. They don't have to be that way."

"Maybe not. But they're always a bad deal for the woman."

"Come on."

"I mean it. Ask your wife sometime if she's gotten everything out of life she wanted."

"Nobody gets everything they want out of life."

Dooley thought he'd scored, finally; she sat there shaking her head for a few seconds, looking a little bit amused. Finally she said, "Marriage is fine. As long as a woman has other choices, too. Marriage shouldn't be the only way to go."

Shrugging, Dooley said, "I'm not arguing with you."

"You better not. I'm buying lunch."

Dooley just looked at her for a while, meeting her cool smile with what he hoped was a confident superior look, until the entrees arrived to break things up. "You're something," Dooley said, picking up a fork. "You're really something, aren't you?"

• • •

"Puig Investigations. What can I do for you?"

"It's Mike Dooley. We had a talk about Tommy Spain a while back." Dooley wasn't sure why he was standing here in this phone booth on Belmont instead of phoning from the office, except that something told him it was a good idea to keep things off the radar for a while yet.

"Dooley, oh, yeah. What's new? You talk to those guys I told you about?"

"Bellisario and Shapiro, yeah. They were helpful. Bellisario put me on to Arnold Swallow."

"Arnie Swallow? Spain's old partner? He talked to you? I'm amazed."

"He didn't want to. I had to use a little leverage."

"I bet that was interesting. What'd he tell you?"

"Nothing yet. I told him to try to find out what Spain's hiding."

"Boy. Step carefully there, will you? I think Swallow's bad news."

"He's kind of dubious, yeah. I'll be careful."

"What about Bernie? He tell you anything useful?"

"I don't know. He told me some strange things, about Mexico and Cuba."

"Tommy's been involved in some strange things, all right."

"He also told me about Spain's wife."

"Marlene? What about her?"

"I'd like to talk to her. Shapiro didn't know what happened to her."

"Wow, I don't either. They got divorced back in sixty-one or two, I think, and she left town. With their daughter. I remember him telling me they were in Florida. Miami, I think. I know he kept in touch because of the daughter. He used to have pictures of her he'd haul out to show people. She'd be, I don't know, maybe eleven or twelve now."

"Do you know what name the wife's using?"

"I don't think I ever knew her maiden name. She might still be using his, I guess. Or she might have gotten married again. I don't think she was the type to let the grass grow under her feet. I'll tell you what, I bet I can find out where she is. Somebody will know. Give me a little time."

"Thanks, John. I appreciate it. Let me know if there's anything I can do for you, any time."

"Oh, I imagine I'll need a friend in the CPD at some point or other."

"Just let me know."

"I will. And hey, Mike."

"What?"

"I mean it about stepping carefully. All these guys, Swallow, Spain, all of them. You're starting to get into serious company."

"I get that impression," said Dooley.

Twenty-eight

DOOLEY PUT ON his uniform carefully, checking everything in the mirror to see that the insignia were right, the tie perfect, the cap squared away. He didn't put on the uniform very often anymore, and it felt strange to him. He looked at himself in the mirror and for just a second he missed wearing it every day; he had to wonder what he would look like in a gold-banded cap, something he'd given up on a long time ago.

In the kitchen Rose's eyes widened when she saw him; she knew what the uniform meant. "Funeral?" she said.

"Yeah. Down on the South Side." Dooley had thrown his suit in a garment bag; he'd take it with him in the car and change out of the uniform at Damen and Grace before roll call.

"Who is it?"

Dooley busied himself with the zipper on the garment bag, not wanting to look at Rose because he couldn't lie to her if he was looking at her. "An old copper I worked with a long time ago."

Rose picked lint off the dark blue dress coat, smoothed his lapels. "You look very handsome in the uniform."

"That's what it's for." Dooley wondered if Rose was thinking wistfully about that gold-banded cap.

She kissed him on the cheek. "Be careful."

He looked into her eyes and felt a brief spasm of anger; he wished he didn't have to lie to her. "You bet," he said.

On the expressway Dooley tried to sort out all his feelings: his heart was heavy because of where he was going and he was irritated with himself for lying to Rose, and he was irritated with her for not being tough enough to take the truth. Dooley had seen the obit in the paper: *4 Area GI's Slain in Viet Nam.* He always read the obits with superstitious attention and the name had jumped out at him: *Marine Lance Corp. George Wilkins, 20, the son of Police Sgt. and Mrs. Raymond Wilkins of 6912 S. Aberdeen, Chicago, was killed by enemy fire in Quang Tri province on August 2.* There had been a notice about the funeral service in the bulletin at work.

Dooley knew that if he told Rose whose funeral he was going to, it would only drive her nuts. As for him, he was all over the map. He'd known all along Kevin was in the thick of it, but this was getting too close. On the other hand, maybe this increased the chances Kevin would be OK, on the theory that lightning didn't strike twice in the same place; maybe George Wilkins had used up the bad luck for both of them. But Dooley knew that was bullshit; in combat, lightning could strike as much as it wanted, anywhere it wanted.

He didn't know what he was going to say to George Wilkins's father. My boy is still alive and yours isn't, he thought. Dooley figured he had to go, and he figured he would know what to say when he got there.

It was a bright hot day and the traffic wasn't too bad and Dooley was past the Loop and on the Ryan before he knew it. The service was at St. Columbanus on Seventy-first Street; Dooley was a Northsider and didn't know the South Side parishes that well, but St. Columbanus was an Irishman and he figured this must be one of the holdout parishes. Aberdeen was far enough west that maybe it wasn't all black yet. The South Side Irish had mostly moved out past Marquette Park, but there were some pockets yet where people were just staying put.

He got off the Ryan and got onto Seventy-first Street and went east, and before he knew it he was there. St. Columbanus was a big handsome brick church with a lot of fake Gothic tracery in concrete, one of the lavish parish churches thrown up in the twenties by a community starting to come into money. Dooley parked on the street a block away. The street had looked pretty black to Dooley coming along from the expressway, but the neighborhood didn't look bad at all, and Dooley figured the church still drew a lot of the original parishioners from farther west. People were milling on the steps of the church and Dooley saw a lot of blue uniforms. He had never met a Ray Wilkins on the department, which wasn't surprising if Wilkins was a South-sider; with a good Chinaman you could work your whole career not too far from home.

There were a lot of Negroes in the crowd around the door of the church, which surprised Dooley a little; Wilkins must have made a lot of friends up in Prairie District. Dooley nodded at a couple of cops but saw nobody he recognized; he was surprised to see a couple of black coppers as well, not a species he was very familiar with. The penny didn't drop until Dooley was inside the church, crossing himself and looking around, seeing lots of dark faces. Jesus Christ, Kevin, you could have told me, he thought.

Dooley made his way up the aisle toward the front of the church, readjusting the picture he'd had in his mind the whole way here. He knew perfectly well there were black marines and black policemen and even black Catholics, but he'd been so sure that a combination of the three had to be someone that looked a lot like him that he was a little bit in shock. He wasn't the only white person by a long shot, but all of a sudden he wasn't so sure he ought to be here.

Dooley joined the line at the head of the aisle waiting to say what there was to say to the parents. The coffin sitting up front was closed, and Dooley knew what that meant. The priest was busy with something up near the altar, and he, at least, was white; Dooley started to get his feet back under him. He waited patiently in line, his hands clasped, casting glances at the Negroes all around him dressed in their Sunday best and looking dazed and forlorn.

Raymond Wilkins stood tall in his sergeant's uniform and accepted condolences with a firming of the lips and a solid handshake. He had very dark skin and just a touch of gray at the temples, and he looked like a man you would think twice about before you messed with him. He had a stack of service bars on his sleeve and a chest full of department commendations and unit meritorious awards. His wife was a handsome woman with a face the color of coffee and big dark liquid eyes that looked like they had all the pain in the world down there in the depths somewhere.

Dooley stepped up and held out his hand. "Mike Dooley, I'm up in Area Six." He had had an idea of what he was going to say, but when he took hold of Wilkins's hand and looked him in the eye he couldn't squeeze out a word. His mouth hung open for a couple of seconds and Dooley tried to force something out of a throat that was clenched tight and finally he had to take a breath and start over, and it was all he could do to get the words out. "I have a boy over there, too. He wrote me about your son. They were friends." Dooley had to take another breath before he could say, "I'm sorry."

Wilkins leaned toward him, still holding his hand. "What's your boy's name?" he said quietly.

"Kevin."

Wilkins traded a look with his wife and said, "Yeah, I think George mentioned him. God bless him, I hope he comes home."

"I'm sorry," Dooley whispered, looking at the wife now, and she took his hand in both of hers and to Dooley's amazement she smiled at him even as a tear broke from the corner of one of her big dark eyes and ran down her cheek.

"We'll be praying for Kevin," she said.

Dooley made his way down the side aisle to an empty pew; he genuflected and slid in and sat down. He laid his cap on the pew beside him and looked up into the far reaches of the vault, at the gilt and the stained glass and the plaster. The mass started and he made all the right responses and stood and knelt when he had to and closed his eyes and bowed his head for the prayers and the whole time he was thinking how you could go your whole life long seeing things one way and all of a sudden something happened and you would never see things the same way again.

Dooley didn't consider himself a prejudiced person; he believed that Negroes had all the rights he had, and he believed in integration as long as they didn't force it down anyone's throat, and he had dealt with black people in all walks of life with decency and courtesy, but until this moment, if you had asked him, he would have said they were different; they just were.

It was funny what your mind retained: Dooley had had a little Shakespeare thrown at him in high school, like everyone else, and it hadn't meant a lot to him but he was remembering something now. *If you cut us, do we not bleed,* he remembered. Dooley sat there looking at the back of Raymond Wilkins's head, watching the man bleed and thinking yes, now he knew: they bleed just like we do, just the same.

• • •

Dooley didn't handle many rape cases; Homicide and Sex were the same unit but you could get a reputation as a specialist and Dooley was a top-notch homicide man. Sometimes, though, you just had to catch what was coming down. Olson was steering west on Foster toward the address of a murder witness who had changed her story a couple of times when the magic number came over the radio.

"Seven six oh two, respond. Seven six oh two."

"Hey, we're being paged." Olson let Dooley reach for the mike; even when he was driving, Dooley got to reach for the mike because he was the top dog.

"Seven six oh two here."

"Seven six oh two, proceed to four five two three North Kenmore. Officers on scene with assault victim."

Dooley repeated the address and hung up the mike as Olson pulled a U-turn at an intersection. "What do you know? A live victim for a change."

The address was a dark red-brick courtyard building on a block that was not as nice as it had been ten or twenty years before. There were a couple of squads parked in front and a crowd of people with not enough going on in their lives milling on the sidewalk. "Lady got raped, up on the third floor," said a laconic patrolman as he pointed them to the right doorway.

The lady was no more than twenty-five or so and she was remarkably composed considering the way her day had gone; she sat on a couch with a child on either side of her and one on her lap held tight in her arms. The apartment was a little on the shabby side and it seemed awfully crowded to Dooley, with a couple of uniforms and a middle-aged lady with rhinestone glasses hovering around the couch. The children's eyes were big and round and they had a hold on their mother that nobody was going to break. They reminded Dooley of a rabbit he had seen once cornered by a dog, frozen and trembling. They were maybe two, six, and eight years old, the oldest a girl with pigtails.

Their mother had dark hair and eyes and a round, pleasant face only a little bit marred by a fresh shiner around her right eye. She was dressed in a yellow sleeveless blouse and a pair of brown nylon slacks, but a couple of buttons were missing on the blouse and it gaped open, revealing the white of her bra underneath. Her eyes came back from far away when Dooley knelt in front of her and the look she gave him said she wasn't expecting much in the way of comfort from him.

"If you need to see a doctor, let's take care of that first," said Dooley. "We don't have to get into the questions yet if you don't want to."

She blinked at him for long enough that Dooley started to wonder if she'd heard him and then she said, "No, I'm all right." She didn't sound convinced.

"Are you in pain? Are you bleeding?"

"No. I'm OK."

He could barely hear her.

"All right." Dooley stood up and looked around the room. "Do me a favor," he said to the two patrolmen. "Check the back, make sure nobody's hanging around, OK?"

They shrugged and left. Dooley looked at the middle-aged woman. "Are you a relation?"

The woman put out a hand to steady herself on a sideboard. She looked in worse shape than the victim. "I'm a neighbor. I live downstairs. She came and pounded on my door. This is just *awful.*"

"Has anybody contacted the husband?"

There was a moment of silence and the woman on the couch said, "My husband's gone."

Dooley nodded and said to the neighbor, "OK. I wonder if you could do me a big favor and take the kids to another room." Dooley looked at the victim. "Can we do that?"

The mother said softly. "Come on, kids. Go with Mrs. Davis. I have to talk to the policemen." She stirred, trying to disengage.

"Noooo!" The little one wasn't having any of it.

"Come on, Billy." The big sister pulled him away, picked him up and carried him. The middle boy went without taking big frightened eyes off Dooley. Dooley watched the neighbor lady herd them back down the hallway and exchanged a look with Olson, who went to stand in the doorway, out of sight of the woman on the couch. She had clasped her hands and she sat with her knees tightly together.

Dooley sat on the edge of a chair a few feet away from the couch. "Can you tell us what happened?"

She was working at it, Dooley could see; she was holding herself together but he wasn't sure how much longer she could do it.

She focused on him and said, "He came in through the back. I had the door open because it was hot, but the screen door was hooked. He must have cut through it with the knife. I was in the bedroom trying to get Billy down for a nap and I heard Debby shout. She said, 'Mommy, there's a man here.' I came out into the hall and saw him coming up from the kitchen. He didn't have the knife, I mean I didn't see it, he didn't have it in his hand. I should have screamed, probably—I almost did, I wanted to—but all I did was ask him what he was doing here. I was trying to stay calm, for my children's sake."

Dooley nodded. "Did you recognize him?"

"No. I don't think I'd ever seen him before."

"Can you describe him?"

It was getting harder; Dooley didn't know how much she had left. She made an effort, put a hand to her head, and said, "Oh, I don't know. Maybe forty years old, not very big, brown hair. He had on an undershirt, you know, sleeveless. I don't know. I could pick him out, but I'm not very good at describing people."

"That's all right. We'll have you look at some pictures when you're ready. Now I have to ask you what happened."

She nodded, briskly, eyes on the floor. "He said, 'I came for the party.' I called to the children to run out the front door—Mark and Debby were up in the front room—but he yelled 'Don't open that door.' And he just kept coming. I told him to go away or I would scream, and he pulled the knife out of his belt. I thought he was going to kill us." Her voice broke a little, and Dooley waited while she got her grip back. She shot him a strained look and said, "I started pleading with him and he said he wasn't going to hurt anybody. He just wanted—he just wanted to get in on the party. He'd been drinking. I could smell the liquor on his breath. I said 'Let my kids go,' and he said 'No, they'll be OK here.' He told them to go stand by the front window. And then he told them—he told them to watch and they might learn something."

She was pleading now, with her look, and Dooley wished like hell he could let her stop. He had a sick feeling in his stomach. He traded a look with Olson and saw he was feeling the same way. Dooley took a breath and said, “All right. We’re going to get you an ambulance, we’re going to take care of your kids. I just need you to tell me, if you can, what he did to you.”

Her head went down then, her face going into her hands, and Dooley knew he’d asked too much; this was why he hated rape cases, hated them with a passion. A murder victim’s pain was over by the time Dooley got there. Her shoulders had started to shake.

“He tore open my blouse and— and put his hands on me. My kids were crying and I was trying to tell them it was OK, and then he got mad and hit me. He put the knife to my throat and he made me sit down and then he—he unzipped his pants and he made me—he made me—”

She keeled over gently sideways, making a noise in her throat, and Dooley sprang out of his chair and managed to catch her before she hit the floor. “Get an ambulance,” he said, and Olson made for the door.

Dooley got her back onto the couch. Her hand was pressed tightly to her mouth. “Are you going to be sick?” Dooley said, as gently as he could.

She stabilized enough to give him a look that was as cold as ice. She took her hand away from her mouth and said, “I already was. Just as soon as he left.” Her eyes rolled up, then squeezed shut, and she toppled over again.

Dooley left her sobbing on the couch. He found the bathroom and looked into the toilet without much hope; sure enough it had been flushed. He went down the hall to the dining room. The kids were seated at the table with the neighbor lady, solemn expressions all around. “Is my mom OK?” said the girl.

“She will be. We’re going to have a doctor look at her. But she’ll be OK.”

Dooley went through the kitchen to the back door. He saw the cut screen, the hook hanging loose. He went out onto the enclosed landing where the garbage cans were and looked at the open back door of the neighboring apartment. One of the patrolman came up the stairs. "Nobody hanging around there."

Dooley nodded. "Are all the back doors open?"

The patrolman frowned. "I don't know. Some of them are. I didn't really notice. Yeah, most of 'em are, I think. Want me to go look?"

"No, that's OK. Just camp here for a few minutes, hold anybody that wanders by for me." Dooley went back inside the apartment. He went through the dining room and walked back up the hall. He looked into the front room and saw that the woman had calmed herself a little and was curled up on the couch with her knees to her chest, sniffling. He went back to the dining room and said to the neighbor lady, "Why don't you go sit with her? I'll bring the kids up in a minute." The neighbor lady nodded and hustled up the hall. Dooley took her place at the table.

"How you doing, pal?" He patted the boy on the shoulder. "Your mom's pretty strong, you know. She'll be OK." He looked at the older girl, who had taken the youngest onto her lap. "You're all tough, I can see that. What that guy did to your mother was pretty bad, but she's OK now. She'll be all right. She's a tough lady." Dooley was just making noise, he knew; he couldn't do anything for these kids that would make the next couple of hundred nights any easier. He waited a beat and said, "What I need you to tell me is if any of you ever saw that man before."

There was silence as Dooley looked around the table, and he didn't have high hopes; kid witnesses were a total crapshoot, but you never knew. The boy was shaking his head and the older girl was just staring at him and he nodded once and stood up. "OK. If you think of anything, let me know. Now, why don't we go try and make your mom feel better?"

"Hooshy bah," said the smallest child, removing his thumb from his mouth for the purpose. He was staring at Dooley.

Dooley said, "What's that?"

"He wants a Hershey Bar," said the older boy. "Not now, Billy."

"Hooshy bah man," the toddler said.

There was a pause. The girl's eyes widened as she looked at Dooley and she pulled the child around on her lap to look at him. She said, "Was that the man that gave you a Hershey Bar?"

"Hooshy bah man *bad*," said the boy, and started to cry.

The girl looked at the older boy for a moment and then up at Dooley. "I think I know who the man might be," she said.

• • •

"Why did he walk all the way up to the third floor?" Dooley led Olson down the alley, hands in his pockets, looking at the back steps of apartments. "Other back doors were open. He could have picked any one. So he had a particular target in mind, but she'd never seen him. How did he know her?"

"The kids, huh? That was a good guess."

"The mom takes the kids to their babysitter's house up at the end of the block here every morning. He probably saw them through a window. The mom caught his eye and he followed them home."

They reached the building at the end of the block. It was a three-flat, with the gray-painted steps leading up to the back porches stacked on top of one another. "The babysitter's on the second floor," said Dooley. "The sister said when the little one came back with the candy bar, he came up the stairs. So we're looking at the first floor. Or else—" Next to the stairs, three concrete steps led down to the basement entrance. The door was open and music was coming from the basement. Dooley went down the steps, followed by Olson.

Dooley stopped in the doorway and looked into a typical apartment-house basement, with the fuse boxes and laundry machines along one wall and the storage bins along the other, lit by naked light bulbs above. There was a table just to the right of the door with a radio, a bottle of whiskey, and a glass on it. A man in a dirty white sleeveless undershirt was sitting at the table with his head in his hands. Dooley rapped on the door frame and the man looked up at him. He had red-rimmed eyes, a couple of days' growth of beard, and a stuporous expression.

"What do you want?" he said. The way he sounded, the whiskey in front of him was not his first glass.

"Police," Dooley said. "You been here all afternoon?"

The man just stared at him. Dooley gave it a couple of seconds and said, "We need you to come with us for a while."

"I didn't do nothing," the man said.

"I didn't say you did. I just need to ask you a few questions."

The man stared some more and then pushed away from the desk. He stood up, reeling a little, revealing the knife stuck in the waistband of his jeans. "Fuckin' cops," he said.

"Tell you what," said Dooley. "I'm going to ask you to step over here and put your hands on the wall before we go any farther." Dooley didn't like that knife where it was. He had moved into the basement and turned, bracketing the man between himself and Olson in the doorway.

The man stood there looking at Dooley with an expression of contempt. He turned to Olson and said, "Fuckin' bitch. I should have cut her throat."

Dooley didn't see it coming; he saw Olson's expression change and then before he could do anything Olson had taken one step and decked the man with a right cross that came out of nowhere. The drunk brushed Dooley on the way to the floor, blood starting to pour out of his nose.

"Hey!" Dooley yelled.

Olson stood there looking down at the moaning drunk with his arms held loosely at his sides, breathing a little heavily. "Piece of shit," he said.

"What the hell's wrong with you?"said Dooley.

Olson looked at him and Dooley could see him coming back from wherever he'd been. "Christ, I don't know."

• • •

"Don't make me go out on a limb again," Dooley said in a low murmur. "You can't pull that kind of shit, Pete."

Olson straightened up from the sink, his face dripping, and reached for a paper towel. He dried his face and said, "It won't happen again." He blew his nose on the towel and threw it in the trash. "You want me to go tell McCone the truth, I will."

"No, I'll back you up. He went for the knife. But don't make me do it again."

"I won't. I promise."

Dooley gave him a long searching look. He could hear voices through the door, out in the office. Olson's right cross had added hours to the evening's work, with a hospital visit complicating the usual process of identification, arrest, and booking. Near midnight now, the paperwork was finally done and all that was left was to haul the rapist over to the 20th District lockup where he would be babysat until the wagon came around at dawn to collect the trash and take it down to Twenty-sixth Street.

"You don't look good," said Dooley.

"I don't feel good." Olson sagged against the toilet stall. "I feel like hell."

Dooley peered at him. It was amazing how you could spend so much time with a guy and never see him; now that he was looking, he could see that Olson had lost weight. "You sick? Take a day off."

"I'm not sick. I'm just not cut out for this."

"Ah, don't give me that. How long you been a cop?"

Olson's eyes were showing things Dooley had never seen before. "I mean it, Mike. It's starting to get to me. I'm having trouble sleeping, the whole thing. I can't get things out of my head. I open a door in my fucking house, I expect to see blood all over the place."

Jesus, thought Dooley. You go along fine for months and then life throws you a big wicked curve ball.

"Well, hell. Go talk to somebody. Talk to your priest, or pastor or whatever it is you people have. Take a day or two off."

Olson shook his head, shamefaced. "How do you do it, Mike? How do you keep it from driving you crazy?"

Dooley shrugged. "I don't know what to tell you, pal. You just don't let it get to you." He waited a second or two and said, "Or you just find a way of being crazy you can live with."

"Thanks," said Olson, brushing past him and making for the door. "That's a big help."

Twenty-nine

. . . The people here are really poor and some of them don't like us much. It makes you wonder what we're doing here. But what do I know, I just do what they tell me to. They're talking about pulling us out early but I'm not going to hold my breath. With our luck we'll be the last unit to go.

You probably heard George Wilkins got killed. That was tough, he was a really good guy. He got killed because he was doing what he was supposed to do instead of ducking out like some guys. You see guys get hurt and you try not to think about it, but when a real friend gets it, it's hard to take. I wish I could say don't worry about me, but I know you have to. All I can say is, keep praying and I should be coming home soon. I miss you all and am REALLY looking forward to that vacation. A cottage on the lake sounds pretty good. I want to just sit and do nothing for a while.

See you soon, love, Kevin

"He sounds different. This is the first time he sounds, I don't know, discouraged." Rose was looking at Dooley, her features tight with anguish.

"That happens. You go through bad periods." Dooley shoved the letter back across the table to her. "He's hanging in there. He'll be OK."

"Did you know this George Wilkins had been killed?"

"I saw it in the paper, yeah."

"Why didn't you tell me?"

"Would you really have been happier knowing?"

"It's not a matter of being *happy,* Michael. I won't be *happy* until our son's home. But I would have liked to know, yes. Did you ever contact the boy's father?"

Dooley shuffled sections of the newspaper, not looking at her. "Yeah, I talked to him."

"And you kept it from me."

"I didn't want you to be upset."

She shook her head, looking at him wide-eyed and open-mouthed. "Michael, I'm a big girl. Don't hide things from me. OK?"

"OK. I'm sorry." He gave up on the paper. "I'm sorry, OK? I wanted to protect you."

"I should call his parents. My God, how awful." She rose from the table and wandered over to the sink, staring out the window with her arms folded.

Dooley opened his mouth to tell her they were black, but he stopped himself. Instead he said, "You want to go see them, I'll go with you. They live way the hell down on the South Side."

Rose said nothing. Dooley stared into his coffee. He said, "How about that cottage by the lake? You find something?"

After a while she turned toward him. "I'm looking into it. There are nice places up in Door County, and it'll be cheaper after Labor Day. But it's still going to cost a lot of money to put us all up for a week."

"Don't worry about the money."

"I have to. I pay the bills. What's happening with you and Rob? Doesn't he have any work for you?"

"For Christ's sake, I've been busy with more important things. I happen to be a police officer, remember?"

"Michael, please don't snap at me. Please."

She was starting to lose control, he could hear, and he got up and went and put his arms around her. "We'll manage it, Rose. Don't worry about it. I'll give Rob a call."

"We can't start fighting," she said into his collar. "We just can't. We have to hang on to each other, whatever happens."

"I know." Dooley stood holding his wife and looking out the window at nothing. After a minute or so she pulled away from him and wiped her eyes with her fingertips.

"I'm going over to the church. You're off today, right?"

Dooley squeezed her hand and released it. "Yeah, but there's a couple of things I have to do. Gotta go talk to a guy. I'll be home for supper."

• • •

There were protesters in Bughouse Square. Dooley found a parking place in front of the Newberry Library and walked around the edge of the park, looking at the hippies and yippies milling with their signs among the usual bums slouching on the benches or sprawled in the shade of the big trees. In some cases he wasn't sure which was which.

He went into the Italian restaurant on the corner of Dearborn and Delaware and was led to a booth in the back. He sat facing the front of the place, watching the lunchtime crowd ebb. Swallow had said two o'clock, but Dooley had come early to do a little reconnaissance. Public place or not, he had taken Johnny Puig's warning to heart.

"Bang." Dooley started as a hand was clapped on his shoulder. "You're dead," said Arnold Swallow, lowering his considerable tonnage onto the seat opposite Dooley. The look on Swallow's face was a lot more confident than the last time Dooley had seen him; there was just a hint of a smirk there. "You're lucky I'm in a good mood today."

The restroom, thought Dooley, trying to keep a neutral look on his face. I overlooked the restroom. "Very funny," he said.

"That's me. The life of the party." Swallow waved at a waiter. "You having lunch?"

"I ate already. A little coffee will do me."

"Suit yourself. The scallopine here is outa this world." The waiter arrived and Swallow ordered without looking at a menu. When the waiter scuttled away Swallow looked back at Dooley with the smirk fading and said, "You know what you are, Dooley? You're a schmuck. That's what. A first-class schmuck. You're the kid in school who tattles on the boys smoking in the restroom. That's what you are."

"That may be," said Dooley. "But you're still the moron who's been sticking his dick where it doesn't belong. Now what do you have for me?"

Swallow sat looking at him for a full ten seconds, putting everything he had into the look, and Dooley sat there looking back at him. Finally Swallow said, "I talked to Tommy."

"That's nice. How are the feds treating him?"

"Fine. They're treating him just fine. A federal jail's a fucking vacation for someone like Tommy."

"Well, he ought to enjoy it. He earned every minute of it. What did he say?"

Swallow leaned forward, elbows on the table. His broad jowly face was a little flushed. "He said she probably brought it on herself."

"How?"

"She got greedy."

Dooley blinked at him. "Keep talking."

Swallow shook his head, a wise man deploring the foolishness of youth. "She tried to peddle something she stole from Tommy. She probably tried to sell it to the wrong people."

"What was it?"

"You don't need to know that."

Dooley reached into his pocket and fished for a dime. He found one and held it up where Swallow could see it. "You gonna shoot me while I walk back to the phone? Is that your plan?"

Swallow glowered. "It won't help you to know what it was. She could have tried to sell it to anyone."

"Don't bullshit me anymore, Arnie. I'm getting sick and tired of it. What did she have?"

Swallow gave it another few seconds for appearances' sake, but Dooley knew he'd been prepared to cough it up from the start; he had to be. "A tape recording," he said.

"What was on it?"

"What I told you the other day. The governor."

"Ogilivie?"

"Yeah."

"Don't make me work so hard, Arnie. What was on the tape?"

Swallow's eyes flicked away and back and he lowered his voice a notch. "Ogilvie and Humphreys."

Dooley squinted at him. "Humphreys. You mean Murray Humphreys?"

"Yeah, the famous Murray Humphreys, the brains of the Outfit. Him and Ogilvie."

"Talking about what?"

"That deal I told you about, for Tommy to come on the sheriff's department, back in sixty-two. Tommy got it on tape without their knowing about it."

Dooley stared at him until the waiter came back with Dooley's coffee and a bottle of wine. Nobody said anything while the wine got opened. When the waiter went away Dooley said, "How did Sally wind up with it?"

"Like I said, she stole it."

"When?"

"When Tommy came back from Mexico. Last year. He got in touch for old times' sake, they had dinner, they went up to his hotel room for a while, had a roll in the hay. He thinks she went through his bags while he was in the shower afterward. He had the valuable stuff in a briefcase."

"How'd she get it open?"

"He was in the shower, his keys were sitting there. He trusted her. What the hell, he made a mistake. He didn't miss it until later. And then before he could get it back the feds scooped him up and he went to jail."

"Why would she steal it?"

"Who the hell knows? Tommy thinks she was pissed off because he wouldn't marry her and she wanted to take what she could get from him. She knew what kind of stuff he was involved in and she probably just grabbed something at random. And then she listened to it and figured out who would want it bad enough to pay for it. Except she wasn't careful enough. She was an amateur. It's not that easy to blackmail someone without getting hurt."

"So we're back to the governor having her killed to keep things quiet."

Swallow shrugged. "I don't know why that would surprise you. You think he's a saint? But like I said, it's not necessarily him. Other people lose leverage if that tape comes to light. Or they gain it if they can get their hands on it."

"Yeah. I see."

"But just in case you got any bright ideas, Boy Scout, think for a minute. You go around making accusations without having that tape to back it up, the only thing that's gonna happen is you make trouble for yourself. You're grown up enough to understand that, right?"

Dooley nodded. "Yeah. I'm grown up enough."

Swallow seemed to relax a little. He took a drink of wine, set the glass down and said, "So, schmuck. Are we even now?"

Dooley stared at him for a while and then said, "I guess so. Go on sticking it to Janet if you want. I'm not going to say anything. Unless I find out you lied to me."

Swallow's brows clamped down again. "You remember what I said, Dooley. About blackmail. It's not as easy as it looks."

Dooley shoved his coffee away untouched and slid out of the booth. "I'll remember," he said. "Thanks for the coffee."

• • •

Dooley gave it a long hard look pushing out Chicago Avenue in the stop-and-go traffic: he thought there was about a fifty-fifty chance Arnold Swallow had told him the truth. He could have cooked something up with Spain, or he could have been just scared enough to give Dooley something real to work with.

The thing with Ogilvie sounded possible; Ogilvie had a clean reputation but nothing surprised Dooley anymore. He knew it was hard to work in the sewers without getting your feet dirty. He wasn't sure how far it got him if it was true, but he knew there was one guy he had to talk to again.

Angelo's had just opened and there was only one customer at the bar, an old-timer in a porkpie hat who gave Dooley a glance and went back to studying the ice cubes in his drink. Lou Molinari was fiddling with the dials of the TV set when Dooley came in. He took a look over his shoulder and then fiddled some more before he came limping up the bar to where Dooley had camped. "Back again, huh?" he said.

"I need you to exercise your memory again, Lou," said Dooley.

"You about wore it out last time."

"I'm sure it's had time to recover. I need you to tell me about a couple of phone calls."

"We get a lot of phone calls here. I don't write 'em down or nothin'."

"You got two calls here at the end of May. One on the thirtieth, one on the thirty-first. They were long-distance calls. You remember?"

Molinari had astute brown eyes under wiry gray brows. He held Dooley's look for a few seconds and said, "How the hell would I know they were long-distance?"

"They might have come through an operator, or the caller might have said so. That ring a bell?"

"Not really. Like I say, we get a lot of phone calls here. How long ago was that?"

Dooley didn't like to lead people, but sometimes you had to. "They were from a woman. Does that help?" He had the barkeep's attention now; their eyes locked again and Dooley watched as the other man's slowly narrowed. Dooley could see him making the connections. "The calls are on record, so don't bother to deny it," he said. "I need to know who she wanted to talk to."

It was the big question, and Dooley figured he had at least a chance of getting a straight answer, because he didn't think a mere bartender would have the authority to lie unless he was rehearsed, and they'd had no reason to rehearse this one because the first time around Dooley had never asked about the calls.

Molinari backed away from Dooley with a frown on his face. He reached down and pulled a rag from under the bar and passed it back and forth over the shiny hardwood a few times. He said, "It don't ring a bell. It was just too long ago, you know?" He tossed the rag back where he'd gotten it and looked at Dooley. "I can't help you."

Dooley looked him in the eye until the other man buckled. He shrugged, flung up his hands and turned away. "Last week, I can maybe remember. Two months ago, that's too much."

"OK," said Dooley. He didn't buy it but he knew he couldn't beat it out of the man. "Where can I find Ronnie Gallo?"

Molinari shrugged. "He'll probably show up here sooner or later."

"I'm not going to wait around. How do you get in touch with him?"

"I got a home number for him, but I don't recommend you try it. Ronnie don't like to be bothered at home. If I were you I'd try the club. He usually starts out there in the afternoon."

"The club. Where's that?"

Molinari tried to stare him down but gave in after a second or two. "The Italian-American Social Club, on Grand Avenue. Grand and Racine, around in there."

"Twelve forty-six," said Dooley. "I know."

• • •

Dooley knew he'd been lied to; he'd seen the look in Lou Molinari's eye. Sometimes a lie told you as much as the truth. He was prepared to make a guess or two: the barkeep had taken the calls, but Sally Kotowski hadn't wanted to talk to him; she'd wanted to talk to Ronnie Gallo.

Dooley went over it all driving back east; he thought it just might hang together. Sally had called Angelo's with the idea of peddling what she had; maybe she had been there before with Herb Feldman or heard Feldman talk about Gallo. Gallo had sent somebody to get her, like his pal Tony Messino from the Grand Avenue club, and consulted the higher-ups. Would the Outfit pay for something like that? They already knew about Ogilvie, presumably. But actually having the tape was a whole different story: that gave them great leverage. If the tape had been Tommy Spain's private project, other people might have been glad to get their hands on it. And maybe somebody had decided there was no need to pay for what they could get Sally to cough up for free.

Dooley didn't think the sheer nastiness of that was beyond what the Outfit was capable of, but on the other hand a killing like that brought heat, and Dooley thought the Outfit was more likely to take the path of least resistance. It seemed like a straightforward transaction; a little bargaining and then thank you very much, it's been a pleasure doing business with you. So what got Sally killed? Dooley didn't think he had it all, not yet. What he needed now was a stick to beat Ronnie Gallo with.

He didn't have one, but sometimes the best thing to do was just to put someone on the spot and see what kind of a lie he told you. Then you could take it from there. He knew Molinari would have jumped on the phone the second he walked out of the bar, but that didn't bother him. It was going to be a lot harder for Gallo to deny any memory of two phone calls from a woman who had been kidnapped from his establishment and killed a couple of days later.

The Sicilians were holding on around Grand and Racine; these days you heard as much English as Italian on the streets and a lot of people had moved out west, but some people would never go. Dooley saw a widow in black sweeping the sidewalk. He parked on Grand and walked half a block west to the club.

It was a modest storefront with a paneled-over front window and a sign painted in green, white and red over the door: *Italian-American Social Club.* In businesslike black letters at the bottom it said *Members Only.* There was an air-conditioning unit over the door that was throbbing like a diesel and dripping water onto the sidewalk. Dooley dodged the drip and pushed open the door.

Inside it was cool and dim after the glare on the street. Dooley closed the door behind him and started counting: he saw six men frozen in attitudes of suspicion under fluorescent lights. There was a short bar to the right with a few bottles and a fat man behind it, a scattering of tables and chairs, mostly unoccupied, a TV on a high shelf, and a couple of doors in the rear. From the look of things he had interrupted a card game, an argument, a soap opera, and at least one nap. "Can't you read?" said a man at a table six feet in front of him, smoking a cigarette with his feet up on the table.

"No," said Dooley, reaching into his pocket. "Saves me a lot of trouble. How about you?" He held up his star.

The man's mouth curled into a sneer around the cigarette. "I can read *that*," he said. "P-O-L-I-C-E. That spells 'sap.' Or is it 'jerk'? I can never remember."

Dooley had taken an instant dislike to this one; he was on the small side but he looked as if he would make up for it in belligerence. He had lots of brown hair combed straight back above a face that narrowed to a pointed chin, with big dark eyes and a narrow mouth built for the sneer.

Dooley put the star away. "Congratulations. Another couple of years and maybe they'll put you up to second grade." He stepped toward the table where three men were playing cards. "I'm looking for Ronnie Gallo," he said.

The three of them were out of the same mold, former tough guys going old and a little soft. A heavy bald man looked at his companions and said, "Ronnie Gallo. Who the fuck is Ronnie Gallo?"

"Sounds kinda familiar," said the dealer, giving the cards an overhand shuffle.

"Try the liquor store. They got Gallo," said the third man.

That brought a laugh, or what passed for a laugh, and Dooley gave it a tolerant smile. "Maybe I will," he said. "I'm going to need a drink when I'm through processing you guys."

They looked at him then, and for a couple of seconds the only sound was the murmur of the television set. "What the fuck are you talking about?" said the bald man.

"The arrest," Dooley said. He jutted his chin at the table, where nickels and dimes were scattered among the ashtrays. "You wouldn't believe the paperwork involved, just to get a wagon over here and take you three over to the lockup for illegal gambling. It'll keep us all busy for the rest of the day. But you do what you have to." He let it lie there, looking at each man in turn. He could see from their looks that they were thinking about calling his bluff, and he could also see them deciding that it wasn't worth risking even the minor annoyance that would mean. The dealer slapped the deck down on the table. "I'm Gallo," he said. "What do you want?"

"A couple of answers," said Dooley. "The questions are easy, I promise."

Gallo stared up at him for a moment. He was a middle-sized weasel-faced man in a yellow checked sport shirt, with steel-wool hair and five-o'clock shadow to rival Nixon's. "It's about the dead girl, ain't it?" he said.

Dooley didn't give anything away. He knew Gallo had to put it out there in case any of his pals were wondering. "You got a place here where we could talk?" he said.

"Back in the office." Gallo got up with an exasperated sigh. "Deal me out," he said.

"Enjoy the game, fellas," said Dooley.

The office was a cluttered room with a desk and piles of boxes and a high barred window on the alley. Gallo sat behind the desk and Dooley took a chair in front of it. "You been bothering Lou at the bar again, I hear," said Gallo.

"That's right. His memory's gone bad on him."

"Well, Lou's getting up there. What the hell you expect?"

"I expect you to remember a little better. She wanted to talk to you, didn't she?"

"Yeah, but I told her to get lost." Gallo gave it a second to see how Dooley would take it. When Dooley said nothing he went on. "Look, officer. I'm giving you this one straight. I ain't gonna bullshit you. I'm a gambler, I had my scrapes with the law, OK? But something like this, what happened to that girl, fuck. How do you think I feel, knowing that happened in my place, those two creeps picking her up in there and doing what they did? That's not honorable people. That's not anyone I want to be associated with."

Dooley just looked at him. "Were you there that night? The night she got killed?"

"No. I own the place, but I don't get out there all that much. A couple of times a week, maybe. Just to check up on things. I pretty much trust Lou to run the place."

"OK. Tell me about the phone calls."

"Lou talked to her the first time. He left a message for me, said this girl had called from Wisconsin and wanted to talk to me. She left her name, but it didn't mean nothing to me. I forgot about it. And then the next night I was out there, and Lou hands me the phone, and it's her. She says are you Ronnie Gallo and I says who wants to know, and she says this is Sally So-and-So, I didn't recognize the name, and I says who, and she says Herb Feldman's girlfriend. And then I said what the hell do you want with me, and she says I can tell you who the snitch is. I says what snitch, and she says the snitch that squealed on Herb to the FBI. She says there's a snitch in the Outfit that nobody knows about and she figured out who it is and she'll tell anyone who'll pay her for her trouble. I says honey, you're a day late and a dollar short, everybody knows how the G got onto Herb, he got careless over the phone. But she says no, there's a snitch and she knows who it is. I says OK, who is it, and she says uh-uh, I'm not saying it over the phone, I'll tell you face-to-face if you'll give me money. I says, you're talking to the wrong guy, why me, and she says Herb liked you. Well, shit, I knew Herbie a little, he used to come in the bar, but we weren't exactly pals. I told her I wasn't the guy to talk to, she should get in touch with somebody more important, like Joe Lombardo or somebody. But she says no, Herbie trusted you and you're the guy I want to talk to. By this time I figure she's got nothing, she's just trying to work something, so I tell her look, I'm not interested, go sell this to somebody else, and she says no, I'm coming down there to see you, and I says I can't stop you, but I'm not giving you no money. She says you will when you hear what I have to say, I'm coming down there tomorrow to see you. And I said fine, knock yourself out, I might or I might not be here. And I didn't work too hard to get out there the next night. I didn't want nothin' to do with her."

Gallo fell silent and Dooley sat there looking at him for a long moment. Gallo threw up his hands in a that's-all gesture and let them fall to the desktop with a thump. Dooley frowned at him some more and then his eyes went to the window high in the wall. It was a good story, a well-tailored story that he was never going to disprove, and it fit with the other parts of the story that the syndicate was trying to sell. The fact that it was completely incompatible with Arnold Swallow's story didn't surprise Dooley at all. Either story or both could be fiction. All he had to do was the impossible: follow them up, check them out, compare them with what could be proven. Dooley felt immensely tired all of a sudden.

"Why didn't you at least want to hear what she had to say?" he asked.

Gallo jabbed at the desktop, suddenly intense. "Because one, I knew it was bullshit. Nobody ratted on Feldman, he was dumb enough to call one of his Vegas buddies on a line the G had a tap on. And two, I don't get involved in pointing fingers and beefs and who said this and who did that. That's too dangerous, that gets you in trouble. I'm just a gambler, I got no ambitions. I tried to steer her to Joey. I didn't want no fuckin' part of her. A crazy broad like that, throwing accusations around, that can get you in a lot of trouble if you start encouraging them."

"Did you tell Lombardo about it?"

"No. To tell you the truth, I thought she was nuts and she'd go away if I ignored her."

Dooley nodded a few times and then stood up. "All right. Thanks for the information."

"Any time, officer. Something like this, it's not our business. It's not what we do. It ain't right."

Dooley lingered in the doorway, trying to keep a straight face looking into Gallo's pious expression. "Yeah. You're a bunch of fucking choirboys, I know."

On his way out he passed the table where the undersized tough guy was working on another cigarette. "You get it all down?" the punk said. "You want me to spell anything else for you?" His feet were back up on the table and the sneer was back on his face. Dooley had been dealing with looks like this since he was six years old and walking past the bullies under the viaduct on his first day of school.

Dooley halted in front of him. "You got a name, mutt?"

The mutt blew smoke at him, the sneer fading to a look of pure hostility. "Write it down, copper. Messino. M-E-S-S-I-N-O. Tony Messino. Remember it."

Dooley had known the answer before he heard it. He smiled at Messino and started moving toward the door. "Now I got what I need," he said.

Thirty

"DID YOU SEE her in *Playboy*? Oh, brother, I'm telling you. Now *that's* a tragedy. Jesus, what a waste."

"Yeah. Breaks your heart, doesn't it?"

"Get a load of the husband. She married this greasy little Polack."

"Watch what you say about Polacks. Some of my closest relatives are Polacks."

"No, but really. Look at the guy."

"What the hell, maybe he has a big dick."

"What he's got is money. That's what they go for."

"He directed that movie she was in. She married the boss. What else is new?"

"How the hell you think she got the part in the first place? It's Hollywood, that's how you get to the top. You spend a lot of time on your back."

"Jesus, look at this. She was pregnant."

"The husband's my number-one suspect."

"He was in London, genius."

"So he hired this kid to do it. This caretaker they arrested. She was pregnant by the other guy, the hairdresser, and he knew it."

"Ah, you're full of shit. The kid did it. He was on drugs or something, you watch."

"Maybe he was in on it, but he didn't do it alone. One guy doesn't kill five people in, what do they say here, 'in ritualistic fashion.' He had to have help. But the drug part, that I believe. Writing on the walls in blood, Jesus. What a bunch of fucking savages."

"This Folger. Is that Folger like the coffee?"

"The daughter, yeah. That oughta nudge their sales up a bit, huh? Any publicity's good, they say."

"Christ, you're sick."

"I been a cop too long."

"You couldn't prove it by me," said Dooley, piping up for the first time. "I can't remember the last time I saw you do any police work."

Dooley had sat there listening until he got tired of it; he had work to do and he couldn't do it with an office full of lazy dicks gossiping over the newspaper like housewives. The crowd broke up and left Dooley with the paper laid out in front of him, the headline screaming *SHARON TATE, 4 OTHERS SLAIN*, the publicity photo of the butchered actress staring him in the face.

Olson drifted over with a cup of coffee. "Who does that remind you of?" he said, tapping the picture with his index finger.

Dooley stared at the picture for a couple of seconds, pretending to work on it; in truth it had struck him when he'd first seen it at home that morning, opening up the paper. Dooley was not an easy man to rattle, but it had given him the creeps all the same. "What's-her-name," he said. "That ex-bunny we interviewed. Sally's friend."

"Yeah. Laura something. Spooky, isn't it?"

Dooley shrugged and reached for the day's batch of cold-case files. "If you pay any attention to that kind of thing."

• • •

Before he hit the street Dooley decided to take a stab at catching up with business on the phone. After a couple of other calls he got Ed Haggerty at the other end of the line.

"Mike Dooley here. You got a minute?"

"Sure. You're gonna ask me about Tony Messino, aren't you?"

"It crossed my mind."

"I did check for you, I really did. But we've never had Messino under surveillance. Not yet. We can't cover everybody. He keeps moving up, we'll probably get around to him."

"I know how it goes. Just to take a swing in the dark, I don't suppose you've ever had a wiretap on Angelo's out in Melrose Park, have you? Ronnie Gallo's place?"

"No, I don't think we could get away with that. The G might."

"Yeah. They might. A lot of good that does me."

"What's going on at Angelo's?"

"My girl called there from Wisconsin, twice, a couple of days before she was killed. I got a story from Gallo about what she wanted but I'd love to have a way to back it up."

"That would be a real stroke of luck. What's Gallo say?"

"He says she was trying to sell him information, about a snitch in the Outfit. According to him, she said somebody had snitched on Herb Feldman to the feds. Gallo said he told her to get lost because they already knew it was the federal wiretap that got Feldman in trouble. He thought she was making up stories to try for a score."

"Hm. Could be. Or there really could be a snitch. I'm sure there's more than one, as a matter of fact. The interesting question is how she would know."

"We didn't get into that."

"Why in the hell did she call Gallo's place?"

"He says she told him Herb trusted Gallo."

"Herb Feldman trusted Gallo? I didn't even know they knew each other."

"I'm just telling you what Gallo told me."

"Huh. That's strange. As far as I know, Gallo and Feldman didn't hang out in the same circles. Feldman was one of those Rush Street guys. And Gallo's a Grand Avenue guy, does his business mostly out on the West Side. That's not to say they couldn't have known each other. I mean, the crews all mix to some extent. But if they were good friends, that's news to me."

"Well, the whole thing could be a lie. I still don't know how she got there the night she was killed, or even if she got there. What I would really like to do is go back and talk to Billy Gaines again, really hammer away at him. But I don't know if I can get McCone to clear it."

"If he's willing to go to jail for that story, I don't know if you'll get him to change it."

"You never know. Now that he's had a little taste of it, his other options might not look so bad. I'll have to find out where they stuck him."

"Might be worth a try."

"What I really need is informants, and I don't have any. I was wondering if you could put your ear to the ground for me. If I'm right that D'Andrea and Messino killed Sally, somebody out there knows it."

Haggerty was silent for a moment. "And the basis of your belief that D'Andrea and Messino killed her is what, again?"

Dooley laughed. "The same basis that makes me think the dog did it when I find a turd on the rug. I can't prove it wasn't one of my kids, and the dog's not talking, but I gotta start somewhere."

"Well, I know I was the guy that first gave you the idea about D'Andrea, so I can't say you're nuts. All I can say is, without anything concrete to go on there's not a lot I can do to help you."

"I know it. I guess I'm just asking you to keep your eyes and ears open. You're the one that knows these people."

Haggerty sighed into the phone. "I been watching 'em for twenty years, Mike. And I know it's damn hard to nail 'em once they've got something stitched up the way they got this one stitched up. I'll keep my antennae out, but I don't know how much I can do."

"You already did a lot. Thanks."

"You still working from the other end? The Tommy Spain end?"

Dooley opened his mouth to tell him about Swallow, but something made him stop. "Still working on it," he said. "I need some help from the feds there."

"Lots of luck," said Haggerty.

Dooley sat with his hand on the phone for a minute after he hung up. All day he'd been thinking about the two stories he'd gotten from Swallow and Gallo, thinking one of them had to be lying. But now he was thinking something different. What if the stories weren't incompatible after all? What if Sally had found something valuable in Tommy Spain's luggage, and then tried to sell it to Ronnie Gallo, only Gallo was telling the truth, too? What if the snitch she was talking about was Tommy Spain?

Dooley wasn't quite sure where that got him, but he had a feeling that wherever it was it was bound to be interesting.

• • •

Dooley and Olson had gone down to the Bureau of Identification at Eleventh and State to get mug shots and record sheets for a couple of bad guys a tip said had killed a liquor store clerk on Belmont back in June. One suspect's Last Known Address was on the second floor of a six-flat on Kenmore in Uptown, the heart of Appalachia in Chicago. Dooley knew they'd come to the right place when Leroy Alvin Pickett himself opened the door, the spitting image of the sullen hillbilly loser in the mug shot, right down to the uncombed ducktail. "Leroy Pickett?" Dooley said.

In Pickett's eyes Dooley saw the whole range of recognition, panic and finally resignation flare and subside in the span of a second. "Who's askin'?" said Pickett, stalling. Dooley could hear a kid crying somewhere inside; odors of bad cooking and worse housekeeping wafted out to him.

"Police. Would you step out here, please?" Dooley had his foot in the door, ready for the slam; he didn't have his revolver out but he knew Olson behind him would at least have his hand on the grip. For a moment he thought Pickett was going to try something after all, but all the man did was say, "What the hell you want with me?" in his cracker drawl.

"We need to talk to you. Now step out here, please." Dooley wasn't going to argue with him; if Pickett didn't come out onto the landing in about two more seconds, Dooley was going to go in and get him. He saw Pickett running through his choices and not finding any good ones.

"Lemme go git some shoes," Pickett said.

Dooley shoved the door wide open and stepped into the apartment, forcing Pickett to back away. "I got a better idea," he said, pulling the cuffs from his belt. "Turn around and put your hands behind you." Dooley shot a glance up and down the hall, looking for threats and seeing only squalor: battered furniture, peeling wallpaper, a girl with a dirty face up by the front window, staring at him.

"Now hold on a minute," said Pickett, his voice rising. "I ain't done nothing."

"You're under arrest," said Dooley, putting a hand on Pickett's shoulder to turn him. "Put your hands behind your back." Make it fast, Dooley was thinking; he could hear chairs scraping on linoleum in a room at the back and he wanted to get Pickett cuffed before he had to deal with any reinforcements.

Olson had moved in behind Dooley and stood well out of lunging range, with his .38 hanging ready at his side, and that made up Pickett's mind for him. "Jesus Christ," he said, letting Dooley snap the cuffs on his wrists. "Don't shoot me."

"*What are you doing?*" All of a sudden the hallway was full of people: what seemed like a dozen ragamuffin kids and a fat woman in a loose cotton dress, coming up from the back room. "Git your hands offa my husband!" She had a voice to shatter windows but not enough teeth to put a dent in a cob of corn.

"He's under arrest," said Dooley. "Hold it right there."

"It's all right, Judy," said Pickett. "It's just some bullshit thing. I gotta go talk to 'em, that's all."

The wife had stopped three feet from Dooley, but she wasn't going to fold; she shook a finger at him. "You ain't takin' him out of here."

"Ma'am, your husband is under arrest on suspicion of murder," Dooley said. "The best thing you can do is take those kids back there and finish feeding them."

"What'd you do?" Now she was glaring at her husband, and Dooley got a glimpse of Leroy Alvin Pickett's domestic life that made him shudder.

"I didn't do nothin'," Pickett said. "Just do what the man said."

"Let's go," said Dooley, putting a hand on Pickett's arm. Olson had holstered his weapon and was waiting by the door; Dooley saw his eyes widen, looking past him, and that gave him the warning he needed to duck just enough to make the pile-driver blow from behind glance off his head.

Dooley gave Pickett a hard shove toward the door and whirled to see the harpy winding up for a second shot, her face contorted; he'd been punched by six-footers that didn't hit as hard as this woman. He warded off her second shot but here came a third and a fourth; she was throwing punches as fast as Sugar Ray Robinson. She was fast but she was wild; Dooley took a couple of blows to the arms and chest and then he'd had enough. He ended it with a right cross that snapped her head back and sent her sliding down the wall to hit the floor like a sack of flour. He spun to check on Pickett, knowing the man couldn't just stand there and let his wife get hit, but Olson had Pickett well under control, pinned to the wall face-first with a gun at his head. "God damn it, Judy," said Pickett.

A little girl was screaming and a boy about ten years old was scowling at Dooley in a way that said just you wait, mister; Judy sat there with her fat legs splayed, looking at blood on her fingers.

Dooley took the cuffs Olson held out for him. "Who's going to take care of your kids now?" he said, breathing heavily. "You're spending the night in jail."

"My tooth," she said. "You son of a bitch. My last God damn tooth."

• • •

"Pickett says he was there but the other guy shot him. We'll see about that when we get the other guy back from Tennessee. Pickett told us where to find him. We sent a teletype to the Tennessee state cops. The wife's waiting for her brother to come down and post bail. She says she's a victim of police brutality." Dooley tossed the paperwork on McCone's desk.

"Is she?" said McCone, giving him the eye.

"She's a victim of generations of inbreeding if she's a victim of anything. She's lucky I didn't shoot her."

"Write it up," said McCone. "Make sure you're covered."

"It's all there." Dooley left the office; he was fed up with being a cop tonight. He stood at his desk looking at phone messages. He checked his watch and decided it wasn't too late to call Johnny Puig. He dialed the number Puig had left and let it ring six times; he was about to hang up when he heard Puig say hello. "Dooley here. Hope I didn't wake you up."

"Nah, here at the agency we never sleep. You still on duty?"

"Just wrapping things up. What's new?"

"I did some snooping for you. Looking for Marlene."

Dooley had to think for a second. "Spain's wife, yeah. You find her?"

"No. But that's the interesting thing."

"What?"

"The reason I didn't. I talked to a few people here, managed to get a phone number for her, in Miami. But the number had been disconnected. So I called in a favor from a friend on the Dade County sheriff's department down there, had him see what he could dig up. He got the address, went and talked to the landlord. Seems Marlene and her daughter skipped out on the lease two months ago, just disappeared. Moved out, left no forwarding address. The neighbor said they just threw all their stuff in the car and went."

Dooley was tired, but the math was simple. "Early June."

"Yeah. First week. The landlord said they were great tenants, never any problems, the last people in the world you'd expect to just vanish."

"That's very interesting."

"Isn't it? It sounds like they got a warning."

"Uh-huh. From who?"

"Somebody that knew what happened to Sally."

Dooley gave it a few seconds' thought. "We didn't even identify Sally until what, nearly two weeks after we found her. End of the second week of June."

There was a long pause before Puig said, "Even more interesting."

"It'd be good to talk to them."

"Yeah. Only I don't quite know where to go from here. I've used up my favors down there."

"Well, you've already done more than I had any right to ask for. I owe you."

"I won't send you a bill. I'll take it all in favors down the line."

"Any time."

"I *will* say one thing. You got me curious, Dooley. Tell you what, if I happen to find out anything more I'll let you know, gratis. I been thinking I needed a new hobby, and Tommy Spain just might be it."

• • •

Dooley couldn't think of a damn thing to say, sitting staring at the letter to Kevin they had left for him on the kitchen table. He had been sitting there for a long time staring at the paper, taking little sips of whiskey every now and again and clicking the pen in and out, in and out. Jesus, he thought. Just write something.

I am sitting here in the kitchen at two o'clock in the morning thinking about you, he wrote. *The house is quiet and everyone is asleep but me. I have a glass of whiskey in front of me and I am thinking about how when you get home we will sit up late together and drink whiskey. You have certainly earned a few drinks. I wish you were here right now so I could tell you about what I did today and you could tell me what you did.*

Dooley stopped and read through what he'd written and swore at himself; if it hadn't been tacked onto what the others had already written, he'd have wadded it up and thrown it away. He went and poured himself another inch of Jameson's and sat down and picked up the pen again.

You will be home soon, I am sure, and we will go someplace, just you and me, and talk about everything. Until then, I will just say be careful and please never forget I am proud of you. When you were a little boy I used to watch you sleep and think how I wanted to keep you safe from everything. I am sorry that I couldn't but that's life.

Jesus, I'm drunk, thought Dooley. He almost started to cross out the last two sentences but he didn't want to make a mess of the letter. He took a drink of whiskey, said hell with it and wrote, *I wish you were here right now so I could tell you how much I love you.*

Dooley signed the letter and laid down the pen. Usually he left the letter out so Rose could see what he had written, but tonight he folded it up, put it in the envelope and sealed it. Rose had put the APO address on the envelope and stuck on the stamps; Dooley double-checked everything. He drained his whiskey and sat holding the envelope in his hands.

This one has to get there, Dooley thought.

Thirty-one

THERE WAS NOTHING but grief in the newspaper, bad news from front to back. There had been more killings in L.A., the same type of scene as the Tate murders; the cops had decided the suspect they'd arrested hadn't done it after all. They were back to square one with a band of maniacs on the loose. Dooley was glad it was somebody else's problem; he had enough of his own. A cab driver had been shot on the South Side; two drifters in Lincoln Park had beaten the living hell out of a father who had refused to let them join in his family softball game.

And the big one from Dooley's point of view, the item on page five: *Inmate Slain in Prison Fight.* William Gaines, serving a three-year sentence for kidnapping, had been stabbed to death in Pontiac state prison by a fellow inmate, a Negro. Apparently it was a racial fight. Dooley sat and looked at it for a long time, thinking. Was the mob's arm that long? Or was it just his usual rotten luck? One thing really bothered him, the idea that he had made a mistake in trusting Haggerty. Dooley'd never heard anything bad about him but you never knew. He did some uneasy calculating and decided that Haggerty was off the hook; even if he'd leaked Dooley's notion from their last conversation, the timing was too quick for that to have set anything off. The long and the short of it was, he had to be right about the fix but it was getting less likely he would ever prove anything.

Dooley would have been happy with all that; the worst news was from overseas. The lull was over in Viet Nam; the communists had launched an offensive all over the country. They were dying like flies, according to the reports, but taking a lot of Americans with them. Nineteen marines had been killed on a ridge two miles south of the DMZ, in Quang Tri province. Dooley shook his head; that was a hell of a lot of casualties for a single action. That was up there with Dooley's worst days out in the Pacific. Get my boy out of there, he thought. Now. He hadn't read anything more about any marines coming home, and he was afraid that was all over.

He looked at the sports pages hoping for distraction: the Cubs were seven up on the Mets and eight over the Cards, and the doubters were starting to shut up. The Sox had lost six in a row, and their first baseman had blown off his thumb cleaning a mortar on army reserve duty. It was a good year to be a North-sider.

• • •

Dooley had forgotten about the parade. The astronauts were in town, fresh out of quarantine, and the city was throwing them a party. The Loop was a mess with the streets closed off and Dooley had to park down past Congress and hike back up to Jackson. The sidewalks were swarming with people hoping for a glimpse of the men who had gone to the moon and Dooley had to shove his way through the crowd.

They'd knocked down a whole block in the south end of the Loop a few years before and put up a complex of big black ugly buildings for the feds to go to work in. The FBI had a floor or two in the federal court building, where a vast empty marble-floored lobby provided a good venue for news photographers and TV cameramen to jostle for angles on the indicted big shots coming and going. Dooley took the elevator up to the ninth floor and flashed his star at a woman behind a long black counter with the FBI seal on it. She picked up the phone and told Dooley to have a seat.

Dooley checked his watch as he sat down; he figured the length of the wait would be a good measure of his clout. He wished he'd brought something to read.

He only had to wait ten minutes, which surprised him a little. Gustafson was a wiry middleweight with a gray crew cut in a summer-weight suit. He shook Dooley's hand and took him through a door and down a long featureless corridor. "You see the astronauts out there?" he asked over his shoulder.

"I saw the traffic jam."

Gustafson laughed, ushering Dooley into a windowless office. "That's all most people will see. But the mayor will look good shaking hands with them."

"I guess that's what counts."

"You said it." Gustafson waved Dooley to a chair and settled behind his desk. "So. You're not giving up on Tommy Spain, huh?"

Dooley crossed one leg over another and gave his trouser leg a tug. "Let's say I'm not giving up on Sally Kotowski."

"That's a good way to look at it, I guess." Gustafson gave him a calculating look and said, "We talked to Spain for you. We had a guy from our Little Rock field office take a day to make the trip."

Everything these guys do is a special favor, thought Dooley.

"I appreciate that. What's he got to say for himself?"

Gustafson reached for a folder on the desk and opened it. He scanned whatever was inside and said, "Well, it's kind of interesting. He claims he has no specific knowledge of what might have led to her death, but he says it could have something to do with something she stole from him."

Dooley met Gustafson's look with a slight nod. "Go on."

The G-man closed the folder and tossed it on the desk.

"Spain says when he got back into town from Mexico last year he looked her up and they went out to dinner. He says then they went up to his hotel room and went to bed. She left late in the evening and after she was gone Spain realized some documents were missing. He thinks she went through his luggage while he was in the shower."

"Some documents."

"That's right."

"What kind of documents?"

Gustafson frowned, firmed the thin line of his mouth and clasped his hands, elbows resting on the arms of his chair. He looked as if he were about to give Dooley a stern lecture on the perils of smoking or looking at girlie magazines. "You don't need to know that," he said.

Dooley sat there staring at him for a while, trying to keep his face a perfect blank. "Don't tell me that," he said finally. "You can tell me you're not allowed to say, or that you don't trust me with the information, but don't tell me I don't need to know that. I'm investigating a homicide, and the nature of those documents could be extremely relevant. Don't insult my intelligence."

Gustafson flinched, just a little; his brows went up a fraction of an inch and then settled. He spread his hands. "I'm not trying to insult your intelligence. OK, you want me to spell it out, I will. I am not authorized to disclose what was in the documents. What I am authorized to tell you is that Thomas Spain said that Sally Kotowski stole material from him that had great potential value as an instrument of blackmail."

"Who's the target?"

The frown was back. "I can't tell you that."

Dooley nodded. "So what am I doing here? Nothing you've told me is worth a damn if you don't tell me who Spain wanted to blackmail."

"You're here because you requested an interview with me. I've told you everything I'm able to tell you. You have to understand that I'm working under constraints. I can also tell you that we are pursuing the matter ourselves. Obviously, if there is incriminating material involved, we are very interested in making a case out of it."

"A federal case."

"Of course."

"Not a murder case."

"That's not our purview."

"I know. It happens to be mine. And I'm just trying to see that somebody gets punished for killing Sally."

"It's my understanding that somebody already has."

"I mean the right person. I think we were sold a bill of goods, and I think Spain knows the real reason she was killed."

Gustafson shifted on his chair, looking irritated. "There was a confession. The case has been closed. Maybe I didn't make myself clear—nothing Spain told us contradicts the confession that was made. That's not to say all the particulars of the case were brought out. But speculation about the reason for the killing is irrelevant as long as there's no evidence that the wrong man is in custody. As far as I know there is none."

Dooley sat there for a few seconds longer looking Gustafson in the eye and coming to the realization that he had run up against a big blank wall put up by experts. "Not yet," he said.

Gustafson waved a hand at him, a vague gesture.

"If you come up with some, let us know." He picked up the folder from the desk top and pulled open a drawer. He took his time finding the right place in the drawer for the folder and Dooley realized he had been dismissed. He put his hands on his knees and got to his feet.

Gustafson shoved the drawer shut and stood up. He extended his hand across the desk. "I know it's hard for a good cop to let go sometimes. But you did your job. Now let us do ours."

Dooley just looked at his hand. "Let me ask you this," he said. "If you come across anything in the course of your investigation that indicates the confession is bogus, will you tell me?"

"Of course." The look on Gustafson's face said, what do you take me for? He let his hand fall to the desk. "We're not trying to obstruct anybody, Mike. We just have our own agenda, and it's a little different from yours."

Dooley nodded, then slowly put out his hand. "I guess so."

• • •

Dooley hiked back to his car and drove straight west to get the hell out of the Loop. So the feds were going to go after Ogilvie? Dooley thought it was just possible. That would make some headlines, and the FBI loved headlines. He was irritated because he didn't think he'd done very well with Gustafson; he kept thinking of all the things he should have said. He had a feeling it was all out of his hands now. Even if the feds were serious, it would take months or years for anything to happen, and Dooley figured when the indictments came down, nobody at the federal building was going to bother much about who really killed Sally Kotowski.

Of course, Dooley reminded himself, there was no guarantee Tommy Spain had told Swallow and the FBI the truth. The discrepancy between 'documents' and 'a tape' was interesting; was that just Gustafson being coy? And Spain's story was different from Gallo's, which was just as interesting.

Who the hell knows, thought Dooley. He was in a rotten mood.

There were messages waiting for him at Damen and Grace, as always; one of them was from *Laura L.* Olson was looking over his shoulder. "I knew it, Dooley. She's got the hots for you. She wants you."

Dooley shoved the slip aside. "She's probably got another random thought about Sally. I told her to keep at it."

"Ah, Mike. How do you do it? I don't get beautiful ex-Playboy Bunnies calling me on the phone at all hours of the day and night. What is it? The Old Spice? Or just your Irish blarney?"

"It's called doing your job."

Dooley didn't look up and Olson got the message and went to sign out a car. Dooley took the opportunity to dial the number on Laura's message, which was starting to look familiar: the Mad Hatter. Laura herself answered for a change.

"It's Dooley."

"Hey, how are you?"

"OK. What's up?"

"Steve Spanos called me."

Dooley had to think for a second. "The fence?"

"Yeah. The one down on Jackson. He says he thinks he knows who has the locket."

"He thinks he knows?"

"That's what he said."

"That's strange."

"How come?"

"I'd expect him to try and sell it to you himself, not direct you to the competition."

"I see what you mean. I'm just passing on what he said. He wants to meet us on Sunday morning and take us to the guy."

"Sunday morning? What the hell for?"

"He wants to take us to Maxwell Street. He says that's where the guy will be. He said to meet him at Lyon's Deli at ten o'clock."

Dooley ran his free hand over his face. "Maxwell Street. Jesus."

"Oh, come on, Dooley. It'll be fun."

Dooley didn't expect to get any fun out of it, but he could think of worse people to share an hour of two of tedium with than Laura Lindbloom. "Sure," he said. "It'll be a blast."

• • •

Dooley could remember when Maxwell Street was where you went to get a suit of clothes; now it was where you went to buy back the hi-fi system the burglars took. When Dooley was a kid his father had taken him down to what he called Jewtown once on some forgotten errand and Dooley had been afraid they weren't going to make it out alive; the aggressive sales pitch was an art form on Maxwell Street.

Now the Jews were mostly gone, but you could still wind up taking home something you hadn't really wanted. A lot of the department stores, tailor shops, shoe stores and furniture houses had closed, but the street still came alive on Sundays when the flea market took over. Start at Halsted and Maxwell and walk a few blocks in any direction, and you could find just about anything you had your heart set on, new or used: auto parts, clothes, electrical equipment, books, records, plumbing fixtures, you name it. Most of it was legitimate, but Dooley knew people who worked burglary and had made more than one arrest down here, finding things that had been sitting in living rooms in Hyde Park or Edgewater a day or two before.

"There's the deli." Dooley pointed up the street through the crowd. He had gotten up early and slipped out of the house while Rose and the kids were at Mass, leaving a note that had been vague on the time of his return. He had been thinking of this as work but now that he was here he was starting to feel guilty, because it felt like he was at a party.

"Slow down," said Laura, putting a hand on his arm. "Let's listen for a second." What made Maxwell Street a party was the music. When the Negroes had moved in after the war they had brought their music with them, and on Sundays they put it out on the street, setting up on the sidewalk, running an extension cord into a shop for the amplifier, putting a hat down for the tips. On a nice day there would be two or three bands on every block. In the last few years the hippies had discovered Maxwell Street and now half the crowd on a Sunday morning was here for the blues.

Dooley stood on the edge of a crowd with a lot of long-hairs in it, watching an old black man howl into a microphone while he played guitar, with a younger man beating on a set of drums. Dooley didn't like colored music all that much but had to admit it had a good beat. "Nice, huh?" said Laura, looking up at him.

"It's OK." Dooley shrugged and started to move away, and Laura came with him after making a face that said he was a drip. She had her hair tied back in a ponytail today and Dooley had decided she really didn't look that much like Sharon Tate. What she looked like was a million bucks, drawing stares in her miniskirt, parting the crowd as they walked, like Moses at the Red Sea. Dooley had put on a suit because he always put on a suit to deal with business, and he felt a little uncomfortable standing out in the crowd. He felt like her bodyguard.

There was another crowd in the deli but Dooley muscled through it until he spotted Spanos sitting at a tiny table in the back. Spanos had an empty plate in front of him, and he grinned at Dooley when he saw him. "You want some breakfast?" he said over the din.

"I ate already."

"Suit yourself." Spanos caught sight of Laura in Dooley's wake and gave her a nod and a smile, then stood up. "You wanna go for a walk?"

"That's what we're here for."

Outside it was easier to talk. Spanos led them west along Maxwell Street, dodging shoppers, gawkers, grifters, past tables loaded with lamps, kitchen utensils, shoes. He gave Laura the eye, up and down, and said, "How's the birthday girl?"

She beamed at him. "Fine, thanks. Did you find a good present for me?"

"I think I might have found what you're looking for, yeah."

Dooley figured it was time for the question. "So why are you doing us this favor?"

Spanos smiled, looking everywhere but at Dooley. "For such a pretty girl I'll do anything," he said. "Besides. I think you might be able to do me a favor or two."

"Says who?" Dooley edged closer to Spanos to hear his answer, cutting out Laura, who trailed behind.

"The suit clinched it," said Spanos. "Who the hell wears a suit down here on Sunday morning?"

"I just came from church," said Dooley. He smiled as he said it, knowing the game was up. Spanos chuckled. "The big red brick one up here at the end of the street?" he said, raising his chin in the direction of the old 7th District station a few blocks ahead.

"Not that one." Dooley didn't want any confusion here; the old 7th District was where Organized Crime Intelligence worked nowadays. "But another one, yeah. I guess I can't fool you."

"There are guys who can hide it and guys who can't. You'll look like a cop lying in your coffin. I saw it the minute you walked into my shop."

Dooley was a little irritated but at the same time he felt flattered. "OK. I'll ask you again. Why are you doing me a favor?"

Spanos walked for a little while, pretending to look at the merchandise out on the tables before speaking. "In my business credit is very important. You build it up where you can, you're careful about giving it out. I'm always looking for a way to build it up. And bankers aren't the only ones I might need credit with."

Dooley had to smile. "I don't know what I can do for you. Your business doesn't come under my department. I'm a homicide dick."

"I thought it might be something like that. But you can still pass the word to your pals in other departments. The ones that occasionally give me a hard time."

"Completely undeserved, I'm sure."

Spanos shrugged, hands in the air. "I'm a legitimate businessman. You've seen my store. Sure, I been burned a few times. People lie to me sometimes. I get taken because I'm a trusting person. That's why I need a little credit sometimes from your side."

Dooley managed to keep from rolling his eyes. "I'm not going to make you any promises."

"I'm not asking for promises. This favor's for free. I'm not asking for anything. Except maybe you put a word in somebody's ear that I helped you. That's all."

It was Dooley's turn to scan the junk spread out along the sidewalk while he thought it over. Finally he looked Spanos in the eye and said, "That I can do. Now tell me about this locket."

Spanos nodded once, suddenly serious. "I was curious after you showed up, because I could tell you were looking for something specific. I asked a few people I know if they'd seen anything like you were asking about. And one fellow said yes. Somebody had brought it to him and he'd made an offer on it, but the seller didn't like his offer. It so happens the seller was a guy we both know, kind of a small-timer, an amateur. And he usually shows up down here on Sundays." Spanos stopped and turned to face Dooley, letting Laura catch up with them.

"And he may still have it," said Dooley, looking for signs in Spanos's face.

"He's got it all right," said Spanos. "I already looked." He smiled.

Dooley stiffened with the thrill that always came with a break. "Where is he?"

Spanos was rocking on his heels, still smiling, the picture of a man just passing the time of day. "Don't look right away, OK? I don't want him to know I fingered him. He's the guy in the fedora over there right next to the hot dog stand. His name's Benny. Unless he's sold it in the last half hour, what you're looking for is laying right out there."

Dooley resisted the urge to look. He nodded and said, "OK. I owe you one."

"Just spread the word in the right places."

Spanos wheeled and took off back the way they had come. Dooley and Laura traded a look.

"I heard," she said, her eyes flicking out over his shoulder. "I see him. Let's go."

The man in the fedora was black and maybe fifty years old, gaunt and light-skinned, with a thin moustache that could have been drawn with a pencil across a wide upper lip. He didn't have a whole suit to go with the fedora but he wore the vest to a nice one over a white shirt with a black tie knotted at his throat. He had staked out a place at the end of a table laden with scarves and handkerchiefs, sitting on a chair with his wares laid out in front of him on a piece of cardboard sitting on a milk crate. He was laughing, having a good time working the crowd jostling to get in line for red hots at the stand next door.

When Dooley and Laura got close enough to catch his eye, he gave Dooley about half a second and then got a reverent look on his face as his eyes went from Laura's head down to her bare toes in the sandals and back up again, taking their time. "Oh my, my, my," he said. "Look at the pretty lady. What part of heaven do you come from, Angel?"

"Iowa," said Laura. "You ever heard of it?"

"Seems to me I heard of it, but I never heard nobody claim it was heaven." His small glinting eyes had made it back to her face, and he was grinning again. "What you doin' here in the big wicked city?"

"Just looking for something nice to take home." She was already scanning the merchandise, an array of rings, bracelets, chains, trinkets, all laid out on the box lid.

"Well, you come to the right place for that. Not like you need anything to make you look nice." Benny shot a look at Dooley. "Who are you, her daddy?"

"How'd you guess?" said Dooley. He was scanning, too, not sure what he was looking for, and suddenly Laura reached down and pulled it out of the spread, a chain with a gold locket on it, little pearls on its face. Laura held it in the palm of her hand, gazing at it. Benny could smell a sale. "You like that? That's nice, all right. That'll look real sweet on you. Go ahead, put it on if you want."

Instead, Laura found the tiny clasp at the side. The locket opened to reveal a minature of a soulful-looking Jesus, eyes raised to heaven. Laura looked at Dooley and said, "This is it. I'm sure."

That was about the worst thing a man peddling jewelry on the street could hear; by the time Dooley looked back at Benny he was already scowling and thinking about damage limitation. "Where'd you get this?" said Dooley

"What's it matter to you where I got it? You like it or not?"

Dooley pulled his star out of his pocket. "I'm a police officer. I need to know where you got it."

Benny knew he had trouble, but he wasn't going to fold. "Same place I get all my stuff, from my suppliers. I'm in the business, I got wholesalers I go to." His tone was indignant, but the look on his face said he didn't expect Dooley to buy it.

"Don't bullshit me," said Dooley. "This has just been identified as stolen property."

"Now hold on. I don't handle no stolen property."

Dooley put his star away. "OK. Have it your way. You got two choices. One, you tell me where you got this locket, and I mean a name, somebody I can go talk to. Two, you're under arrest. I take you in on suspicion of receiving stolen goods, we catalogue all this and see how much of it has been reported missing. Those are your choices."

They weren't good ones, Dooley could see. Under the brim of the fedora he could see a man trying to choose between the frying pan and the fire. That was the kind of situation Dooley liked to have a man in. The glinting black eyes narrowed and Benny said, "You want a name? That's all?"

"It's gotta be the right one."

"But then no arrest?"

"If I find you lied to me I come back and jump all over you. You give me straight dope, I don't give a damn what you sell. I'm interested in the man that gave you this. I'm not even a robbery dick. I'm in homicide."

Benny gave it some more thought, things sinking in, and then the brim of the fedora dipped once. "All right. But you got to make it look like you're takin' me in. I can be seen getting arrested, but I can't be seen squealing."

"Fair enough. Pack it up. You're under arrest."

A little space had cleared around them as the crowd had read the situation. With a few quick motions Benny swept up his merchandise and stowed in in his pants pockets, then shoved the milk crate under the neighboring table. "You gonna cuff me?" he asked.

"Not if you don't make any trouble. I might hang onto your arm."

"Let's go then."

Dooley marched him back down Maxwell Street toward the vacant lot where he'd parked the car. Laura trailed them and the crowd parted as they went, recognizing a bust in progress. Benny walked with the dignity of a man unfairly maligned; Dooley heard a few people call to him as they passed, laughing at his bad luck.

When they got to the car Dooley patted him down, partly for show and partly because it was a bad idea ever, under any circumstances, to just assume a man was going to play it straight. He found nothing but the jewelry, keys, a roll of cash. He put Benny on the back seat of the car, told Laura to get in front, and drove out of the lot onto Newberry and turned north. "Talk to me," he said. "Who gave you the locket?"

"This ain't gonna come back on me, is it? I mean, I'm not gonna have to testify or nothing?"

"I can't guarantee that. It might come to that. But maybe not. What I'm going to do is ask you to sign a statement. That means you come up to Area Six with me now for an hour or so. And I'll need to be able to find you again."

"Man, you don't want much, do you?"

"Hey, Benny. I can just drive over here to the district at Monroe

Street and tell them to charge you with receiving. Look, level with me and I'll do my best to keep you out of it."

A few seconds went by. Dooley drove slowly, waiting. Benny said, "Because, you see, this guy I got it from, he worries me some, you know?"

Dooley could see him in the mirror, looking sullen. "Who is it?"

Benny was silent for a moment as Dooley pushed north, away from the market, into deserted streets. "He's one of them Italian guys. I know him from a crap game I get in on sometimes, up Halsted a ways. A few weeks back when I was up there he come to me with that locket. I gave him twenty-five bucks for it. I think it's worth a lot more, but I guess I'm just out twenty-five bucks."

"You're breaking my heart. What's his name?"

"I only got a first name."

Dooley flicked a look in the mirror and said, "OK then, what I'm gonna do is, we're gonna drive back to the station there on Maxwell Street and you're going to come in and look at some pictures with me."

"No, you don't need to do that."

"Then I need a name. I really need this guy."

"All right, lemme think a second." Benny made them wait for it, almost all the way to Roosevelt Road. "Messino," he said finally. "Tony Messino."

Thirty-two

DOOLEY PULLED UP in front of the Victorian house on Cleveland and threw it in park. He looked over at Laura and saw her leaning over against the window, staring at nothing. "Here you go," he said. "I'm sorry you had to wait around so long."

"That's OK. Everyone was nice to me."

"I bet they were. They don't get to see people like you up there very often." Laura had kept a roomful of second-watch dicks distracted from their work while Dooley took Benny's statement and then did the inventory paperwork on the locket.

She went on staring out the windshield. Dooley waited a little while and then said, "This is a big break, Laura. This busts it wide open again."

"I know." He could barely hear her.

"You OK?"

She roused herself and managed a shrug. "Want to come in for a while?" she said softly.

"I gotta get going. I have to drive back downtown to deposit this with the evidence section, then I gotta go back to the office and write up a report."

"Please." Dooley had never seen a look on her face like this one: he hadn't imagined she could look desolate, hurt like this. "Please come in just for a while," she said. "I really don't want to be alone. Please."

Dooley had the thrill of the chase running through him and all he wanted to do was go inventory his evidence and then track down McCone and have a heart-to-heart talk, but he couldn't drive away and leave her looking like this. "OK," he said.

Upstairs it was hot; all the windows in Laura's place were open but there wasn't much of a breeze stirring. Dooley sat on the couch while Laura went back to the kitchen to make them some iced tea. He took off his jacket and sat there in his shirt sleeves and shoulder holster, looking around the room. There were posters on the walls, prints of paintings he vaguely recognized, some Oriental-looking landscapes. There was a stereo and lots of records, books on shelves made from boards laid across cinder blocks. Dooley wondered what he was doing here. He got up and went to the front window and looked down into the street. People went by on the sidewalk, laughing.

Laura came back and handed him a glass of tea. "I didn't put sugar in it," she said.

"That's OK." Dooley took a sip and went on looking out the window. Laura stood beside him, arms folded. She hadn't brought any tea for herself and Dooley didn't really want his; he set it on the windowsill. He looked at Laura and saw tears tracking down her cheeks.

"I feel awful," she said. "It never really sank in, what happened to her, until I held that thing in my hand." Laura had clutched the locket, the gold chain trailing out between her fingers, all the way from Roosevelt Road. In the office at Damen and Grace he'd told her it was evidence and she'd handed it over, saying, "Yeah, I guess that's all it is now."

Dooley murmured, "It's over. She's at peace."

The sobs caught Dooley by surprise; all of a sudden Laura had her face in her hands, shoulders shaking. Dooley stood there paralyzed for a moment. He wanted to sprint for the door, but instead he put a hand on her shoulder and said, "Hey," and then Laura was wobbling, tipping toward him.

He caught her and held her, and after a few more sobs she took her hands away from her face and put her arms around him and sagged a little, and pressed her face to the side of his neck. Dooley stood there with a weeping woman in his arms, just holding her while she shook, and after a while it seemed like the right thing to do. "It's OK," he said.

"It's not OK." The words came from deep in her throat. "It hurts."

He held onto her through a few more sobs. "You get over it. Believe me."

It took a while, but in a few minutes she had stopped crying and they were just standing there by the window hearing street noises and hanging onto each other. It felt good to Dooley but he knew it couldn't go on forever. He was starting to get a little restless when she finally drew back from him enough to look up into his face. "You're good," she said, her big brown eyes shining, very close.

"What are you talking about?"

"You're a good man."

Dooley opened his mouth but couldn't come up with anything intelligent to say. He was starting to get hypnotized, with this beautiful woman, her face full of pain, staring at him like this. All he could do was look back at her. Her face came a little closer and Dooley stiffened just enough for her to get the message, and she stopped moving. "It's OK, Dooley," she whispered. "There's nothing wrong with this."

"Maybe not." Dooley didn't know where he was going with that thought, so he shut up. He tried to pull away from her but she held onto him.

"Don't run away from me, please. I really need someone right now."

"I don't think it's me you need."

"Why not?"

"I'm a married man."

"Does that mean you can't be my friend?"

"No, I guess not."

"So comfort me. That's what friends do."

"I don't know how to comfort you."

"You're doing just fine. It feels great. Doesn't it feel great to you?"

"It feels fine, yeah."

"So OK, then." Her head went down again, resting on his shoulder. Dooley couldn't figure out how to extract himself, so he gave her a couple of pats on the back, for lack of anything better to do. Finally Laura let go and pulled away from him. She had stopped crying and she looked drained. She managed to smile at him. "It really is all right. I'm not going to make you do anything you don't want to do."

"You're right about that."

"Jesus, Dooley. What are you afraid of?"

"I'm not afraid of anything. I'm just thinking about my wife."

She searched his face with her big brown eyes for a while. "Do you love your wife?"

"Of course I love my wife."

"Then what could I possibly do to hurt your marriage?"

Dooley knew there was an answer to that, but he couldn't come up with it. "Nothing, I guess."

"Your marriage is between you and her. Nothing that happens between you and me has to change that."

"Nothing's going to happen between you and me."

"It already has." She let Dooley work on that for a few seconds and then she said, "Look, I'm not going to seduce you. I have no designs on your home and family. I want you to go home to your wife, believe me. I just want you to go home happy."

"I am happy."

"That's good. You know what? I'm happy too, when you're around."

Dooley stood there nodding like an idiot.

"You OK now?"

"I'm all right, I guess. Thanks."

"Don't mention it."

She laughed then, still wiping tears away, and she looked so beautiful Dooley almost grabbed her again. She said, "You're funny."

Dooley didn't know what he'd said that was so hilarious. He didn't like the way she confused him, but he had to admit he had liked holding her. "I need to get going," he said.

"I know. Come back soon." She was looking wistful now, big brown eyes wide open. "Business or pleasure."

"OK," Dooley said, making for the door. "There will be business, that's for sure."

At the door he paused, turning to say good-bye, and he half expected it when she put a hand on either side of his face and stood on tip toes and kissed him lightly on the lips, drawing back with a grave look. "Friends?"

"Sure," said Dooley, and made a beeline for the stairs.

• • •

"Jesus Christ, Dooley." Kowalcyk stopped in front of the desk, coffee in hand even though it had to be ninety degrees in the office. "Does your wife know what kind of informant you're hanging around with these days?"

"Not unless some jealous copper's told her."

"I mean, Jesus. What a looker."

"I didn't notice."

"No, of course not." Kowalcyk took a sip of coffee. "So, you banging her yet?"

"Fuck off, will you? I got work to do." Dooley kept pounding the typewriter keys. Kowalcyk stood there looking at him for a moment before moving off with a shake of the head. Dooley hacked at the keys for a while longer, wiped sweat off his forehead with a wadded-up Kleenex, and pulled the form out of the machine.

He stared at the strange creation in his hands. It was something that in theory couldn't exist: a Supplementary Report on a case that had been cleared, closed, wrapped up and filed away. He'd put some time and effort into it because he knew the report had to be damn good to get McCone's attention. He'd checked the schedule and seen that McCone was on today. He looked at his watch. McCone should be coming in before too long. Dooley could go grab a bite to eat somewhere and come back. He had already blown most of a rare Sunday off anyway and another hour wasn't going to matter.

"Go home, Dooley." Kowalcyk had his feet up on a neighboring desk. "This place will still be here tomorrow."

"Don't I know it," said Dooley, heading for the door.

• • •

"Can she prove it?" said McCone, looking weary, his head resting on one hand. Dooley could tell this was the last thing he wanted to deal with today. "Can she absolutely swear it belonged to the victim? Is there a number, an identifying mark?"

"She was positive. We can go back to the sister, too, see if she can back her up. Look, the guy got it from Messino. That's too much coincidence."

"I'm not arguing with you, Mike. I'm saying you have to have something solid to take to the State's Attorney, that's all. They're going to ask some tough questions. What's this Spanos up to, for example?"

"I can't answer that. You want me to go back and interview him again, I will. All I know is that he found it, my informant identified it, and the fence came up with a name, without prompting. What more do you want?"

McCone sighed. He pulled Dooley's report toward him. "I can take it to the lieutenant, he can take it to the Chief of Detectives. But they're going to have to take a long hard look at things before they'll re-open it."

"That's their job. I've done mine." Dooley pushed back his chair and stood up. "You want to know how much time I've spent on this? My own time?"

McCone looked up at him, thoughtful. "Nobody's ever accused you of not doing your job, Mike. If all my dicks worked as hard as you do, I could retire a happy man."

"And it doesn't mean a God damn thing if somebody at Eleventh and State buries this."

"Why would anyone down there bury this?"

Dooley made a who-are-you-kidding face. "Because this is all about keeping the lid on something, and you know as well as I do there are people down there who owe their jobs to the people that want the lid there."

McCone's eyes narrowed. "What do you mean? What are they keeping the lid on?"

Dooley had been wanting to confide in somebody but he wasn't sure he was ready. "I don't know."

McCone stared at him for a few seconds and then tapped on the report with a finger. "Nobody's going to bury this."

"I'm taking that as a promise."

"Mike, I'll do what I can. But you've just handed me a job that's going to make my life a little harder for a while."

"Show 'em the pictures," said Dooley, making for the door. "Show 'em what they did to Sally."

• • •

"Where have you *been*?" The instant he walked into the kitchen Dooley knew he was in trouble; the look on Rose's face would have struck a lesser man dead at ten paces. She was rising from her chair at the kitchen table, giving off sparks. Dooley stood there for a moment groping frantically for what it was he'd forgotten. "I had to go in to work." It came out sounding feeble.

"I see," Rose said, folding her arms. "Was it an emergency?"

"No, but it was damn important."

"More important than your daughter's birthday lunch at DiLeo's we've been talking about for days?"

"Shit," he said.

"That kind of language doesn't help anything." She was getting frosty now, nose in the air; Dooley hadn't seen her like this since the time he stumbled in drunk after Dan Newman's retirement party. "We talked about it *last night*. Are you going to tell me you forgot?"

Dooley shoved the door closed behind him. "I had to go meet a guy. I wound up getting a big break on a case out of it. I went into the office to write it up and it just drove everything else out of my mind. Where is she? I'll talk to her."

"She has to work tonight. She left already. She was making light of it but she was *very* disappointed. This would have been a good occasion for you two to make up a little bit, but you missed it."

"So I'll take her out somewhere tomorrow, big deal."

"Michael, the party's over. You missed it. Everybody was there but you."

"I'll make it up to her." He draped his jacket over the back of a chair. He wanted a drink. Rose wasn't ready to give up. "You were off work today, you told me."

"I am off. But when something comes up you have to take care of it. You don't clear a case by being lazy."

"Couldn't the paperwork at least have waited?"

Dooley ran himself a glass of water at the sink. "Yeah." He drank half the glass. "It probably could have. Look, I forgot, OK?"

"How could you *forget*? You have a *family*, Michael. We have at least as much of a claim on you as the city does. Don't we?"

Dooley made a mistake then; instead of saying of course, how could you think otherwise, he gave it a half-second's honest thought, and the slightly dubious look on his face was enough for Rose. Her face contracted and darkened and he knew he'd done it now. Rose shook her head a few times, trying impotently to find words scathing enough, and then stalked out of the room. He heard her go up the stairs; he heard the door to their bedroom slam.

Dooley stood motionless for a minute or so. He could hear the television going up in the living room, the sounds of a ball game, Jack Brickhouse rambling. Dooley shook his head and got down the bottle of Jameson's. He put ice in a glass and set the glass on the counter beside the bottle. He leaned on the counter, wondering why he felt so damn guilty when he had a perfectly clean conscience.

Dooley put the glass in the sink, put the bottle back in the cupboard, and left the kitchen. He walked up the stairs slowly and went to the door of his bedroom. He tapped on the door and pushed it open. Rose was lying on the bed, her back to the door, her shoes off and her feet drawn up. Dooley locked his star and his .38 in the drawer and then changed into a pair of slacks and a sport shirt, waiting for her to say something. When he was finished he sat on the edge of the bed with his back to her, elbows on his knees. "I'm sorry I missed it," he said. "Did she have a good time?"

She made him wait for an answer. Finally she said, "Well, she laughed a lot. Her best friends were there. But she wanted you there. She told me so."

"You give her the watch?"

"Of course I gave her the watch." Rose sighed. "I went out and bought it, I wrapped it, I gave it to her. But I put your name on it along with mine, I'm not sure why."

Dooley scowled at the rug. "Don't forget, I paid for it."

"No, Michael, I won't forget."

"I wasn't just out having a good time, Rose. I was working."

"I know that. You like to work. You'd rather work than be with your family."

Dooley could feel himself getting steamed again, like when Kathleen had said the only thing he understood was violence. He didn't have the words to tell her how she was wrong; he couldn't explain it. He took a deep breath and said, "That's not true."

Dooley sat there listening to distant sounds, the faint drone of the TV downstairs, kids yelling outside, a car purring by on the street. Rose said, "It's hard being married to you."

He laughed, a short bitter exhalation. "Well, you're kind of stuck with me, aren't you? I guess you married the wrong guy. Too bad."

"That's not what I'm saying and you know it."

"I'm sorry it's so tough being married to me. Yeah, I really got the easy part, didn't I? All I have to do is deal with dead people all week long."

She stirred now, rolling toward him. "Well, there are some live people in this house that would like it if you paid a little more attention to them."

Dooley gave her a glance over his shoulder. She looked like hell, her hair disheveled, her face puffy. Suddenly Dooley had had enough. "So who pays attention to me?" he said. He stood up and made for the door.

"You're never *here*," Rose said, her voice rising as he left the room.

• • •

Dooley knew he ought to hang around, watch the ball game with Frank for a while, wait for Rose to get over it and come downstairs, apologize a few more times and be nice to everybody, get down whatever leftovers Rose came up with for supper, settle in front of the TV with her and watch *Bonanza,* then *Mission Impossible.* But he couldn't do it.

Dooley had to get out of the house; he had to talk to somebody that wasn't furious with him. Somebody who understood why he had spent his whole God damn Sunday off doing what he did every other day of the week. Somebody who appreciated it. He jumped in the car and went.

He was supposed to have his piece with him even when he was off-duty, but tonight he didn't give a damn. Dooley had given the department enough for one day. He was going to take the evening off and mean it this time.

Even on a Sunday night it was tough to park near Wells Street. Dooley found a spot on North Avenue and hiked a block or two. He almost got cold feet at the door to the bar but made himself go in. "She called in sick," the long-haired bartender said to him, spotting him as he stood there at the end of the bar gaping stupidly, not finding Laura. Dooley thanked him and left.

He went back to the car and started it up immediately; he wasn't going to waste any time trying to make up his mind tonight. He drove up Cleveland and said hell with it and parked too close to a hydrant on Laura's block. He walked back to the house and rang her bell.

There wasn't any answer for what seemed like a long time and Dooley was about to give up and go around to try the back when the buzzer went off. He opened the door and went up the stairs. She called out asking who it was when he was halfway up and he said, "It's Dooley." She was standing in the doorway waiting for him, and the look on her face was full of wonder. "You came back," she said.

"How you feeling?" He stopped on the landing, three feet from the door.

"I'm fine. Come on in." She was barefoot and her hair was hanging free and she was draped in a loose cotton dress that came halfway down her thighs and left her shoulders bare. She looked like at least ten million bucks.

Dooley didn't move. "I looked for you over at the bar. The guy said you were sick."

"I called in because I couldn't face it tonight. But I'm OK. What are you standing there for?"

"I'm taking you out for dinner."

She blinked at him. "I just ate."

"So we'll go get a drink." Dooley figured that as long as he didn't go into her apartment he was OK. He knew he was playing with fire, but he needed the warmth. "Come on."

Laura stood there wide-eyed for a second or two, and then she laughed a little bit. "I have things to drink here. Come in, will you? I don't want to go anywhere tonight." She took a step back, opening the door wider.

Dooley shrugged and walked into the apartment. "I wanted to tell you how it went with my supervisor," he said as Laura closed the door. "I think he's going to go to bat for us. I think he's going to do his best to get the case reopened."

"That's good news." She waited a beat and said, "Is that why you came over here?"

"Yeah." Dooley shoved his hands in his pockets. "And because I wanted to see you."

"I'm glad. God, I'm glad."

Dooley stood speechless while she took two steps and threw her arms around him. He just got his hands out of his pockets in time to catch her and squeeze back, and they stood swaying for a moment, cheek to cheek. Laura pulled back far enough to say softly, "There's nothing wrong with this, Dooley, is there? Isn't it a good thing?" Her lips were two inches from his. He could feel her body through the thin dress, lithe and strong. Dooley knew he ought to let go of her but he didn't. He took a deep breath and made his last desperate stand. He said, "I've always been faithful to my wife."

Her eyes were enormous, big brown eyes. "Your wife's a lucky woman. But you're not going to run out of love if you give me some."

That was all Dooley needed in the way of logic. He was through fighting it. He kissed her, and when her tongue touched his there was suddenly nothing in the world he wanted as badly as what he knew, with a flash of astonishment, he was about to get.

• • •

"Can I still call you Dooley? Or is that too formal now?" Dooley could barely see her in the weak light from the streetlamps outside, propped up on an elbow above him, her hair brushing his shoulder. The gauze curtains stirred in the night breeze. Beyond the open windows the city murmured, restless and vast.

"That's OK by me."

Laura ran a fingertip down the ridge of his nose, traced the line of his lips. "I don't even know your first name. Isn't that weird?"

"Doesn't matter."

Dooley was still drifting, at peace on a calm dark sea. He'd forgotten; he'd forgotten what it was like, this easy carnal communion, the sheer blissful oblivion of desire fulfilled. He'd forgotten what peace was like. Laura caressed him, smoothing tendrils of slightly damp hair back from his brow, his temple. "You make me happy," she whispered. "I feel safe with you."

Dooley wanted to tell her things, too, but he couldn't find the words. He put a hand on the back of her neck and pulled her down and kissed her. After the kiss she slid down and put her head on his chest and they lay like that for a while. Cars purred up and down the block outside; the thump of rock and roll music sounded faintly through the floor from the apartment above. Dooley said, "I have to go home."

Some time went by and then Laura stirred and rolled off him. She stretched to kiss him on the cheek and said, "No regrets, I hope?"

"No," said Dooley. "No regrets."

Thirty-three

So how did you do this, Dooley thought, looking in the mirror. Did you just stop shaving past the earlobe and go through a few days when it looked crummy, or did you shave a quarter-inch lower every couple of days so they crept down the side of your face gradually? He thought of the guys he knew who had gone to sideburns. How had they done it? Hell with it, he thought finally, and pushed the foam up past his earlobes.

Downstairs the kitchen was vacant but the paper was waiting. North Korea had shot down a U.S. chopper. First the *Pueblo* and now this; Dooley wondered why they didn't just drop an A-bomb on Pyongyang and be done with it. A hurricane was raking the Gulf Coast with 160-mile-an-hour winds, and in upstate New York thousands of people had overrun a farm to listen to a rock concert. Hundreds of them were sick or hurt and the highways were jammed, making it impossible for ambulances to get through. Who the hell signed the permits for that one, thought Dooley. Out in California, Ronald Reagan was saying he wouldn't run for president again. Dooley shook his head in wonder; washed-up in two careers now and the guy could still find a way to get his name in the paper.

In Viet Nam the Marines were going toe-to-toe with the NVA near the DMZ. It didn't say what units were involved, which irritated Dooley, but he knew up near the DMZ it had to be the Third

Division. There was fighting all over the country, but the Department of Defense was saying the troop withdrawals would go on. Dooley read the article twice and shoved the paper away. He took his coffee out onto the patio. It was nice outside, not too hot with a little breeze. It was a new world this morning.

Last night had been a little strange, stopping for a drink on the way home so his breath would back up his story if anyone asked, walking into the house contrite, not having to act too much to play the part of the chastened prodigal, slinking home. Rose had been cool but civil, on her way to bed; he'd said he was sorry, meaning it more ways than she knew but feeling more amazed still than guilty. He'd talked baseball with Frank a bit and waited up for Kathleen to get home from her waitressing job. She'd listened to his apology, said it was OK, and gone up to bed. Dooley had sat up late in the back yard with a glass of whiskey and finally gone in a little drunk to lie beside his sleeping wife, thinking about Laura. The whole thing had been a bit unreal.

This morning he felt good. He had looked at himself in the mirror and thought, I cheated on my wife last night. But it didn't feel like cheating. Laura had put it just right: he wasn't going to run out of love. Dooley felt full of love this morning.

He heard a car pull into the garage. When he went into the kitchen Rose and Kathleen were bringing in sacks full of groceries. Rose set one down on the table with a thump. "You're up early."

"It was too nice a day to stay in bed. Need some help?"

She looked a little startled but said, "I think there are a couple of bags still out there. You have to go in early today?"

Dooley put his cup in the sink. "Not today. I thought maybe I might take my eighteen-year-old daughter out to lunch today. My wife, too, if she wants to come." Rose and Kathleen traded a look, not sure they wanted to buy it. Dooley went out to the garage and got the last couple of bags of groceries.

When he came back in Kathleen said, "It's OK, Daddy. You don't have to strain yourself to make it up to me." Her look and her tone were on the cool side.

Dooley put the groceries down. "It's no strain."

"Actually, I already agreed to go someplace with Nancy."

"OK, that's all right."

"I'll take you up on it," said Rose.

Dooley looked her in the eye. He was pleased to find he could do it, pleased to see something in her face other than the usual patient suffering. "It's a date," he said.

• • •

"I'm sorry about yesterday," said Rose. "Maybe I was too hard on you." She looked at him across the rim of her Coke; after spending all that money yesterday she had refused to let Dooley take her anywhere expensive today and they had wound up at a diner on Milwaukee, nothing to shout about but decent for lunch.

"No," said Dooley. "I had it coming. It was inexcusable to forget her birthday. And I should spend more time at home, I know I should." It made Dooley feel good to be contrite; he was going to show Rose how good a husband he could be.

"You've been putting in a lot of overtime."

"I've been working this one case real hard, and mostly on my own time because the geniuses at the top think they already cleared it. But I have a feeling it's going to be over soon. Then I'll have my free time back. Of course, I should probably fill it up working for Rob so we can afford to go someplace nice when Kevin comes home."

"We'll find a way to afford it. Don't fill up all your free time." Rose toyed with her glass, her look vacant. She said, "When are they going to pull out Kevin's unit?"

"Soon. I haven't read anything specific recently, but they're not going to cancel the troop withdrawals. The Ninth Marines are coming out already, and the Third Marines are supposed to be next. I think it could be real soon." Dooley waited until his wife raised her eyes to his and then he said, "He's going to come home, Rose. The odds are in his favor."

Rose nodded. "All right, I believe you." They sat there looking at each other the way they had been looking at each other since 1948 and for a moment Dooley forgot all about Laura Lindbloom. "Michael," Rose said.

"What?"

"I haven't been much of a wife to you lately."

"What do you mean?" said Dooley, knowing exactly what she meant.

"You know what I mean. That part of our marriage hasn't been very—active for a while, and I'm sorry about that. But that's going to change. I'm going on a diet, I'm going to take better care of myself. I may not have too much time left before—before I'm old. But what time I have left is going to be better. I promise you that."

Dooley couldn't find anything to say. He had just realized like being hit in the face that it was mainly the assumption that his sex life with Rose was essentially over that had allowed him to justify sleeping with Laura. He sat there with his mouth open, starting to see that things could be more complicated than he had expected. The earnest look on his wife's face was driving a stake through his heart. He closed his mouth and swallowed hard. "That will be good," he said.

• • •

I haven't told her any lies, Dooley thought, driving down Elston. I didn't actually lie to her about anything. I made one mistake, and maybe it has to be a one-time thing, but I haven't lied to my wife, not in words.

Up on the third floor there were messages waiting. Dooley went through them quickly: requests for information from dicks in other divisions, a response from a witness he'd been trying to track down. There was nothing from a Laura L. and Dooley stepped hard on his pang of disappointment. The last thing he needed was to go mooning around like a lovesick schoolboy.

But God, that feeling. Laura on her back beneath him, all that hunger, all that heat. Dooley had to close his eyes for a second.

The office was crowded at shift change, McCone trying to get organized for roll call, second watch tying up the loose ends. A telephone rang and somebody shouted, "Dooley!"

He had to make himself slow down walking over to take it. "Dooley here," he said.

"Listen good," a man said. "You want proof Chuck Steuben didn't kill Sally Kotowski?"

Dooley put his hand over the mouthpiece and said, "Hey, shut up!" to two dicks who had burst out laughing next to him. Into the phone he said, "Who are you?"

"I asked you a question," said the man. He sounded like a heavy smoker and there was something, traffic noise maybe, in the background.

Dooley waited a beat and said, "Sure. What you got?"

"Not so fast, ace. Here's what you do. You know a place called Lenny's, on South State Street?"

"Lenny's. Lenny's Liquors?"

"You got it. State south of Van Buren. Be there at one o'clock tonight."

Dooley gave it two seconds' thought. "I got a better idea. Why don't you come to me?"

"Sorry, that's the deal. One o'clock. By yourself."

"I don't go anywhere by myself. You got something to say, you can say it to my partner, too."

"Fuck you, then. Good-bye."

"Wait a minute." Dooley was sure he'd lost him but a second or two went by and he hadn't heard a click in his ear. "Let me ask you one question. Why would I *not* bring my partner? I'm going to share everything with him anyway."

"Because nobody wants to talk to your fuckin' partner. That's a take-it-or-leave-it offer. One o'clock, by yourself. You'll figure out who to talk to."

Now the click came and the line went dead. Dooley hung up the phone and stood there for a moment with his hand on the receiver, then picked it up again and dialed the number Haggerty had given him at O.C. It was shift change there, too, and Dooley managed to catch Haggerty in the office. "Mike Dooley here. Did you by any chance come up with an informant for me, give somebody my number?"

There was a short silence and Haggerty said, "How come?"'

"I just got a call offering information about my case. The old come-alone-at-midnight deal. At Lenny's Liquors, downtown."

"It wasn't anything I did," said Haggerty. "Who you supposed to meet?"

"He just said I'd know who to talk to. I didn't recognize the voice. He asked me if I wanted proof Steuben didn't kill Sally."

"That's interesting."

"Yeah, it's interesting. I'll tell you though, I'm not sure I believe in Santa Claus anymore."

"You never know. You've been shaking the tree, maybe something just fell."

"Could be. Anyway, I have to go, don't I?"

"You gotta go, yeah. Just one piece of advice."

"What's that?"

"Take backup."

"You better believe it," said Dooley.

• • •

"One o'clock, huh? Will McCone approve the overtime?" Olson didn't look happy. He sat twirling the key ring to the Plymouth around his index finger, frowning.

"What if he doesn't?" Dooley said, irritated.

Olson grinned. "Then the drinks are on you." He stood up. "Jeez, Mike. I'm with you all the way, you know that."

Dooley rolled his eyes and got to his feet. "He already approved it, I talked to him. It's still officially a cleared case, but he said he'll back us up as long as we come back with the proof."

Olson was leading the way to the door. "Well, hell. For once I can tell the wife I had no choice. I was ordered to go to the bar."

Eight hours later, Olson was sounding a bit less enthusiastic. They had spent most of the shift driving all over the North Side looking for a Mexican girl who might have seen her boyfriend shoot another seventeen-year-old in the head with a .22. "I think Marisa's skipped town," said Olson. "I think she's gone south."

"Could be," said Dooley. "But then somebody would have told us. We'd be getting 'She's gone' instead of 'I don't know where she is.' I think she's still around. I just hope she's still alive."

"What, you think Luis popped her, too, to shut her up?"

"Not Luis, probably, but one of his friends maybe. It sounded like she was ready to talk to us."

"Christ."

"Hell with it. Tomorrow's another day. Now we get to go downtown for our nightcap."

"Ah, shit. I forgot."

"Think about the overtime."

"Yeah, the overtime. And the drinks. Or are we still on duty?"

"We're on duty. But I'm not going to tell anybody about the beer you're going to drink. You're going to need it for cover."

"What about you?"

"I'm planning to go in there, talk to whoever wants to talk to me, and get the hell out. You're not supposed to be there anyway. What we'll do is, you go in first, by yourself, and just do a little recon. If you see anything that looks funny, you come right back out."

"Oh, I get to walk into the ambush? Thanks a lot."

"Look, genius, they're expecting me, not you. They won't know who you are."

"I know, I'm kidding you."

"Loosen your tie and try to look harmless. If you don't like what you see, come back out and look for me. If it looks OK, just sit down and have a beer and wait. And keep your eyes open. I'll come in a few minutes after you. Remember you don't know me."

Olson drove in silence for a few seconds. "You really think it's a set-up?"

"No, I don't. I think it's probably somebody who's got an axe to grind. But you never take chances."

South State Street was not where you took your kids to look at the Christmas lights. Establishments on State Street south of Van Buren had names like the Rialto, the Follies and the Pink Lady, and if there was anything in the windows advertising what was inside, you covered your kids' eyes when you passed it. South State Street had come down in the world since Dooley was a kid, and it had never been all that great to begin with. Coming up on one in the morning it was not quite deserted, but a stray conventioneer might have been happier if it had been, to judge by the look of the people that were out.

Lenny's Liquors had been there since Dooley was riding in a patrol car, and he remembered being in there a couple of times, but he didn't know much good or bad about it. It was a package store with a bar, a place where you could buy a pint to take back to the flophouse or sit at the bar and drink if you couldn't wait to get home. Dooley had Olson cruise past the bar, then pull over on Congress and get out to walk back around the corner to the bar. He got in the driver's seat and negotiated the one-way streets until he wound up parked at a bus stop on State pointed north with a good view of the door of Lenny's Liquors. There was some flickering neon over the door that looked as if it had been there since the Depression and a front window with the name of the joint painted on it. Dooley checked his watch, kept an eye on the sidewalks and the mirrors, and waited. There was no sign of Olson and at one on the dot Dooley switched off the ignition and got out of the car.

He walked across the street and went into the bar. It was the usual arrangement with the brightly lit package store through an archway to the right, coolers along the wall and a cash register at the front, with the gloomy barroom stretching back from the street door, a long room with a high stamped-tin ceiling and black linoleum on the floor. The bar ran down the left-hand side, the booths down the partition wall on the right. What light there was came from a line of fluorescent tubes on the wall behind the bar.

There were seven people at the bar, three pairs and a lone man. Three of the booths were occupied, the one nearest the front by a pair of old-timers, one halfway down by two Negroes, and the one farthest back by Pete Olson, who sat with a beer in front of him, leaning back in the booth, the picture of unconcern. Dooley nodded at the bartender, a worn-out sourpuss in a dirty white shirt and a black tie, and went slowly down the room scanning. When he met Olson's eyes Olson gave him just a hint of a shrug. Dooley looked away and veered toward the loner sitting two-thirds of the way down the bar, because he had immediately recognized him as Tony Bellisario.

Bellisario was perched on his stool like an oversized toad with an elbow on the bar and a cigar in his mouth, facing the door. He had recognized Dooley, too, and they frowned at each other as Dooley drew near.

"Don't tell me," said Bellisario.

Dooley shoved a stool out of the way with his foot and moved in close to the bar.

"Don't tell you what?"

"Don't tell me it was some dumb-ass cop trick."

Dooley stared at him for two or three seconds, with a little warning bell going off in his head. "Aren't you the guy who's supposed to prove to me Steuben didn't do it?"

Bellisario's brow crinkled and he took the cigar out of his mouth. "What the fuck are you talking about?"

"Why are you here?" Dooley said, suddenly intent.

"I got a phone call."

Dooley went cold. "That's bad," he said.

"NOBODY MOVE!"

Dooley didn't have to look to see who had yelled behind him; voice and location told him it was one of the Negroes, and now he wished he had paid them more attention. In the mirror behind the bar he could see them coming up out of their booth ten feet behind him, one with a revolver in his hand and the other one shaking a grocery bag off a double-barreled sawed-off shotgun. He turned his head to the left, moving as little as possible, to get a direct view over his shoulder. His hand had gone inside his jacket in the first second after the shout, but it had never come out because the mirror had shown him how close that shotgun was. Too late, thought Dooley. I needed to get the jump in the first second and I didn't.

"All right people, this here's a hold-up!" the shotgunner yelled, bringing the gun up and sweeping the room with it. "Wallets on the bar, NOW! You, mister, clean out the register and throw it all in the bag." His partner scooped up the bag and jumped to the bar to throw it across at the bartender, who had frozen with his hands halfway up. Dooley's mind was running a mile a minute; he turned back to trade a look with Bellisario, and he saw that they both understood exactly what was going on. He shot a look at Olson, who had jerked upright but was frozen on his seat. What are you waiting for? thought Dooley.

He looked over his shoulder again. The shotgunner swung the gun away from the bartender and pointed it at Dooley. He said,

"Let's go, Jack. Take it out." He was a tall thin black man with a wild Afro and glittering black eyes that weren't quite wild enough for a hold-up man's, and the last doubt that his primary job here was to kill two men disappeared from Dooley's mind.

Come on, Pete, Dooley pleaded. I need you to do something. Anything, just give me the second I need. Dooley's mind was moving so fast he had time to think about everything: how he was going to die because Pete Olson was too scared to go for his gun, too scared to yell *police*, how he could hardly blame Pete for being sane, for not wanting to attract the attention of a man with a sawed-off shotgun within easy killing range.

Dooley had his left hand planted on the bar, his right hand on the butt of his .38 inside his jacket, finger on the trigger inside the holster, but he was never going to get it out in time; the twin barrels of the sawed-off looked as big as sewer pipes six feet away. It's going to be a closed-coffin funeral, Dooley thought.

"*Police!*" Dooley heard Olson's yell from the back of the bar, almost a scream, and saw the shotgun jerk toward Olson, and it was time. With a wrench of his wrist Dooley twisted his gun in the holster, hoping there was enough give in the leather to let him get the muzzle high enough, and fired through his jacket, scorching his armpit, blowing out the side panel of his Sears and Roebuck gray worsted suit jacket and punching a hole in the shotgunner's stomach.

One barrel went off as the gunner doubled over, but Dooley couldn't wait to see if Olson was hit or not; he had the second he needed now and in the midst of screams and the thump of falling bar stools he managed to rip the .38 out of the holster and bring it up to train it on the second Negro, who had not yet figured out who had shot whom and was looking for a target with a wide-eyed frantic look on his face. Dooley sighted on his chest and squeezed off two rounds that punctured the gaudy fabric of his Hawaiian shirt, pulling through the stiff double action of the revolver effortlessly under the wondrous effects of adrenaline. The wide-eyed look stayed put as the man started to crumple but Dooley couldn't afford to stand and watch him; the other man was still moving. He had sat down hard on the floor as if someone had pulled a chair out from under him and he was grimacing at Dooley, crooked white teeth shining in the black face, trying to bring up the shotgun. Dooley knew a wounded man with a sawed-off shotgun was just as dangerous or more so than a healthy man, but he wanted somebody alive, so he leveled his gun at him and said, "Drop it." The Negro appeared to think about it for a second, but then instead of dropping it he brought up the gun with one last convulsive effort.

Dooley shot him through the head.

• • •

"You guys are kind of far from home, aren't you?" The lead dick was somebody Dooley didn't know, a youngster of maybe thirty-five or so. He was thin and intense; he looked as if he never got enough food or sleep. He chewed gum with his mouth open, ferociously. "What were you doing down in this neck of the woods?"

"We were supposed to meet an informant." Dooley stood with his hands on his hips, watching the crime scene techs step gingerly around the bodies. The bar had filled up with 1st District coppers fast in the few minutes after the shooting. Dooley had managed to keep the witnesses from running out the door and sent Olson out to the car to call it in on the radio, keeping him busy to get him through the shakes. Dooley had taken off his jacket and hung it over a bar stool. The coppers had shaken their heads over it, poking fingers into the hole in the fabric, looking at Dooley with reverence.

"Who's your informant?" the dick said.

"He didn't show up." That was the literal truth, even if there was more to it than that, and Dooley wasn't going to go into it all now; he figured that all this dick had to be concerned with was whether he'd been justified in blowing holes in these two pieces of shit. At some point he was going to have to write up his suspicions, but for now he was going to hold to the bargain he'd made with Bellisario while waiting for the detectives to get there. "Keep me out of it and I'll take care of Swallow," Bellisario had said in a low voice at Dooley's elbow.

"I can't keep Swallow out of it if it was really him that set it up," Dooley had murmured, and Bellisario had given him a long look and said, "Then I guess we'll have to see who gets to him first."

"So you shot this one and your partner shot the other one, is that how it went?" the dick was saying.

Dooley shook his head. "I got 'em both."

The dick's eyebrows went up and he shook his head once. "OK. Lemme get some statements and then I'll let you go. You're probably gonna be up all night writing up your own report."

"You know it." Dooley walked over to where Olson was standing with his hands in his pockets, watching the proceedings. "How you doing?" Dooley said.

"I'm sorry, Mike." Olson turned haunted eyes on him.

"For what?"

"I didn't even get off a shot. I almost didn't get my piece out."

Dooley shook his head. He put his hand on Olson's arm and squeezed. "Hell, if you'd started shooting you might have hit me. You did all you needed to do when you stood up and yelled. That saved my life. By the way, did I say thanks?"

"I froze. I should have spotted them in the first place, anyway."

"You stood up, didn't you?" Dooley gave him a slap on the shoulder. "Sometimes that's all you need to do. Just stand up."

• • •

Dooley got home near dawn. He skipped the whiskey and went directly upstairs to his bedroom. Rose stirred when he came in and he went over and kissed her, then locked his star and his gun away and got undressed. He got into bed and put his arms around his wife and held her, just lying there with his face in her hair. She made a soft satisfied noise in her throat, still half asleep.

It was your family you thought about after you felt death's cold dank breath on your cheek; Dooley lay there thinking about Rose and Kevin and Kathleen and Frank and seeing the whole thing play out in his mind again, the terror, the shots, the blood on the floor. He'd had hours to think about all the rest of it, the implications and the urgencies and the threats that were still out there. Now he just wanted to go to sleep with his wife in his arms.

He thought about Laura Lindbloom barely at all.

Thirty-four

"WHAT IN GOD'S name happened to your jacket?" The look on Rose's face as she held up the perforated suit coat said she wasn't sure she really wanted to hear the answer.

Dooley laughed, trying to make light of it. "A bullet went through it." He watched his wife blanch and go slack-jawed. "Don't worry. It was going out, not coming in." Dooley closed the paper and drained his coffee. Serious now, he said, "I killed two men last night."

Rose just made it to the chair across from him before her legs gave out. "Oh dear God. Oh Michael, what happened?"

Dooley shrugged. "It was a tavern hold-up. Olson and I happened to be there. On business, by the way."

She closed her eyes for a moment. When she opened them she said, "Was that why you were so late getting in?"

"Yeah. You shoot somebody, they really put you through the wringer. But I'm in the clear. It was justified, all the way. They'd have shot me if I hadn't shot first."

She shook her head, the horror too much for her. She reached for his hand. "Oh, Michael, I pray for you every single day. I pray for you all the time."

He smiled at her even though the horror was starting to come back to him, too. There were times when Dooley just wanted to grab his wife and hang on for dear life, but you had to keep your chin up. "I guess it works. Keep it up."

She let go of his hand after a while. "That's the first time, isn't it?"

"That I shot somebody? As a cop, yeah. The war, you don't want to hear about it."

That was the wrong thing to say, he realized instantly. He could see Rose's thoughts flash straight to her son out there in the middle of a shooting war. "Hey," he said. "Let's go out to lunch again, what do you say?"

• • •

"That's a hell of an accusation," said McCone, his eyes narrowed. "Are you sure you're not getting a little rattled?"

"Look at it. Why was Bellisario there?"

"Bellisario is who, now?"

"The guy that gave me the dirt on Swallow."

"Did I see a report on this?"

"No, because this was on my own time, after the case was cleared, remember? I'll write it all up for you now, don't worry. Bellisario pointed me to Swallow and gave me a way to pressure him. The reason he was there last night is because he got a phone call, just like I did. The caller claimed to have money for him, a loan payment from a guy he'd been leaning on. And the minute I walk in and start talking to Bellisario, the shit hits the fan. It was a setup and the two of us were the target. The robbery part was just a cover. Swallow was cleaning house."

"OK, that's pretty damn suspicious all right. How the hell are you going to prove it?"

"I don't know. Look at the two dead guys and try to find a connection with Swallow maybe. But that's not my main concern, and it's not Swallow's main concern. His real worry is Bellisario. Syndicate guys don't fool around. I think Swallow's time is up, and if he has any brains he's already on his way out of town. I wouldn't mind talking to him again, but I think he's already given me all he's going to give me. Maybe somebody with more to offer him, like the feds, for example, could get him to cut a deal. But then maybe Bellisario will get to him first."

McCone sat there chewing on it and not liking the taste. "Write it up," he said at last.

"What's happening with the last report I gave you?"

"I sat down with Donovan. He's going to take it downtown. He didn't make any promises."

"Don't let 'em sit on it."

"I already promised you I'd do what I could, Mike. Now you promise me something."

"What?"

"From now on, you do everything by the book."

"I've tried to do everything by the book."

"I know it. Just don't let it get—personal."

"I'll follow the rules," said Dooley, rising. "But it's personal. You look up the snout of a sawed-off, see how personal it feels."

• • •

"Dead-eye Dooley. Fastest gun in the West."

"That'll teach 'em to try to bust up Miss Kitty's saloon."

"What'd you use, Dooley, your Fanner-fifty?"

"Two-for-one deal, Jesus. That's some shooting."

"Hey Olson, where were you? In the john?"

"Hell, I was under the table. I knew Mike would take care of it."

"Well, you made a good start, Dooley. Now why don't you go out there on West Madison and take up where you left off?"

"You better watch it, they'll get you for coon hunting out of season."

"Stuff it, will you?" Dooley was trying to go through his messages, and the crowd was starting to irritate him. "Just hope you never have to do it."

That shut everyone up; they drifted off in an embarrassed silence. Nyman slapped Dooley on the shoulder as he passed and said quietly, "You done good, Mike."

Dooley went to a phone and made his calls: routine stuff, except for two. One was from Haggerty, who wasn't in; the other from Laura. Dooley folded the paper and put it in his shirt pocket. "Let's go find Marisa," he said to Olson.

They hadn't found her by dinnertime. Dooley was a little jumpy, hitting the streets again after looking up that shotgun the night before. The world was a little less safe for him tonight and would be for a while. He wondered if Arnold Swallow had shot his wad and decided probably, just probably.

They ate at a place Dooley liked on Lincoln Avenue south of Belmont. Dooley went back to the restroom, and when he came out he stopped at the pay phone and shoved in a dime. He dialed and waited; Laura answered, bar noises in the background.

"It's Dooley."

"Dooley!" Her tone of voice obliterated all the resolutions Dooley had made in the last two days in an instant. "How *are* you?" she said.

"I'm OK. What's up?"

"I wanted to see you." He said nothing, and after a moment she added. "Business or pleasure."

Dooley could hear all kinds of things in her voice, none of them related to business. It's all different now, he thought. Everything is different and everything is complicated. "Me too. I'm not sure when."

"You working?"

"Yeah. I'm not sure tonight would be good."

"It doesn't have to be tonight."

"OK. Sometime soon."

"Tomorrow? You could come by the bar after you get off."

"Maybe." Dooley knew he was making a poor showing. He wanted to be with her but he was having doubts, serious doubts. "Sure. Tomorrow would probably be OK. It depends on how things go."

"OK. Dooley?"

"Yeah."

"Is everything OK? I mean, after the other night? Still no regrets?"

Dooley had to laugh a little. He wasn't going to go into it all on the phone. He closed his eyes and said, "No regrets."

• • •

There were riots in Czechoslovakia now to go with the ones in Northern Ireland; sometimes it seemed like the whole world was going up in smoke. Closer to home, a Black Panther leader had gotten himself arrested for torturing an informer to death. You can dress them up in funny hats but they're still just gangsters, Dooley thought. Gustafson had been busy; the FBI had scooped up a whole flock of Outfit gambling bosses and put them in front of a federal grand jury downtown. Dooley scanned the names: Ferriola, Angelini, Cortina, Cerone. He didn't see anything that was likely to help him but it would be interesting to talk to Haggerty.

In Viet Nam, nine GI's had been killed by fire from one of their own tanks. Dooley turned the page, trying to ignore the leaden feeling in the pit of his stomach. Here it was: *Off-duty Cop Shoots 2 in Tavern Robbery.* The reporters had gotten it wrong as usual but Dooley didn't care; he was happy to have people think he'd been off duty. He read his name and got the same funny feeling he had before when he'd made the paper: half proud, half embarrassed. He would be getting a few phone calls today.

"Did you see this? Did you see what Holtzman did yesterday?"

Frank tugged the sports section out from under Dooley's elbow, jarring the mug in his hand.

"Watch it, will you?" Dooley glared at him, dripping coffee on the tabletop.

"Sorry. Look, he threw a *no-hitter.*" Frank slapped the paper down in front of Dooley, covering the section he was trying to read.

"Terrific. Now get me a napkin."

"A no-hitter! And you know what? I *almost went to the game.* Jim called and wanted me to go, but I had to work. Jeez, I wish I'd called in sick or something." Frank flung a paper napkin at him.

"You better not let me catch you skipping work to go to a ball game."

"OK, I didn't."

"You better not ever let me catch you lying to your boss. Or anyone, for that matter."

"OK, OK. I won't. But man, a no-hitter. I *told* you it's their year. Do you think we can get tickets to the Series?"

Dooley shoved the sports section aside. "Calm down. It's early yet. How many games are they up now?"

"Seven and a half. They got it in the bag."

"Well, they've got a ways to go yet. It's still August."

"We gotta go to another game soon. The Braves are here today and tomorrow and the Astros are coming in this weekend. Are you off?"

"Nah, I had last weekend off, remember? I have to work for a while now."

Frank stood there for a moment while Dooley turned over a page of the paper. "When are we gonna go play ball again?"

Dooley pretended to read for a few seconds, trying to come up with an answer. He looked up and said, "I don't know. Not today. I gotta go in early."

"We should go play again some time."

"Sure. Say, you're planning to get a haircut today, are you?"

"What?" Frank stood blinking at him. "No, why?"

"Why do you think?"

"Come on, it's not that long."

"Get it cut. I'm assuming this job of yours pays you enough to afford a trip to the barber."

"Ma always pays for my haircuts."

"Not anymore. You got your own money now."

"Aw, *man.*" Frank slouched toward the door, then stopped and wheeled to face him. "You're a real drag sometimes, you know that?"

Dooley nodded, turning over a page. "That's my job."

• • •

Maxwell Street was deserted on a weekday; now it was just another slum. Dooley parked by the big red-brick station and made sure to lock the car. Haggerty's office was on the second floor, where O.C. Intelligence lived; he'd offered to come meet Dooley somewhere but Dooley had told him it was no problem for him to make the drive; when somebody was doing you a favor you went out of your way to make it easy for him.

Up to now Dooley had only talked to Haggerty on the phone, but he had pegged him pretty closely from his voice: a big gruff old-school copper, gray-haired and black-browed and gimlet-eyed. "Mike," he said, rising and extending a massive hand across the desk. "You look younger than I expected in the flesh. You must be pure of heart and pure of mind."

"Used to be, a long time ago."

"Weren't we all, weren't we all." They settled onto chairs and Haggerty's chuckle faded. "I heard you were in a fight the other night."

"Yeah. Made the papers today."

"I saw. That's all it was? A stickup?"

Dooley took a casual look around. There were other people in the office but nobody looked too close or too interested in what he was saying. "Actually, I had my doubts. I think it was a setup, to tell you the truth."

"I wondered. You got an idea?"

"Yeah. I think it was Arnold Swallow behind it."

"Swallow? Tommy Spain's old partner?" He'd caught Haggerty by surprise. "Why?"

"Because I leaned on him. With information I got from Tony Bellisario. Who was also there that night. It almost worked, too. The message was pretty clear. Bellisario and I had just enough time to figure out what it was about and then the shooting started."

Haggerty peered at him. "That's unbelievable. If you're right, that's dynamite."

"If I'm right, I don't think Swallow will be around too long."

"You went after him because he and Spain were in cahoots, huh?"

"Yeah. I thought Swallow knew what it was all about. But I'm not so sure. He gave me a story I think came from Spain, but I don't know if I believe it."

Haggerty laughed gently. "I'd say that shows pretty good judgment."

"I have to find another angle to go at it from."

Haggerty cocked his head on one side, considering. "Well, Dave Novotny just got out of jail."

Dooley had to think for a second. "Spain's wire man."

"Yeah. He might know a few things. Of course, he might also want to keep his mouth shut. But the word is he's back in town."

"Where would I find him?"

"Well, he had a house with a wife and kids somewhere on the South Side if I recall correctly. I can look it up for you."

"That would be great."

"No problem. You see what the feds did yesterday?"

"Yeah. Is it going to make any difference?"

Haggerty shook his head. “Not much, not now. They’ll do a little time and somebody else will take over the books for a while. But I think in the long run it’s the feds that are going to bring down the Outfit. I hate to say it because I don’t like the bastards much. But in this town we need ’em. I’m not telling you anything you don’t know, I’m sure.”

Dooley gave a half-hearted nod. “I didn’t see anybody I knew personally on the list.”

“No, everyone you’re interested in is still in operation, I’m afraid.” Haggerty frowned, getting his thoughts lined up, getting to the reason he’d called Dooley. “I went and looked at some informant reports for you.”

“I appreciate it.”

“There wasn’t a whole lot there on Tony Messino. He hasn’t been on our radar that long, and so far he’s been reasonably careful.”

“He’s got an attitude, I can tell you that.”

“I’m sure he does. I did find one thing that might be interesting to you.” Haggerty put his hand on a folder that lay on the desk, as if he were about to open it, but seemed to think better of it. “One of my officers wrote up an interview with an informant he had on the Grand Avenue crew a couple of months ago. The informant reported a conversation he happened to hear at the beginning of June, on June third to be exact.”

Haggerty paused and Dooley knew it was for dramatic effect. “That’s interesting, all right. That’s the day.”

“Yeah. He overheard one side of a brief telephone call from inside the Italian-American Club on Grand. He heard your pal Messino on the phone in the back room. He heard him say, ‘Tell Joe it’s done.’ That’s all.”

“Tell Joe it’s done.”

“That’s it. No context, no nothing.”

“What time was this?”

“Late afternoon is all it says.”

"That would work. We found her the next day."

Dooley and Haggerty looked at each other for a long moment. "Joe D'Andrea," said Dooley.

"Aiuppa, DiVarco, LaBarbera," said Haggerty. "There's a lot of Joes. Joe Lombardo's the crew boss."

Dooley frowned. "You have anything else on him?"

"In connection with your girl? Not a thing in the world. This proves nothing. It's just a teaser. It just points to Messino a little more. If you can nail Messino you might go up the tree from there. But you have to nail Messino first."

"I'm working on it," said Dooley.

• • •

I'm going to see her home, and we're going to have a talk, thought Dooley. And that's all that's going to happen. He stood on the sidewalk watching as Laura exchanged a few final words with the shaggy bartender, who was dousing lights inside the bar. She came out of the bar and slipped her arm through his and they walked up to North Avenue where he had parked the car. "Rough day at the office?" Laura said.

"Not too bad. We found a girl we'd been looking for, a witness to a murder. She was reluctant, but I think she's going to testify."

"That's good. Anything new on Sally's case?"

"It's out of my hands now. Now we're waiting for the higher-ups downtown to make a decision."

"A decision about what?"

"About reopening the case."

"How can there be any doubt?"

"There's always doubt. The brass likes cleared cases, and this one has already been cleared. Besides, the people that killed Sally have ways of influencing what goes on down there."

They walked a few steps in silence. Laura said, "That's terrible."

"That's life. There are some good people downtown, but . . ."

"But what?"

Dooley wasn't sure what he wanted to say. "The system's not perfect."

"You sound like a dangerous radical, Dooley."

He laughed. "There is nothing perfect in the world and never will be. Get used to it."

She squeezed his arm. "This is perfect. Being with you."

Dooley found nothing to say and they were silent on the drive up Cleveland and the search for parking. It was a warm night and the street was quiet; it was pleasant to walk back to her house in the gloom under the trees. Dooley was trying to get his thoughts in order. Up in the tower, he thought. We'll sit up in the tower with something cool to drink and we'll talk about how we can be friends. Laura unlocked the front door and led him up the stairs; she opened her apartment door and then closed it behind him. She threw her arms around his neck and said, "Let's go to bed."

Dooley couldn't believe she was in his arms, couldn't believe this electrifying kiss was for him. "OK," he said, when he came up for air.

"And this time," said Laura, "I'm going to teach you a few things."

Until this moment Dooley would have said he knew pretty much what there was to know, but the way she said it suddenly opened wonderful new vistas for him. "Start at the beginning," he said. "I don't want to miss anything."

• • •

Dooley woke up and swore; it was just starting to get light outside. Moron, he thought, swinging his feet to the floor. Of course you fell asleep. He grabbed his pants and pulled his watch out of the pocket: it was nearly five. Laura stirred as he scrambled into his clothes. "Dooley," she said, softly and thickly, barely awake.

"I have to go home."

She stretched a hand out across the sheet but he let it lie there. "Come back soon," she said.

He concentrated on buttons and shoelaces for a while. "I will." He bent to kiss her when he was dressed.

"Be careful out there," she said, releasing him.

"Don't worry."

She stopped him at the door. "Dooley?"

"Yeah?"

"Are you going to lie to her?"

Dooley just stood there blinking for a moment. "No. I'm not going to lie to her."

"That's good."

So maybe I just lied to Laura, he thought, speeding home through empty streets. Maybe I'll lie to both of them.

When he got home it was light out and Rose was waiting for him in the kitchen, sitting at the table with a mug in her hands and strain showing in her face. "Thank God," she said. "I was worried." She got up and came into his arms.

"Don't tell me you've been waiting up for me."

"I got up a little while ago. I couldn't sleep. After what happened the other night I was worried."

"You ought to know by now, as long as you don't get a phone call, there's nothing to worry about."

"Where were you?"

Dooley hadn't prepared anything, but the answer came immediately, effortlessly. "I was talking to an informant."

"All this time?"

"Sometimes you have to buy 'em a few drinks."

"I see. I thought there might be a few drinks involved."

"It's not what you think," Dooley said, standing there holding his wife and thinking: not yet. Technically, I still haven't told her any lies.

Thirty-five

THERE WASN'T ENOUGH money to fund the schools but the mayor was saying he was going to find some. Dooley had to laugh, imagining Daley going through drawers up on the fifth floor. Let the Outfit fund the schools for a year, he thought. That's where all the money is.

Bernadette Devlin in her miniskirt was in New York and Bernadine Dohrn in hers was in custody. The Arabs were shelling Jerusalem and the Reds were shelling the hospital at Cam Ranh Bay. All over Viet Nam things were going to hell: near the DMZ a platoon of exhausted GI's had refused to advance. Dooley shook his head; he knew how bad things had to get before troops would disobey a direct order under fire. The Seventh Marines had lost twenty KIA in the Que Son Valley; there was nothing about the Third Marines in Quang Tri, and nothing more about the planned troop withdrawals.

Dooley gave up on the paper and stared into his coffee for a while. The previous Sunday's paper had said the troop pullout was in danger because of the escalation in the fighting. Dooley had tried to hide the news from Rose but she'd overheard it on the TV news, and she had gone up to the bedroom to cry. Dooley had told her there was a good chance the withdrawal would go ahead as scheduled, but he was whistling in the dark. Dooley was just holding his breath, trusting to the odds.

He set down his coffee and sighed and reached for the sports section. The Cubs had lost to the Reds and were four and a half games up on the Mets.

• • •

The stockyards were dying; the big meat companies, Swift and Armour and the rest, were pulling out, and people were saying before too long the yards were going to close down. The interstate highways had made the railroads obsolete and the railroads were the reason the stockyards and maybe even the city itself were there. The Jungle had been there for a hundred years but it was about to close up shop.

Nobody will miss the smell, Dooley thought, heading west on Forty-seventh Street along the southern edge of the yards. Rose had had an old uncle who used to be a livestock handler out in the yards, one of the better jobs and hence the province of the early-arriving Irish, and he remembered him shaking his head at mention of Upton Sinclair and saying, "That boyo didn't know the half of it."

Dooley crossed Ashland and started looking at street signs. For a neighborhood that was losing its economic foundation, it didn't look too bad; people were hanging on. The Back of the Yards would still be here after the yards were long gone, and the Bohemians and Poles and Mexicans who had bought these houses with money earned the hard way on the docks and the killing floors and the packing tables were not going to give them up without a fight. They would put a little money into a used car and drive somewhere to work. God knew what the blacks would do; they had never lived this far west.

Dooley turned south and drove a couple of blocks, looking at house numbers. He found the house he was looking for just shy of a railroad viaduct and pulled over. It was a block of small houses, jammed together shoulder-to-shoulder, with tiny front yards fenced off from the sidewalk; if you didn't have a lot of land you had to protect what you had. There were old trees shading the street and a few flower beds suffering in the heat; after the constant showers of early summer August had been mostly dry. Dooley went up a flight of steps and rang a doorbell.

The woman who answered the bell in a yellow house dress had seen better days, just like the Union Stockyards; she was tall and thin and brisk in her movements but her hair had gone gray and hadn't had curlers in it anytime recently or even possibly been combed, and her eyes had the suspicious look of the debtor or the protective spouse. "What do you want?" she said.

"I'm looking for David Novotny," Dooley said.

She looked him up and down and said, "You the FBI?" The resigned way she said it told Dooley she was familiar with the species.

Dooley pulled out his star. "I'm a Chicago police officer, ma'am. Area Six Homicide. Mr. Novotny is not in any trouble that I'm aware of. I'm hoping he can help me with information related to a case I'm working on."

She wasn't sure she could believe him, he could see, but she was tired of fighting somebody else's battles. "He's around back. You can go down the gangway." She pointed and shut the door in his face.

Dooley went around the corner of the house. He had to duck to get by a laboring air conditioner and then he came out into a narrow back yard bisected by a concrete path that ran straight back to a ramshackle garage. A man sat with his legs crossed on a folding lawn chair at the south edge of the yard, in the shade of the neighboring house. He wore Bermuda shorts and white sneakers and a plaid short-sleeved shirt and he was tapping idly on the ground with a golf putter, staring at nothing. A golf ball lay on the parched grass a yard from his feet.

"Mr. Novotny?" The man looked up at Dooley as he came across the grass and Dooley could see him making the same assessment as his wife, sizing up and then giving up. This man was whipped, Dooley could see.

"Who wants to know?" the man said in a half-hearted tone. He had a long mournful face that hadn't gotten shaved that morning, under a slightly tattered straw hat. Dooley went through his routine with the star and the man said, "I told the U.S. Attorney everything I know. Every damn thing. I paid my debt to society. I been out of jail a week, for Christ's sake. Can't you leave me alone?"

Dooley put the star away and tried to put a sympathetic look on his face. "I didn't come here to make you miserable. I'm just hoping you can help me out."

"Help you out? Who's going to help me out? I'm the one sitting here with no money, no job, no friends."

Dooley looked around and saw another lawn chair folded up and leaning against the back steps. He went and got it and set it up in the shade next to Novotny's. He sat down and said, "Yeah, you were the fall guy, weren't you?"

"You know all about it, do you?"

"I heard a few things. You got indicted along with Spain, the other guy walked."

"It was Spain's idea. He got what he deserved, Fisk got probation, I got the shaft. All I did was try to be a stand-up guy."

"Well, the G frowns on perjury."

"Tell me about it." Novotny took a feeble swipe at the grass with his putter. "Especially by sworn officers of the law." He hefted the putter, pointed at the house with it. "My old man bought this house in 1923. He worked in the stockyards over there. He gave the place forty-three years and three of his fingers. He had four children and he used to tell us we were too good to live here. When I went on the sheriff's department he wiped tears out of his eyes and told me he was proud of me. Now here I am back home, Back of the Yards again. I'm just glad he was dead before I got indicted."

Dooley didn't usually get treated to witnesses' family histories. He waited a couple of seconds and said, "You got a bad break."

"I had it coming." Novotny swiped at the ball and missed. "So you're a homicide dick up in Area Six. What the hell do you want with me? I never killed anybody."

Dooley took a deep breath and jumped. "I want you to tell me what's on one of those tapes you recorded for Tommy Spain that got a girl killed a couple of months ago."

Dooley had expected Novotny to laugh, scoff, tell him to go to hell. He hadn't expected what he got, which was a total freeze lasting eight or ten seconds. Finally Novotny turned to face Dooley and what Dooley saw in his eyes almost made him feel sorry for the man. "I don't know," Novotny said. "I never listened to the God damn tapes. I just collected them and turned them over to Tommy."

Dooley knew the man was lying to him; he could see it in his face. The stark terror in Novotny's eyes made a liar out of him. Dooley just sat there and looked at him with his blank patient interview face on. "You want to try again?" he said.

Novotny's head sagged. He looked at the ground between his feet for a little while, resting his forehead on his hands clasped on the handle of the putter, and then straightened up and looked up into the hazy sky. "I never listened to any of it." He turned to look Dooley in the eye and said, "I'll go back to jail before I tell you anything different, and jail nearly killed me."

Dooley gave it a few seconds and said, "I know how to protect a witness."

Novotny laughed at last, a dry exhausted sound. "Sure you do. Let's say, just for the hell of it, I did know what you're talking about. I tell you, you do whatever you do with it, what happens? Sooner or later somebody's going to figure out where you got it. It'll be in your God damn report, for one thing, and don't tell me they can't look at your reports, because I know they can. And once they figure out where you got it, how long do I have? Twenty-four hours? Less? How you gonna protect me? I'm too damn old to run and hide. If I did know anything, which I don't, I'd be a God damn fool to tell you. Put that in your report."

Dooley didn't know how to refute that; it was an ironclad argument. He thought for a while, listening to a TV babbling faintly through an open window. "What did Spain do with the tapes? Where did he hide them?"

"I don't know that, either. I don't know a damn thing, officer. I'm like Sergeant Schultz. *I know nossink!*" Novotny snapped off a salute and went back to whacking at the grass with his putter. "All I know is, I'm an ex-con and about as employable as a three-hundred-pound jockey. But at least I'm alive, and I plan to stay that way."

Dooley nodded, conceding. "Spain's got something on somebody, somebody with real juice. The somebody thought Sally Kotowski had it or knew where it was, and that's why she got butchered. I don't think she had it, or she'd have given it up and died faster or maybe even lived. So it's out there, and if I can find it I'll know who the somebody is. I don't give a damn about what Spain has on him. But I want to nail him for Sally."

With disgust in his voice Novotny said, "She got butchered, huh? For you, that's a reason I should help. For me, that's a damn good reason to keep my mouth shut." He looked at Dooley and smiled, but there wasn't any humor in it. "That's what they call a deterrent."

"So how would I go about getting a hold of that tape?"

"I can't tell you that. And that's no bullshit."

"Who could?"

They sat there not looking at each other for a minute or so. Finally Novotny said, "The tape won't help you nail the killers. People that are big enough to blackmail have other people do their killing for them."

"I know who killed her. If I know why, I can put it all together, make a conspiracy case."

"You don't want to know. It'll only bring you grief, believe me."

Dooley was through trying to coax him. He stood up and shoved his hands down in his pockets. "Your old man would be proud of you," he said, and wheeled to go.

Novotny let him get almost to the corner of the house. "Go see Fay," he called.

Dooley halted and looked back. "Who the hell is Fay?"

Novotny just stared at him. Dooley walked slowly back across the ragged grass. "Who's Fay?"

"You don't know who Fay is? That's Tommy's wife."

"I thought her name was Marlene."

"Nah, Marlene's his second wife. Fay was number one, the real one. She's the one Tommy really loved, the one that got away. And she knows Tommy better than anyone."

"Where is she?"

Novotny's face took on a look of disbelief. "You really don't know, huh? Man, she did a better job than I thought."

"What are you talking about?"

"I mean she did a good job covering her tracks. Fay married on up the ladder, and I guess she didn't want people knowing she started out as a poor crooked copper's wife out on the West Side. Fay's quality now."

"Who are we talking about?"

Novotny laughed softly, and this time it sounded like he meant it. "Fay Blackman, Howard Blackman's wife."

Dooley just blinked at him. "You're shitting me."

"No. She used to be married to Tommy Spain. And I bet she knows where all the bodies are."

• • •

McCone collared Dooley as soon as he came into the office. "The lieutenant wants to talk to you."

"Donovan? What's he want?"

"He's got a couple of questions, that's all."

Dooley dumped his briefcase on a desk and followed McCone toward the lieutenant's office. He felt like a kid going in to see the principal. He caught a couple of glances but most of the dicks were caught up in the routine of shift change, too busy to notice or care.

Mack Donovan was the Commanding Officer of Area Six Homicide/Sex and a decent copper as far as Dooley knew. He was a burly man just vain enough to comb long strands of brown hair from the side of his head over the bald patch on top. Other than that Dooley had always found him to be a straight-shooter. "Sit down, Mike," Donovan said without looking up from the report on his desk.

Dooley sat down and waited. In a few seconds Donovan looked at him over the top of his reading glasses and said, "This is quite an accusation."

"About Swallow?"

"Yeah. Can you prove it?"

"I haven't tried yet."

"If you're going to accuse a fellow officer of attempting to kill you, you'd better be prepared to back it up."

"I'm aware of that. That's why I didn't mention Swallow to the officers investigating the shooting. You want me to go after Swallow, I will."

Donovan and McCone exchanged a look. Donovan said, "That might be kind of tough."

"Why?"

"Swallow's gone."

"What, you mean dead?"

"No. I mean he's gone, as in absent. He asked for emergency leave two days after the shooting and hasn't been seen since. IAD talked to his neighbors and they say they think he left town."

Dooley had to smile a little. "I would too, in his shoes. Do you believe me now?"

Donovan gave Dooley a long searching look. "How sure are you about all this? About your new take on the case?"

"One hundred percent sure. You read the report, right? Where did I go wrong?"

"I'm not saying you're wrong. I'm saying you have to have proof."

"The locket's proof."

"Only if you prove it came from the victim."

"I've got a sworn statement from a witness to that effect."

"And only if you can prove your fence got it from someone other than the man who has already been identified as the killer. All you've got is an allegation from a convicted felon implicating this Messino. That's not proof."

Dooley didn't like the look on Donovan's face. "I know it's not. I thought it was sufficient reason to proceed with an inquiry."

"I'm not sure about that. This is one we got a confession on."

"You didn't get a confession. You got an accusation of a dead man. And the guy that made it is dead now, too."

"That doesn't make any difference. We still got a credible account of the killing by a man who admitted participating in it. That's about as good as it gets."

Dooley could feel himself starting to get steamed. He said, "You're satisfied, are you?"

Donovan's brow clamped down. "What matters is if they're satisfied downtown. It's going to take a lot more than you've got to reopen this one, Mike."

"You don't like the locket, huh?"

"I don't like the setup. It sounds to me like maybe this Spanos is using you to get at Messino for some reason. I'm not sure you were sufficiently skeptical on that one."

"Could be. So do I have official clearance to go back and talk to him again, try and shake him?"

Donovan sighed, closing the folder. "I'll have to get back to you on that. For now, it's a closed case. I'm sure you have plenty of other cases to keep you busy."

Dooley sat there nodding, stone-faced. "Yeah," he said, rising. "That's for sure."

• • •

Dooley didn't think much of reporters as a rule, but he had known Pat Fallon since they had first collided as a rookie patrolman and a wet-behind-the-ears stringer at a murder scene on West Jackson in the late forties. Fallon wrote a column in the *Daily News* now and Dooley had set him straight on a few things over the years. He respected Fallon because he mostly got it right and never embarrassed him. While Olson went to sign out the car, Dooley dialed the number he had for Fallon at the paper.

"Fallon."

"Pat? Mike Dooley here."

"Mike, hey. How's the crime-fighting business?"

"Busy. How's the newspaper business?"

"Slow. Tell me you've got a nice juicy scandal for me."

"The scandal is, I still see your byline in the paper every day. I guess drunkenness isn't grounds for dismissal any more."

"Au contraire, my friend, it's an important qualification. How do you think we get people to talk to us? Especially cops."

"Cops only talk to reporters because they know you'll just make something up if we don't."

"You bet. That's the fun part. That and the drinks, of course. Seems to me I've bought you a few in my lifetime. What's going on?"

"You got a minute to talk?"

"I've always got a minute for you, Mike. What you got for me today?"

"Not a damn thing. Today I need something from you."

"Whoa. Stop the world. You mean it's finally time for the quo after all those quids?"

"Whatever you say, pal. What do you know about Howard Blackman?"

"Blackman? What do you mean, what do I know? I know what everybody knows. Rich as Bejeezus, major philanthropist. Nixon just named him ambassador to Ireland."

"Yeah. You know anything about his wife?"

"His wife? You mean the new one?"

"Fay's her name."

"Yeah, the new one. Not really. I know his first wife died a few years ago and he remarried a year or two after that. I've seen her a couple of times. She's a typical rich man's second wife—younger and better looking than the first one."

"You know anything about her background?"

Fallon was silent for a couple of seconds. "Not really. Why? What's going on, Dooley?"

"I might want to interview her, that's all. Her name came up in connection with something. Did you know she used to be married to Tommy Spain?"

"Get out of here, Dooley."

"I'm serious. That's what I'm told, anyway."

"That's real interesting. I wonder if the people in Washington know that."

"Well, I'm not going to tell them. I just need to talk to her. And I don't even know how to find her. Somehow I doubt the Blackmans are in the phone book."

"No. Lemme see, they've got a place on the Gold Coast and a big spread up in Kenilworth, I think, on the lake. You could go through his office, I guess. Global Properties, on Michigan Avenue. You better hurry. I think I read he goes to Dublin in a couple of weeks."

"Yeah. I'm sure I can track her down. I just didn't want to go in cold. I like to know who I'm dealing with."

"Well, with her you're dealing with a very rich lady."

"That'll make a change."

"Jesus, Dooley. You got me curious now. Will you keep me posted?"

"It's just routine, just an interview."

"Don't give me that. Nothing's routine when you're that rich."

"That's kind of what I'm afraid of," said Dooley.

Part Three

Get Ready

Thirty-six

DOOLEY COULDN'T BELIEVE it was September already. He had blinked and the summer was gone. The heat was over but it still hadn't rained; the farmers were grousing downstate and Dooley's lawn looked like something you might wipe your feet on. The nights were cool. Dooley was off on Labor Day for once, and they all went to a cookout at his sister Barbara's place, where Dooley sat on a lawn chair drinking beer and listening to his brother-in-law Ted explain to him how the world worked, which was always good for a laugh. He drank too much beer and drove home a little bit exuberantly, Rose tight-lipped with alarm on the seat beside him, Kathleen in the back muttering "Daddy, slow *down*," and Frank just snickering, enjoying the ride.

Kathleen was going off to college, only as far as DePaul, it was true, but she was going to live in the dorm and she might as well be going to California. Dooley had read about what they were getting up to in college dorms these days and it bothered him; he had to trust that a Catholic school would keep his daughter, or more importantly her male classmates, in line. He watched her move around the house in her last few days at home, packing and making plans, and it made him sad. He was losing his little girl.

Rocky Marciano was dead, killed in a plane crash; there was rioting in Fort Lauderdale and in Camden, New Jersey. Down in

Brazil the generals had ganged up to dump the president, but in Libya all it had taken was a colonel to kick out the king. Nixon was at the governors' conference, making promises; Dooley couldn't find anything in the paper about the only promise that mattered to him, the one involving the Third Marine Division. He had missed some excitement on his days off: a nun had been shot out on the West Side and two Wood Street coppers had been jumped by seven Negroes and beaten and robbed. Dooley shook his head; things were going from bad to worse.

The Cubs had been rained out in Cincinnati after sweeping the Braves, and the Mets had lost; the Cubs were four and a half games up. Dooley was a believer now; the Mets were the real threat but he figured the Cubs were going to hold on; they just plain had a better team. Over the course of a season the cream always rose to the top. He shoved the paper away.

"Can I talk to you for a second?" said Rose, sitting across the table from him, looking up from the checkbook and the pile of bills.

"What's up?"

The look on her face was peculiar: uncertain, almost timid. "It's about this place up in Wisconsin. You know, with the cabins on the lake. Where we're going in October."

"Yeah, what about it?"

"Well, they want a deposit. They want fifty dollars."

Dooley shrugged. "Do we have the money?"

"Sure, we have the money. It's just . . ."

"What?"

She opened her mouth but nothing came out; she fought for control and said in a quavering voice, "What if Kevin doesn't come home?" Then she hid her face in her hands and began to sob.

Dooley watched in amazement for a few seconds. He pushed away from the table and got up and went around to stand behind her and put his hands on her shoulders. Kathleen appeared in the doorway, wide-eyed. Dooley scowled at her. He squeezed Rose's shoulders and said, "Write the check. Kevin's coming home, and we're all going fishing. Send 'em the God damn money."

• • •

Somebody had written *Shapiro called— Pooch in County Hospital* and then followed it with *???* Dooley shoved the message into his jacket pocket. "Ready to go?" he said.

Olson took his feet off the desk. "Yeah. What are we doing tonight?"

Dooley gathered up the papers on the desktop and threw them in his briefcase. He had his marching orders for the evening but figured he could justify a little side trip if the need arose. "We'll be canvassing around Lincoln Park, on that kid that got shot. First we're going to Cook County Hospital, though."

Olson's brow wrinkled. "Who's in the hospital?"

"A guy named Pooch."

"Pooch? What the hell kind of a name is that?"

"It's some kind of Spanish."

"That doesn't sound Spanish."

"He can explain it."

"Who the hell is he?"

"He's a guy that knows a lot about Tommy Spain."

"Who?"

Dooley snapped the briefcase shut. "I'll fill you in in the car."

• • •

Johnny Puig looked like hell; he looked like Boris Karloff about halfway through the make-up job for *The Mummy.* "I feel great, though," he said, a little indistinctly. "They give you good drugs." He didn't sound convincing. The eye that was not covered by gauze was swollen nearly shut; Puig's lower lip looked like a sausage with stitches in it. One hand was splinted and bandaged and the other had skinned knuckles.

"What the hell happened to you?" Dooley stood over him, with Olson loitering by the door. Dooley had had to deploy his star and a fair amount of forceful persuasion to get past a tough-looking nurse.

"I got a special delivery message," Puig said, working at getting the words out. "At my office." Puig had to stop and get his breath; Dooley knew the effects of broken ribs when he saw them. "Two big ugly postmen."

"Take it easy. Don't try and talk. We can come back later."

"No. Listen." Puig panted gently for a while and tried again. "I set something off. Someone I talked to told someone."

"Who was it?"

"Dunno." The single eye closed for a while. When his breathing stabilized it came open again and Puig said, "They said forget all about Tommy Spain. I never heard of—fucking Tommy Spain. Their words. Fucking Tommy Spain."

"OK. Stay quiet." Dooley patted him on the shoulder.

"I didn't tell anybody about you. I think you're still OK."

"Fine, that's good."

"Dooley." Puig reached for him with the bandaged hand. "There's a guy."

"Later. Take it easy."

"No. Found a guy. Informant. Inside, inside the mob. You gotta talk to him."

Dooley waited; he wasn't going to rush a man in pain. He and Olson traded a look. Dooley had filled him in on the way down and Olson had been amazed and a little hurt by all the things Dooley had done without telling him. Now he stood watching, eyes narrowed. Out in the hallway, hospital noises echoed: subdued voices, a door banging far away.

Puig said, "He has to be careful, real careful. Here's what you do." Puig had to rest for a while, and Dooley hoped he was close to done, because he could see he was wearing the man out. He was expecting to be chased away at any second, but this was County Hospital and the nurses were busy with more urgent matters. "There's a tavern . . . in Elmwood Park, Carlo's. You call . . . and you leave a message for Grady. Say it's about the Corvette . . . and leave a number . . . not a cop number. Your home number, or . . . a neutral number, better. Someone who can take a message. Then just wait. He'll get back to you."

"Grady."

"Yeah. He's got—"

Dooley waited, but Puig didn't finish. "He's got what?"

"Dynamite," Puig whispered. "He's got dynamite."

• • •

"So Mike, what's the story?" said Olson as he steered up Lake Shore Drive. "What's going on?"

"I told you. The Steuben story is bullshit, D'Andrea and Messino killed Sally to keep something Spain has from coming out. What that is, I don't know, but it will help us put it all together."

"Can't we nail D'Andrea and Messino with what we have?"

"Not yet. With a little more work, maybe. Just maybe. But then it's the same old shit. They take the fall, the guy that ordered it doesn't lose an hour's sleep. I want 'em all, top to bottom."

Olson shook his head. "Sounds like a tall order."

"It's never been done. It's too hard. You need a case the brass can't smother, all those crooked lawyers and judges can't fix. You need proof and you need noise, lots of it."

Olson drove in silence for a while. "Is McCone up to date on all this?"

"More or less. It's the higher-ups I'm not so sure about. This stuff with Puig is all off the record so far."

"What happens if the higher-ups don't go for it?"

"Hell with 'em. All they can do is tell me they won't pay me for my time. They can't stop me from working on it."

After a silence Olson said, "What about me? What do you want me to do?"

"I'm not asking you to do anything. It's my thing, it bothers me."

"I thought we were partners."

"Four o'clock to midnight, we're partners. This is just my hobby."

Olson put on his signal and slid over to get off the Drive. "What the hell? I'm with you, Mike. Whatever you need."

"Thanks," said Dooley. "I'll let you know."

• • •

An eighteen-year-old kid from Milwaukee had been shot to death in the alley between Orchard and Howe just south of Armitage, late the previous night; first watch had caught it and come up with a witness who had come up with a description that had generated a sketch of two suspects, the usual cartoon villains, with long hair. The word was they had run south.

"Wells Street," said Dooley. He was not thinking of Laura, not primarily at any rate; it was a legitimate guess based on the notion that two long-haired low-lifes prowling between North and Armitage would have left tracks somewhere in the Old Town swamp. Laura was just a bonus.

Olson parked on North Avenue just about where Dooley had parked the last time he'd been here and they walked to Wells Street. "Split it up again?" said Olson.

"Sure." Dooley was thinking hard; how could he maneuver this without looking too obvious? "Which side of the street do you want?"

"Seems to me last time you had the east side."

"Yeah, OK." Dooley managed to make it nonchalant. He wasn't

going to start letting Laura affect his work. He watched Olson cross to the east side of the street with a pang of regret; he could see the Mad Hatter's sign lit up just down the block.

He made his way south, working the sidewalk and the bars, pulling out the sketches, repeating the descriptions, prodding memories, getting a lot of shrugs and shaken heads. He met a certain amount of reserve, a certain amount of resistance. Dooley was used to it.

He heard a whistle and looked across the street to see Olson in front of the Mad Hatter, beckoning. Dooley strolled across the street, not hurrying. "What's up?"

Olson had a smile on his face, cocking his head at the door of the bar. "Guess who works in here?"

He's forgotten I went in here back in July, thought Dooley, but he'll remember if he thinks about it. "I know," he said. "Sally's friend."

Olson looked a little deflated but said, "Yeah, I guess she's kinda hard to forget, isn't she? She asked about you."

"No shit?" Dooley allowed himself a grin. "I guess I better go say hi, then."

Olson put a finger on his chest, mock-reproachful. "If you're not out of there in ten minutes I'm coming back for you."

"You just tend to your work, partner, and I'll tend to mine." Dooley went into the bar.

Laura looked up from a drink she was mixing and saw him, and the way her face brightened made Dooley's heart kick; Dooley had forgotten what it was like to have this kind of combustion set off just by a look. He waited for her at the end of the bar, watching her move, looking at her long bare legs beneath the miniskirt and thinking that where they led wasn't quite such a mystery to him anymore. When Laura came up the bar toward him he had to work at keeping his expression under control.

"Hi there." She was working at it, too, he could tell. "You can't stop for a beer, your partner tells me."

"We're on the job, I'm afraid. Did he show you the pictures?"

"Yeah. They didn't really ring a bell, but I'll keep my eyes open."

"OK. How you doing?"

"I'm fine. Hey, I got a postcard from Jenny."

"Who? Oh yeah, your little friend. What's she up to?"

"She was at Woodstock."

"Where's that?"

"That big rock festival a couple of weeks ago, in New York."

"Oh, sure. Did she manage to keep her clothes on?"

"I don't know. She said it was a pretty wild time." She hesitated, and they smiled at the same time, both of them conscious of the humor in having to put on this show. "What are you doing after work?" she said.

Dooley had had the best intentions in the world, hadn't even thought of her until half an hour ago, but Laura's smile obliterated everything. He gave a fleeting thought to the amount of back-and-forth driving involved and said, "Meet you here at closing?"

"I'd love that," she said, and Dooley had trouble stopping himself from leaning over the bar to grab her.

• • •

Dooley got up in the dark to piss. He found his way to the bathroom, and while he was there he took the opportunity to wash himself; he wasn't going to go home to Rose with Laura's smell all over him. He could still taste her, an amazing thing. He hated to wash her off but he had to.

He went back and sat on the edge of the bed in the cool breeze coming in through the open window, stirring the gauze curtains. He thought Laura was asleep, but she rolled over and put an arm around his waist. "Don't go," she whispered.

"I gotta."

"Not yet. It's only three."

Dooley lay back down beside her, took her in the crook of his arm, her head on his chest. He lay there and held her and was glad for everything that had happened between them but troubled, too; he wished he could make sense out of his feelings. He could see tree branches tossing gently outside, could hear their restless whisper. He wasn't sleepy at all this time. He lay with his eyes wide open and stared out the window.

After a while Laura nuzzled him, then kissed him in the hair on his chest. She raised her head, propped herself up on an elbow and said softly, "What you thinking about?"

Dooley didn't want to tell her, but he did. "I'm thinking about my boy."

"Which one?"

"Kevin, the one overseas."

She caressed him for a while, big luminous eyes close to his. "When's he coming home?"

"Soon. But he's in the thick of it. They're supposed to pull him out, but I don't know when they're going to do it."

"God, that must be hard."

"The worst part of it is, I'm afraid I used up all my luck."

"What do you mean?"

Dooley stared out the window and said, "I was out in the Pacific for three years. I won four Purple Hearts and came home on my own two feet. That's damn lucky. I used up all my luck over there and I'm afraid I used up my son's luck along with it."

Suddenly Dooley was scared to death, eyes squeezed shut. Laura threw her arms around his neck and held him, murmuring his name. Dooley squeezed back and concentrated on not crying; he wasn't going to give her the satisfaction. "Jesus," he said. "Just gimme my boy back."

Time went by while they lay there, Laura stroking his head, kissing the tears from the corners of his eyes. After a while Dooley pushed her away gently and sat up.

"I gotta go."

Laura watched him pull on his pants and said, "Do you talk about this with your wife?"

"No."

"Why not?"

"She's got enough problems of her own. She doesn't need to take on mine."

"Jesus, Dooley. And you wonder why your love life went south."

"Who the hell made you an expert on my marriage?"

"You did. You just told me a lot about your marriage."

"Since when do you give a damn about my marriage?"

A few seconds went by and she said, "I care about you. If your marriage is important to you, I care about your marriage."

That confused the hell out of Dooley. He tucked in his shirt tail and said, "I need to think about all this."

"Yeah, I'd say you do. Look, my side of it is simple. I believe you can love more than one person. *I* can, anyway. So I would like to think that we can love each other and you can still love your wife. But I can tell you that your wife needs you to trust her, if she's going to go on loving you."

"I trust her."

"When was the last time you let her wipe your tears away?"

"Hell, she's never seen me cry."

"Well, there you go, Dooley. That's your problem right there."

Dooley finished getting dressed in silence, irritated by the whole topic. When he was done he stood there looking at Laura's pale shape on the bed, trying to get a grip on the things that were flying around inside his head. "I'm no good at talking about this kind of thing," he said.

He expected more lectures, but all Laura said was, "That's OK, Dooley. You're really good at other things."

Dooley was exhausted all of a sudden. "'Bye."

Laura came up off the bed and reached for him and he held her, naked and warm. She kissed him on the lips and said, "Don't be mad at me, OK?"

Dooley's heart fluttered; she was tying him in knots. "No," he said. "I'm not mad."

• • •

It was cool outside and the streets were empty. Driving home, Dooley suddenly couldn't believe what he'd done. Things seemed clear all at once; it seemed like he'd been living in a fog for weeks and suddenly it had blown away and he could see again. He swore at himself in an undertone, making the tires squeal a little on the turns. What the hell am I doing? he asked himself, over and over.

It wasn't until he was nearly home that Dooley figured out what was happening. He was still thinking about Kevin. Dooley realized that there were certain aspects of Kevin's coming home that he hadn't thought about until now. Now he had an image in his mind that wouldn't go away: trying to explain to a battle-hardened marine fresh off the line how he had cheated on his mother.

"What the hell did I do?" said Dooley out loud, sitting at a red light at a deserted intersection. There was nobody in sight and he hit the accelerator, leaving behind a patch of rubber and a squeal to make old men mutter under their blankets.

Thirty-seven

HO CHI MINH was dead. There was a picture of him on the front page, with his little goatee, looking harmless, smiling at the camera. See how far that grin gets you down in hell, you cocky bastard, thought Dooley. His only concern was whether this made any difference to the war. The North Vietnamese were announcing a truce in Uncle Ho's honor but they had broken truces before. There was still scattered action across Viet Nam; an ARVN unit had been badly mauled, not a good sign if you were hoping to leave the country in their hands. Dooley looked in vain for news about the withdrawal.

The first-watch dicks had made an arrest for the Milwaukee kid after some good sharp work; the kid had fallen in with bad companions, the oldest story in the book. Philly Alderisio had been arrested again, for a weapons violation this time; he was already awaiting trial on the fraud charges and Dooley wondered if this would finally be enough to keep the son of a bitch behind bars.

The Cubs had lost but so had the Mets; big deal.

Dooley shoved the paper away and sat staring into his coffee. He'd been avoiding his wife for a couple of days, trying to get his emotions in order. His conscience had finally kicked in, but it was having to slug it out with some fairly intense memories, visual, tactile, visceral, you-name-it, of Laura Lindbloom. Dooley had always been a strong-willed person, and it was a new thing for him to contend with desires that were stronger than he was.

Frank came into the kitchen. He slunk to the refrigerator and took out the orange-juice pitcher and poured some into a glass. Dooley said good morning and got a muttered reply. Frank slunk out of the kitchen again, glass in hand, not looking at Dooley, head down. Dooley watched him go up the hall. After a moment he got up and followed.

Frank was sitting on the couch sipping his orange juice and scowling out the window. Dooley saw he hadn't been imagining things: the kid sported a ripe shiner on his left eye and a big fat lip. He went on staring out the window, not looking at Dooley.

Dooley walked slowly across the living room and sat on an armchair opposite the couch. "What the hell happened to you?"

"I got in a fight."

"Anybody I know?"

Frank gave him an irritated look. "You don't know any of my friends."

"OK. What was it all about?"

"Nothing. It was stupid. This greaser at the park was making fun of me. So I hit him."

Dooley nodded. "Did you at least win?"

"Uh-uh. I got the shit kicked out of me."

Dooley's first impulse was to tell him to watch his language, but he stopped himself in time; as miserable as Frank looked, he knew that would just be piling on. He was trying to decide if he was proud of his boy for sticking up for himself or ashamed because he'd lost. "Sometimes it's smarter to walk away," he said finally.

Frank looked up at him with the kind of piercing look that Rose was so good at and said, "Kevin wouldn't have walked away."

Kevin wouldn't have lost, Dooley almost said, but once again he stopped himself in time, and all of a sudden lights went on. "You're not in competition with Kevin," he said.

"That's news to me," muttered Frank, staring at the floor.

Dooley sat there looking at his younger son, seeing things he had been blind to. It seemed to be that kind of week. After a long silence he said, "Son, if I've ever given you the impression that I favor Kevin over you, that was wrong of me."

Frank drained the glass and set it down on the coffee table. "You *do* favor Kevin over me. And you know what? I don't blame you." Before Dooley could say a word, Frank was up off the couch and out of the room.

"Frank," he called after him, hearing him run up the stairs. Dooley sat there in the quiet house, and the longer he sat there, the worse he felt.

• • •

Dooley had thought for a while about how seriously to take the cloak-and-dagger business. He had to respect the desire of Puig's informant for insulation, and police numbers were recognizable by their prefixes, so he wasn't going to leave his work number. The question was whether leaving his home number posed any danger; finally he decided that Mike with a Northwest Side exchange number asking about a Corvette was not likely to get anyone in trouble. He got the number of Carlo's in Elmwood Park from directory information and called and left the message as instructed with a sleepy-sounding barmaid.

His second item of business was tricky for different reasons. Just as he had figured, there was no trace of Howard Blackman, tycoon and ambassador-designate, in the phone book or directory assistance. At Global Properties he was informed by the third or fourth layer of insulation that Blackman's home number was not available. "I'm a police officer, and this is official business," Dooley said. "I can give you a star number, and you can call and verify it."

"I'm sorry," said the functionary. "I'm just not authorized to give that out."

"You're not listening. I'm a police officer."

"In any event, Mr. Blackman is in Washington now."

"Actually, it's his wife I need to speak to."

"Ah." There was a silence and then the voice said, "Perhaps I can give you the number of her social secretary."

"That would be good," said Dooley, recognizing a skillful side-stepping of responsibility.

The social secretary sounded as if she'd never spoken to a policeman before and didn't quite believe in their existence. "What on earth could you want with Mrs. Blackman?" she said.

"That's between me and Mrs. Blackman."

"I see. Well, I'm sorry to inform you that she is in California at the moment."

"When do you expect her back?"

"I believe she's intending to return next week."

"Can you get a message to her?"

"Of course."

"Then tell her I would like to speak to her as soon as she returns. She can call me at the following number. Do you have a pencil handy?"

"Of course."

Dooley repeated his name and read off his work number. "One more thing," he said.

"Yes?"

"Tell her it's regarding her first husband. That ought to get her attention."

"I'll see that she gets the message," said the lady at the other end of the line, but she didn't sound enthusiastic at all.

• • •

It was time to go to court again. Dooley had arrested a man in May for hacking his mother to death in the kitchen of their apartment, and after a few months of nonsense involving determinations of competence it was finally time to stand the bastard up in front of a judge. Dooley had no doubts at all about the man's competence; it had taken a firm hand to sever all those major blood vessels. The principal item of evidence was a foot-long bread knife Dooley had rescued from the mess on the floor, covered with Mama's blood and Junior's fingerprints.

He drove down to 11th and State and went up to the eighth floor to ERPS, where Evidence and Recovered Property were stored until somebody found a use for them. Like all dicks he was on good terms with the old sergeants who ran the place; a detective was responsible for getting his evidence to the courtroom and if he had any sense he stayed on the good side of the men who hoarded it. ERPS was like a deli counter with dicks jostling for service; when it was your turn you ordered up an envelope full of incriminating evidence instead of a pound of salami. "You got one of my toys back there somewhere," Dooley said, shoving his copy of the inventory form across the counter to a white-haired copper.

"Goin' to court, are we?"

"Going to put an ungrateful son where he belongs. Careful and don't cut yourself." The clerk peered at the form, looking for the inventory number; Dooley reached into his briefcase and made a spur-of-the-moment decision. "Say, while I'm at it. Could you grab this one for me too? That would save me a trip tomorrow." He pulled out the form for Sally Kotowski's locket and shoved it across the counter.

"Making an old man like me work twice as hard, shame on you." The old copper took both forms and hobbled away down an aisle between high shelves. Dooley waited, wondering if he was crazy, wondering what the hell he was going to do with the locket. All he knew was that he would feel better having it with him.

After a few minutes the old copper came back holding a big manila envelope with a buff-colored form attached to it. He tossed the envelope on the counter with a clunk and handed Dooley his forms. "There's your toothpick. The other item isn't there."

I knew it, Dooley thought. My hunch was one hundred percent right and one hundred percent too late. "What do you mean, it's not there?"

"I mean it's not there. It's already been retrieved."

"How could it have been retrieved without the form I just handed you?"

"You got a partner? Maybe he came in and got it. Happens all the time."

"Without the form?"

"What the hell do I know? Maybe he took it out of your case there. Were you off recently? All I can tell you is, the item with this inventory number ain't back there."

"Can you check the file copy for me?"

The old sergeant gave him a look that said don't push your luck. "Why don't you check with your partner first?"

Dooley was getting steamed. "My partner wouldn't have any reason to come and get it. Now, if somebody retrieved my evidence, he had to sign for it. I'm asking you to check the copy and tell me who took my God damn evidence. OK?"

"Keep your shirt on. What was the number?" He looked at the form and went, trailing a murderous look. Dooley stood there and waited, thinking about what was happening to his case. The sergeant was gone for what seemed like a long time. Dooley checked his watch and swore; he was going to be late for court. When the sergeant came back, he had a scowl on his face. "The copy's not on file."

Dooley scowled back at him. "Which means the evidence has to be back there, right?"

"Except it's not. What probably happened, one of the dumbshit civilians they got working here misfiled it. Either that or we never had it. You intended to bring it in and didn't, or told your partner to and he didn't."

"Then I would still have the other copies with me, wouldn't I?" Dooley waved the yellow form at him.

"How do I know what you did with the forms?"

"Don't give me that shit. Check the master file."

"Oh, come on, now."

"When I dropped off the evidence I handed in a pink form, too. I want to see it. If it's in the file, it means you had my evidence and lost it. If it's not in the file, you not only lost my evidence, you tampered with the files, too. You try and tell me I'm making all this up again, I'm going to come over this counter after you."

"I didn't do a fucking thing to your evidence."

"Somebody did. Now go find my form."

Business had come to a halt in ERPS; Dooley had gotten everyone's attention. The sergeant tried to stare him down but gave up on it and shoved off. Dooley could feel the stares of the other waiting detectives. At his shoulder a voice said, "What'd you lose? Jewelry? That figures. They steal it. The amount of evidence that walks out of here is a fucking disgrace." Dooley looked to see a robbery dick he knew slightly, shaking his head.

"Or they just lose it," put in another man. "Lazy bastards."

When the sergeant came back he was carrying a pink form and he had a neutral expression on his face. He laid it on the counter in front of Dooley. "That what you want?"

Dooley scanned the form; it was a copy of the yellow one he held in his hand, with a description of the locket on it. "That's it. That proves I left the item here."

"I wasn't calling you a liar," said the sergeant. "It's just that guys do make mistakes."

"I don't make that kind of mistake," said Dooley. He turned to the dick at his side. "Do me a favor, will you?" said Dooley. "If it comes down to it, back me up on this. You saw the pink copy."

The other man scanned the form. "I'll back you up, don't worry."

Dooley slid the pink copy back across the counter. “Put that back in the file. It better be there when the IAD people check.”

“You got no need to threaten me.”

“Then find my evidence.” Dooley grabbed the manila envelope, signed the form for it, and threw it across the counter. “I have to go to court now. But I’ll be back. And when I come back, I want to find my evidence waiting for me.”

“I’ll do my best.”

“Do better than that,” said Dooley, shouldering his way to the door.

• • •

“It’s gone, McCone. Somebody took it. They’re covering it up.”

McCone didn’t like what he was hearing, but he wasn’t going to fling up his arms and run around in circles. “You checked with Olson?”

“Olson never knew it was there. The only people that knew it was there besides me were the people who read my report.”

“So what are you saying?”

“God damn it, you know what I’m saying.”

“Don’t raise your voice in here.”

“I’m sorry. Look, you and I both know there’s crooked coppers in this department. There’s coppers in this department that owe their God damn jobs to the Outfit. Some of them are down at Eleventh and State, and one of them made that locket disappear because it proves I’m right. What are you going to do about it?”

Francis McCone was a good copper, Dooley thought, but like anyone who had put in his thirty years he had found ways of coexisting, of being a good cop without rocking the boat too much. It just wasn’t worth the trouble. Dooley knew that, and he knew he was asking a lot of an old copper drawing in sight of a comfortable retirement. “I’ll speak to the lieutenant about it,” McCone said after a silence.

"Do that," said Dooley, getting wearily to his feet. "Me, I'm filing a complaint. I'm not going to let them get away with another one."

McCone sighed, the sigh of a much-burdened man. "I'll back you up, Mike," he said. "But don't expect miracles."

• • •

Dooley never had any trouble getting through his shift; he knew how to work, and he knew watching the clock only made it move slower. Tonight was different; he had a lot on his mind. He couldn't wait to get off.

"You OK?" Olson asked him, steering north on Broadway toward the address of a woman who had filed a rape complaint.

"I'm fine."

"You don't seem like yourself tonight."

"Who do I seem like?"

"I don't know. You're not saying much."

"What do you want me to say?"

"I don't know, how about, 'Would you look at the legs on that broad,' or 'God, that meat loaf was bad.' You know, just regular stuff."

Dooley ran through all the things he might say: They're smothering my case, I cheated on my wife, I'm a lousy father. He opted for "I need a vacation."

"Jesus, now I'm scared. When Iron Mike Dooley needs a vacation, we're all in trouble."

"Is that what they call me?"

"Nah, I just made that up. Mostly people call you 'that asshole Dooley.' No, Jesus, Mike, I'm kidding. You serious? You're the best dick on the squad and everyone knows it."

"I could still be an asshole."

"What is it with you tonight? You having an identity crisis or something?"

Dooley laughed softly to show him he was fine. "I'm OK. I got a lot on my mind, that's all."

"You're the fuckin' Rock of Gibraltar, Dooley. Don't go soft on me now."

"Not a chance, pal." Dooley felt better for about five seconds. Then he remembered where they were going and felt worse again; he hated rape cases.

This one was not too bad; the victim had had time to get angry, a reaction Dooley always liked to see. Even better, she knew the man who had assaulted her and they had found him, arrested him and processed him by one in the morning. "The booze is on me," said Olson, signing off on the report. "Personally, I don't think you've been spending enough time in J.J.'s. That's your whole problem right there."

Dooley looked at his watch; Laura didn't get off for another hour, but he didn't want to miss her. "I'm gonna pass," he said. "I promised the wife."

"What, to stop drinking?" Olson gaped at him.

"To spend less time with you shiftless sons of bitches." Dooley snapped his briefcase shut. "No, really, I'm just worn out. I'm gonna go home and get in bed for once." Dooley didn't wait around to argue; he jumped in his car and headed north in case anybody was watching before cutting over to Lincoln to slice down toward Old Town.

He could tell Laura was surprised when he walked in just before closing; he waited on the sidewalk while she and the moptop shut things down. "I'm glad you came by," she said, taking his arm.

"I had to see you."

"God, me too. I've been thinking about you a lot."

They made small talk on the short drive. Upstairs in her place, Laura kicked off her sandals and spun to face him; she grabbed him just like before and kissed him. Dooley had to kiss back, he couldn't help himself, but he had had all evening to make up his mind and he broke it off early. Laura looked up at him and said, "What's wrong?"

"This is."

"What do you mean?" He could see in her eyes that she knew what he meant. Dooley pulled away from her; he had to or he was going to crumble again. He walked to the couch and sat down. "I can't sleep with you anymore."

That rocked her back on her heels a little; her eyebrows went up and then came back down. "I see," she said. "Any particular reason?"

"It's wrong," said Dooley. "I'm a married man."

Laura wandered a couple of steps away toward the window, her arms folded. Just from the way she was holding herself Dooley could see she knew it was over, but he knew he wasn't going to get out of it without some unpleasantness. All over but the shouting, he thought. Laura wheeled to face him. "I wondered if that might not come up again," she said.

"I should have stuck to my guns."

"I don't recall holding one to your head."

"You didn't. I made a bad choice."

He could see that hurt her; he could see it as clearly as he was seeing everything else these days. "I'm sorry you think it was bad."

"How could it not be bad? I hurt my wife."

"Did you tell her?"

"No. Not yet. But I hurt her even if I never tell her."

"I don't understand that. But that's OK. I get the message. Just remember, nobody made you sleep with me."

"I'm not blaming you. But *you* remember, you made the invitation."

"Yes, I did. And excuse me, but I had the impression for a while that you were glad I did."

Dooley could feel himself crashing into the limits of what he knew how to say. He felt like smacking something. "God damn it,

Laura. I had the time of my life and you know it. But it was wrong. All that free love stuff, you won't run out of love, all that stuff. It sounds great, it sure as hell got me going. For a while there I was having as much fun as everyone else was, for once in my life. I wasn't smart enough to resist it and I'm not smart enough to tell you why it's wrong. You did a hell of a job on me. I don't blame you for a thing, but it can't go on."

She had a stricken look on her face. She said, "I did a hell of a job on you? Is that what it felt like?"

"I don't have the words for it. I'm no good at words."

"Can I tell you what it felt like from where I was standing?"

Dooley felt exhausted and all he wanted to do was go home to bed. "I can't stop you."

"From my end it felt like I was drowning in the ocean and you pulled me out."

His head snapped up to look at her; he wasn't sure he'd heard her right. "What?"

"I was sitting there in the dark and you turned on the lights. I was having bad dreams and you woke me up. I was lonely and all of a sudden you were there and I wasn't lonely anymore."

She was still standing there by the window with her arms crossed, but something about the way she said it made him able suddenly to see right in past the stricken look to the real her. He just stared at her for a few seconds. "You?" he said. "How could you be lonely?"

She did the last thing he expected and started laughing, but then Dooley couldn't tell if it was laughter or crying, because the tears were rolling down her cheeks, and then it was pretty clear she was crying. "Oh God, Dooley, you idiot. What do you think I am?"

He had to then; he couldn't sit there and watch her cry. Dooley got up off the couch and went and put his arms around her and held her while she got his collar wet for a while. Through the window he could see tree leaves, shimmering in the light from the street lamps. "I'm sorry, Laura. I don't know what to do." That's not true, he thought as he said it.

"You do what you have to do," Laura said, drawing back far enough to look at him. Her cheeks were glistening and her nose was running a little. She sniffed. "Just don't hate me for having needed you."

Dooley was struck dumb; he had never ever, not for an instant, thought of it in those terms. He looked into her eyes for a while and said, "I didn't think that was how it was."

"That's how it was," said Laura, lovelier than ever with her eyes full of tears. "That's how it was."

Thirty-eight

FRIDAY NIGHT IT finally rained, making up for lost time. The heavens opened up and dumped enough water on the city to shut down O'Hare and knock out the power in a dozen places. Rush hour was madness, the roads backed up and the viaducts flooding again. Dooley and Olson spent the evening looking in vain for the older brother of a Puerto Rican girl who had been raped the week before; the accused rapist had turned up with six bullet holes in him a few hours after making bail.

On Saturday the paper was full of misery: An ex-marine who had been home from Viet Nam less than a month had been shot to death riding on the back seat of a convertible out on the West Side. That one hit Dooley in the gut; where the hell would his son be safe? In Northern Ireland the Protestants were rampaging through Catholic neighborhoods and in Viet Nam the Reds were shelling Da Nang, ignoring their own truce. Dooley didn't even look at the sports section; he was too disgusted.

He had to go to work but not till four; his wife and his kids were all out somewhere with friends, making the most of a nice Saturday at the tail end of a dying summer. Dooley didn't know what the hell to do with himself. He did some work around the house and yard and made himself a sandwich and sat on the patio eating it and thinking about Laura Lindbloom. At two-thirty he took a shower and put on his suit and tie, took his star and the .38 out of the locked drawer. He picked up his briefcase from the corner in the kitchen and went out to the car.

Dooley hadn't been to confession since Eisenhower was in the White House, probably in his first term. He still went to Mass at Christmas and Easter, but the other sacraments had more or less fallen out of his life. He wasn't sure why; he still believed there was a God and that it was important to follow the rules, but on the whole he hadn't had much time for religious observances. Dooley figured that making sure his kids were brought up in the Church was his main obligation at this point in his life.

But then it wasn't every day he cheated on his wife. Dooley drove over to the church and parked on the street. He felt a little bit conspicuous walking up the wide front steps; he didn't particularly want to meet anyone he knew, but if he did he didn't want it to be any big deal.

Inside it was cool and dim. There were four people waiting in the aisle near the confessional, a mom with two kids and the usual elderly female. Either they were all a little early or the priest was a little late; nothing seemed to be happening. Finally Father Doyle came hustling down the side aisle. He did a double-take when he caught sight of Dooley and gave him a big smile and a nod before ducking into the confessional.

Dooley stood there waiting, trying not to look at anybody. He sneaked a glance at his watch; if things didn't move along quickly he was going to be late for roll call. How much sin could a couple of grade-school kids get up to?

When it was his turn he stepped into the booth and knelt in the dark.

He cleared his throat and said, "Bless me Father, for I have sinned. It has been—" Dooley realized he should have given a little thought to this. He also realized he was talking too loudly; there was no need to broadcast his confession to the whole parish. He lowered his voice and said, "It has been at least fifteen years since my last confession." Dooley waited for some expression of disapproval, but there was only silence beyond the grate. Here goes, he thought. "I killed a man," he said.

Jesus, where did that come from? Dooley felt as if somebody else were suddenly in control of his tongue.

Softly from beyond the grate Father Doyle's voice came: "I thought it was two."

"No," said Dooley. "I don't mean recently. Those two had it coming, that was self-defense. I mean in the war. I mean, I killed a lot of men in the war." Shit, he thought, how did I get started on this? It was too late to stop. "But there was one in particular maybe I shouldn't have, and I don't think I ever confessed it."

Dooley hadn't thought about it in years, but all of a sudden it was vividly with him: the hot Luzon sun on his head, the pleading of the Filipino collaborator dragged out of hiding by his newly liberated compatriots. Dooley had had a decimated platoon to get into a secure position by nightfall and no time to bother with local scores to settle; when the village headman tried to insist that he take the scoundrel into custody, he'd raised his Garand and blown most of the scoundrel's brains out the back of his head. He could still see the blood pooling in the dirt.

"I killed a man in cold blood, Father," Dooley said, and it chilled him to say it.

Some time went by, and Dooley was starting to think he'd shocked a priest, something he'd always assumed was impossible. Finally Father Doyle said, "What made that one different?"

"I should have taken him prisoner. But I didn't want to bother. It was easier to kill him."

Softly the voice came. "The war had brutalized you, you're saying."

"I guess so, Father."

"But you remain able to make the distinction between right and wrong."

"I guess so."

"Then God will forgive you."

Dooley sure as hell hoped so; he was amazed to find how much it still bothered him after all these years. "That wasn't what I came in here to tell you," he said. Dooley opened his mouth but nothing came out; he closed it, took a breath and tried again. "I committed the sin of adultery."

Dooley was giving Father Doyle a workout today. There was another long pause and the priest said, "How many times?"

"Three times." Each one was crystal clear in his mind but Dooley knew that was a bad direction for his thoughts to go in at the moment. "But it's over. I've ended it and I'm sorry. And ashamed."

A little time went by and the priest said, "If you are truly repentant, you can count on God's forgiveness."

"All right, father." Dooley hesitated; he wanted to ask the priest if he should tell Rose about it; he wanted to talk about the whole thing, but he knew the confessional wasn't the place.

"Was there anything else?" the priest murmured.

For a moment Dooley was tempted to open the floodgates. I am ill-tempered with my wife and children, I have favored one son over the other, I have bullied my daughter. He could be in here all day. He said, "That's all, Father."

He could practically hear Father Doyle counting up the prayers for his penance; what did they do, look it up in a table? "Say ten Our Fathers and ten Hail Marys," the priest said.

I got off light, Dooley thought, and felt guilty for thinking it. "Now make a good act of contrition."

Dooley wasn't sure he could remember it. "Oh my God, I am heartily sorry for having offended Thee . . ." He groped for the words. "I detest all my sins . . ." There was something about the pains of hell here, he thought, but he wasn't sure. ". . . most of all because they offend Thee. I firmly resolve to sin no more . . . and to avoid the near occasions of sin." Dooley hoped that was close enough, and apparently it was, because the next thing he heard was the absolution coming through the grate. *Ego te absolvo. . . .* He crossed himself and got up and left the confessional.

He went up to the front of the church and genuflected and slid into a pew and knelt and said his penance. Then he crossed himself and hoisted himself up onto the pew and just sat there for a moment, trying to decide if he felt any better. He wished he could go on sitting there looking up into the high vault of the church, doing nothing, but he didn't have that luxury; it was time to go to work.

• • •

Dirksen was dead, the old senator finally giving in to lung cancer. He had looked dead for at least two years in Dooley's estimation; it was about time. Out in the Judean desert they had found the missing bishop, also dead, and down in Brazil they were bargaining for the kidnapped ambassador, who was presumably still alive. The silence from Viet Nam was deafening. There was no word about truces, troop withdrawals or prospects of victory, but on the obituary page a headline said *Two area marines killed in Viet action.*

The Cubs had lost four in a row and their lead was down to two and a half games, but they were heading into New York for the big showdown. Dooley was off tonight and he had a sudden picture of Frank and himself sitting in front of the TV, together.

He found Frank in the living room with his feet up on the couch, reading a magazine. Dooley quelled his irritation and even smiled a little when Frank hustled to sit up. The kid's face was looking better, except for the pimples. "You want to go hit the ball a little?" Dooley said.

Frank looked at him open-mouthed for a couple of seconds and said, "Uh, sure. I guess."

Dooley was lacing up his tennis shoes when the phone rang. Frank answered it and held it out to him. "It's for you."

Dooley took the phone and said hello. "Michael Dooley?" a man said in his ear.

"Yeah."

"This is Sergeant Davis down at ERPS. You filed an IAD complaint about some missing evidence?"

"That's right."

"We have located the evidence for you."

Dooley just stood there for a moment, with the phone to his ear. "I don't believe it," he said.

"What was that?"

"Where was it?"

"Right where it should have been. We're trying to determine why you were unable to locate it the other day."

"It wasn't me that was unable to locate it. It was the officer in charge."

"Well, it's been located. Are you willing to withdraw your complaint?"

Dooley looked at Frank, standing there patiently with his bat and glove, just waiting for him. The last thing in the world Dooley wanted to do was put on his suit and drive downtown. Suddenly he was angry. "Not until I have a look at it," he said. "Give me an hour."

Dooley hung up the phone and watched Frank's face go through a couple of changes. "I'm sorry," Dooley said.

Frank shrugged. "It's OK, Pop."

"Later," said Dooley. "Maybe tomorrow."

"Whenever," said Frank, heading back up the hall.

• • •

Davis was a tall and loose-limbed specimen with gray hair that matched his unwelcoming eyes; he had the severe look of a man whose professional life was dealing with other people's displeasure. "You make some serious allegations in your report," he said.

"That's right, I do." Dooley wasn't ready to concede anything.

"Are you willing to reconsider them in the light of the item reappearing?"

"I'd like to know why it disappeared in the first place."

"It didn't disappear. I was able to locate it without any difficulty this morning."

"Then what happened the other day? Did you talk to the officer I dealt with?"

"I saw no reason to consult him."

"Consult him. He'll back me up. The item was missing."

"The point is, it's here now." Davis tapped on the manila envelope lying on the desktop.

Dooley held his icy gaze for a few seconds, wondering. It was impossible to say where Davis fit in. It was possible he was on the level and just rushing through things, grateful to have an out; supervisors hated IAD investigations. "Let me see it," Dooley said.

The sergeant slid the envelope across to him. On it were written the inventory number along with the original R.D. number of the case. Dooley opened it and slid out the smaller plain white envelope he'd stored the locket in. He opened the envelope and shook the locket and chain out onto the desk.

Dooley stared at it for three seconds and said, "It's not the same one." He looked up at Davis, starting to get steamed again. "They switched it." Dooley threw the bauble across the desk. It was a locket, on a chain, but there were no tiny pearls. "It's not even close."

Davis glared at him. "It matches the description on the form."

"That's just because I didn't make it detailed enough. I foolishly assumed I could entrust my evidence to your department."

Davis's eyes narrowed. "I'm going to let that slide for the moment and suggest you withdraw your complaint unless you have some way of supporting this new allegation." Davis was giving him the full wattage, no doubt a look that had cowed many a troublesome patrolman.Dooley was way past letting desk officers intimidate him; he'd stared down armed madmen. "And I'm going to suggest you find out who's trying to kill my investigation. Unless you're in it with them."

Davis's look changed; suddenly he looked more amused than angry. He eased back, looked down at the form in front of him and said, "I'm going to report a finding of 'unfounded' on this complaint. You're free to file another one if it makes you happy. But I'd recommend that you learn not to throw around wild accusations. It undermines your credibility. Now, you want your evidence back, or not?"

Dooley laughed. "Keep it. File it where it was. It's a fake, but who gives a shit? As long as the paperwork's in order, I know you'll be happy."

Davis watched him stalk out of the office. "Yeah, I'm ecstatic," he said to Dooley's back.

• • •

"Dooley, what the *hell* are you doing here?" Kowalcyk stopped in his tracks, coming in at the end of his shift.

"Writing a poem about you. What rhymes with moron?" Dooley didn't look up from the typewriter; he had a full head of steam he was hoping would carry him through to the end of his report. He had fumed all the way from 11th and State, swearing out loud in the car. The fix was in and he didn't know what to do besides write it up, make sure it went in somebody's file. He'd even found a sheet of carbon paper; he was sure as hell going to keep a copy for himself. *This officer finds it extremely disturbing to think that police personnel would carry out such tampering in aid of criminal elements,* he wrote. He paused, scowling at the paper, wishing there were words to express his outrage.

Kowalcyk dropped onto a chair. "Does your family recognize you when you visit them?" he said.

"Family?" said Dooley. "You mean those people that live in my house?"

• • •

Tell her or not? Dooley was going around in circles. He remembered a conversation in J.J.'s, a few months before, about a dick whose wife had divorced him after he confessed his infidelity. "He brought it on himself, the idiot," somebody had said. "You don't ever tell her that."

"You'd have to be out of your mind," someone else had thrown in. "What they don't know don't hurt 'em."

Everyone had gotten in his two cents' worth: "They're better off not knowing. It only makes them miserable to know. If you want to patch things up, you keep your mouth shut. Hell, my wife fuckin' told me, if I ever cheat on her, for Christ's sake don't tell her."

That had been the consensus, and Dooley kept coming back to it; it had a certain common-sense authority to it. But it bothered him; Dooley had a feeling that something he and Rose had always had would be lost if he tried to keep this from her. Hiding bad news from her was one thing; that didn't ask her to believe anything false. But if he hid this from her he would be asking her to love somebody that didn't really exist.

He took her out for lunch again. This time they went east, toward the lake, Dooley wanting to get off the beaten track a little. They found a place on Sheridan Road near Pratt Avenue, nothing fancy but decent, and it was a block from the lake. Conversation over lunch was a little strained. They talked about the children, Kathleen's breathless phone reports on her first week of college, Frank's grousing about going back to St. Patrick, but they kept bumping up against events overseas that were holding their oldest child's life hostage. Beyond that there were periods of silence; after more than twenty years of marriage it was hard to remember what they used to talk about.

They walked out on the breakwater at Farwell Avenue after lunch. It was a gorgeous day, cool and sunny, with hints of fall coming. They could make out the tallest buildings in the Loop eight miles south, the Prudential Building, the new Hancock building. The breeze ruffled Rose's hair. There were a few fishermen along the pier but at the very end, out past the light tower, there was nobody. They stood in silence for a moment and then Rose put her arms around him and Dooley hugged her back and thought, never, I'll never be able to tell her. "Rose," he said, after a long moment.

She could read the tone of his voice, and she pulled away just enough to look at him. "What is it?"

"I did a bad thing." Dooley looked into his wife's eyes and knew it was too late to go back and hoped he was doing the right thing. "I cheated on you." Dooley had owned up to mistakes large and small in his life; in the army and on the department he'd learned that the only thing to do was admit it and take the punishment like a man; cringing was something Dooley didn't do. "It was short, it's over, it won't happen again. I've confessed it and I just have to find a way to make it up to you."

He had no idea what to expect; he'd been hoping for a knowing nod, an I-thought-so crossing of the arms, maybe followed by a slap in the face. Anger he could deal with. What he got was an instant of obvious shock, the very worst thing he could have seen, followed by dawning dismay. Get ready, thought Dooley. It's going to be bad.

Rose's face stabilized a little; she took a deep breath, drew herself up and said, "I see."

Dooley figured as long as he kept talking he was OK, up to a point. "I know it was wrong. I don't have any defense. But it's over, and I'm telling you because I can't lie to you. And I'm going to spend the rest of my life making it up to you."

She stood still, and he could see her face hardening. After a moment she said, "Anybody I know?"

"No."

Rose was getting wiser by the second, the shock being replaced by scorn. "I did wonder about the late nights. This was the informant you had to buy all those drinks for?"

"That was a lie." It was and it wasn't, thought Dooley, but explaining all that would mean admitting to professional mistakes that were just as bad as the personal ones.

"How long has this been going on?" said Rose quietly.

"Not long." How much detail does she need, he thought. How much does she want? "Three times, Rose. That's all. And then I came to my senses."

She started nodding then, just standing there nodding with her hair flying in her face, not bothering to brush it away. "Well," she said, "I have to say, this is the last thing I expected from you, Michael."

That one hurt. "I'm sorry," Dooley said; he'd run out of words.

Rose wasn't going to let it go at a simple apology; he could see trouble in her eyes. "Take me home, please," she said, and wheeled and started walking toward the shore.

• • •

The lead was down to a game and a half. The Cubs had lost the first game in New York the night before, three to two, Koosman beating Hands, a close call at the plate going against the Cubs, Hundley losing his cool and practically needing to be roped and shot with a tranquilizer gun. There had been a picture of him in the paper, jumping up and down. Tonight it was Seaver versus Jenkins, Jenkins going on two days' rest. "I'm worried," said

Frank. "Durocher's wearing them out. I don't know if they have enough gas in the tank."

"Don't worry," said Dooley. "We'll get 'em tonight. This is where class tells, when the race gets tight." He wanted to forget all about his troubles tonight and just lose himself in a ball game. Rose had sleepwalked through dinner and then told them she was going over to Emily's for a while; Dooley figured his reputation was about to crash and burn around Emily's house. He just hoped it wasn't all over the neighborhood by morning.

The worst thing was, he missed Laura tonight, missed her like hell. He missed everything about her, her looks, her voice, her laugh, her body. He knew it was bad for him to dwell on it, but he was just starting to feel the loss. He had done the right thing but it was going to hurt for a while. He wondered if he would ever be able to see her again, just have some kind of a friendship. Something told him he was dreaming. He had promised to call her but he knew that would be a mistake, at least for a while. Temptation, serious temptation, was not something Dooley had a lot of experience with. He wanted Laura so bad he ached with it.

"What the heck?" Dooley's mind had been wandering and Frank's squeak jerked him back. On the TV screen there was a shot of the Cub dugout, Santo standing in the on-deck circle, and what looked like a black cat walking across the grass toward him. While Dooley watched, it circled, got spooked by the ballplayers lining the bench, and scampered away across the diamond. "Is that *weird,*" Frank said.

Dooley started to laugh; he couldn't help it. A black cat in a baseball game fit right in with the way his life was going.

"That's it," he said. "It's all over. The Cubs are screwed."

Thirty-nine

All hell was breaking loose, all over the world. The Israelis had shot down eleven Arab jets in the Middle East and the Russians and Chinese were meeting in Peking to decide whether they should keep shooting at each other. In Northern Ireland the Protestants were still chasing Catholics through the streets. In Viet Nam the truce was over; the Marines had killed 20 NVA near An Hoa while sustaining only one casualty but the communists were shelling American and ARVN bases all across the country.

Closer to home, it was just as bad: there had been rioting near the Taylor Homes on the South Side and at Cabrini-Green somebody had trapped three coppers in an elevator between floors and set it on fire. The cops had made it out, but just by the skin of their teeth, and nobody had been arrested.

Dooley was sick; he didn't know what the country was coming to. He couldn't look at the paper anymore. He put his face in his hands and just sat there for a while. He didn't know what his own life was coming to, either. Rose had hardly talked to him at all for the past three days. He couldn't blame her but it was driving him nuts. He kept waiting for the other shoe to fall.

Dooley sighed and took his hands away from his face. His eye fell on the sports section. The Cubs had lost again in Philly and were in second place, a game behind.

• • •

The message had read simply *Mrs. Blackman* followed by a phone number. Dooley had called the number and talked to someone who was not Mrs. Blackman and been told that he could see the lady at home on Friday at two o'clock. Home was in Kenilworth, which was why Dooley was driving north along the lake, going through towns he could never afford to live in. The streets were shaded by old trees and the houses were very large; there were glimpses of blue water on his right. It was a beautiful day for a drive but he was weighed down by things that were happening. He went through Wilmette and almost missed the sign announcing Kenilworth. Dooley turned off Sheridan Road and after a little wandering managed to find the police station, which was about the size of a small branch library in Chicago.

The Chief of Police was close to retirement and looked fairly comfortable behind his desk. Dooley introduced himself and showed his star and they compared notes for a while; the chief had put in twenty years down in the city and then jumped at the chance to finish his career in a place where enforcing parking restrictions was the major law enforcement task. "So what can I do for you?" he said.

"I'm just checking in," Dooley said. "I've got an appointment to talk to Howard Blackman's wife and I'm not sure I can even find the place. I didn't see any house numbers as I was coming in."

The chief chuckled. "No, they don't make it real easy, do they? I can take you over there if you want. Blackman's got a big chunk of land on the lake. But the entrance is kind of inconspicuous." He reached for his hat. "And people do tend to be a little nervous about strangers since the Percy murder."

Dooley remembered the senator's daughter getting beaten to death in her bed, three years back; it had made the news all over the world and never been solved. "I don't blame them."

"That happened six months after I took the job," the chief said. "So much for the peace and quiet."

"You caught a lousy break."

"That's life. I just wish we could have caught the bastard." Outside in the parking lot the chief said, "You mind my asking what this is about with Mrs. Blackman?"

"Probably nothing at all," said Dooley. "She used to be married to a guy whose name came up in connection with a case I'm working on. The guy's not available so I'm hoping she can answer a few polite questions. Just shaking the tree, really."

Dooley could see the chief wondering if anything falling out of the tree could hurt him. Part of a job like his was insulation; rich people didn't like to be bothered by policemen. "She's agreed to see you, has she?" the chief said, not looking at Dooley.

"That's what her people tell me."

"OK, follow me." They got into their cars and the chief led Dooley back toward the lake and up Sheridan Road a couple of hundred yards. He put on his signal and pulled over just shy of a narrow blacktop drive that pierced a screen of trees. Dooley drew even and the chief pointed and touched the bill of his cap. Dooley returned the salute and turned into the drive.

The drive ran for a few yards, past tennis courts, and bent left and then the trees ended and all of a sudden Dooley thought he was in another country. Ahead of him was a huge rambling house built of gray stone with ivy climbing up it, with terraces and balconies and gables and chimneys poking out here and there, surrounded by a vast garden with hedges and flower beds and clumps of small neatly trimmed trees that stretched to the edge of the shimmering blue lake. Dooley thought he'd blundered into Disneyland.

He followed the drive to what looked like the front door, a big iron-studded hunk of wood that sat at the top of a flight of steps. He stopped the car and got out and went up the steps, looking for a doorbell. He found one and pushed it and waited, looking out over the park and wondering who the hell mowed all that grass.

The door opened and a maid was there, in a black dress with a white apron. She looked Mexican but her English was perfect as she said, "Can I help you?"

"I'm here to see Mrs. Blackman. She's expecting me." Dooley handed the maid one of his cards. She took it and beckoned him in and closed the door behind him and told him to follow her. He followed her across a high-ceilinged hall past the foot of a wide staircase and down a short passageway and around a corner into another passage, where she motioned for him to wait and knocked on a door. She opened it and went inside and Dooley heard voices and then the maid came back out and waved him in.

Dooley went into a room dominated by the lake, bright and restless beyond a line of windows. A woman had risen from a chair and was coming to meet him. She was tall and slender and not at all hard to look at, and Dooley's first impression with the light behind her was that she was ten years younger than he was. "Mr. Dooley?" she said, holding out her hand. "I'm Fay Blackman."

Dooley shook her hand. "Pleased to meet you." Close up he revised his opinion; she was maybe his age, maybe a couple of years younger, but she had the best care money could buy. She was fighting middle age and winning so far. Her hair was a rich auburn; her clear skin showed a few lines but all they did was give her character. She had a long face with fine features that gave her a slightly fragile look, but her intelligent brown eyes made her look shrewd enough to take care of herself. "I appreciate your taking the time to talk to me," he said.

"Not at all. Would you like some coffee?"

Dooley didn't really want any coffee, and he didn't want to make a social occasion out of it, but he had already figured out that, as much as he hated to play the peasant in the manor house, he was going to get farther with this woman if he let her feel she was doing him a favor. "That would be great, thanks."

"Elena, would you bring us some coffee, please?" Dooley thought she was talking to the air until he realized that the maid had been hovering just outside the door, waiting for this. "Sit down, won't you?" Fay Blackman waved him to a chair facing the one she'd been sitting in. Dooley padded across a thick carpet and sat down with the lake on his left, a room full of books on his right, and a very wealthy woman six feet in front of him. She was wearing a sleek gray pants suit, and she crossed her legs and folded her hands in her lap.

"This is a beautiful house," Dooley said.

She smiled, but there was irony in it. "It's a long way from Taylor Street, isn't it?"

"Is that where you grew up?"

"Close. More like Racine and Polk, actually. But you tell people Taylor Street, that tells them all they need to know. Or so they think."

Dooley nodded. "Is that where you met Tommy Spain?"

She took a deep breath, as if she were about to go off the high board. She said, "His name was Tommy Spagnola when I met him. But then my name was Fay Ciccone in those days. I met him in a butcher shop on Racine when I was running errands for my mother. He was good-looking and he flirted with me and wound up walking me home and asking me out. We went out off and on for four years before we got married. We broke up and made up a couple of times. My parents didn't like him but he kept coming back, pleading and making it up to me. Finally we got married. That was in 1954. We were divorced two years later. I should have listened to my parents, I guess."

Dooley had the impression she had been rehearsing that all morning. He said, "When did he become Tommy Spain?"

"Before he went on the police department. He thought it would be better not to have an obviously Italian name. I don't know if it made any difference."

The questions were about to get tougher and Dooley was trying to find the right formula. "Were you aware of . . . his connections?"

"You mean did I know he was a gangster? Not when I married him. I knew about his Uncle Mooney. That's what he called Sam Giancana. I knew who *he* was. Tommy told me Mooney was just a friend of his father's and a good guy and he wasn't going to tell an old family friend to get lost because he did a few shady things. I bought it. It wasn't until after we were married that I started to realize that Tommy was in the rackets himself. It's harder to hide things from a wife. That's why I divorced him. I gave him an ultimatum and he chose the mob over me. And that, Mr. Dooley, was the end of my involvement with Tommy Spain. I went on to build a new life. I went to college, I made a career for myself, eventually I met Howard and we were married. I saw Tommy a few times over the years, heard about him certainly, but at this point I haven't seen him in at least four years, and I certainly don't know anything about what he's been involved in. In fact I have worked very hard to distance myself from all that. So I really can't imagine what could have brought you here today."

She had grown chillier over the course of the speech until at the end her gaze was arctic. Dooley blinked at her a few times and suddenly he became aware that she was rigid with tension. She's scared shitless, he thought.

"Well," he said. "I certainly didn't come here to cause you any trouble." Dooley knew that what Fay Blackman was scared of was the damage a mere Chicago police detective could do to an ambassador-designate's prospects if the detective wanted to make an issue out of his wife's first husband. Dooley didn't have anything at all against the new ambassador, but he also knew he could use that fear if it turned out to be necessary; he knew he had a big stick to wave at Fay Blackman, *neé* Ciccone, if he had to. "What I came for was insight," he said. "I was hoping you could help me get inside Tommy's skull."

The fine features had settled into a look of disdain. "I have a limited amount of time to devote to this. I'll be happy to answer any specific questions you might have."

"I really have just one question. And I'll get to it in a second. But first let me tell you about a girl named Sally Kotowski." Dooley looked out the window, getting his thoughts in order. "I spent a fair amount of time with Sally, at the beginning of June. I feel like I got to know her fairly well. And I kind of liked her, to tell you the truth." He looked at Fay Blackman now and saw her wondering where the hell he was going. Dooley said, "I wish I'd had a chance to meet her when she was alive. Sally was murdered on June third, we think. She was tortured to death. And she used to be Tommy Spain's girlfriend."

Dooley had hoped to make an impression, but he got more than he bargained for; for a moment he thought he was going to have to go run after the maid. Fay Blackman's eyes widened, then closed; the color drained from her face, and she put a hand to her fine high brow. "Oh God," she said.

Dooley sat and watched her. He saw her take a few deep breaths and then open her eyes, her hand dropping away. "Did Tommy do it?" she whispered.

Dooley shook his head. "No. Tommy's in a federal prison. Somebody else did it because they wanted something they thought Sally had."

This was even worse; Fay froze with a look of horror on her face, and when she spoke she could barely get the words out. "Something Tommy gave her."

"That's what I think."

"Oh God, that's horrible."

"Yes, it is."

Fay got out of her chair and went to the window. She stood there looking out at the lake and composing herself and finally she turned around. She had a new look on her face now, one that suggested a slowly kindling anger. "Tommy did the same thing with me. Tried to, anyway. He had me hide things for him, hold money, carry messages. He said nobody would expect a woman to do it. And he laughed off the risks. The ones he was shifting to me. That was one of the things that spoiled our marriage. Tommy liked to use people. Especially women."

"That's the impression I get, and it brings me to my question. I don't think Sally really had what they wanted. I'm not sure Tommy trusted her enough."

"I certainly couldn't say."

"So the question is, who else would he use? Who else would he leave something really valuable with? Something he had to keep safe but always have access to? Who else did he trust that much?"

For a second he thought she was going to faint; in a breathless voice she said, "He didn't give it to me. Is that what you think?"

The idea had crossed Dooley's mind, but he said, "No, I don't. But I'm wondering if you don't know who he did give it to."

She steadied and said, "I haven't had anything to do with him in thirteen years. I don't have any idea who Tommy's friends are anymore."

"I think the person I'm looking for is somebody he's known a long time. I don't think gangsters trust each other very much, so I don't think I'm looking for a gangster. I'm just guessing, but I think I'm looking for someone from the period in his life when he knew you. Somebody from the old neighborhood. Somebody you might know."

In the silence Elena arrived with the coffee on a tray. Fay told her to put it down on the table and waited until she was gone. "I don't know if I can help you," she said, looking out the window again. "That was a long time ago."

Dooley stood up. He still didn't want any coffee, and he'd done what he came to do. "You have my card," he said. "If you come up with any ideas, please give me a call. Thanks for your time."

She let him get to the door before she stopped him. "I can give you a couple of names," she said. "I don't even know if they're still alive. And they're just guesses."

"That's two more guesses than I have right now," Dooley said.

• • •

Dooley stopped at the first phone booth he saw and dialed Haggerty's number at Maxwell Street. He had to wait, watching cars zoom by on Sheridan Road, while somebody went looking for him, but in a minute or two he was there.

"What's up, Mike?"

"I need to look at your surveillance records for Tommy Spain. The ones you mentioned, when he got back from Mexico a couple of years ago."

There was a pause and Haggerty said, "You're still on that, are you?"

"I'm on it, all right. I'm close to busting it."

The silence this time went on until Dooley said, "Ed?"

"I'm still here. You got your supervisor on board with this?"

"Sure. Why wouldn't I?"

"I got a warning about you."

"You're shitting me. From who?"

"Brass. You don't need to know. But the word is, the Kotowski case is cleared, any further investigation is unauthorized. I was told to refuse any further cooperation with you."

"How'd they even know—Shit. I put you in my report, didn't I?"

"I guess you must have. I was told you've been filing unfounded complaints and in general making a nuisance of yourself. Basically, the idea is you're going off the rails."

It was Dooley's turn to stand in silence for a moment. "Ed. Do you think I'm off the rails?"

If anyone was taping this conversation, there was going to be a lot of empty space on the tape. After a while Haggerty said, "I don't think you're off the rails, Mike. I don't know that you're right about this case, but nobody's right about everything. I'm going to have to take a harder look at this before I can give you anything else, though, I'll be honest with you."

Dooley nearly hung up on him; he had the phone halfway to the cradle before he pulled it back. He blew out a deep breath and said, "OK, Ed. I understand. Give me a call." Then he hung up.

• • •

Dooley wasn't surprised when McCone called him into the office; he'd been waiting for it. "Sit down, Mike," McCone said, busying himself with papers. Dooley sat down and waited. McCone shuffled the papers for a few seconds more and finally looked at him. "I just talked to Donovan."

"Let me guess," said Dooley. "I've gone off the rails, making unfounded complaints and a general nuisance of myself."

McCone frowned. "That's not how he put it. Not in so many words."

"Whatever. Anyway, the Kotowski case is closed and any further investigation is unauthorized."

Suspicious, McCone said, "Who'd you talk to?"

"I didn't have to talk to anyone. I could see how the wind was blowing."

"Well. I want you to know I stuck up for you."

"Thanks."

"It's just tough to get a cleared case reopened. It takes a hell of a big surprise."

"I had one. They made it disappear."

"ERPS recovered it. They said you chose to disregard that."

"They switched lockets on me. Somebody went in there and tampered with it."

McCone glowered at him. Dooley could see him fighting, trying to decide whether his professional conscience or his professional comfort was more important to him. Dooley had always respected McCone, and he figured there was a chance the outcome was still in doubt. Finally McCone said, "If you can prove it, file another complaint. I'll back you up."

Dooley got to his feet. "I'll think about it. But I think they've got it pretty well stitched up."

"So what are you going to do?"

Dooley mused for a moment; for once he really wasn't sure. "Ask me tomorrow," he said.

• • •

The second Dooley walked into the kitchen he knew something was wrong. Usually when he got home the light over the sink was on and that was it; now the overhead light was on and he could see light from the living room coming down the hallway. Dooley closed the door to the garage softly behind him, listening. The line of work he was in, the frame of mind he was in, all the things that had happened to him recently, he wasn't going to assume somebody had forgotten to turn off the lights before going to bed.

The house was quiet. Dooley set his briefcase gently down on the floor and eased his .38 out of its holster. He held it at his side and walked slowly up the hall. The dining room was dark; Dooley paused to look around the door frame but saw nothing. He went on past the stairs to the living room.

Rose was sitting in the armchair by the window. She sat with her legs crossed; her robe had fallen open to reveal most of one pale, slightly lumpy thigh. She was looking at Dooley. "Don't shoot," she said. "I'm innocent."

Dooley put his gun away. He stared at his wife in amazement as she got slowly to her feet and came toward him. She was wearing her bathrobe and slippers but her face was made up with bright red lipstick, mascara, rouge, the works. Dooley had seen Rose with a light touch of lipstick, but never like this. It wasn't that she looked bad exactly, but it wasn't Rose; she looked like a stranger. The smell got to him before she did; the smell was explained by the bottle of Jameson's and the empty glass stitting on the table by the lamp. Rose stopped a yard away and folded her arms. She said, "Welcome home, officer. What's the matter, no informants to interrogate tonight?"

Dooley thought to himself, here we go. "You're drunk," he said.

"Yeah. So what ? Why should you have all the fun?"

Dooley had been tired when he walked in the door; now with the alarm ebbing he was about to drop. He said, "I'm going to go upstairs and put a few things away. Then I'll come down and we'll talk." He started to turn away and stopped to add, "Pour me a drink, will you?"

Upstairs he locked away his star and the .38 and took off his jacket. He stood for a moment rubbing his face and then went back downstairs. He found Rose sitting in the chair again. She had put a glass on the coffee table in front of the couch, with ice cubes in it, and poured enough whiskey over them to knock Dooley out. She had refilled her glass too; two inches of whiskey, no ice. Dooley sank onto the couch. "You're going to be sick," he said.

"Well, that's my business."

He took a drink of whiskey. He felt ashamed; he felt embarrassed. "Rose," he said.

"That's me. Your wife. Remember?"

"I'm sorry, Rose."

"Like what you see?" She lifted her chin like a fashion model and made a flourish with her hands, spilling a little whiskey. "I did it for you."

"You didn't have to. I like the way you look."

"Not quite enough, apparently."

"Rose."

"I spent eighty dollars on a new dress today, too. And then when I got it home and put it on I looked at myself in the mirror and cried."

"I'm sorry."

"Me too. I'm just feeling sorry for myself, I know. I'll get over it." She put the glass to her lips.

"Dammit." Dooley came up off the couch and was across the room in two strides. He tore the glass out of her hand, spilling whiskey on her robe. He slammed the glass down on the coffee table, spilling more. "That's enough."

Rose was giving him a sullen look. Under the makeup it looked a little comical, but Dooley didn't feel like laughing. "Michael, how could you do this to me?" she said.

"I don't know."

"How could you do it to me *now*?" Her look had changed; now she looked desolate. Dooley sat on the edge of the coffee table facing her. "I don't know, Rose. I guess I did it because I'm weak."

"Don't lie to me, Michael Dooley. You're the strongest man I know."

Dooley ran through all the honest answers he could give: I did it because I was mad at you; I did it because I was feeling sorry for myself, I did it because she is so wonderful. He said, "I didn't do it to hurt you. I just lost my head. First time in twenty-five years, Rose. I lost my head. It happened once. One time. Now it's over." He drank whiskey, grimaced and set the glass down beside hers.

There was a long silence while Dooley stared at the rug. "Is she pretty?" said Rose.

This is your punishment, Dooley thought, take it like a man. "Sure."

"How old is she?"

"She's twenty-nine."

"I guess that explains it, then. Men are like that, aren't they?"

Dooley looked up at his wife. "I don't know what men are like.

I only know about me. She's good-looking and she made a play for me. That's what happened."

Rose was killing him with that forlorn look. "It's all over for me, isn't it? You're never going to look at me and want me again, are you?"

"That's not true."

"I have a mirror, Michael. I know what I look like now."

"Rose. Stop it."

"Of course, you're not exactly Tyrone Power anymore yourself."

"I know that."

"The difference is, you don't have to be. You just need to *have* power. Young women love power, don't they? No young man is ever going to want to sleep with me, ever again, but you, a big tough copper, you could have just about any woman you want, couldn't you?"

"I don't want anybody else, Rose. I just want to make it up to you."

"Well, good for you, Michael Dooley. I'm glad your conscience is bothering you. I don't suppose you'll let that spoil the memories, though, will you?"

Dooley had to shut up because he knew he deserved every word of it. As he looked at his wife her tears started to come, welling up and rolling down her cheeks, taking little trails of mascara with them, and then her eyes were squeezed shut and she put her hands to her face and twisted on the armchair, drawing her legs up, and she was sobbing.

Two in one week, Dooley thought, rising slowly, wearily to his feet. You fucked everything else up but you got really good at making women cry.

Dooley cleared the glasses and the bottle and turned out all the lights while Rose's sobs grew quieter and less frequent. It had been years since he had carried her in his arms, but he wasn't going to leave her here. He got his arms under her neck and her knees and strained. She was heavy but she didn't fight him and he made for the stairs, staggering just a little. He had to rest on the landing but he made it; he dumped her on the bed a little harder than he would have liked but he was beat. He stripped to his underwear and lay down beside his wife and put his arms around her and waited for her to go to sleep.

He felt bad. Dooley felt like hell tonight.

Forty

IT RAINED OVER the weekend, just as it had rained on most of the weekends in the early part of the summer, but this time it didn't seem like an injustice. It was just the summer passing away. On Saturday morning Dooley nursed his wife through a hangover, bringing her coffee and toast in bed, bringing her cold cream and Kleenexes so she could clean her face, sitting with her while she dozed, holding her hand. They didn't mention what they had talked about the night before. Frank asked if she was OK and Dooley told him she was going through a rough time, with Kevin overseas and all; he wondered if the kid had heard anything the night before but it didn't seem as if he had.

Dooley worked all through the weekend. On Saturday the Puerto Ricans rioted on Division Street and three cops were hurt; Dooley missed the riot but caught a stabbing in an Uptown bar, one drunk Indian slicing up another one who bled to death on the floor before an ambulance got there. On Sunday he and Olson tracked witnesses through the rain, nobody wanting to talk about a shooting that happened in front of twenty-three people at a dance in a rented hall on Southport at one o'clock Sunday morning.

The newspapers brought no relief. Thirty thousand Navy personnel were going to be pulled out of Viet Nam but there was no word about the Marines. U Thant was saying a solution might be in sight, but the B-52s had started bombing the North again. On the West Side a man had fired a .32 into a protest march and hit a Negro boy in the head; the boy was in critical condition. The man who fired the gun was black, too. Nothing made sense anymore.

The Cubs were three and a half games behind the Mets and Frank was in mourning.

• • •

"Man, they're serious, aren't they?" said Olson.

"Yeah. They are. They don't want the case reopened." Dooley sawed at his Salisbury steak. He should have known better; by this time in the evening, even in a decent place, the Special of the Day had been sitting around for a while and wasn't so special anymore. "All they need is one crooked copper with access to ERPS. And you can bet they've got more than one."

"So what happens if you pursue the complaint?"

"Probably not a lot. It just goes nowhere. And if I go on investigating, my reports go nowhere. The Chief of Detectives has ruled on it. I'd have to come up with another break like the locket, and this time make a hell of a lot of noise about it, so if they try and bury it again somebody raises a stink. I'd have to take it to the papers or something, I don't know.'

Olson watched him eat for a moment. "You keep saying 'I.' Remember, I'm here, too."

"OK. We'd have to take it to the papers. But first we'd have to come up with something. And I don't know if there's anything else out there."

They both picked at their food. Dooley was tired of thinking about it.

Olson looked up from his plate. "Run one thing by me again. Why did she call the bar?"

Shrugging, Dooley said, "I got two different stories. According to Swallow, she had a tape she stole from Spain and wanted to sell. According to Gallo, she knew about a snitch and was willing to rat on him. Either one of those could be true, or both. Or neither, what the hell."

Olson worked on it in silence for a while. "Seems to me if we knew who she said the snitch was, we'd have somebody with a motive."

"Except why did they torture her? If they just wanted to shut her up."

"We got a little glimpse of D'Andrea at play that night. D'Andrea at work might do all that to Sally just for the fun of it, along with shutting her up."

"That could be."

"Maybe we need to lean on Gallo again. Or that bartender. Find a way to get at them. I don't know, that phone call always bothered me."

Dooley washed down a mouthful with coffee. "Me too," he said, frowning.

• • •

Dooley woke up just before dawn, the bedroom just starting to take shape in the pale light, and all of a sudden he knew. Sometimes it happened: your mind worked on it while you were asleep and then when it was solved you woke up. Dooley wondered why it had taken so long for him to figure it out. Never make assumptions, they told you on day one at detective school, and here Dooley had made a huge one and it had been misleading him for weeks, months even. Twenty years on the job and still showing signs of stupidity; Dooley amazed himself sometimes.

He got up even though he hadn't had nearly enough sleep and got dressed and went down to the kitchen. He made coffee and thought about his day. The mind was an amazing thing: here it had thrown up an answer for him on a day he happened to have off. He'd promised to go help Rob on a job and he'd promised Frank he'd play ball with him, but he figured he could beg off both of those; he had a feeling of urgency about this one. He went back up to the bedroom and grabbed his tie and jacket and star and the .38. Rose stirred in the bed and he bent to kiss her. "What time is it?" she murmured.

"Too early. Don't get up. I have to go see somebody. About a case." He lingered for a moment, holding her warm hand, sitting there hurting with guilt and love and resentment all mixed up. Then he went downstairs and got ready to go. It was six o'clock and he figured Rob would be up; he called and begged off, pleading police business. Rob was used to that and wished him luck. Dooley left a note on the kitchen table: *Gone to Wisconsin. Back this afternoon. Frank, I'll try to be back in time to play ball.*

He checked the map he kept in the car and took off. He caught the expressway at Touhy and headed north. There was a little of the anticipation he usually felt at the start of a long trip but today it was overshadowed by other things. Dooley took the family to Wisconsin for a few days just about every year, so it was a familiar drive for him. Wisconsin was full of retired Chicago cops and Dooley had thought about it himself, finding a house on a lake somewhere, maybe a little bar to invest in.

He put the news on the radio. Nixon was saying more troops were coming home from Viet Nam soon; Dooley would believe it when he saw it. A cop had been shot answering a call in the projects; he was expected to live. The Cubs had lost in Montreal and were four and a half out. The Cubs were dead, gone, history. Dooley turned off the radio.

He pushed through Milwaukee without too much trouble and got on 57 going north. Summer was not officially over until the twenty-first but to Dooley it felt like fall; there was no change in the leaves yet but the hay was all cut, the signs out by the roadside.

Apples for sale—Pick your own. Dooley liked the Wisconsin landscape; it looked just like every city guy's idea of the countryside, with green rolling hills and red barns and white farmhouses. West of Sheboygan he turned off, checked the map, and made his way along county roads to Elkhart Lake.

Dooley had never been there, but it was like a lot of Wisconsin resort towns, cottages and a few hotels clustered around a lake, the town strung out along a main street with a couple of bars, a little grocery store, antique shops, and a church or two. Dooley hadn't been sure how to find where he was going, but it turned out to be simple: he just followed the signs to *Radke's.* The road wound through the woods with glimpses of water shimmering below, nice-looking homes hidden in the trees. Dooley pulled into a gravel parking lot in front of the hotel.

It was a big ramshackle frame structure painted a dull green, with a veranda all around on the ground level and peaks and turrets and rows of windows with shutters. It was a big place and it would take a lot of upkeep, but if they had managed to fill it during the summer it would probably pay for a quiet winter. A sign on the veranda roof said *Radke's Resort Since 1927.*

Dooley sat in the car for a moment thinking about his approach. He got out of the car but instead of going up the steps onto the porch he headed to the right around the end of the building, just strolling with his hands in his pockets like a man looking at the property. Behind the hotel there was a clearing with some beat-up playground equipment and a few picnic tables, and then the land sloped down through trees to a beach. A dock jutted out into the water but there was nothing tied up there. There was nobody in sight; Labor Day had come and gone and everyone was back in school, back at work. It gave Dooley a melancholy feeling, the good times over and winter ahead.

He found Radke by a tool shed at the business end of the property, a hundred yards through the trees from the hotel, a garage and a couple of sheds hidden from view behind a line of brush. Radke was on his knees by a little John Deere riding mower, poking at the engine with a monkey wrench. He looked up when he heard Dooley's footsteps, looked back at the engine, snapped his head up again and froze. "Morning," said Dooley.

Radke stood up like a man whose joints were giving him trouble, wiping his grease-stained fingers on his overalls. "Morning," he said. He looked a little worse than Dooley remembered him, the long horse face showing some strain. "What can I do for you?"

"What's wrong with this thing?" Dooley said, nodding at the mower. He still had his hands in his pockets, the city slicker in a suit, slumming with the locals. He had a cold hard feeling in his guts but he put a smile on his face; he felt like a cat with a mouse in its paws.

Radke said, "It's a piece of shit, that's what's wrong with it." He tossed the wrench on the ground. "What do you want?" The face he turned to Dooley showed he knew exactly what Dooley was here for.

Dooley held the smile for a moment, amiable and relaxed, propping him up for the haymaker. "I want you to tell me about a couple of phone calls you made back on May thirtieth and thirty-first." He let the smile fade.

Radke pulled a rag out of a pocket of the overalls and worked on his fingers in silence for a few seconds. "That was a long time ago," he said, but without much conviction. "How do you expect me to remember?"

Dooley was guessing, but he knew it was a damn good guess, the only possible guess. "You called a bar named Angelo's in Melrose Park, Illinois. I don't know who you talked to, but I can guess what you talked about."

Dooley stood listening to birdcalls in the trees, the faint sound of a motorboat in the distance. He was prepared to hammer at Radke, meet the bluff, chip away at the wall, but all of a sudden

Radke caved in. He turned, staggered a little, and sank onto the seat of the mower, lowering himself with a hand on the steering wheel. "I didn't know they were gonna kill her," he said.

Dooley had to take a deep breath at that. He exhaled and said, "What did you think they were going to do, give her an award?"

Radke looked up at him with pain in his eyes. "I thought they'd maybe slap her around a bit, take back whatever it was she ran off with. She was a woman. I didn't think they'd kill her."

"They'd kill the fucking Pope if he held out on them," Dooley said. He watched Radke shake his head a couple of times and look up at him, whipped. Dooley said, "What did she do, slap you?"

Radke shot him a look of pure malice but Dooley knew where the malice came from: shame. Radke's head dipped back down and he said, "She led me on. Friendly as could be, waggling her ass around here in her little short pants, and then when I try to grab a little of what she was advertising she gets all—indignant. You know."

"I can imagine." Dooley said. With as much contempt as he could muster, he said, "How much did you get for her?"

Radke didn't look at him this time. In a strangled voice he said, "Not nearly enough."

"No, it never is, is it?" Dooley wanted to knock Radke off the seat, take the wrench to him, break his long nose in a couple of places. "You stole from her, too, didn't you? After she was dead. You went through her things." Dooley was guessing, but again he knew it was a good one. "How much did you get out of that?"

"A couple of thousand." Radke said it to the ground, barely loud enough for Dooley to hear. "I figured she wasn't gonna need it."

"No, I guess not. Is there any left?"

Radke shook his head. "I spent it all already."

"Well, I hope you had fun with it."

Radke looked up at him with big pleading eyes. "You tell Vickie yet?"

Jesus, Dooley thought. "That's not your biggest worry," he said. "Believe it or not. Your biggest worry is you're an accessory to murder."

Now Radke was holding up his hands, pleading. "I swear to God I didn't know they were gonna kill her."

"Doesn't make any difference. Your only chance is to cut a deal, and that means telling me everything. Every single fucking thing."

Dooley had hooked him, gaffed him, hauled him into the boat. "What do you need to know?"

"How did you know who to call?"

Radke looked off through the trees and said, "I knew Ronnie Gallo because of my father. This place used to be pretty popular with the hoods from Chicago. In the old days all the resorts had gambling. Dive down to the bottom of that lake, you'll find all the slot machines they threw in when they closed it all down. My old man and Ronnie's father got to be friends. And when he was a kid Ronnie would spend summers up here, and we used to hang around together. And we kept in touch. I had his number, at the bar, and I called up and asked for him."

Out of all the places in the country she could have run to, thought Dooley, she had to run here. "And what did you tell him?"

"The first time I called he wasn't there, but I left a message. I said tell him if anybody was interested I could say where Sally Kotowski was. But it would cost them. I said I'd call back the next day."

Dooley waited a couple of seconds. "So you did."

"Yeah. And Ronnie was there, and he said he got the message and there were some people who were really interested, and they were willing to pay. He said they'd call me if I gave them a number where they could talk business. I gave him the number over at the Legion Hall and a time to call."

Dooley was losing patience with the pauses, the head-shaking. "And what happened?"

Radke was through looking to Dooley for anything; he told the rest of it in a mumble, with his eyes on the ground. "I told them drive up to Sheboygan and call me with a number where I could reach them. They called a couple of days later, they were at a motel. Then when she went out the next night I called and told them to drive over here and meet me down the road a ways. I slipped out and met them and showed them where to wait for her on her way back from the bar. They gave me a hundred bucks."

Dooley wanted to vomit. He said, "A hundred bucks."

"Don't get started. I know I did a bad thing."

"No, I won't get started. I'll let the prosecutor do that."

"I guess I deserve it."

Dooley opened his mouth to tell him what he deserved was a slug in the head but thought better of it. He had a decision to make: he was freelancing here where he had no jurisdiction, but he'd just gotten an admission that blew the recorded version of events out of the water. There was no way he could just drive away from this. "You're going to need to come with me and make a statement," Dooley said. He was thinking about how to locate the sheriff or the nearest State Patrol office; he wanted witnesses, a stenographer, the works.

Radke looked up then, and Dooley made sure there wasn't anything in his face that might give the man hope. "OK," said Radke quietly. He stood up. "Lemme go clean up a little."

Dooley followed him back toward the hotel. "Is your wife here?" he said.

"She's around somewhere. Let me talk to her, OK?"

"That's fine with me."

"What do I tell her? You taking me to jail?"

"Tell her you'll be gone for a few hours." Dooley wasn't sure how things were going to go. They went up on the porch and Radke turned at the door and said, "Do you have to come in with me?"

Dooley hesitated; he wasn't sure he wanted to watch the Radkes' marriage go up in flames, but there were rules you followed. "Yeah, I'm afraid I do," he said.

Radke shrugged and pulled open the screen door. Inside, the lodge was cool and dim. They went through a big empty pine-paneled hall with a fireplace at one end toward a counter with pigeonholes behind it. Radke said, "I think she's back in the office." He lifted a flap at the end of the counter and went through a door, moving slowly. Dooley edged along the counter just close enough to hear whatever was going to get said. He stood with his hands in his pockets, looking around the big hall and thinking it was too bad; it looked like a nice place to spend a week with the family.

A door at the far end of the room opened and Victoria Radke came through it. She stopped dead when she saw Dooley and they stared at each other for a brief moment. In the office behind him Dooley heard what might have been a drawer sliding gently open. He started moving, fast. He ducked under the flap at the end of the counter and made it to the open door of the office just in time to see Radke put the revolver to his temple. Radke looked right at him with big melancholy eyes and Dooley drew breath but his shout was drowned out by the big bang as the shot punched a hole in Radke's head. The light went out in the eyes and Radke toppled off the chair.

"You son of a *bitch!*" Dooley yelled. He stood in shock for a couple of seconds and then reached for the doorknob, because he heard footsteps coming rapidly across the polished floor and he didn't want Victoria Radke to see the mess her husband had made of the office.

Forty-one

"I KNOW I fucked it up. About as bad as it can be fucked up. I should have seen the signs. But I didn't." Dooley had refused to sit down and was leaning on McCone's desk. He was in the worst hurry of his life; he had broken all the traffic laws there were coming back from Wisconsin after finally extricating himself from several hours' worth of explanations to the Sheboygan County Sheriff's Department and the Wisconsin State Patrol. It was close to ten o'clock at night and Dooley was straining at the leash.

McCone threw up his hands. "I don't know what you can do. With Radke dead, you've got nothing."

"I know. The question is, what can I salvage? There's only one chance, and that is to go after Gallo, fast, and hope I can trick him into an admission before he finds out Radke's dead. That means it's a matter of hours, maybe minutes. The radio could have it any time. If it hits tomorrow's papers, we're cooked. It'll be in the Milwaukee papers for sure, and since I was involved, it could get out here."

"There's nobody else who can back up what he told you? The wife maybe?"

"Christ, he never told her. That's why he killed himself, because he was so ashamed. She's a fucking basket case now anyway. I'm afraid it's just me."

McCone was giving him the evil eye and Dooley thought he'd lost him. McCone said, "Mike, swear to me this is all on the level."

Dooley just gaped at him. "Jesus Christ, McCone. I thought you knew me better than that."

"I'm just asking because I've seen officers let cases become crusades and do things that were ill-advised."

"Give me a shot at Gallo. If I can break him it'll bust things open. You can watch me, for Christ's sake. But we have to go get him fast."

McCone glared for a moment longer and said, "All right. Go get him. I can't give you any help. Everybody's out on the street. You know where to find him?"

Dooley was already moving toward the door. "I know where to look."

• • •

Dooley had to guess, and he knew his first guess had to be good; if word got out that the cops were looking for Gallo, Gallo would get hard to find instantly. Dooley figured that Gallo's work day was in full swing by now and he wouldn't be wasting time at the social club on Grand Avenue; his best guess was the bar in Melrose Park. Dooley took thirty seconds to call home and tell Rose he was OK, just working, and then he jumped in his car and went.

The problem was, in Melrose Park Dooley had all the legal authority of a kid with a tin badge out of a Cracker-Jack box. Normally he would have asked for help from the Melrose Park cops, but he was not too sure about that department; with all the mobsters that lived in their town, right or wrong the feeling was that they were all on the pad. He could go to the sheriff's police and have them pinch Gallo and then turn him over, but that would take all night; they would want a warrant and Dooley wasn't going to waste time with judges tonight. The best thing would be to spot Gallo somewhere in the city, but that was just dreaming. If he found Gallo at the bar, he was going to have to make something up.

It was close to eleven by the time he walked into Angelo's, and the place was about half full. Molinari was behind the bar, and Dooley didn't waste any time. He stalked down the bar and leaned over it to crook a finger at the old man. "What the hell you want now?" Molinari said.

"Where's Gallo?"

"How the hell should I know?"

"You got an emergency. How do you contact your owner?"

"What's the emergency?"

"Somebody's about to bust up his bar."

Molinari looked a little skeptical, but not for long; the look on Dooley's face planted just enough doubt in his mind. "I'll see if I can find him," he said. He stepped out from behind the bar, making for a hallway at the rear. Dooley watched him for a couple of seconds and then followed; he wasn't going to be had for the second time that day. There were a lot of hostile eyes on him but he didn't care. Molinari looked over his shoulder and said, "Wait at the bar."

"He's back there, isn't he?"

"I said wait at the bar." Molinari tried to stop him but Dooley brushed past and went down the hall. The first two doors were restrooms; Dooley opened the third without knocking.

Gallo looked up from his desk with an angry glare. Dooley had caught him in mid-count, licking his thumb with a stack of bills in his left hand and a dozen or so bundles on the desk, with rubber bands around them. "What the fuck?" Gallo said. There was a second man across the desk from him, a leather-faced old villain in a black suit jacket whose hand started inside his jacket as he twisted on the chair.

Dooley knew he was on thin ice any way he looked at it, legally and otherwise, but sometimes the best thing to do on thin ice was skate like hell. "You're under arrest," he said. He dug out his star and flashed it at the second man, which stopped the movement of his hand.

"What the hell for?" barked Gallo.

"You're wanted for questioning in the murder of Sally Kotowski. You coming quietly, or does it have to get ugly?"

Behind Dooley, Molinari said, "I tried to stop him, Ronnie."

Dooley knew he had big trouble if anyone got a notion to resist, but he didn't care; he was running on adrenaline and outrage. Gallo said, "You can't arrest me here."

"The hell I can't. I'm looking at the proceeds of an illegal enterprise right now. I can claim extraterritorial jurisdiction under the gambling statutes." It was pure horseshit but Dooley didn't think Gallo was much of a lawyer. The scary part was how seriously the old bruiser was going to take his role as Wells Fargo guard; he still had his hand inside his jacket. Dooley looked him in the eye and said, "What are you gonna do, shoot a cop? I don't give a damn about the money. Keep your hands where I can see 'em."

The hand slid out of the jacket. Gallo stared at Dooley for a moment longer and said, "You're out of your mind."

"You said it," said Dooley. "That makes it a bad idea to cross me. Now move your ass."

• • •

In the interview room Gallo sat examining a thumbnail, looking like a man in the dentist's waiting room who has read all the magazines. When McCone came in Dooley shut the door behind him and sat down across from Gallo. McCone walked around behind Gallo and leaned on the wall. "OK," said Dooley, "you know why you're here."

"Like hell I do." Gallo looked up from his thumb, but he didn't look particularly concerned.

"You're here because I didn't like the answers you gave me the last time I talked to you, so I'm going to give you a chance to give me the right ones."

"What, like I flunked a test?"

"That's it. It's the stay out of jail test."

"OK, so what are you charging me with?"

"Nothing, so far. Lie to me again and we'll try on obstruction of justice and accessory to murder just for a start, see how they fit."

Gallo snickered, a little contemptuous sound. "You're fuckin' hallucinating," Gallo said.

"On May thirty-first you received a phone call from Elkhart Lake, Wisconsin. Who did you talk to?"

Gallo rolled his eyes. "Christ, not this again. I told you already. I talked to that broad, that Sally girl that got killed later. I fuckin' told you all about it."

"You are prepared to swear that you spoke with Sally Kotowski on the telephone on May thirty-first of this year?"

"I couldn't swear about the day. That was your idea. But I talked to her, yeah."

Dooley couldn't see any point in beating around the bush any longer. "Do you know a man named Robert Radke, residing in Elkhart Lake, Wisconsin?"

Dooley always loved this moment, when their eyes locked onto his and he could see they knew he had them. Gallo had little weasel eyes that didn't give much away, but there was no way he could hide his sudden spike in attention. Dooley leaned back on his chair, allowing himself the very faintest of smiles. "Do you want me to repeat the question?" he said after a few seconds had gone by.

Gallo's look had gone totally blank. He looked at his thumbnail again, worked at it with a callused fingertip. "I ain't saying another word," he said. "Not without my lawyer here."

"You want a lawyer, do you? We're to that stage already? You haven't even heard what Radke told us yet."

Gallo gave Dooley a bored look. "I want my lawyer."

"Fine. But you get him in here, we're past the point when we can work something out. You get your lawyer in here, what's he going to tell you? Keep your mouth shut. You keep your mouth shut, there's nothing we can do. Then we call in the State's Attorney and they take a look at a whole menu of charges they can bring. I mean, you helped kill the girl, Ronnie. That's serious jail time. You talk to me, maybe it doesn't get to that stage."

Gallo had to be going through a bad moment; even hoods were human. But Gallo was a pro, and he knew how it went. "I want my fucking lawyer," he said.

• • •

"We lost," said Dooley. He and McCone were huddled in McCone's office. "He called my bluff."

"You're giving up awful easy, aren't you?"

"He gets a lawyer in here, it'll go just like I said. He'll shut up and before I can get anything out of him, the lawyer will get word that Radke's dead. It's over." Dooley wanted to throw something, put his fist through the wall. He had gambled on being able to rattle Gallo and lost. "I shot my wad in there. I've got nothing left."

McCone scratched at his neck, rubbed his eyes. He was technically off duty now; the first watch sergeant had taken over. Dooley could tell he was wishing he'd made his escape before Gallo had come in. McCone said, "The faster you get the lawyer in here, the better chance you got. Get somebody in here, lay out what Radke told you, see if you can get him to cut a deal before morning. As long as he doesn't know Radke's dead, you got a chance."

"Right." Dooley went back to the interview room. Gallo had his eyes closed, head resting on his fist. "Who's your lawyer?" Dooley said.

Gallo opened his eyes. "Jerry Rodkin."

"Who else?" said Dooley.

• • •

Dooley didn't know how a man could look as good as Jerome Rodkin did at two o'clock in the morning. He looked as if he had just come from the barber shop by way of his tailor's. "Why is my client in here?" he said, shooting his cuffs and frowning faintly, as if perplexed by a slight delay in the dinner service.

"Because a man in Wisconsin finally stood up and told the truth." Dooley had brought in another chair for Rodkin and the three of them were sitting at the table like housewives in the kitchen. "Your client has been implicated in the killing of Sally Kotowski."

"Who's the man in Wisconsin?"

"Robert Radke." Dooley knew he couldn't hide it; he could only hope that he could break Gallo down before his lawyer found out Radke was history.

"What's his allegation?"

"He spoke to your client regarding the whereabouts of a woman who was subsequently abducted and murdered. He sold her out, and your client passed the message." Dooley turned to Gallo and said, "He spilled it all, Ronnie. How he knew you as a kid, the whole thing. How he called you and sold you Sally Kotowski for a hundred bucks. That's good for accessory right there. How much worse it gets depends on how much you're willing to say up on the witness stand. Finger the killers for me and I'll fight for you with the State's Attorney."

Gallo looked at Rodkin but it was a foregone conclusion. Rodkin gave a very slight shake of the head, and Gallo shrugged and said nothing.

"Is Radke here?" said the lawyer in a tone of idle curiosity.

"He's in Wisconsin, in the custody of the Sheboygan County Sheriff's Department."

"I assume you took a statement from him."

"Sure."

"Can I see it?"

Dooley knew this was the beginning of the end. "It's being retyped."

"When can I see it?"

"When it's ready."

Rodkin gave him a bland look. "I'll want to review it before we even begin to discuss these allegations."

"Suit yourself." Dooley got up and left the room. He knew it was over.

• • •

It was nearly dawn again when Dooley got home. He had put in twenty-four hours straight, on his day off, and he would never be paid a dime for it because none of it was authorized. He had gone through the motions of charging and processing Gallo, only to see him walk out immediately on bail; Rodkin had peeled the bond money off a roll he pulled out of a pocket. The charges had nothing to back them up but Dooley's word and would be thrown out instantly when they got to a grand jury.

Dooley pulled into his garage but instead of going inside he walked out and stood in his driveway, looking into the lightening eastern sky. He was past exhaustion and into light-headedness; he couldn't believe he hadn't slept since he had gotten up to drive to Wisconsin. It seemed like a month ago. He had seen a man blow his brains out; that was yesterday but it all seemed like the same day.

Dooley was through; he was done with the Kotowski case. It was over, and the bad guys had won again. Dooley had given it a shot but fucked it up, and it was time to toss in a bad hand. Hell with it, he thought. He went back in, closed the garage door, and went into the house. Rose woke up when he came into the bedroom and just watched him as he put away his gun and his star; he knew what she was wondering. He had fucked up his case, fucked up his marriage, fucked up everything. He got into bed and kissed Rose and passed out.

He woke up in daylight; his watch said it was nearly two o'clock. The house was quiet and Dooley lay there in the bed listening to the occasional passing car outside and not much else. He didn't want to get up. He was off again today but had nothing he wanted to do. Dooley just wanted to be left alone for a while, a couple of years, maybe. He heard the doorbell ring.

He listened for Rose's footsteps downstairs but didn't hear them; instead he heard footsteps outside, going down the walk away from the door. Dooley got up and went to the window. He parted the curtains in time to see a car pull away from the curb in front of his house, a car he didn't recognize. Dooley thought for a moment and then put on his bathrobe and went downstairs. He went to the front door and opened it. Sure enough, there was a manila envelope sitting there inside the screen door. Dooley picked it up and closed the door.

His name was written on the envelope and in the upper left corner the words *City of Chicago Department of Police* were printed. Dooley opened it and pulled out a thin sheaf of papers just far enough to see the words *Intelligence Division*.

Haggerty. Dooley shook his head. He went back upstairs and locked the envelope in the drawer with his gun and star. He was through; it was all over.

He got dressed and went back downstairs. In the kitchen he made himself some coffee and glanced at the paper: Nixon had said it was time to end the war and 35,000 troops were coming home. Make it fast, thought Dooley.

He ate some toast and went to turn on the TV, something he almost never did. The Cubs were playing on channel nine. They were at home against the Phillies, and the camera showed mostly empty stands. On the field everyone was going through the motions. That was about what Dooley felt like doing, so he sat down to watch, and he was still sitting there when Frank came home from school.

Frank stood in the doorway looking at the TV screen with a glum look on his face. "What are you watching those bums for?" he said.

"That's a very good question. Because they're more interesting than the wallpaper, I guess. But it's close."

"I hate them."

"Boy, that's a switch."

Frank dumped his books on the coffee table and flopped beside Dooley on the couch. "How could they blow it like that?"

"It's a tough game. It keeps you humble. And sometimes the other guys just beat you."

"They were in first place the whole year. From Opening Day on. Till a week ago."

"They got worn out."

"They folded, that's what happened. They choked."

Dooley had to laugh a little. "Hey, it was fun while it lasted." They sat in silence for a while, watching. Jenkins was pitching, going for a twentieth win that wouldn't mean a damn thing now. Dooley was in a strange mood; it wasn't often he was content to just sit and do nothing. He realized that for the first time in a long time he was glad his boy was there with him. He looked over and was startled to see a glint of moisture at the corner of Frank's eye. Hastily Frank wiped it away and his face settled into a scowl.

Dooley was amazed. "Frank, it's just a game. Nobody died."

"I thought they were going to do it. This was their year." He was working hard to control his voice.

"So did I. We'll get over it." Frank sat there glaring at the TV, and suddenly Dooley envied him with a pang so sharp it nearly took his breath away. Dooley could just remember a time in his own life when losing a baseball game was the worst thing that could happen, and now all he wanted was to protect his boy somehow from all the things ahead of him that were going to be a lot worse than seeing a ball club go down in flames. He reached over and put a hand on Frank's shoulder. "Hell with 'em. Let's go hit the ball around a little. Break a few windows, maybe."

Frank said nothing, didn't move, and Dooley thought he was about to get the brush-off. "OK," said Frank. "But if you break a window, that's your problem. I'm taking off."

• • •

Rose was making dinner when they got home. Dooley hadn't talked to her since before his trip. He kissed her on the cheek and she gave him a quizzical look. "So what's in Wisconsin?" she said, a little timidly, as if she didn't really want to know.

"A witness. But it turns out he's dead. Big waste of time. Last night, that was a waste of time too. Sometimes the big ones get away." She saw that was all he was going to say by way of explanation and went back to her vegetables; Dooley went to take a shower.

The phone rang as he was coming down the stairs. He picked it up in the hall.

"Mike?" a man said.

"Yeah."

"This is Grady. You called about the Corvette?" The voice was a little on the high side, but gravelly.

Dooley froze; he had to think for a second who he was talking to. "Yeah. Johnny Puig gave me your name."

"Right. OK, you interested in talking to me?"

Dooley had to stand there and think about it. A lot of things went through his mind. He wanted to tell the man it was all over and he was done with it; he had written it all off. He wanted to tell him he didn't give a damn about whatever he had to say. He stood there thinking about it and finally he said, "Sure. But I pick the place."

Forty-two

AL'S TAP WAS a square little building on Central a couple of blocks south of Lawrence, the type of establishment you could miss if you were going over thirty miles an hour. Dooley's brother-in-law Ted had taken him there once; Dooley had chosen it because it was boring. It was an old-fashioned neighborhood tavern in a nice safe neighborhood, with a long sturdy bar with ranks of bottles behind it and chairs and tables like you might find in somebody's kitchen, all chrome and plastic. There was a TV on a high shelf at the end of the bar and it looked like *Hawaii Five-0* was winding up; it was getting close to ten.

Dooley sat at the end of the bar, facing the door to keep an eye on the comings and goings. He ordered a beer and settled in to wait, nursing it. There was a decent crowd, some watching TV and some talking. People came and went. Three lone men came in but none of them seemed to be looking for anyone, and they all joined parties already there. On the TV the news came on after a spate of commercials, with Nixon leading it off, saying something Dooley couldn't hear.

"You Mike?"

The man at Dooley's elbow was maybe fifty years old and had not had an easy half-century. He'd spent a lot of it in the sun and a lot of it working with his hands, and it had cost him a couple of teeth and etched some lines in his face. He had dark, slightly watery eyes that didn't look like they missed a lot.

"Yeah. I thought you said you'd be in a red shirt." Dooley's alarm bells were going off; he'd thought he'd been watching pretty carefully but he hadn't spotted this man.

"You think I'm nuts?" the man said. "I had to watch you for a while before I was gonna give away my position."

"How'd you know me?"

"You're the only guy in here that looks like a cop."

"OK. So you're Grady."

"That's me." He settled onto the empty stool next to Dooley, bottle in hand, looking at the TV. "Tricky Dick. Something about that guy, I don't know. I don't trust him." He drank beer. "Puig said you're clean. I hope to God he's right. I'm taking my life in my hands talking to you."

"Well, you must have believed him. You're here."

"I don't know why I believed him. I guess I'm just desperate."

"It's not too late to walk out. I don't have the slightest idea who you are."

"Puig didn't tell you, huh?"

"Nope."

Grady drank more beer and set the bottle down. "I'm the guy that drives the dice game around."

"What do you mean?"

Grady laughed softly. "You don't know about the dice game? I guess they keep it pretty quiet. See, there's a big craps game. I mean, there's a lot of games, all over. But this is a big one. This is a big moneymaker for the Outfit. This is where the high rollers play. And the high rollers don't like getting busted. You play in one place a few times, word gets around. So a few years ago the guys that run the game got the idea of putting it on wheels."

"On wheels?"

"Yeah. First it was a bus. An old school bus. Now it's a semi. They've got a custom trailer, air-conditioned and everything, with a built-in bar, bathroom, the works. No windows to see in, completely secure. They load up the truck with gamblers and take off."

"You're kidding me."

"Nope. Drive down to Peoria and back, wherever. Drive all night, and all the time they're shooting craps back there. Morning comes, you drop them all off back at the parking lot."

"Unbelievable."

"Swear to God. And I'm the guy who drives."

Dooley shook his head. "How'd you get that job?"

Grady laughed again, a worn-out mirthless laugh. "Long story, but basically, the Outfit owns me. Body and soul."

"How's that?"

"I got in over my head. Long time ago. I gambled, what else? And I didn't know how to stop, and I lost my fucking shirt, and borrowed from their God damn sharks, and couldn't pay. And then one day I realized I was at that point."

"What point?"

"Where you realize they own you. You realize you got no choices left. You will never, and I mean never, be able to pay what you owe, because they're counting up the juice on the juice by this point, and you could work for the next five hundred years and never pay them off. And so your choices boil down to number one, run away and hope like hell they never find you, or number two, you say OK, guys, I'm yours."

Dooley shook his head. "Some choice."

"Yeah. I wasn't gonna run because I got a wife and three kids and whatever bad things I done, I love my wife and kids, so I said hey, whatever you want me to do, I'm your man."

"How long you been at it?"

"Too fuckin' long. But you don't want to hear my life story. You want to bust Tommy Spain, right?"

"Not exactly. He's already busted. I'm trying to find out what he's got on other people that could get them busted. Puig told me you have something big."

Grady laughed in his throat, a nasty wet sound. "Big, is that what he said?"

"He said it was dynamite."

"It's better than that. It's TNT."

Dooley was used to informants talking up their product. He picked up his beer and said, "Sounds like it could do some damage."

"Only if somebody wants to use it. The FBI didn't."

"You talked to the FBI?"

"First people I went to. I figured the local cops were a waste of time. No offense or anything. But I've seen too many cops stuffing envelopes into their pockets. I thought I'd go straight to the top."

"And what happened?"

"Nothing. Not a fucking thing. I got an hour of their time and a polite thank you. And then nothing."

"It takes them a while. The G takes its own sweet time."

"I waited two years. Then I called them. They'd never fucking heard of me. I asked for the agent I'd talked to and they said he was transferred out of town."

Dooley let a few seconds go by. "I have to ask this. You sure it was all that good?"

"Wait till you hear it."

"That's what I'm here for."

"OK. You want another one?" Grady ordered two more beers. When they were set up he said, "This goes back a few years. What I am, see, my real job I mean, I do construction, home repair. When I got in trouble with them, they said OK, you can work off the debt. There's always things we need done. So I became the guy they called when they needed any kind of construction done. And I could tell you some stories too—hidden rooms and shit like that, but that's not what we're here for. What happened was, they put me to work at the Armory Lounge. Know where that is?"

"I've been there."

"Know who used to hang out there?"

"Giancana."

"That's right. And all his boys. Including Tommy Spain."

"Right. OK, what happened?"

"Well, by that time, I'd been working for them for a couple of years already, and they were used to me being around, right? So it was like they didn't see me anymore. And this one night, I was at the Armory, doing some painting in the back hall, by the johns, and Giancana and Spain were sitting there in a booth in the back room talking. And I could hear every fucking word they said. At first I wasn't paying any attention, but then a couple of things caught my attention and I started listening. And then I wished I hadn't, and then I didn't know what the hell to do. I thought about trying to bang shit around, you know, so they'd be sure to notice me and tell me to get lost, but I was too scared. So I just kept painting, and they kept talking. And then they broke up and went off somewhere and I finished the job and went home. And I didn't think too much about it till a few months later, when it happened."

"When what happened?"

Grady took a drink of beer and said, "When the president got shot."

• • •

"Come on," said Dooley.

"Swear to God. I heard 'em talking about killing the president of the United States."

Dooley realized he was staring at Grady. He made himself look at the TV screen, but he wasn't seeing anything. After what seemed like a long time he said, "When was this?"

"Summer, six years ago. July, maybe. I don't remember exactly. And I didn't think too much about it because Mooney was always talking big, talking about getting rid of guys he didn't like. But then when it happened, a few months later, I remembered what I heard."

Dooley was wishing like hell he'd stayed home tonight, told Grady to take a hike. "You're gonna have to tell me exactly what you heard. You sure they were talking about Kennedy?"

"They never said his name. But what got my attention was when Giancana said, 'That son of a bitch wouldn't even be in the White House without me.'"

Dooley thought about it while he drank beer. "OK, big deal. He was mad at Kennedy for siccing his brother on the rackets. Everybody knows that. That's a long way from planning to kill him."

"Wait. Giancana said he wished he could get rid of the guy, and then Spain said, 'Well, say the word and we could probably do it.' He said something like, 'There's a lot of guys in Washington that don't like him, either, and I've got the contacts to rig something up if you want to do it.' And the thing was, Spain sounded like he really knew what he was talking about. He sounded serious."

"And what did Giancana say? Did he give the word?"

"Not right then. Spain told him he could find people to do it and get away with it, and Giancana said it was something to think about, and then they left. But shit, what do you want? It happened."

Dooley was starting to feel a little better. Grady didn't have a thing. Dooley had dealt with it dozens of times: somebody thought they had something that made them important, but all they had was smoke. "I'm sorry, pal, but it doesn't prove a thing. What it sounds like to me is Spain bragging."

"Yeah, that's what the FBI said. They said it didn't mean shit. Not without something to back it up."

Like a tape, Dooley thought suddenly. "Christ."

Grady gave him a sidelong glance. "The FBI didn't want it. Nobody else believes it. Who does that leave?"

Dooley looked back at him and said, "I guess that leaves me."

• • •

Dooley sat staring at the newspaper, trying to stamp on the queasy feeling in his belly. He was looking at a headline that read *23 Marines Chosen to Leave Viet Slain in Battle*. The article below the headline said that elements of the Third Marine Division, recently selected to be withdrawn, had been hit hard by the North Vietnamese Army near the DMZ. Until now Dooley had always been able to step back, trust to the odds, keep a lid on his feelings. It was getting harder; he was starting to lose confidence in the odds.

He shoved the paper away. Dooley had not slept well; he had gotten up too early without feeling rested and gone and sat in the yard for a while in the early morning cool, trying to sort out his thoughts.

Somebody had dumped something in his lap that he had to do something about. He had tried to write it off but he couldn't. It went beyond Sally now.

Dooley went upstairs to his bedroom. Rose was just getting up, sitting on the edge of the bed looking tousled and sleepy. "You're up early," she said.

"I couldn't sleep." Dooley sat down beside her and put an arm around her; she stiffened a little but when she saw that was all he wanted to do, just sit there with her, she relaxed and laid her head on his shoulder. Dooley wished he could tell her about everything. He wished he could tell someone. He wished he could go back to the way things used to be. He kissed Rose and got up and went to unlock the drawer where he kept his gun and his star. He pulled out the manila envelope.

• • •

Dooley had seen the university buildings from the expressway, but he hadn't ever looked at the campus up close; he couldn't believe how ugly it was. They had torn the heart out of the Taylor Street neighborhood to pave over a hundred acres and put up a lot of concrete blockhouses. It looked more like a housing project or a prison than a college. He couldn't blame the Italians for being hostile. A lot of them had moved out west, but there were a few diehards around what was left of Taylor Street. There was a stretch of three or four blocks where you could still get a good dish of *pollo al pomodoro* or a glass of the finest grappa, provided you didn't look too much like an academic.

The church was a couple of blocks north of Taylor, a little west of the university. Dooley didn't know a lot about it, but it was named for an Italian saint. The church was built of yellow brick with a big green copper dome on top, and tacked onto it was a rectory built of red brick. Together they looked as if they could weather whatever the city threw at them, whether the university to the east or the housing projects a few blocks south.

Dooley parked on Loomis and got out of the car. He had spent a little time with Haggerty's surveillance records in the morning. A lot of them were useless, with a fair amount of *lost subject in traffic* and similar notations, but the flatfeet had managed to stick with Spain a few times, and Dooley had come up with one match between the places Tommy Spain had visited just before he went to prison and the people Fay Blackman had told him Tommy might trust. One match made for one decent guess, Dooley figured; if it wasn't the right one he wasn't sure what he would do next.

He walked around the corner of the church and found a door in the side of the rectory and rang the bell. He waited for a minute and was about to ring it again when he heard footsteps clapping across tiles inside and the door was pulled opened by a nun. "Hello," she said. She was a young nun, with dark eyes in a round pleasant face set off by her wimple, in a habit that exposed at least twelve inches of her shins. "Can I help you?" she said.

"I'm looking for Father Piccolo," said Dooley. "Have I come to the right place?"

"You have," the nun said. "Can I tell him who's calling?"

Dooley pulled out his star. "I'm a police officer. I'd like to talk to him about one of his former parishioners."

Her eyes widened just a little but she hesitated only a moment before stepping aside. "Please come in." She closed the door and led him down the hall. There was music playing somewhere in the house, and it surprised Dooley because it didn't sound at all like what he imagined priests listened to. It sounded familiar to him; he thought maybe Frank or Kathleen had the same record.

The music got louder as they went, and it turned out to be playing in the room she led him to, a big wood-paneled room at the back of the house with windows that looked onto a small enclosed garden. An old priest sat at a large table with stacks of ledgers and piles of papers spread out in front of him. He was white-haired and craggy-faced, but the look in his eye was keen and he was tapping his fingers on the table in time to the music. Somebody was singing about a warm gun in a toneless voice.

Reacting no doubt to the look on Dooley's face, the priest smiled and gestured toward the record player, and the young nun hurried over and lifted the needle off the record. In the sudden quiet the priest said, "I've asked Sister Mary Catherine to take charge of my musical education. The more cacaphonous the music has gotten, the more seriously the young people seem to take it, and I realized I must be missing something."

"You and me both," said Dooley. "My kids tried to educate me, and I flunked."

"It takes persistence, I'm finding." The priest and the nun traded a brief look as she stuffed the record back into its sleeve, and Dooley thought he detected the beginnings of a blush along with her smile. The priest said, "And what can I do for you, officer?"

Dooley showed him the star. "I wanted to talk to you about a man named Tommy Spain. Spagnola, his name used to be."

The smile on the old priest's face went away, and as he sat there looking at Dooley it was replaced by what looked like melancholy, or even regret. "Tommy Spain," he said. "I never got used to the name." He sighed and pushed away from the table. "I think the garden would be a good place for us to talk. Can you carry on here for a while, Sister?" As he made for the door he said, "We're going through the archives to write a history of the parish. Our fiftieth anniversary is coming up."

"Congratulations."

"Thanks. When this parish was established you could walk along Taylor Street from Halsted to Racine and hear nothing but Italian. People were poor, but they took care of one another. A lot of things have changed."

The garden was mostly in shade, with the church looming above it. There was a patch of grass, a brick walk leading to a bench, roses along the wall. "Prohibition was the worst thing that ever happened to this neighborhood," the priest said. "No matter what some will tell you. When they finally repealed it, only the thugs had gotten rich. And we've been suffering for it ever since. Ninety-nine percent of the people in this parish are honest, but it's the one percent that isn't that made Taylor Street famous."

They reached the bench and sat down. "I had high hopes for Tommy. I thought he might escape all that. His mother was a good woman, his father wasn't worth much. There was a moment, a point when he was maybe eighteen or nineteen, when I could see he was wavering. He could have gone one way or the other. He was running around with the wrong kind of people but he still liked to come and talk to me sometimes. I tried to push him in the right direction and I failed. Maybe I pushed too hard."

Dooley waited for more but the priest was frowning at the roses. Dooley said, "Tommy came to see you on February 13, 1967."

There was a long silence. "Yes, he did. He had just gotten back from Mexico."

"And he knew he was about to be indicted."

"I remember."

"He gave you something to keep for him."

The priest didn't move for a while and Dooley sat there looking at the back of the rectory and listening to the hum of the city beyond the walls. "You're just guessing, aren't you?" the priest said finally.

"That's right. But I think I just got my answer."

"Do you know what it is?"

"I have a pretty good idea. Do you?"

The old priest passed a hand over his face. "No. All Tommy said was that it would be breaking no law to keep it and it would be a kind of insurance that might keep him alive. Maybe my judgment was bad, but I said yes. Did Tommy lie to me?"

"No, I'd say he told you the truth."

"Are you going to ask me to give it to you?"

Dooley knew he had gotten to the tricky part. "I'm not sure yet. What did Tommy tell you to do?" he said.

"He said just keep it safe, and if he died a violent death I was to send it to a man at the *Chicago Tribune* who would know what to do with it."

Dooley nodded. "That's about what I figured." He thought for a moment and said, "Is it a tape recording?"

A few seconds went by and Father Piccolo said, "Your information is pretty good."

"Here's what I'm going to ask you to do," said Dooley. "I'm going to ask you to listen to it. And then decide what should be done with it."

Dooley knew better than to rush things now; he and the priest sat there together for what seemed to him like a long time. Dooley was comfortable and in no particular hurry, and he wouldn't have minded sitting there a while longer, but at last the priest said, "What will happen to Tommy if I do?"

"He won't have his insurance anymore."

"And his life would be in danger."

Dooley almost told him that Tommy was safe where he was, but it occurred to him that he couldn't say that, not by a long shot. "Maybe. But then I would hope to be able to take some action against the people who would be threatening him. If I had the tape."

More time went by and the priest said, "I would give it to you on one condition."

"What's that?"

"I'll have to warn Tommy. That's only fair."

Dooley thought about that for a while. "OK. Just don't tell him who came and got it. Can you agree to that?"

"I suppose so." Father Piccolo stirred at last, rising to his feet on creaking joints, and Dooley stood up with him. The priest looked older, or maybe just more beaten down, than he had when Dooley had first walked into the room. "Why don't you wait in the hall?" he said. "I'll go and get it."

Forty-three

THE THIRD DIVISION had lost thirty-five more marines killed in action in the last twenty-four hours; there was still no mention of what regiment they belonged to. Dooley was starting to feel it, the first deep stirrings of dread. Bad things were going on over there and it didn't look as if anybody was coming out soon; someone on TV had said that the Third Division was going to be tough to replace because they held so much territory and the ARVN wasn't ready to take it over.

Dooley heard Rose coming in from the garden and quickly got up from the table; if she saw him brooding over the paper she would know what he was brooding about. He went to pour himself some more coffee from the percolator. "Morning," Rose said.

Dooley shot her a look, trying to read the signs; the freeze had been thawing little by little but he still felt as if he were on probation. "Morning. What's it like out there?"

"It's nice. It's sunny, but it's not too hot." She went to the sink and ran a glass of water.

Dooley watched her drink and said, "You look like you lost weight."

She turned to him with an expression he wasn't used to seeing; she was challenging him. "I've lost ten pounds," she said. She drank some more water, keeping her eyes on him. "Some of it was diet but a lot of it was wear and tear."

Dooley just stood there. "You look good," he said finally.

The look softened just a little. "We could go out for lunch again," she said.

That was a good sign but it came at a bad time; Dooley had a lot on his mind today. He gave it a few seconds' thought and he could see the disappointment just starting to show in her face. Hell with it all, Dooley thought. "Sure."

She blinked once or twice and said, "Just promise me you don't have anymore surprise announcements."

"No surprises." He set down his mug. "I do have one thing to do, but maybe we can work it in. Does Phil still have that tape recorder?"

Phil was her brother-in-law, married to her sister Maureen, noted for his love of gadgets. Frowning at the sudden curve he'd thrown her, Rose said, "As far as I know. Why?"

"Maybe we can swing by Maureen's after lunch. I've got something I need to listen to."

• • •

It wasn't as easy as Dooley had thought it would be. First there was the fact that he wasn't an electronics expert; he'd seen Phil set up the machine but had never done it himself. Maureen said she didn't have a clue and left him to it. He had been worried that maybe the tape was some nonstandard variety that wouldn't fit the machine, but it seemed to be the right size; it didn't take him long to figure out how to thread the tape through and get it going on the other reel.

Then there was what he was hearing. He'd expected to sit down and listen to the tape and have the whole thing laid out for him, but what he had was a series of scratchy, barely audible conversations that didn't mean a lot to him. He kept stopping the tape and rewinding it to go over things he had missed. In the intervals of silence he could hear Rose and her sister back in the kitchen, talking quietly. He was going to have to wind things up and leave for work soon. He had put his notebook and pen on the table but hadn't written anything down because he hadn't figured out quite what he was listening to.

Or who; that was going to be the hard part. Maybe Haggerty would recognize these voices, but to Dooley they all sounded the same. He stopped, rewound, punched the play button again. *Can they really do that?* someone said on the tape. *Joe, it's the G,* said someone else. *They can do anything they fucking want.*

There were about twenty minutes of conversation on the tape. Dooley reached the end and then rewound it and listened to the last five minutes or so straight through. He sat for a while just thinking about what he had heard, thinking about all the Joes he knew of. Then he rewound the tape the whole way and took it off the machine. He put it back in its flat cardboard box and put the box in the plain brown envelope Father Piccolo had handed him at the foot of the stairs in the rectory. He started to put the envelope in his briefcase but stopped. He thought for a second and took the box out of the envelope. He got up and walked across Maureen's living room to the built-in shelves where Phil kept his tapes in labeled boxes. The box in Dooley's hand looked about the same as all the others, and he reached up and slipped it in at the end of a row.

Dooley threw everything back in his briefcase, closed it and walked back to the kitchen. "All through?" Rose said.

"Yeah. Thanks, Maureen. Tell Phil it was a big help."

"So what's on this mysterious tape?" Maureen said, thrilled to be involved in the workings of the law.

Dooley smiled, making light of it. "A bunch of gangsters, talking business."

"How exciting. Any big secrets?"

He shook his head. Dooley was a bad liar, but if ever there was a time for a fib, this was it. "Not really," he said.

• • •

Dooley and Rose slept with the windows open; fall was in the air. The Sunday paper was full of college football. Kathleen came home for dinner and Rose made an occasion of it, with a roast and mashed potatoes and gravy and green beans and jello salad and rolls, the works. They ate in the dining room. Kathleen was full of herself, full of the novelty and the excitement of going to college. She talked non-stop. The work was hard but not too hard and she had made a ton of new friends and she was learning about things she had never suspected existed. Dooley had never been to college, and he was proud of his daughter but a little jealous, too. It was changing her already.

"There's going to be a big demonstration downtown next week, and I'm going to go."

There was a freeze and Dooley said, "What kind of demonstration?"

"Against the war. A peace demonstration." Kathleen was giving him the same challenging look her mother had given him the day before, and Dooley had the feeling all of a sudden that she had been saving this up, working up to delivering the bombshell since she walked in the door. He laid down his fork. Frank and Rose were looking at him warily. "Don't forget you've got a brother over there in the middle of that war," Dooley said.

"I haven't forgotten, Daddy. Why do you think I want the war to end?"

He shrugged. "It's one thing to want it to end. It's another thing to support the other side."

"What makes you think I support the other side?"

"I don't know, the demonstrations I've seen, I wouldn't exactly call them pro-American."'

"Daddy, you don't have to be anti-American to be antiwar. It's a bad war. We shouldn't be there."

"Maybe not, but we're there. And as long as we're there, you have to support our men. How do you think Kevin would feel if he saw you out there?"

"I would hope he would know I'm doing it for him."

"For him?"

"Yes, for him. I want my brother back home, the sooner the better. Don't you?"

"Sure, but—" Dooley couldn't finish; he'd run out of words.

"But what?"

Dooley jabbed at the tablecloth with a finger. "Just don't tell me your brother's on the wrong side. Don't try and tell me that. That's what steams me, these punks running around saying we're on the wrong side in this war. Maybe it's a mistake to be over there, but not because the communists are a bunch of angels."

Kathleen held his gaze but there was a little fear in her look now. "I'm not saying they are. I'm saying it's not our fight. I'm saying my brother Kevin shouldn't be over there risking his life for a corrupt regime."

Dooley sat there glaring at his daughter, trying to suppress the sneaking feeling that he had been bested, and by a slip of a girl at that. He came close a couple of times to opening his mouth but couldn't quite put his finger on what he wanted to say. Rose and Frank were tensed, waiting for the storm, Kathleen was just sitting there looking at him, and suddenly Dooley realized that when you got right down to it, he wasn't sure he disagreed with Kathleen all that much. He realized something else, too: that look in her eye was the look of somebody who was scared but not backing down.

Dooley picked up his knife and fork. He cut off a piece of meat, but before he put it in his mouth he looked at Kathleen and said, "All right, I can live with that. Sounds like you've given it some thought."

Nobody said anything for a while; Dooley chewed and tried to ignore the looks going around the table. The next time he looked at Kathleen, he saw something different in her eyes; he could see he had his daughter back again, as much as he was ever going to.

• • •

The G-men showed up after lunch. When the doorbell rang, Rose and Kathleen were back in the kitchen doing the dishes, and Dooley and Frank were in the living room, watching the Bears losing, up in Green Bay. Dooley went to answer it and there was Gustafson, standing on his doorstep along with another agent, both of them decked out in their Sunday best and looking like they meant business. Jesus Christ, thought Dooley, that was fast.

"Mike? I'm sorry to bother you at home, but it's fairly urgent. I wondered if you had a minute to talk." Gustafson had on his Official Business look, a long way from the affable smile he'd tried out on Dooley in the office downtown. The other agent looked like a fullback just out of the shower after the big game, crew-cut and square-jawed and still pissed off after a loss.

Dooley put on an innocent look and said, "I'm heading into work in an hour or so. Couldn't it wait? I could see you down at the Area."

"I'm afraid not, Mike. You get into work, you'll have distractions, it'll be hard to make time for us. This is something we wanted to discuss outside the regular channels anyway." Gustafson was keeping his voice down, terse and quiet. Dooley looked at the scowling fullback. Good cop, bad cop, he thought.

"OK," he said. "Let's go out back."

He took them out onto the patio, Rose and Kathleen goggling at them as they passed through the kitchen. Gustafson said good day to the ladies, giving them a tight smile. Outside, Dooley shoved three chairs together and they sat down. "This is Special Agent Krause," Gustafson said. "He's one of our top guys on the C-1 squad." Krause nodded, just barely.

"How you doing?" said Dooley. He looked at Gustafson. "What's going on?"

"You interviewed a priest down on Taylor Street a couple of days ago. Father John Piccolo."

"Yeah." Dooley's mind was working fast. "I'm still interested in Tommy Spain. Piccolo knew Spain when he was younger, and I thought he might be able to tell me about Spain's associates. I'm looking for people Spain might have trusted with compromising material he collected, because I'm starting to think that's the key to the Kotowski murder." Dooley was a bad liar, but he knew how to edit.

Gustafson didn't take the trouble to pretend to believe it. "He gave you a tape."

Dooley stared, then frowned. "Who says?"

"We need that tape, Mike. Don't try and bullshit us."

Dooley was impressed; he was getting the full industrial-strength treatment without any beating around the bush. He didn't have to fake the look of resentment that he could feel settling over his face. "Somebody else has been bullshitting you," he said. "He didn't give me anything but a few names, which I mostly knew anyway."

Krause spoke up for the first time. "The tape he gave you is evidence in an ongoing federal investigation, and it's extremely sensitive material. It has nothing to do with any current case you're working on, and any attempt to publicize its contents or pass them on to any interested party or use them in any way would be extremely prejudicial to the work of our agency. We need it, and we need it now."

Dooley was getting steamed. He glared back at Krause and said, "Just supposing he did give me something, it would be evidence in a CPD investigation, and I would have to be the judge of what it pertained to and who had a right to it. And if you went through the proper channels, I'd probably be happy to share it with you. But I don't like being braced at home on a Sunday like I've done something wrong."

"I assume you've listened to it?" Gustafson said.

That almost tripped Dooley up but he managed to keep the slightly puzzled frown on his face. "I don't know what the hell you're talking about. Did you get this from Father Piccolo himself?"

Gustafson and Krause traded a look and Gustafson turned back to Dooley. He said, "OK. You've made your position clear. I'm disappointed, but not really surprised. I've worked in this town long enough to know how it goes."

"Wait a second. Are you trying to tell me you think I'd pass something along to the mob?"

"I'd hate to think it. You don't have that kind of reputation. But in this town, you never know."

"That's an insult, mister. I don't care if you are from the fucking FBI. You don't sit there in my house and insult me like that."

"If I'm wrong, the best way to prove it is to hand over the tape."

Dooley peered at him. "I'm starting to think you're more worried about my giving something to the papers than you are about my giving it to the mob."

"Either way," said Gustafson. "That would be a very bad mistake on your part. Now let me make *my* position clear. If any of what's on that tape gets to the wrong people, or, yes, hits the papers, we'll make a federal case out of it. Literally. We'll prosecute you for obstruction of justice so fast you won't know what hit you."

"We'll have your ass in a sling," said Krause.

Dooley sat there looking from one to the other and trying to keep his mouth clamped shut. He knew they had used up all their bullets for the moment; the interesting question was what they would try next. "I'm a homicide cop," he said. "I don't give a damn about anything but clearing homicide cases. If this tape of yours turns up and has something I can use to convict Sally Kotowski's killer, I'll use it. If not, you're welcome to it, and I'll come and lay it on your fucking desk. But you don't come into my house on a Sunday and accuse me of lying and misconduct. You don't try to intimidate me. I don't care if you are the G. *That's* my position, and I hope it's clear." Dooley also hoped like hell he'd left just enough ambiguity in the situation to give him a little breathing room. Gustafson stood up and Krause did the same a second later.

Gustafson's face was blank. "OK, Mike, have it your way. Just don't make any mistakes."

Dooley got slowly to his feet. Eye to eye with the G-men he said, "If you're questioning my integrity, you're the ones making a mistake. A big fat one."

• • •

Sometimes detective work was unbelievably tedious, but that was what Dooley needed tonight; his mind was fully occupied with things other than the fruitless canvass he and Olson spent virtually the whole shift on. A kid had shot a man dead on Chicago Avenue and run up an alley; somebody had to have seen where he went but nobody was owning up to it. Dooley and Olson knocked on a lot of doors and got nothing.

Nothing didn't generate much paperwork and Dooley was home by one in the morning. He drank his Jameson's sitting at the kitchen table, thinking about Tommy Spain's tape and what it meant, and then turned out the lights and went upstairs.

When he bent down to kiss Rose she caught his hand. "Don't put on your pajamas," she whispered.

Dooley just sat there on the side of the bed for a moment. "OK," he said finally.

When he slid in between the sheets Rose pulled him to her; she was naked, too, something he hadn't felt in a while. She wasn't Laura Lindbloom but she felt good. "Nothing has to happen if you don't want it to happen," Rose whispered in his ear. "I just wanted to get used to this again."

Dooley was tired as always and one part of him just wanted to go to sleep; another part of him wanted desperately not to disappoint her. He lay there for a moment and sure enough things started to happen.

• • •

"Did you learn that from her?" The question surprised Dooley; it jerked him awake. Rose's hair was tickling his cheek and her breath warmed his neck. Their bodies were slick and warm against each other. Dooley felt good; he was glad it had happened. It had been a little work, but it was worth it.

"Does it matter?" he said.

Rose took her time coming up with an answer and Dooley started to worry a little; the last thing he needed was for this to get spoiled. "I guess not," she breathed.

I love my wife, thought Dooley, close to sleep again. It felt good to think it. The telephone rang.

Rose started; Dooley swore. Kevin, he thought. No, Kathleen; something happened to Kathleen. Rose let go and he rolled over and snatched the phone off the hook. "Hello."

"Michael Dooley?" said a man.

"Yeah. What is it?"

"This is Tommy Spain."

Dooley just lay there propped up on an elbow until the voice said, "Hello?"

"Horseshit," said Dooley. He swung his feet to the floor.

Soft laughter came over the wire. "No bull, Officer. Speaking to you direct from Texarkana, Texas, courtesy of the federal government."

Dooley put a hand over the mouthpiece. "It's just work," he said to Rose. Into the phone he said, "I'm going to switch extensions. Hang on." He laid the receiver on the table and pulled on his pajama pants. "When you hear me talking downstairs, hang up," he said to Rose.

He didn't bother to turn on any lights. He almost picked up the phone in the hall but decided it was a little close to the stairs and went on back to the kitchen. He took the wall phone off the hook and said, "Still there?"

"I'm here, pal."

Dooley heard the soft click of Rose hanging up the phone upstairs. "Prove you're who you say you are," he said.

"Prove it? How do you want me to do that?"

"Tell me what's on the tape."

"Hey, I don't know who's listening besides you and me."

Dooley didn't much like that idea. He thought for a moment. "Where did you meet your first wife?"

Spain laughed again. "At the butcher's. You talked to Fay, huh? Man, you must have a surplus of that Irish blarney. What the hell did you say to old Father John to make him cough up the tape? I thought I could trust a priest to keep a promise."

"I think Father John's seen through you, that's all."

"You ought to be ashamed of yourself, taking advantage of an old man."

"What the hell do you want, Spain?"

"What the hell do you think I want? I want you to stop trying to be a fucking hero. I want you to turn the tape over to the FBI."

"Why? How does that benefit you?"

"It doesn't, particularly. But they'll take better care of it than you will."

"What do you think I'm going to do with it?"

"I wish to God I knew. I don't see what possible good it can do you, except let you do some grandstanding. It's sure as hell not going to bring Sally back to life."

"No, we never manage that. But sometimes we manage to convict the people that do the killing. Even the ones who order it, once in a long while."

"That's what you think you're going to do?"'

"The thought crossed my mind."

"Man, and here I thought I was talking to a grown-up. How long you been a cop, Dooley?"

"Long enough to get disgusted."

There was a brief pause, Dooley listening intently to the faint cosmic noises coming down the wire. Spain said, "Let me tell you the facts of life. You take that tape public, all that's going to happen is, you're going to start a war. A lot of people will die. And at the end of it, nobody will be better off."

"Yeah, especially you. You won't have your leverage anymore."

"That's true, but that's not the main thing. The main thing is, something like that has to be handled with care."

"And the FBI will handle it with care, I know. I guess that's the part that really disgusts me."

"The G knows you don't upset the apple cart. They know that some things are inevitable and the best you can do is control them."

"And you're going to help them control things, huh?"

"I've got a role to play, let's say. I've been training for it all my life."

"I got a word for that kind of role."

"Save it. Look, Dooley, I didn't call you just because I was having trouble sleeping. I called you to give you the word. And the word is, cough it up. Otherwise you got all kinds of problems."

"From the G?"

"For Christ's sake, Dooley. It's not the G you have to worry about. The G didn't kill Sally."

"So let me ask you this. How are the people who killed Sally going to find out I've got the tape?"

"Well, let me put it this way. I don't want you to use the tape, the FBI doesn't want you to use the tape. Either one of us might decide things were serious enough to drop a hint in the right place. You know how the brains in the Defense Department are always talking about deterrence? Well, consider Sally deterrence. You don't want to risk it. There's a reason they came to your house today."

Dooley had ice water running in his guts. "You're a low-down piece of shit, Spain."

"I'll take that as a compliment. But listen to me, Dooley. It doesn't have to go that way. I waved the stick at you, now here's the carrot."

"Save your breath, asshole."

"Hear me out. When's your son due to come home from Viet Nam?"

That one hit Dooley in the gut; he had to put his hand on the wall. "What the hell do you care?"

"It could be tomorrow, Dooley. It can be arranged."

"Don't make me laugh."

"Dooley, listen to me. Do you think they let the average federal prisoner make secret phone calls in the middle of the night from the warden's office? I've got major league clout, Dooley. And if I don't have enough, you know the G does. We have the contacts in Washington that can pull the strings. We can have your boy on a chopper tomorrow, heading for DaNang and that big silver bird home. All you have to do is call up Gustafson and hand over the tape."

Dooley stood there listening to the thumping of his heart. This is how they win, he thought; this is how they always win.

He thought about Kevin, up on the line. He thought about Rose, lying awake upstairs; could he possibly pass up a chance to save her son? He thought about dead marines and he thought about a dead girl lying in the weeds by the river. He thought about his dead brother Patrick, his dead father. He closed his eyes and put the phone to his ear.

"Go fuck yourself, Spain." Dooley hung up the phone.

Forty-four

"THAT'S IT, HE'S out." Dooley jumped up from the table, knocking over his chair. "He's out, Kevin's coming home. Rose!" Dooley didn't know where his wife was; he'd come downstairs to an empty kitchen and made himself some coffee, then looked at the paper. He went to the back door and looked out into the yard, but he didn't see her. He looked into the garage; her car was gone. Frank was at school and there was nobody to share the news with; Dooley felt like shouting it out the front door. "He's out of it," he said aloud again. He picked up his chair and sat down to read the article again.

Marines Leaving Bases Near DMZ the headline read, but the important part was the first paragraph: *The U.S. Marine Corps announced today that it is reducing the length of a tour in Viet Nam for combat troops from 13 to 12 months, effective immediately. The period is measured from the date of departure from the United States. The decision affects most of the 72,000 marines currently serving in the country.* Kevin had left the U.S. on September 14, 1968, a date burned into Dooley's memory; as of a week ago yesterday, Kevin's tour was up. "He's coming home," Dooley said again, quieter this time.

Dooley stood up and went to the window. He couldn't wait for Rose to get home. He had hardly slept, lying awake agonizing about his conversation with Tommy Spain. He had even started to think about where he could move his family, at least until it was all over. He had always thought the Outfit had rules about people's families but he wasn't sure anymore; he was afraid he'd made a big mistake. He had felt like hell when he'd gotten up but now he felt like he could handle things, especially with Kevin coming home. "Fuck you, Tommy Spain," he said, looking out the window.

Dooley didn't know what to do with himself; he knocked around the house looking for jobs to do, went out into the yard and stood looking at the cracked board in the fence, couldn't settle to work. He heard Rose's car pull up.

He helped her bring in the groceries, suppressing the desire to blurt it out. She could tell something was up and eventually asked him; he showed her the paper, the smile breaking out.

Rose read it and closed her eyes; he thought she was going to faint. She swayed a little and he reached out and held her. The paper dropped to the floor as she put her arms around him. "Thank God," she said. When she pulled away, her eyes were moist. "When?" she said. "When will he be home?"

"Soon," Dooley said. "They fly them home these days. He'll probably call from wherever he lands first."

"I want to see him. I won't believe it until I'm holding him."

"Believe it," said Dooley. "Kevin's coming home."

• • •

Dooley couldn't concentrate worth a damn; the files he was looking at could have been written in Chinese. Things in the Area had been quiet and he and Olson were supposed to be looking at cold cases. There was always something to work on, somebody who had gotten away with murder, but there wasn't always anything obviously useful to do. The case that was most on Dooley's mind had been declared solved and he hadn't decided what to do with the bombshell he'd been handed. Between that and his son coming home he couldn't keep his mind on his business.

He decided to try to chase down a kid who had claimed to witness a shooting back in May and then disappeared; enough time had gone by that the kid might have decided it was safe to turn up again. It was a good assignment for the mood Dooley was in; it involved a lot of driving around looking for addresses. It ate up the clock and left him time to think.

When he got home Rose was still up, sitting in the kitchen with a mug of hot chocolate. Dooley's heart jumped when he came in and saw her, but she smiled at him right away to reassure him and got up and kissed him. "I couldn't sleep," she said. "I'm too excited."

"It could be a few days," Dooley told her. "There's always nonsense to go through in the military, paperwork and processing and God knows what. He's probably in Da Nang now, getting ready to fly home. The point is, he's out of the field. They'd have pulled him out right away."

"Wouldn't he have called? He called once from Da Nang, remember?"

"Look, I don't know how it goes. Maybe he's in transit somewhere. Don't worry, he's on his way home." Dooley wanted to reassure her, but the truth was he was having a little trouble himself; Dooley knew there were a million things that could go wrong. He was still bothered by the heavy casualties the division had taken over the past few days. Every day that went by without a telegram from the Defense Department or a somber-faced marine officer knocking at the door made it a little more likely Kevin had survived, but in spite of his euphoria of the morning he knew they weren't out of the woods yet.

It's a race, he thought, slipping into bed next to Rose. It's a race between a phone call and a telegram.

The next day was cool, the first day that really felt like fall; it was sunny but the temperature never got above sixty-five. Dooley spent the early part of the afternoon fixing the fence in the back yard, at long last. He needed something to occupy him; every time the phone rang the bottom dropped out of his stomach. Dooley finished the fence and got ready to go to work.

The phone rang again as he was coming down the stairs. Rose answered it again with the same note of eagerness in her voice that went straight to Dooley's heart; just like the previous times he heard the let-down as she came back to earth. "Just a moment," she said. "For you," she said as he came into the kitchen, holding the phone for him. Dooley took it and said hello.

"Dooley?" It was a man's voice, not one he knew.

"Yeah. Who's this?"

"You don't give a shit. Just listen. You got something we want."

Dooley froze. Here we go, he thought. "What would that be?"

"Don't get cute. Just get ready. Here's what's gonna happen."

"Hold it a second. Since when do you tell me what's gonna happen?"

"Since I got something you want. Got it?"

"I don't know what you're talking about."

A noise came down the line, what sounded like a sigh, maybe of exasperation. "Hold the line."

At the other end there were indistinct noises and then something very distinct that made Dooley go cold: Laura Lindbloom's voice. "Dooley? Is that you?"

Very conscious of his wife at the sink behind him, Dooley said, "Yeah, it's me. You OK?"

"I'm scared, Dooley." There was a hint of a tremor in her voice.

All of a sudden Dooley was, too; he had to take a deep breath. All right, don't panic. Where are you?"

"I'm not sure. They put me in a van." More than a hint: he could tell she was terrified.

"OK. It's gonna be all right. Let me talk to the guy again."

He was back in a hurry. "All right, asshole. You get it now, right? You got something we want, we got something you want. Now listen good."

"I'm listening."

"No monkey business, no cops. You come alone, ready to deal. Is that simple enough for you?"

"I guess so."

"There better not be any tricks. Anything happens that we don't like, everything's off. You understand?"

"Where?"

"That's the spirit. You know the Sears at North and Harlem?"

"I know it."

"You park in the lot at midnight. By yourself. And you wait. Somebody will tell you what to do. Got it?"

Dooley leaned on the wall, thinking desperately. "Make it one o'clock," he said. "I'm working tonight."

"That's your fuckin' problem. We'll be there at midnight, and if you're not, *she* has problems." Click went the phone in his ear.

Rose was looking at him as he turned around after hanging up. "What was all that about?"

Dooley shook his head, feeling things crashing down around him. "Monkey business," he said. "Just monkey business." He looked up to see her staring at him. "Just work," he said. "Somebody trying to be cute."

"Nothing dangerous, I hope." She'd been a cop's wife for a long time, but the risks still worried her.

Dooley looked right through her, without seeing her. "No," he said. "Not for me."

• • •

He knew it was futile but he had to check. Dooley drove down to Laura's house on Cleveland. He rang her bell and got no answer; the street door was locked. He checked for signs of forced entry and saw none. He rang the other doorbells but got no response. He went around to the back and up the stairs to the studio. The door was closed and locked. Dooley knocked and rattled the knob but nobody came to open it. The house was deserted.

Dooley sat in his car thinking. Things were much worse than he had thought; somewhere he had fucked up bad, really bad. Dooley had been worrying about his family and forgotten all about Laura. A man's family might be off limits, but not his mistress. But what the hell were the connections?

Schroeder. There it was; had to be. Schroeder, Swallow, the mob. Crooked vice cops and gangsters; there wasn't much separation. Schroeder would have carried a grudge and done some snooping, then put the word around about Dooley and Laura. He might have talked to Swallow. And Schroeder knew people who knew where Laura lived. Dooley had thought he was being discreet, but had he really given any thought to it? He'd been seen in a Wells Street bar with Laura; he'd had dealings with a mob-linked fence with her beside him in the role of his mistress. And God knew who Laura had talked to about it. Dooley had forgotten how the grapevine could work. And when Tommy Spain had passed the word that a cop named Dooley needed to be pressured, it wouldn't have taken too much for the right people to put two and two together.

Dooley swore out loud; he'd been an idiot. This is your punishment, he thought. You did a bad thing and it came back to bite you. He started the car.

Dooley did something he almost never did: he called in sick. "I'm puking my guts up," he said into the pay phone, not exaggerating by much. "Tell Olson he's on his own tonight." Dooley hated to do it, but things were serious. He had given five seconds' thought to playing it by the book: going in and laying it all out for McCone. He had decided that nothing McCone could possibly suggest would make things better. Dooley was afraid of what an official response would mean: lots of cops on the scene to spook the men who had Laura. He had thought about bringing just Olson into it because he would have felt better with some backup; he knew Pete would help but he was afraid of what might happen if he was spotted. Dooley had decided he was going to have to be on his own tonight, too.

He drove back north and rang his sister-in-law Maureen's doorbell, praying she was home. She was, and her face lit up when she saw Dooley. "Well, it's our secret agent man. You need the tape recorder again?"

"I left something the other day," Dooley said, pushing at the limits of courtesy as he barged into her living room. He took the tape off the shelf where he had left it. He looked at Maureen and said, "Does Phil know how to copy a tape?"

Astonished, standing there in her apron, she said, "I think so. But I remember he told me once you need two machines. He'll be home in an hour if you want to talk to him."

Dooley frowned, nodding. "I might do that. Do you have a typewriter I could use while I wait?"

Dooley sat at the dining room table and typed while Maureen worked in the kitchen, looking in every few minutes with wonder in her eyes. He typed steadily for nearly an hour, finishing just before Phil walked in the door.

Phil was tall and going bald and Dooley had always thought he was a bit goofy, but today he was Dooley's best friend. "Sure, I can borrow my neighbor's portable," he said, eager to help.

"Terrific. One copy. Can I come back in a couple of hours and pick it up?"

Dooley drove west and south, to the Sears store at North and Harlem. He sat idling in the parking lot, trying to imagine how it would go. He was at the edge of the city here: due west across Harlem was Elmwood Park; River Forest and Oak Park were on either side of Harlem south of North Avenue. Dooley cruised a few blocks each way, trying to anticipate. Harlem and North were busy commercial streets but a block off them in any direction took him into residential streets that would be deserted at midnight.

He went back to Phil and Maureen's. Phil had copied the tape for him and wouldn't take any money for the blank tape. "Jeez, Mike, I'm happy to help."

"Then could you do me one more favor?" He handed Phil the copy of the tape and the sheets he'd typed. "First chance you get, could you mail these to me, at my house? Just put them in an envelope and mail them to my address."

Dooley left Phil and Maureen rigid with excitement. He still had hours to get through before midnight. All he knew how to do was work. He drove down to the Mad Hatter and found the bartender pissed off that Laura hadn't shown up for work; that told Dooley something. He went back to the house on Cleveland and found Danny the artist at home; he had thought he'd heard Laura's doorbell ring in the morning but hadn't thought much of it. He hadn't noticed any van in the street.

Dooley canvassed. He found a man who had seen a blue van in the alley behind the house; Dooley looked and saw that they could have hustled Laura out the back and through a gate into the alley without being seen. The witness hadn't noticed anything besides the color of the van.

Dooley tried to think it through; they would need a place to keep Laura on ice for a day. He had a few guesses about neighborhoods but knew there were too many places they could use. He wasn't going to go in with guns blazing and rescue her anyway.

Dooley decided there was really only one thing to do: show up.

• • •

The dark-colored Olds Cutlass Supreme crept into the parking lot off North Avenue and rolled to a halt twenty feet from Dooley's car. Dooley was leaning on the car with his arms folded in the cool night air. From the passenger side of the Olds a voice said, "Dooley?"

Dooley walked toward the car. He couldn't see the face very well under the high lamps lighting the lot, and he doubted he would have recognized anybody anyway; they had an endless supply of foot soldiers for jobs like this. "Walk west to the furniture store," the man said. "You better be alone."

"I'm all by myself," said Dooley.

The man motioned with his hand and the Cutlass accelerated, wheeling around in a wide arc through the empty lot to exit back onto North Avenue, heading west. Dooley started walking.

He crossed Harlem and saw the sign for the furniture store, a couple of blocks ahead, on the south side of the street. Dooley tried to spot the watchers as he walked, hands in his pockets, a man out for a bedtime constitutional. A few cars went by but there wasn't much action out here just past midnight in the middle of the week. Dooley didn't see anything that stuck out but he knew they would be there.

The parking lot for the store occupied the southeast corner. Dooley stayed on the north side of the street until he had drawn even with the lot and could scan it. There were two cars parked on the lot, backed up against the storefront, a Coupe de Ville and a Buick Riviera, sitting a few feet apart. Dooley spotted the Cutlass parked a little farther along North Avenue on the other side. He stood there for a moment looking at parked cars, on North and the cross street running south, trying to see which ones were occupied. He decided it didn't much matter; any way he looked at it he was outnumbered. He let a car go by and then crossed the wide deserted street.

Two men emerged from the Riviera as Dooley ambled across the parking lot. They came to meet him, not hurrying. When he was ten feet away the one on the right said, "Hold it." He was short and squat in a windbreaker stretched by his gut. "Just stand right there."

Dooley said, "Where's the girl?"

"You'll find out when it's time."

Dooley didn't like that. "Before we go any farther I gotta know she's OK."

"You're not making the conditions." He jerked his head toward the Caddy. "The man wants to talk to you."

Dooley didn't like it at all, but he was in a weak position. He wasn't going to just walk away. He stared into passionless eyes for a couple of seconds and said, "That's what I'm here for." He took a step toward the Cadillac.

"Not so fast. Just hold still." The second man stepped toward Dooley. This one was ugly as sin, a pug with a nose that had been broken a few times. He started to reach for Dooley's jacket but Dooley knocked his hand away. "You don't put your hands on me," he said.

"Look, asshole," said the short man. "You don't get in that car until we're sure you're not wired up. We'll keep your gun for you, too. Don't worry, you'll get it back."

Dooley was losing all the battles so far, but he figured he had to put up a fight. He hated to just roll over for anyone.

The pug reached inside Dooley's jacket and took his gun out of the holster. He stuffed it in his own belt and then started checking pockets. He looked at Dooley's star and put it back; he took the tape out of the side pocket of Dooley's jacket, opened the box, closed it again and tossed it to the other man. "Keep looking," the man said.

The pug probed Dooley's waistband and ran his hands over his back and sides and down his pants legs. "That's it," he said, stepping back.

"OK," said the short man. "Now just sit tight." He walked over to the Cadillac and handed the tape to somebody on the back seat through an open window. The driver's side door opened and a man got out. He wandered away across the asphalt and lit a cigarette. The short man bent down and listened to a low voice from inside the car for a moment and then straightened up. "You're on," he said, beckoning to Dooley. Then he walked away.

Dooley went slowly over to the Cadillac. He opened the back door and climbed in and looked across the seat to the man he had come to see. He got a good look at him before the dome light went off with the closing of the door. He was an old man now, older than in the pictures Dooley had seen, and not a very big man. He had once been thick-chested and powerful, powerful enough to beat two men to death with a baseball bat for Al Capone, but now he was an old man carrying a little too much weight under a light nylon jacket. The wavy hair had gone gray but he still had the brooding face dominated by the dark eyes. "Joe Batters," Dooley said. "The only Joe that matters."

"Nobody calls me that except friends," the old man said. .

"Sorry. I guess it's Mr. Accardo, then."

"That'll do. You're Dooley?"

"I am."

"You're a stubborn son of a bitch, Mister Dooley."

"That's what they tell me."

"What did you think you were going to do with this?" Accardo held up the tape in its box.

"Put somebody in jail, I hoped."

"Well it ain't gonna happen now. You listened to it, right?"

"Yeah, I listened to it. Of course. What else was I gonna do?"

"Sure. But you understand how things are, right?"

"I do now. I was confused at first. Somebody threw me a big fat curve ball on this one. I thought it was all about Dallas."

Accardo gave a little grunt of laughter. "Dallas? You think I'd ever let that fucking Giancana pull something like that? Why do you think he's in Mexico now? Whoever pulled the trigger in Dallas, it wasn't us."

"That's good to know. I guess you're on the side of the angels now."

"You said it, brother. I'm with the good guys."

"Except all that money keeps flowing up to you, doesn't it? I can see why you'd want to keep it quiet. Although, who'd believe it anyway? Joe Batters, an FBI snitch."

The temperature dropped, fast. "You watch your fucking mouth."

Dooley was fed up. He was going to have to keep his mouth shut for a long time after he got out of the car, and there were some things he wanted to get off his chest. "Don't get me wrong," he said. "I understand. When the G offers to intervene with a federal judge to get the only conviction anyone ever pinned on you overturned on appeal, and all you have to do in return is feed them information, I guess the choice is pretty easy. Then you can go on saying you never spent a night in jail."

"And I never will. I don't have to explain to you how things work, do I?"

"No, you don't. I can sure as hell see why *they* don't want this getting out—you're the best informant they could possibly have. You can't do any better than having the other side's top guy on your team."

"I'm not the top guy anymore. I'm retired. And business is still good. I haven't hurt anybody that didn't have it coming."

"I'm not sure Jimmy Hoffa would agree. You gave him to the G, didn't you? It took me a while to figure out what I was hearing, but Spain had all the goods on there."

"You know what, Dooley? You're in a bad fucking position. You know too damn much."

"Look, Mr. Accardo. I don't give a shit, you understand? I don't give a damn what the G gets up to. They're the experts. I'm just a lowly homicide dick. I'm not going to rock the boat. I got a job to do and a family to feed. I gave you back the tape, now I need to see the girl."

Accardo said, "First let's talk about all the copies you made."

Dooley took a deep breath. "I only made one. I put it in my safety deposit box, at my bank, along with a written account of what it means. The only way it could come to light is if I die. Then they'll look in there for my life insurance policy and things like that and they'll find the tape. As long as nothing happens to me, nobody's going to know about it. If I were you I'd worry about all the other copies Spain made. You gotta know there are others out there."

"You're not telling me nothing new."

"Well, see how you like this. The FBI's grooming Spain as your successor. He wants the top job, and they've already got him on the roster."

"I know all about that. Lemme ask you something."

"What?"

"Why do you think I'm not worried? No matter how many copies you made?"

This is where you have to watch yourself, Dooley thought. He was having trouble keeping the lid on an immense surge of anger. "Deterrence," he said. "You established your credibility with Sally." Dooley turned to look at Accardo now, and he couldn't keep the bitterness out of his voice. "That's all she died for, wasn't it? Just deterrence. She never had the tape. She never had anything you wanted. You were just sending a message to Tommy Spain, weren't you?"

Accardo sat rock-still for a long moment, and then he said, "It wasn't supposed to be so rough. But I hope you got the message, too."

"I got it," said Dooley, barely getting the words out.

"Then it's time for you to get the fuck out of my car. They'll tell you where to find your girlfriend."

"Just a minute." Dooley knew he was pushing limits, but he was going to finish what he had come for. "There's one more piece of the bargain."

"What the fuck are you talking about?"

"I told you, I'm a homicide dick. I don't care about gambling or prostitution or anything else you do. Your business is your business. But when somebody gets killed, especially the way Sally got killed, now it's my business. I'm never gonna implicate you in anything. You can count on that. But you have to give me the guys that did Sally. You have to give 'em to me because I'm an honest man doing an honest job, and even you benefit when there are limits. I'm not gonna say anything more about Sally except I think that was outside the limits. You give me the guys that did it, and we're square. The limits are back in place and nobody will ever know what we talked about in here."

"I don't *have* to give you a God damn thing."

"No, but I think you will. Because on some level I think you're honest enough to know that guys like the ones that did Sally don't deserve to be walking the streets. You don't want 'em on your side. So give 'em to me."

"You're fuckin' dreaming."

"I'm not talking about a trial, Mr. Accardo. I mean you give me the names, and I will take care of them myself. Do you understand me?"

Accardo just stared at him through the gloom for a while. This time Dooley stared back; he had looked the Imperial Japanese Army in the eye, and after that a Grand Avenue dago tough guy was nothing. "You're nuts," Accardo said.

"That's what they tell me."

Accardo laughed, one brief grunt. "I'll give you one of them," he said. "But we'll take care of it ourselves. You stay out of it."

Dooley sat there staring at him, drawing it out as long as possible. He knew he'd gotten all he was going to get, more than any sane man would have tried for, but he wasn't going to bow and scrape. He put his hand on the door handle. "When?" he said.

Accardo waved a hand at him, dismissing him. "Tomorrow. Now get the fuck away from me before I change my mind."

Dooley got out of the car and shut the door, gently. He made for the three men standing together smoking fifty feet away. "All done?" said the short man, tossing away a glowing butt as he drew near.

"I need two things," said Dooley. "Right now."

"Catch," said the pug, tossing his gun to him. Dooley caught it and holstered it. "That's one," he said.

"Let me guess," said the short man. "Number two has tits and a pair of lips that were just made for sucking on my big Dago dick."

"Where is she?" said Dooley, fighting the urge to pull his piece right back out again and shove it down somebody's throat.

The short man wasn't intimidated by Dooley's eight-inch height advantage; he jutted his chin up at him, sneering. "About eight miles due east of here," he purred. "Right where you found her friend."

• • •

Dooley ran; he didn't give a damn who saw him. He ran back to his car and peeled out of the lot, and he drove east like a madman. He got pulled over just past Cicero and had to flash his star at the officers, explaining that he had just gotten a tip on a possible homicide. He could see them wondering why he wasn't in a department car, but they let him go.

Dooley wouldn't let himself think about it; he had enough on his mind just driving without hitting anybody. In the back of his mind he was going over options, all of them extreme, if what he was afraid of was true. Dooley was going a little bit crazy tearing east on North Avenue in the middle of the night.

Weed Street was dark; there was a lamppost near the end of the street but the light was out. Dooley screeched to a stop and jumped out of his car. The gap in the fence was still there; nobody had bothered to fix it. Dooley tore the sleeve of his jacket on the wire as he ducked through. It wasn't raining this time, but it was dark; through the brush Dooley could see reflections shimmering on the dark river but he couldn't make out a thing on the bank below him. He thrashed through weeds, stumbling and nearly pitching headlong down the slope, grabbing a branch to steady himself. He was going from memory, and getting it wrong; all of a sudden he was teetering above the black water and all he had found was old tires and empty bottles. He got his balance and looked back up the slope. He couldn't see a damn thing; he would have to wait for daylight.

Dooley swore at himself; he would beat the bushes on his hands and knees all night if he had to. His eyes were starting to get used to the dark and suddenly he saw it, the faintest hint of fair hair in the gloom, a huddled shape that might be a woman tossed in the weeds, and his heart nearly failed him because it was perfectly still. "Laura," he called.

The sound was muffled, inhuman.

"Laura?" Dooley started up the slope toward her, slipping to his knees, crawling. The sound came again, a stifled moaning, a torment to hear, and then Dooley was touching her leg, and unlike Sally she was warm.

Forty-five

DOOLEY HAD HIS gun drawn as he went back through the gap in the fence. He knew there was always a chance Joe Batters had a surprise up his sleeve. He looked hard into the shadows but saw nothing. Reaching back with his free hand he grabbed Laura's and led her to the car.

She was steady on her bare feet, and she hopped into the car briskly enough; apart from the dirt on her legs and the shock on her face she looked more or less intact. They had gagged her and wired her to a tree; Dooley had gotten the tape off her mouth without too much trouble but the wire had been hard. He had made her talk to him while he worked on the wire, and after she got her sobbing under control she had told him she wasn't hurt. Dooley wasn't sure he believed her, but it was a good thing to hear.

"Are you sure you don't need a doctor?" he said, turning onto North Avenue again, heading east.

She was crying, slumped over against the window. "No. I'm OK. I'm just—scared. I was scared out of my mind. I've never been scared like that, ever. It was hell. Oh, God, Sally."

Dooley didn't know where he was going, but he drove fast. "Laura, I have to ask. Did they do anything to you? Anything at all?"

She took a deep breath and steadied herself. "No. But they made it pretty clear it wouldn't bother them."

Dooley could imagine it. "I don't know if you can press any charges on this. I don't know if we can risk it."

"I don't care. I just want to feel safe again. But I don't know where."

"Do you have some place you can go? Out of town, I mean? You gotta have friends someplace."

"Sure. Someplace."

"I don't know if you have to stay away forever. Probably not. But a long vacation would be a really good idea."

"What about my apartment? My things?"

"To tell you the truth, I don't even think we should risk going back there to pick up a change of clothes."

"I don't even have my purse with me."

"Can Danny get into your place?"

"Yeah, he has a key."

"Then I think it's time to wake him up with a phone call. He can grab a few things and meet us somewhere. How much money do you have?"

"I don't know. Not enough for a plane ticket."

"Enough to get you on a bus? I can kick in a little."

"Probably." A few blocks went by and Laura said, "Dooley, what was all that about?"

"Evidence. I had some and they wanted it back."

"Did they get it?"

"Yeah."

"So they won again."

Dooley drove, keeping an eye on the mirror. "Maybe not. Not completely."

• • •

They found a bar open on North Avenue; Laura washed up in the restroom and called Danny. He showed up in twenty minutes, bringing Laura's purse and a pair of shoes and a Pan-Am flight bag packed to her instructions. "What's going on?" he asked Dooley. For the first time since Dooley had met him he looked as if he were taking something seriously.

Dooley didn't feel like explaining. "She's a witness," he said. "That's not a real safe position to be in sometimes."

"When's she coming back?"

"I don't know. It's not forever."

Danny and Laura embraced on the sidewalk and then she and Dooley got back in the car. Dooley turned down LaSalle Street, heading for the Loop. Lights flashed by, cars veered in and out of their path. "It's all over," said Laura in a dreamy voice.

"What's over?"

"This part of my life. It's over. I don't know what's going to happen next."

"You can come back. Just give it a while."

The blocks passed by, lit up by neon and sodium vapor but empty of life. "Do you really want me to come back?"

Dooley scowled into the night. "I do and I don't. I shouldn't but I do."

They were crossing the river, lights from the high buildings shimmering on the dark uneasy surface, when Laura said, "No, Dooley, it's over. I think this whole thing is over for me. I did a lot of growing up here, but I think it's time to go."

Dooley was amazed at the black depths of the sadness that came over him all of a sudden. "Where?" he said, a little louder than he intended.

"I don't know. California maybe. I always wanted to see California."

"That's a long way away."

"Yeah," Laura said. "A long, long way."

The big hall of the bus station on Randolph was nearly deserted, just a scattering of marooned travelers drifting or dozing. Dooley was still nervous and he stuck close to Laura, watching people as she talked to a ticket agent. She came away from the counter with a ticket. "In half an hour I can catch a bus coming from Cleveland that'll get me to Des Moines," she said. "That'll take me close to home. Maybe I'll stay with my mom for a while."

They found a corner to wait in, away from the lights. They stood in an embrace; Dooley didn't give a damn anymore who saw them. After a while Laura started to cry again, softly. Dooley didn't know what to do except hold her tighter. When it was time to go down the escalator to the dock he walked with his arm around her.

The bus pulled in and two or three passengers picked up their things and started to shuffle toward it. Laura sobbed once, squeezing him, and drew back to look at him. "I love you," she whispered. "I shouldn't but I do."

Dooley looked into her big gleaming eyes, knowing he had hit one of life's big jackpots and knowing it was gone; he was never going to see her again. He wished he had the words to tell her. "You've got a hell of a lot of life ahead of you," he said. "Be happy."

"I was happy with you." She kissed him quickly and pushed away.

• • •

Dooley went home; he went home to his wife and got into bed with her in the darkness and put his arms around her. She stirred and murmured and went back to sleep. Dooley lay there thinking about Laura until he lapsed into uneasy dreams.

When he woke up he was alone in the bed and the light told him it was midmorning. He found Rose at the kitchen table, looking at the newspaper. "I'm worried," she said. "Why haven't we heard anything? Shouldn't he at least have called?"

"I don't know, Rose." Dooley pulled the paper across the table.

"There's nothing in there," Rose said. "It just says the Marines are coming home. It doesn't give any details."

Dooley scanned the front page: there was going to be a trial downtown at the federal building, the eight protesters arrested at the convention last year finally going before a judge. Protests were expected. Dooley pushed the paper away; he didn't give a damn. "I don't know. He should be safe by now. He's probably in some depot at the end of a long line for the phone. All we can do is wait."

"I want to go over to the church. Will you come get me if he calls?"

Dooley looked at the clock. "I have to leave in an hour or so."

"Aren't you off today?"

"Yeah. But I've got to go meet a guy."

"About a case? I thought all that was over."

"This should do it, today. I think this should be just about it."

• • •

Get ready, thought Dooley. It's going to be bad.

The first time Dooley had said that to himself, he had been sitting in a hole on a ridge on the island of Bougainville, with remnants of the Japanese 17th Army massing for a banzai charge in the trees at the bottom of the hill. The succeeding frenzy had taught Dooley that even very bad things could be survived, and he had found the formula helpful at stressful moments over the years.

Now Dooley stood at the kitchen sink, looking out the window at his yard, the trees across the street, a patch of blue sky. He wished he could go on standing there forever, stuck in that moment in time, because he was afraid of what was going to happen when he had to move.

Dooley couldn't have said exactly when the conviction had settled on him that his son was dead. Maybe it was the dream he'd had just before dawn, his little boy Kevin calling to him for help; maybe the look on Rose's face at the kitchen table, maybe just the fact that two days after Kevin should have been pulled out of the line they still hadn't heard from him. Maybe he just hadn't had enough sleep. But Dooley was suddenly sure their luck had finally run out.

The certainty made things easier in one way: he had shaken off all doubts about what he had planned to do today, ever since talking to Tony Accardo the night before. Now he had nothing to lose; he was an angry man and he had unfulfilled business to take care of. He just hoped he got it taken care of before he had to deal with telegrams and sympathy and a wife going mad with grief.

Get ready, thought Dooley. It's going to be bad.

• • •

It was all guesswork, but Dooley's guesses had been pretty good so far; they had experience behind them. He figured the place to start was Joe D'Andrea's house. D'Andrea lived in a brick bungalow near Harlem and Diversey out on the West Side, in a quiet neighborhood that never gave the Austin district coppers any trouble. Dooley had memorized the address when he'd first gotten interested in D'Andrea, and he found it without any trouble.

The problem was going to be watching. D'Andrea's house was on a corner, with a garage behind it that opened onto the side street. A high board fence stretched along the sidewalk from the house to the garage. There was a gate in the fence. Dooley made a pass or two and found a place to park half a block down the side street on the same side as the house. He had a clear view of D'Andrea's garage, which was all he needed. He wasn't too worried about being spotted; the neighbors were probably used to seeing men in parked cars staring at D'Andrea's house, and at this angle D'Andrea couldn't see him from the house, which was the important thing.

Dooley settled in to wait. It was almost one o'clock, and he figured D'Andrea might be up and around soon. He had not bothered to get here any earlier because he knew how a mobster's schedule went. Now that he was here, he hoped things got rolling soon; he could be patient when he had to be but today it was hard to sit doing nothing. Dooley had a lot on his mind today.

My son is dead, he thought. Dooley knew it wouldn't hit him until he saw the telegram in his hands. He wondered how it would read. *We regret to inform you* . . . Was that the formula they used? Dooley tried to remember how the telegram announcing Patrick's death had gone. One of those in a lifetime was enough. One war was enough, for that matter; he couldn't understand how this one had happened. Nobody had dropped any bombs on the U.S. that he could remember. Dooley had always figured the government knew what it was doing, but now he wasn't so sure.

The back door to D'Andrea's house opened and shut again. Dooley couldn't quite see who had come out; the garage gave him only a partial view of the doorway. He waited for the garage door to go up; that would be the signal to start the car.

He waited, and the garage door stayed shut. When after a while he saw a thatch of white hair showing above the high fence, he remembered Joe D'Andrea talking about working in his yard. Dooley took a deep breath and blew it out; he was starting to think he was in for a long wait.

My son is dead. Correction, he thought, one of my sons is dead. Dooley knew he had been a bad father to Frank; he couldn't really explain it. Maybe it was the fact that Rose had started talking early on about how Francis would be the priest in the family; Dooley respected priests but secretly thought of them as inadequate somehow, less than men. It was wrong, he knew, but there it was. Frank had seemed to like the idea for a while, and maybe that was what had affected Dooley's attitude. In any event it was time for him to make it right. Frank was a good kid, a smart, good-hearted boy with his share of guts, and by God Dooley was going to treat him like a number-one son from now on.

Dooley knew he had to keep a lid on things here; he was going to need all his resources, and choking up at the thought of his boy was not going to be helpful.

A car went by. Cars had been going by at intervals ever since Dooley had parked there, but this one caught his attention because it was going slowly and there were two men in it. As it approached the end of the block it slowed even more, and suddenly Dooley realized he'd been making assumptions again.

Dooley had figured if Joe D'Andrea was going to get hit today it would be somewhere else; he'd get a summons or be ambushed in some spot he was known to frequent. They didn't hit guys at home, Dooley had always thought. But here he was watching a car creep to a halt at the curb next to D'Andrea's house. Dooley put his hand on the door handle.

He wasn't really surprised when he saw the man get out of the car and cross the sidewalk to the gate in Joe D'Andrea's fence; the only surprising thing was how slowly he walked, considering he was wearing a Mickey Mouse mask and carrying a shotgun. There was nothing furtive or even remotely concerned in his bearing; he could have been the plumber coming to clear out the drain.

Dooley waited to open the door until he had gone through the gate. The timing was going to be tricky. He got out and eased the car door shut and started walking, fast. His mind was going a mile a minute; wait to hear the shots or start running now? He started running.

He still hadn't heard any shots by the time he reached the gate, and he wondered if he was misreading the whole thing or had hallucinated something. Ahead of him he saw the car idling at the corner, the getaway driver at the wheel. He looked through the open gate.

He saw a small back yard with neatly tended flower beds along the fence on the far side and an open door in the side of the garage at the back of the lot. He could hear voices coming from inside the garage. Dooley stepped into the yard in time to hear

Joe D'Andrea's voice rise in panic: "Tony, kid, you can't do it. Not to me."

Get ready, thought Dooley, drawing his .38. Things had already taken on that strange slow-time effect they always had in combat, like a car wreck except that a car wreck was over in a couple of seconds and a fire fight could go on for a couple of hours. Dooley moved toward the garage door figuring distances, angles, seconds. The shotgun blast startled him but at the same time settled him down; the waiting was over.

Dooley went through the garage door leading with his gun. He saw D'Andrea's Torino filling most of the space; to his left he saw a vast splatter of D'Andrea's blood staining the end wall. D'Andrea had slid to the floor out of sight beyond the car, leaving a smear down the wall, and the man with the shotgun was racking the slide for a second shot when Dooley yelled "Police! Drop it!" The man with the shotgun snapped a look over his shoulder; he had pushed the Mickey Mouse mask up on top of his head to show D'Andrea who was killing him. Dooley leveled his .38 at Tony Messino and said, "Drop it. Now."

Messino's eyes flicked past Dooley just as Dooley heard footsteps behind him. Dooley spun in the doorway to see Ronnie Gallo coming across the yard, dragging an automatic out of his waistband. Dooley had time to think what an idiot he was for assuming again, assuming the driver would take off instead of coming to his partner's aid, and then it was time to move. He jumped out of the doorway just as Messino fired the shotgun again. Splinters flew out of the doorframe and pellets smacked into the high wooden fence; Gallo flinched as they flew by him. Dooley hit the grass and rolled, winding up on one knee facing Gallo. Gallo had an astonished look on his face as he got his balance and brought the automatic up in slow motion. Dooley's first hurried shot hit him in the left shoulder and spun him a little; Gallo fired the automatic into the lawn and then Dooley put one in his chest and he took a couple of steps backward, still looking amazed, before his legs gave out and he collapsed. There was a great silence.

Dooley was listening hard for footsteps inside the garage. All he heard was the sound of the shotgun being pumped, once again. "Messino!" Dooley yelled. "Throw out the gun and come out with your hands up!"

Dooley knew it wasn't going to happen, even before he heard Messino's feet scraping on the concrete floor. He could see how it was going to go, Messino relying on superior firepower and a rush for the car. Instinct took Dooley toward the garage; Messino would have a widening arc of yard to scan as he emerged, and the closer to the edge of the arc Dooley was, the better.

Messino came flying out through the door with the shotgun held high. He saw Dooley right away, but right away was too late; Dooley was almost close enough to grab him. Messino tried to bring the barrel around to bear on him but Dooley fired at point blank range into his chest and then knocked the barrel aside with his gun hand as it swept toward him. The gun went off as Messino stumbled but the pellets went up into the trees this time.

Messino wasn't going to be able to rack the slide again, not in time, and Dooley could see he knew it. Messino's momentum had carried him a few feet out into the yard, and he lay on his side trying to work the action of the gun but not finding the strength. Dooley walked toward him, holding his gun at his side. He kicked the shotgun out of Messino's hands and stood looking down at him. "What's the matter, Tony? Nobody ever fought back before, huh?"

Messino looked bewildered now, and blood was oozing through the hole in his pale blue sport shirt, making a very dark stain. Dooley knew he didn't have much time to get his message across. He bent down and spoke softly. "I want you to think about Sally," he said. "I made her a promise, and I kept it."

Messino's eyes widened just for a moment and then Dooley could see he had lost him. Gallo was quiet now, too, crumpled on the grass. Dooley went and took one look inside the garage and saw that Joe D'Andrea wasn't going anywhere, not with half his head missing. Dooley came back out and stood in the yard with his handiwork, feeling disgusted. He was finished.

• • •

Dooley's last shooting had drawn only a couple of first-watch dicks; this one brought out the brass. He even rated an Assistant Deputy Superintendent with this one. Joe D'Andrea's yard filled up with gold-banded caps and in the street beyond the fence a crowd gathered, drawn by the cluster of squad cars at the corner. A lieutenant with an irritated look on his face said, "What the fuck were you doing here?"

Dooley went through it again, patiently. "I came here to question Joe D'Andrea about a killing I think he was involved in. I've been working on the case since June. I was just in time to see these two hit him. I tried to arrest them and they resisted." Dooley knew he was in for a rough ride; three Outfit guys dead and a dick from outside the area with a smoking gun was going to raise a lot of eyebrows. Dooley was just glad everybody but him was dead. Sometimes things worked out better than you expected. Dooley had honestly intended to arrest Tony Messino and let him make up whatever story he wanted; charging him for D'Andrea's murder would not have been as good as nailing him for Sally's, but it would have worked.

But maybe this was better. Dooley spent a couple of hours at Area Five, answering more questions. "You the same Dooley that shot those two guys down in Central a few weeks back?" a sergeant asked him.

"I've had a busy summer," Dooley said.

It was nearly five o'clock by the time he got in his car and left. He didn't particularly want to drive into the Loop, but he didn't particularly want to go anywhere else, either. He pushed east along Grand, looking at what time had done to the city he grew up in, wondering where things had gone wrong.

Something was going on in the Loop; the traffic was snarled and there were coppers everywhere. Dooley ditched the car on Franklin and started walking. As he got close to the federal building he started to hear the noise of the crowd. It was a random and angry noise, the noise of chaos. He heard windows breaking. Jackson was closed off and he had to show his star to get within two blocks of the federal building. "What the hell's going on?" he asked a copper in a riot helmet.

"The Panthers and the hippies are rioting, because of the trial. Where the hell you been all day?"

Dooley came around a corner into the plaza and there they were, ragged bands of them, running and throwing things and yelling. The cops seemed to have secured the area and it was down to skirmishing, little groups here and there taunting and singing and just milling. He had to show his star a few more times, but he finally got to the door of the building. "You think you're going inside there, do you?" said the U.S. marshal on the door.

"I gotta talk to Gustafson in the FBI office. Call up and ask him if you want."

The marshal didn't need another argument on his hands and he waved Dooley in. Inside there was a siege atmosphere, with cops and marshals and God knew who else walking around with wide eyes and jumping at noises. Dooley took the elevator up to the ninth floor and went into the FBI office. "I need to talk to Gustafson," he said. "Tell him Dooley's here."

It was Krause who came out and got him and took him back to Gustafson's office. "You got what we need?" Krause said as they walked down the hall.

"Not anymore," Dooley said.

Krause gave him a look but said nothing. Gustafson was waiting behind his desk when Dooley walked in. "Things any calmer out there?" he said.

"I got a message for your good friend Joe Batters," Dooley said.

Gustafson's eyes went hard. "Accardo? He's no friend of mine."

"Don't give me that. You told him I had the tape. Did you tell him you didn't care how he got it back, or did he just know you wouldn't care?"

The two G-men exchanged a look and Gustafson said, "Mike, you have to let me explain the situation."

"I understand the situation. I just don't have to like it. Now take a fucking message. Write it down if you have to."

Gustafson gave him a long cool look and said, "What's the message?"

"Tell Accardo we're square now. Tell him I got both of them, just like I wanted to, and now we're even."

"What are you talking about?"

"Accardo knows. Tell him he's got nothing to worry about from me as long as he sticks to business. But tell him if I ever catch another homicide that has anything to do with the Outfit, I'll work it to death, just the same. Tell him there's one copper he can't buy."

Gustafson nodded, very slightly. "Where's the tape, Mike?"

"Ask Accardo." Dooley was finished here, too; he turned and headed for the door.

Gustafson called after him. "Dooley."

"What?"

"We're on the same side. You understand that, right?"

Dooley was tired, beat to death. He took in Krause and Gustafson with a look. "That's what they tell me."

On the sidewalk outside things were still happening. Dooley had almost gotten clear of the mess when a punk with hair like the Wild Man of Borneo veered toward him. "Hey, *pig!*" he screamed. "Guess what? You're *outnumbered!*"

Dooley wound up and decked him. The punk went flying and Dooley kept walking. He felt a little better. He thought for a second that the punk might be right, but nobody seemed inclined to come after him. He walked all the way back to his car. His feet were getting sore.

My boy, he thought, driving north. I don't know what kind of country you would have come back to anyway. It made Dooley sad to think how much all those people back at the federal building would have hated his son.

Dooley drove to Damen and Grace. He didn't really have to, but he wasn't ready to go home. He went up to the third floor and put his jacket over the back of a chair. "I thought you were off today," Nyman said, frowning at him.

"I'm never off," said Dooley.

"There's a bunch of phone messages for you."

"I'll get to them." Dooley sat down to type up his last report on Sally Kotowski. He typed up everything he knew about it except for the truth behind it. *It is my belief that the victim was killed to deter release of information in the possession of Tommaso Spagnola a.k.a. Tommy Spain, currently in federal prison in Texarkana, Texas,* he wrote. *Any subsequent inquiries should be directed to him.* Dooley tore the report out of the typewriter and took it in and laid it on McCone's desk. "That's the end of it," he said. "If the brass doesn't like it, they can kiss my ass. Tell 'em that."

McCone gave him a thoughtful look. "Mike, you got a vacation coming up, right?"

"You bet," said Dooley. "I'm going fishing with my boy."

I have a daughter, too, thought Dooley, driving north up Elston, toward his home. It was late at night now and he drove with the window down, cool air ruffling his hair. A daughter with brains and courage, a grown-up woman now. He thought about Laura, all alone on a bus heading west through the night. Laura was a gift, but I have better ones I get to keep, he thought. We'll take that vacation, my boy, my girl, and my wife, and we'll sit by that lake and talk about Kevin and start getting over it.

Dooley hadn't really believed it, deep down, until he pulled into his driveway behind his brother-in-law Ted's car and saw all the lights on, the other cars parked on the street in front of his house. That was when it sank in at last, seeing all the relatives gathered; that was when Dooley knew it was real. He bowed his head and squeezed his eyes shut and thought, This is it, and it's bad, all right. He sat there fighting it for a while and thought about his wife inside needing him and took a deep breath and wiped the corners of his eyes with his fingers and made himself get out of the car.

Dooley walked up the path toward the front door of the house where he had raised his children, wondering how much pain a man could take in his life and thinking he was about to find out. His heart kicked when the door flew open with a bang and he couldn't think for a second why his son was tearing across the yard toward him screaming, and then as Frank jumped at him, almost knocking him down, he heard what the boy was screaming.

"Kevin's home! Kevin's home!" Frank had gone crazy, leaping around him, waving his arms, and just as the words were starting to register Dooley looked at the doorway to his house and saw himself standing there. He saw a young Michael Dooley there, lean and tired and burned by the sun, worn out from hard fighting and long journeys, and then he realized he was looking at his boy; Kevin had come home.

Dooley started to smile, swaying a little on his feet and wondering now if sudden joy could kill a man, as Kevin stepped off the porch, Rose and Kathleen and the rest jostling in the doorway behind him, and came to meet him. Dooley shook his head in amazement. He held out his hand and Kevin took it and said quietly, "Hey, Pop. It's good to see you."

They embraced and Dooley clapped him on the back a few times and then stepped back to look at him. "Jesus, it's good to have you back," he said.

Kevin was grinning his old mischievous grin, a beautiful sight, and he said, "What the hell, Pop? You told me the Cubs were going to win it all."

Dooley threw back his head and laughed at the stars, laughed until his eyes were running with tears. "Ah, forget about the Cubs," he said, walking up the path with his arms around his sons. "It's football season. And I got a feeling the Bears are gonna do great this year."

Afterword

WITH THE SINGLE exception of Tony Accardo, all the characters given speaking roles in this story are fictional creations, though many of the organized crime figures mentioned existed in fact, and the character of Tommy Spain is only thinly fictionalized. The central premise of the plot is of course sheer speculation, but the profound influence of the the Capone gang and its descendants in Chicago and American society in general is factual, documented in numerous works including Ovid DeMaris's *Captive City* and Gus Russo's *The Outfit.*

The Chicago Bears' record in 1969 was 1-13.